MOON
月
つくよみ
詠
PHASE 5

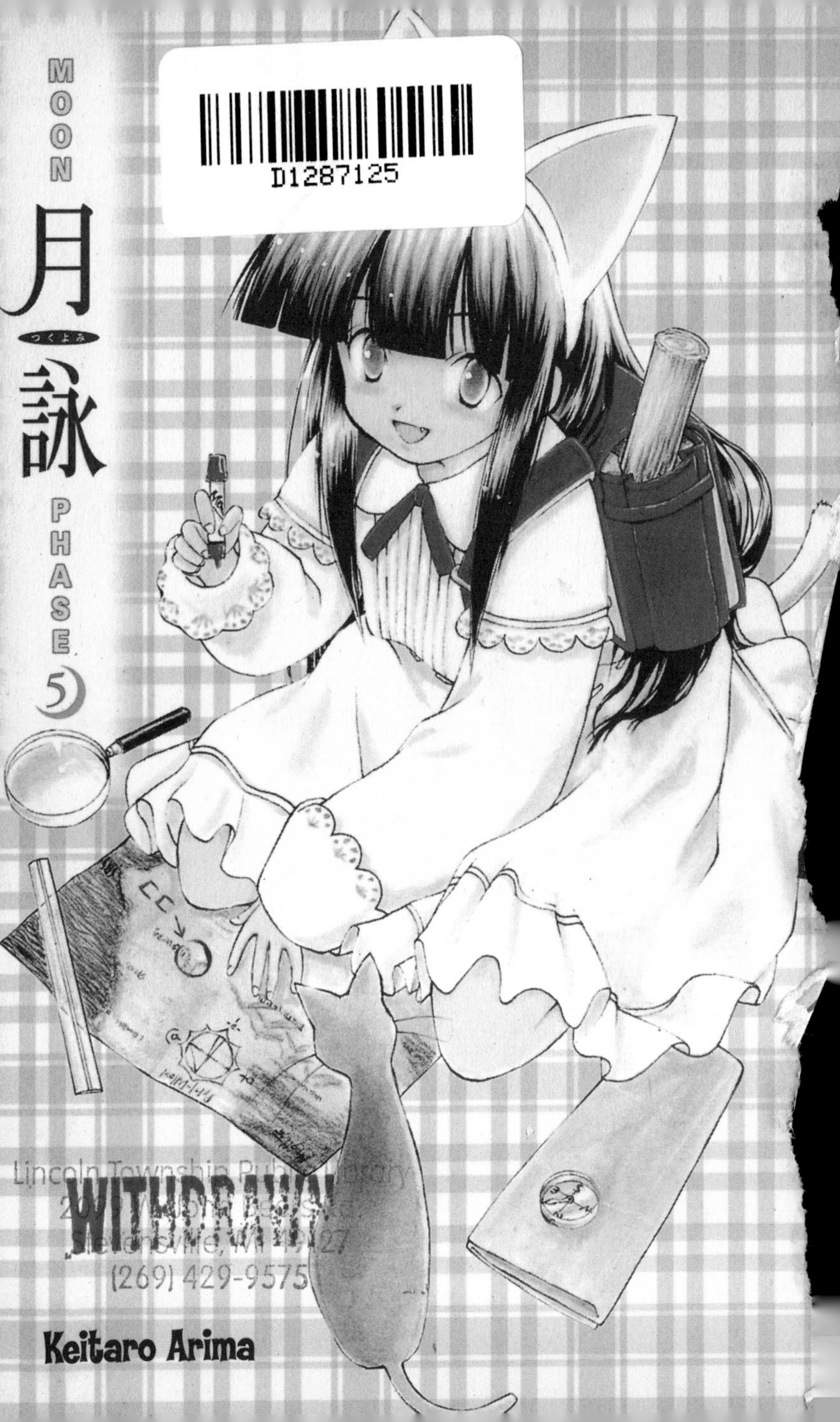

Keitaro Arima

STORY SO FAR

Kouhei Mido has never had a close encounter with the supernatural kind, so why are ghosts showing up in every photo he takes? Things get even kier when he meets up with the cute adorable (but watch out, she bites!) ampire, Hazuki at the spooky old German castle. Before he knows what's happening, Hazuki suddenly volunteers to move in with him back in Japan, as the team struggles to find her long lost mother. Easier said than done.

The vampire Count Kinkle and is accomplice Elfriede stubbornly attempted to take Hazuki back with them. During their final battle, Hazuki risked her own life to jump out into the sunlight and rescue Kouhei from a bitter end, causing her to lose consciousness. After the defeat of Count Kinkle, with the help of Elfriede, the team can finally catch a break. But when Hazuki awakens, she's taken on an entirely new persona and calls herself..."Luna".

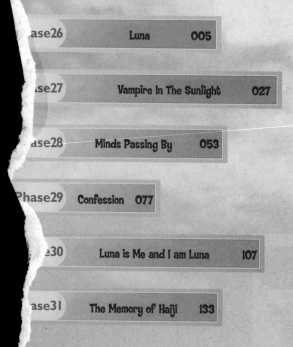

TSUKUYOMI
Moon Phase 月詠

CREATED BY: KEITARO ARIMA

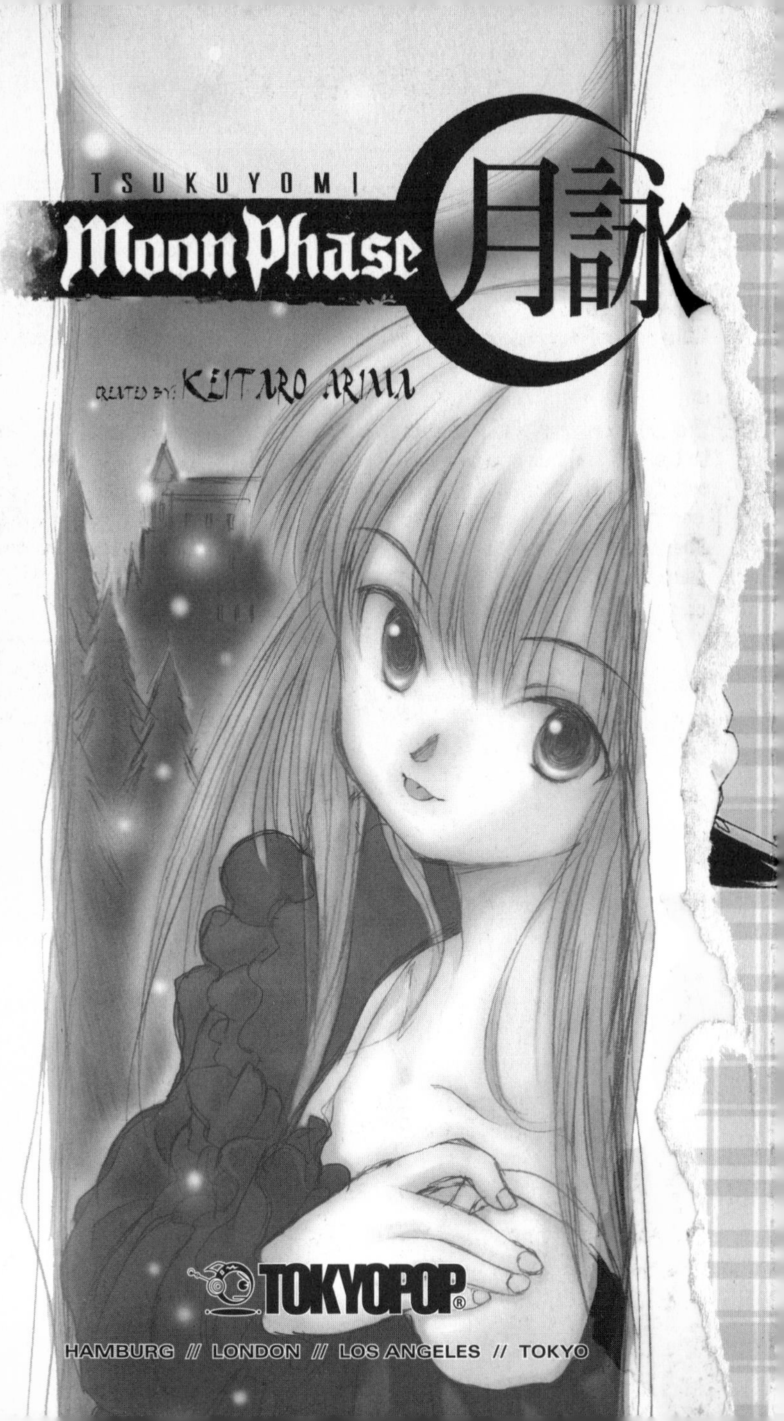

TOKYOPOP®

HAMBURG // LONDON // LOS ANGELES // TOKYO

Tsukuyomi: Moon Phase Vol. 5
Created by Keitaro Arima

Translation - Yoohae Yang
English Adaptation - Jeffrey Reeves
Retouch and Lettering - Nancy Star
Production Artist - Mike Estacio
Cover Design - Fawn Lau

Editor - Katherine Schilling
Digital Imaging Manager - Chris Buford
Pre-Production Supervisor - Erika Terriquez
Art Director - Anne Marie Horne
Production Manager - Elisabeth Brizzi
VP of Production - Ron Klamert
Editor-in-Chief - Rob Tokar
Publisher - Mike Kiley
President and C.O.O. - John Parker
C.E.O. and Chief Creative Officer - Stuart Levy

A  Manga

TOKYOPOP Inc.
5900 Wilshire Blvd. Suite 2000
Los Angeles, CA 90036

E-mail: info@TOKYOPOP.com
Come visit us online at www.TOKYOPOP.com

ISBN: 1-59532-952-8

First TOKYOPOP printing: December 2006
10 9 8 7 6 5 4 3 2 1
Printed in the USA

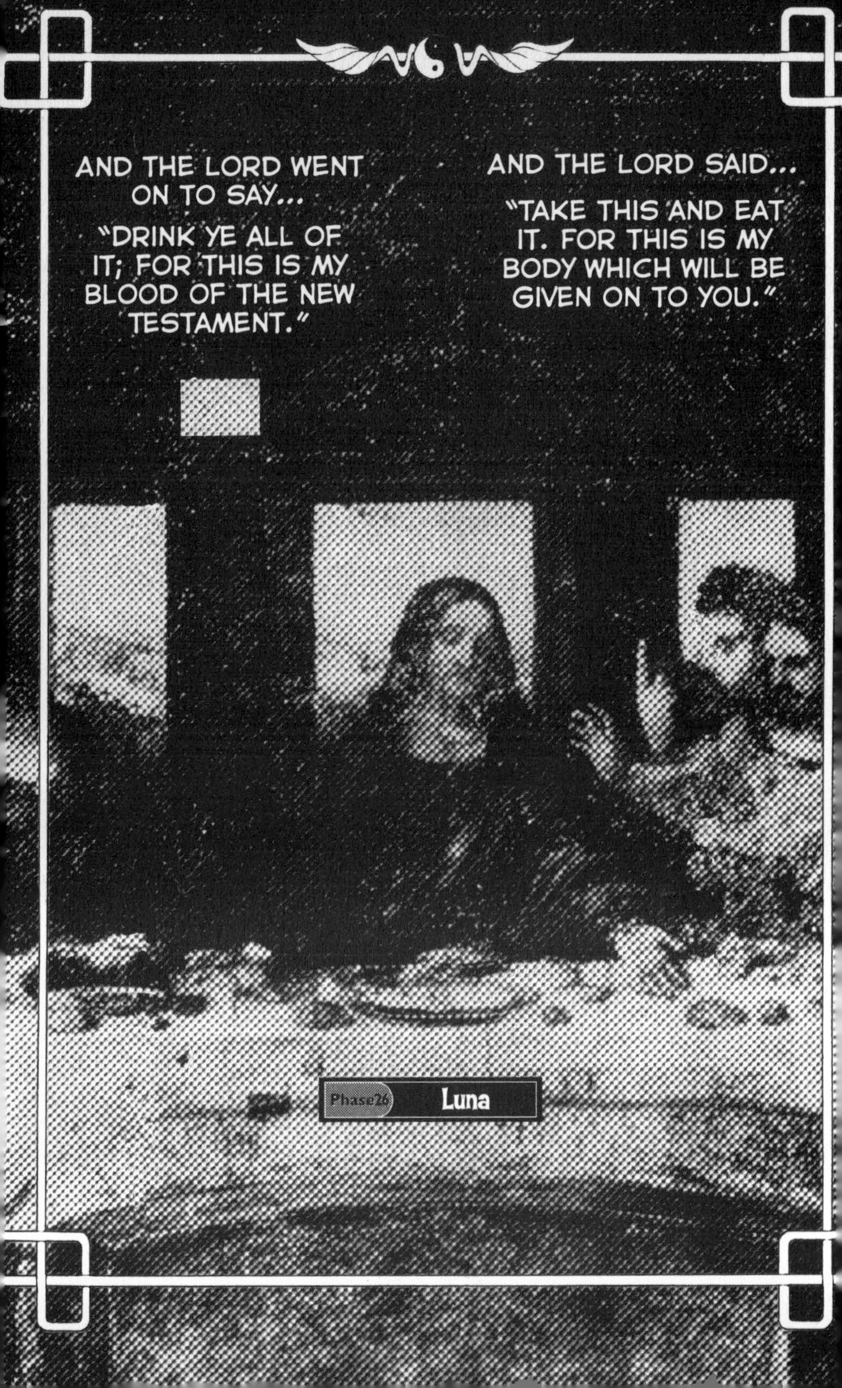
AND THE LORD SAID...
"TAKE THIS AND EAT IT. FOR THIS IS MY BODY WHICH WILL BE GIVEN ON TO YOU."
AND THE LORD WENT ON TO SAY...
"DRINK YE ALL OF IT; FOR THIS IS MY BLOOD OF THE NEW TESTAMENT."
Phase26 Luna

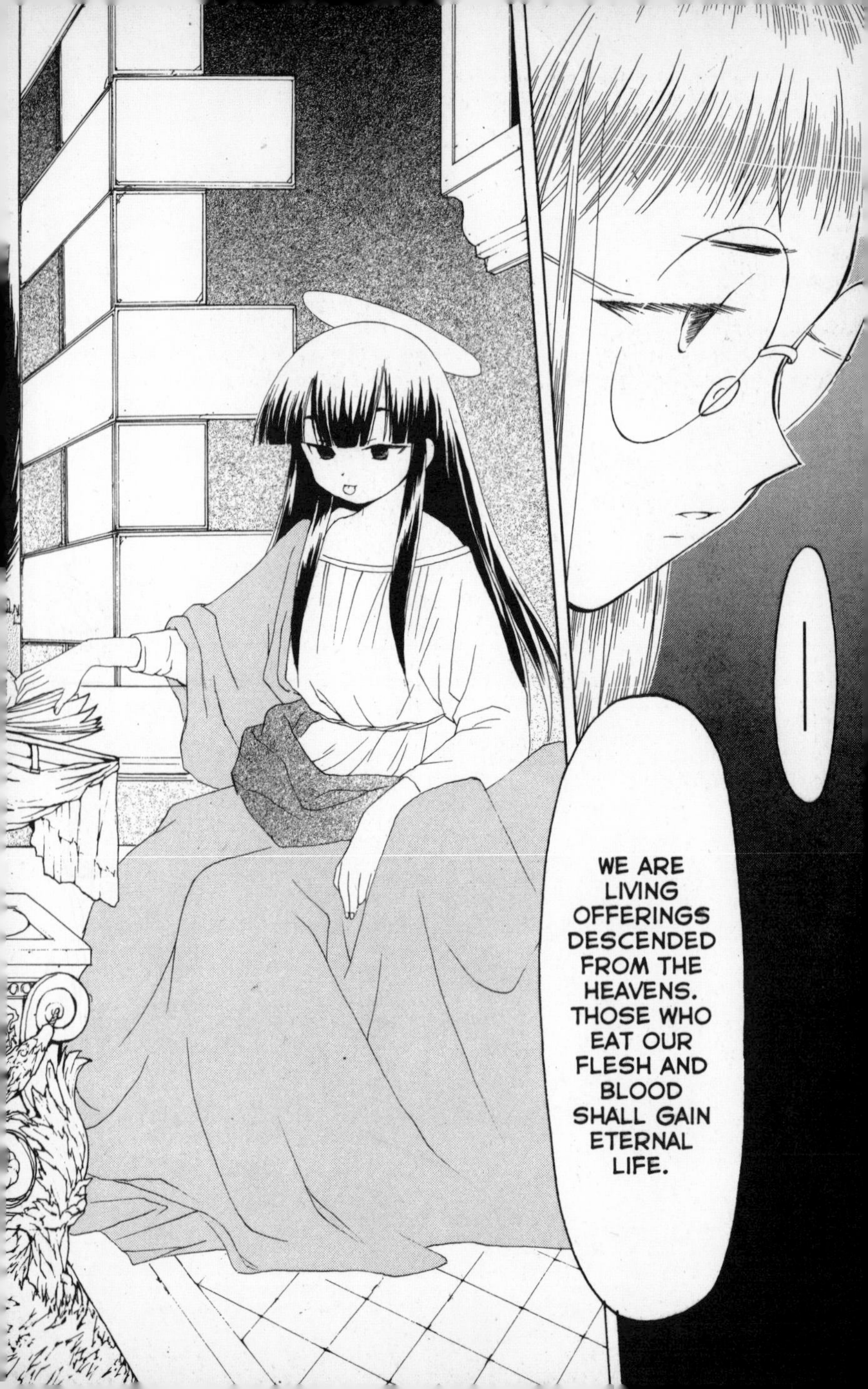

—
WE ARE LIVING OFFERINGS DESCENDED FROM THE HEAVENS. THOSE WHO EAT OUR FLESH AND BLOOD SHALL GAIN ETERNAL LIFE.

Phase26 Luna

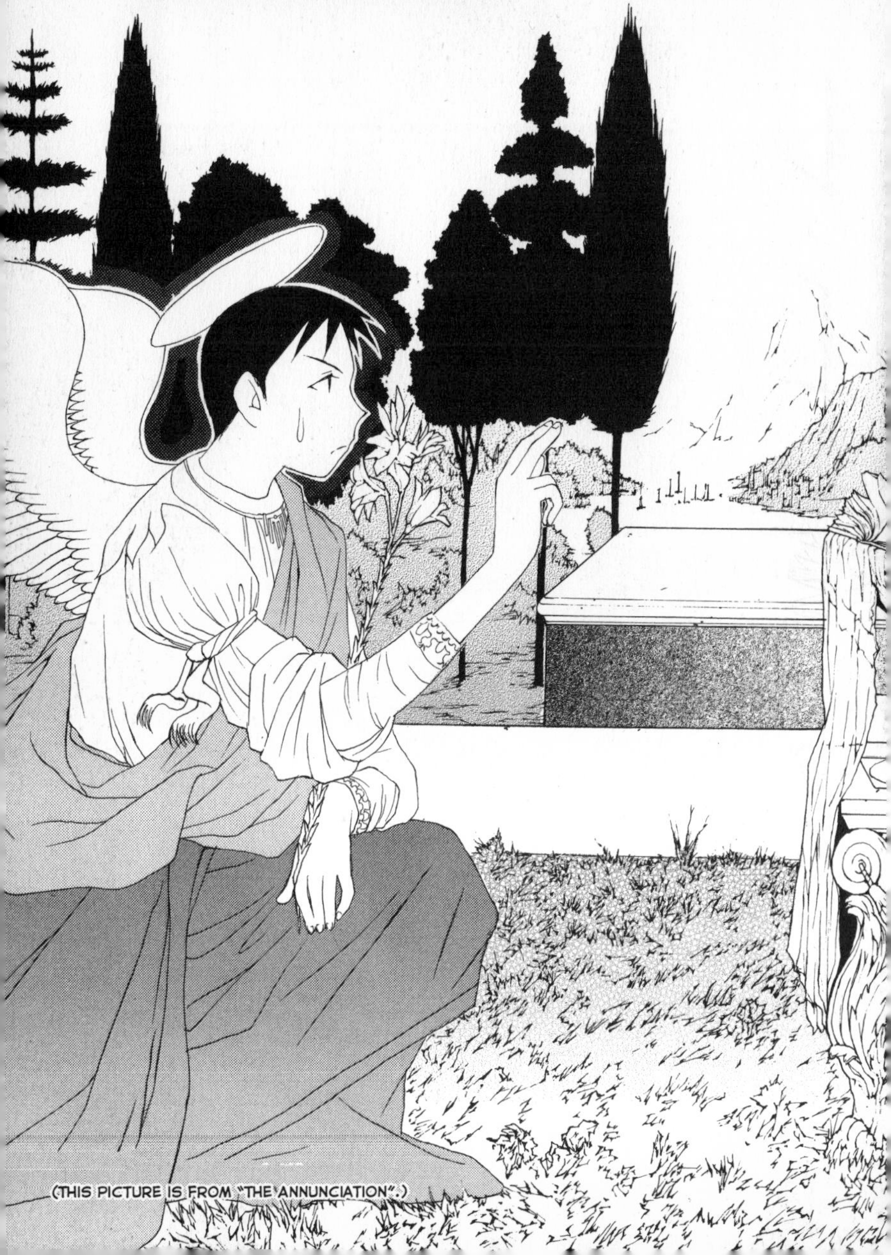
(THIS PICTURE IS FROM "THE ANNUNCIATION".)

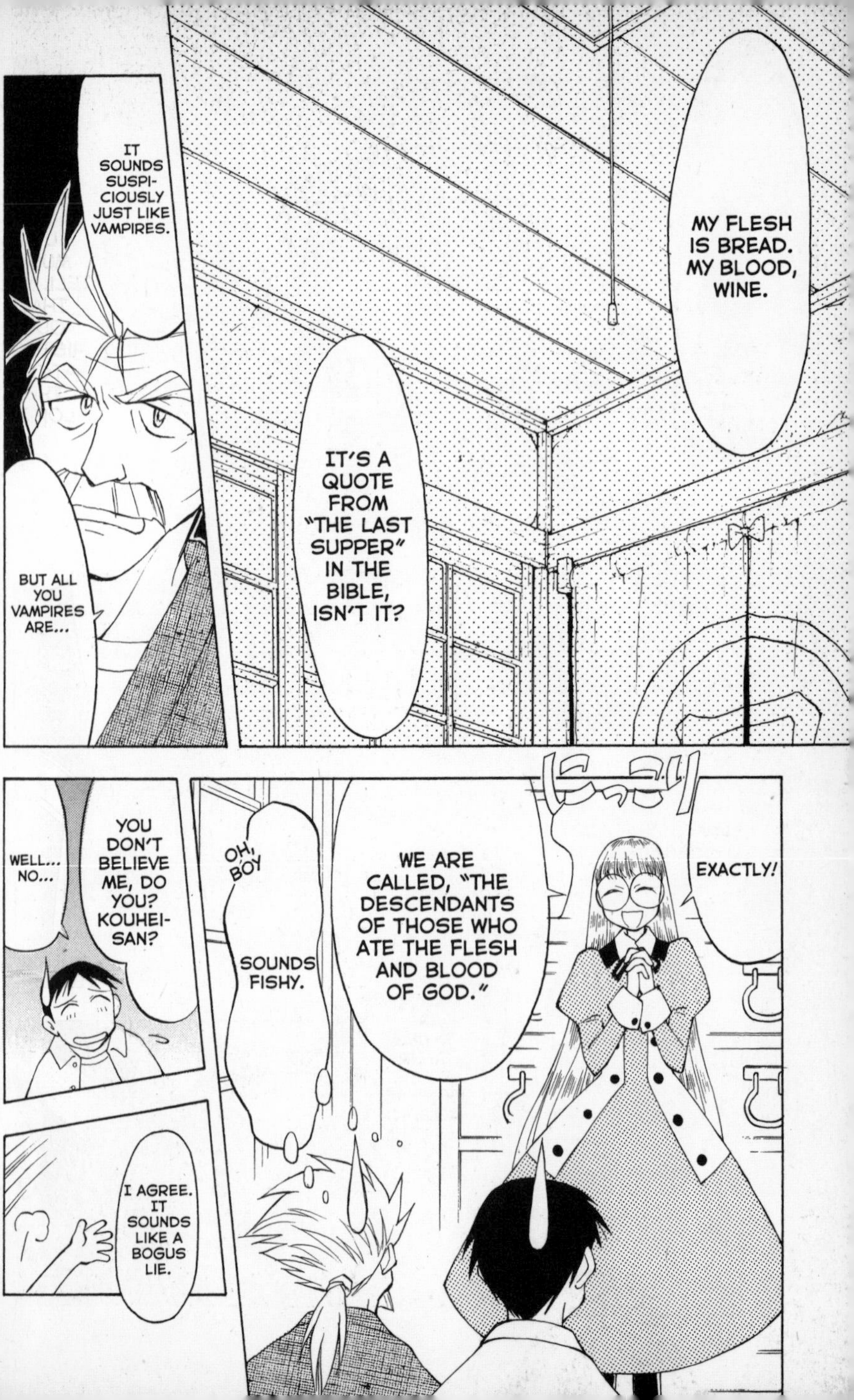
MY FLESH IS BREAD. MY BLOOD, WINE.
IT'S A QUOTE FROM "THE LAST SUPPER" IN THE BIBLE, ISN'T IT?
IT SOUNDS SUSPI-CIOUSLY JUST LIKE VAMPIRES.
BUT ALL YOU VAMPIRES ARE...
にっこり
EXACTLY!
WE ARE CALLED, "THE DESCENDANTS OF THOSE WHO ATE THE FLESH AND BLOOD OF GOD."
OH, BOY
SOUNDS FISHY.
YOU DON'T BELIEVE ME, DO YOU? KOUHEI-SAN?
WELL... NO...
I AGREE. IT SOUNDS LIKE A BOGUS LIE.

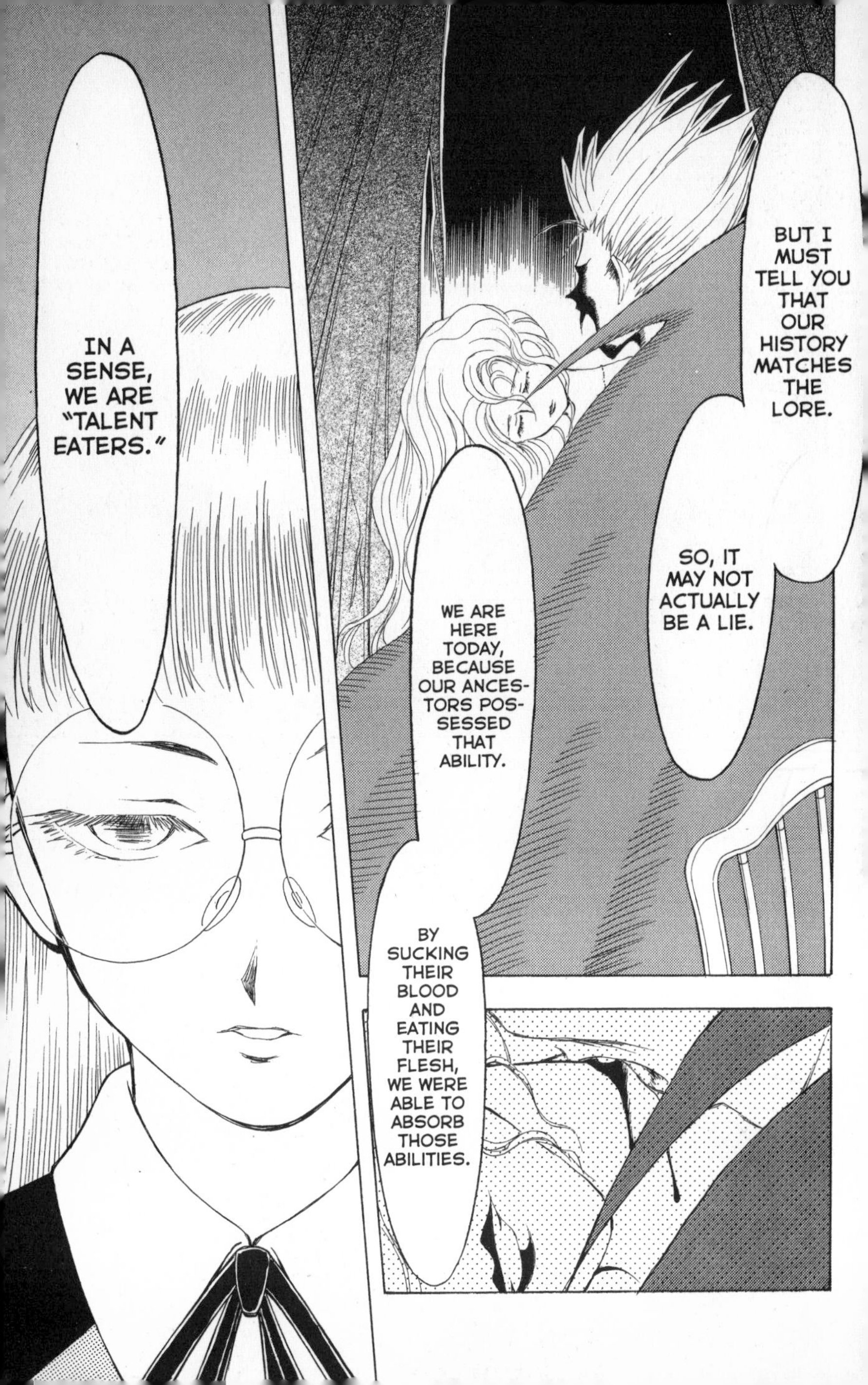
BUT I MUST TELL YOU THAT OUR HISTORY MATCHES THE LORE.
SO, IT MAY NOT ACTUALLY BE A LIE.
WE ARE HERE TODAY, BECAUSE OUR ANCES-TORS POS-SESSED THAT ABILITY.
BY SUCKING THEIR BLOOD AND EATING THEIR FLESH, WE WERE ABLE TO ABSORB THOSE ABILITIES.
IN A SENSE, WE ARE "TALENT EATERS."

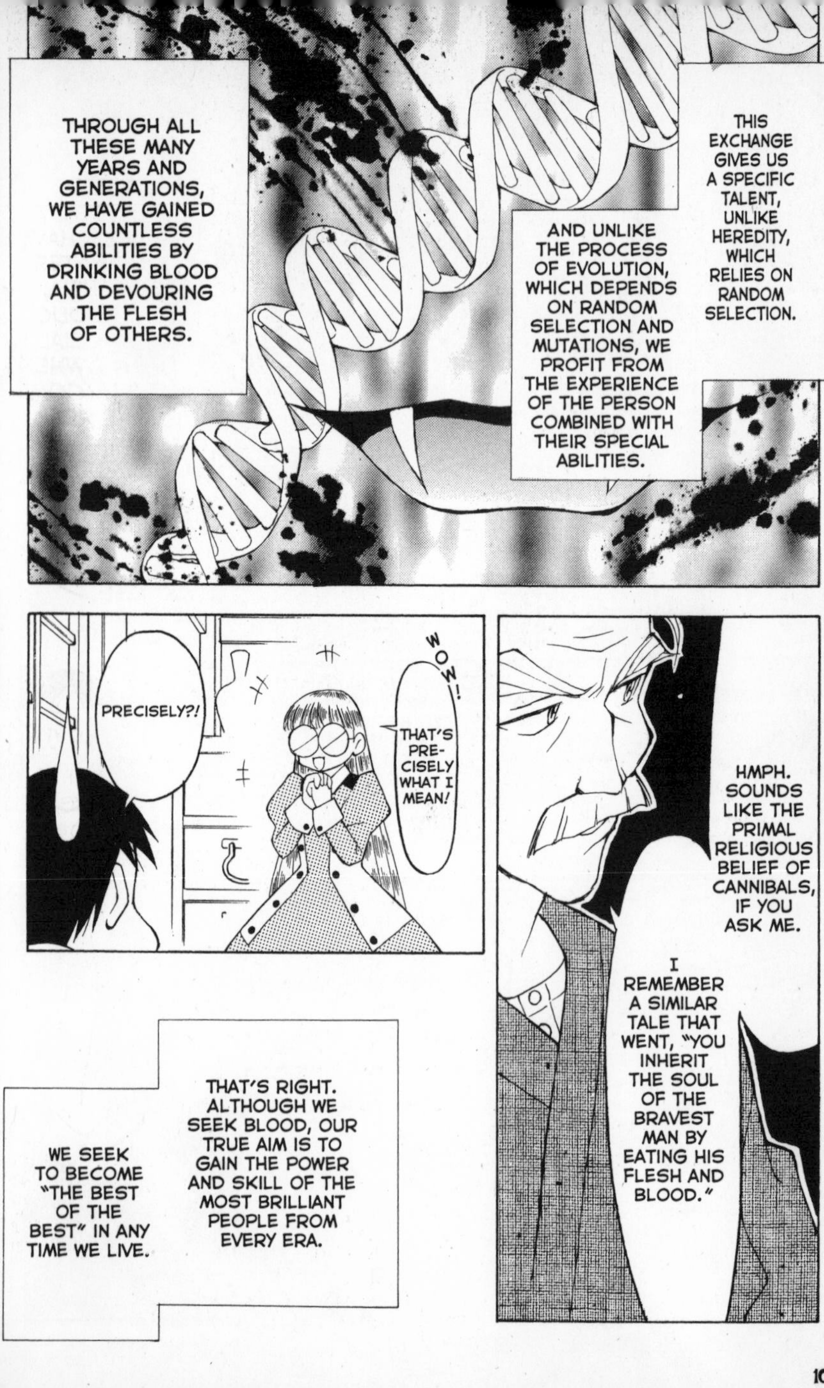
THROUGH ALL THESE MANY YEARS AND GENERATIONS, WE HAVE GAINED COUNTLESS ABILITIES BY DRINKING BLOOD AND DEVOURING THE FLESH OF OTHERS.
THIS EXCHANGE GIVES US A SPECIFIC TALENT, UNLIKE HEREDITY, WHICH RELIES ON RANDOM SELECTION.
AND UNLIKE THE PROCESS OF EVOLUTION, WHICH DEPENDS ON RANDOM SELECTION AND MUTATIONS, WE PROFIT FROM THE EXPERIENCE OF THE PERSON COMBINED WITH THEIR SPECIAL ABILITIES.
WOW!
THAT'S PRECISELY WHAT I MEAN!
PRECISELY?!
HMPH. SOUNDS LIKE THE PRIMAL RELIGIOUS BELIEF OF CANNIBALS, IF YOU ASK ME.
I REMEMBER A SIMILAR TALE THAT WENT, "YOU INHERIT THE SOUL OF THE BRAVEST MAN BY EATING HIS FLESH AND BLOOD."
THAT'S RIGHT. ALTHOUGH WE SEEK BLOOD, OUR TRUE AIM IS TO GAIN THE POWER AND SKILL OF THE MOST BRILLIANT PEOPLE FROM EVERY ERA.
WE SEEK TO BECOME "THE BEST OF THE BEST" IN ANY TIME WE LIVE.

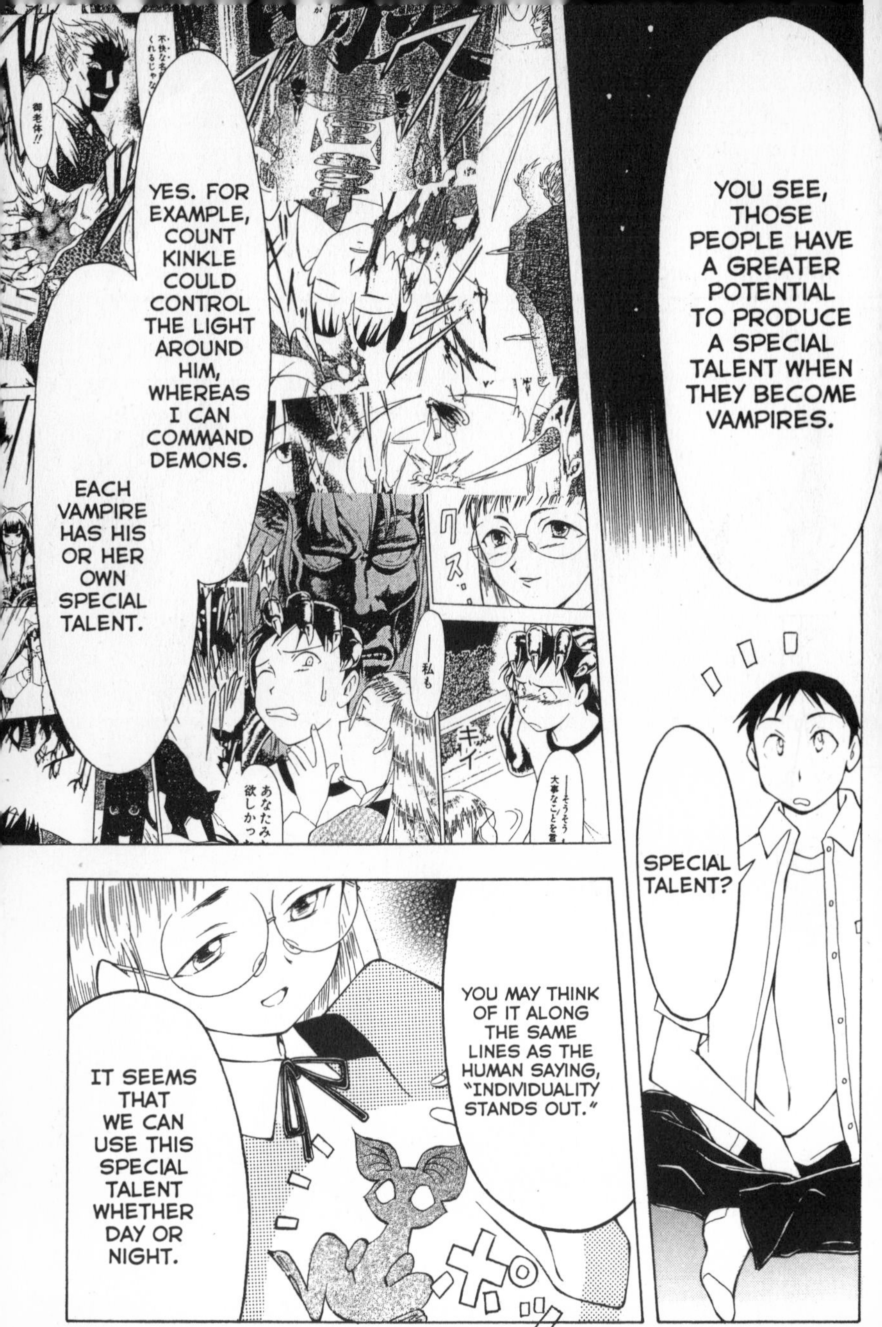
YOU SEE, THOSE PEOPLE HAVE A GREATER POTENTIAL TO PRODUCE A SPECIAL TALENT WHEN THEY BECOME VAMPIRES.
SPECIAL TALENT?
YES. FOR EXAMPLE, COUNT KINKLE COULD CONTROL THE LIGHT AROUND HIM, WHEREAS I CAN COMMAND DEMONS.
EACH VAMPIRE HAS HIS OR HER OWN SPECIAL TALENT.
御老体!!
私も
クス
キイ
YOU MAY THINK OF IT ALONG THE SAME LINES AS THE HUMAN SAYING, "INDIVIDUALITY STANDS OUT."
IT SEEMS THAT WE CAN USE THIS SPECIAL TALENT WHETHER DAY OR NIGHT.

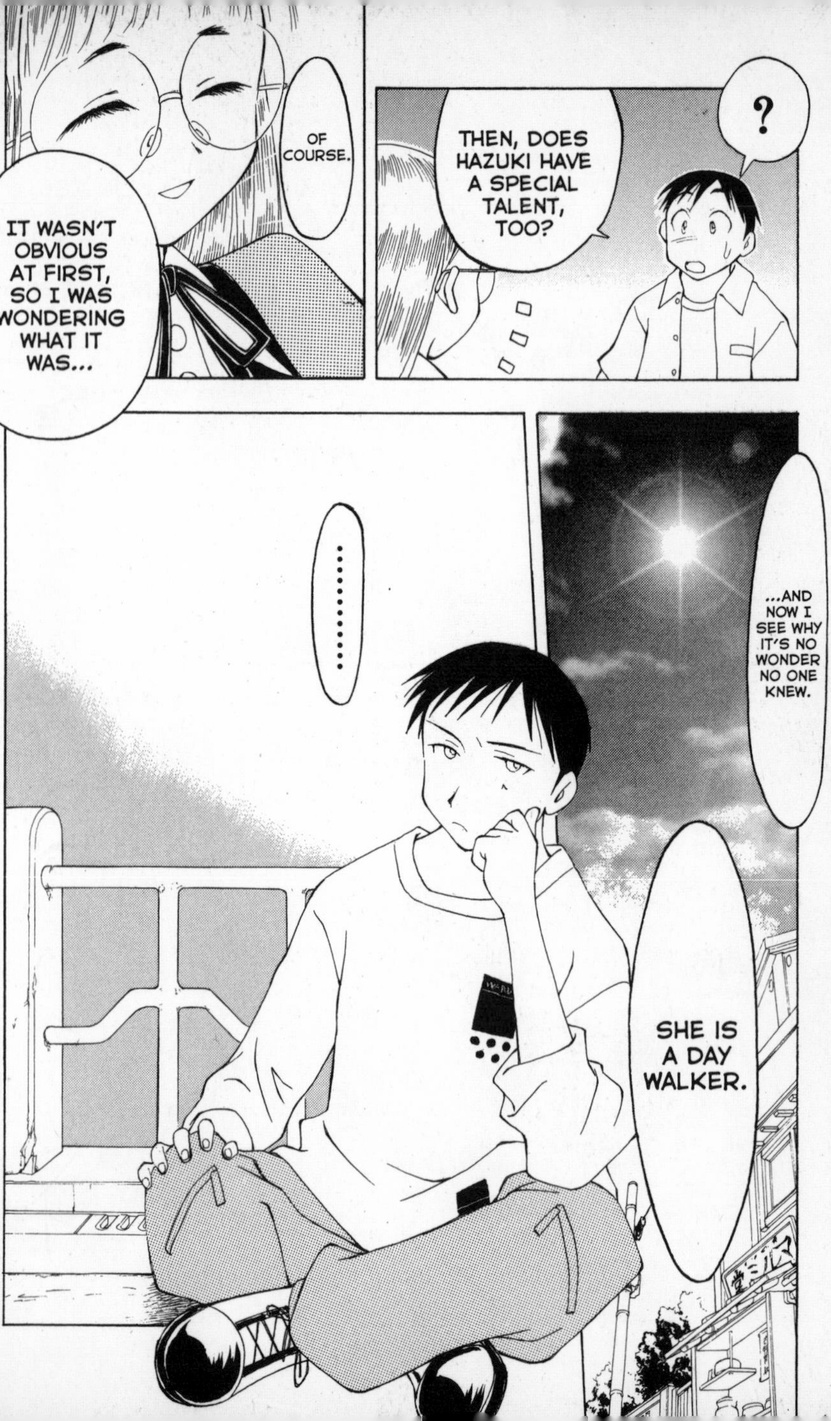

THEN, DOES HAZUKI HAVE A SPECIAL TALENT, TOO?
?
OF COURSE.
IT WASN'T OBVIOUS AT FIRST, SO I WAS WONDERING WHAT IT WAS...
...AND NOW I SEE WHY IT'S NO WONDER NO ONE KNEW.
SHE IS A DAY WALKER.
....

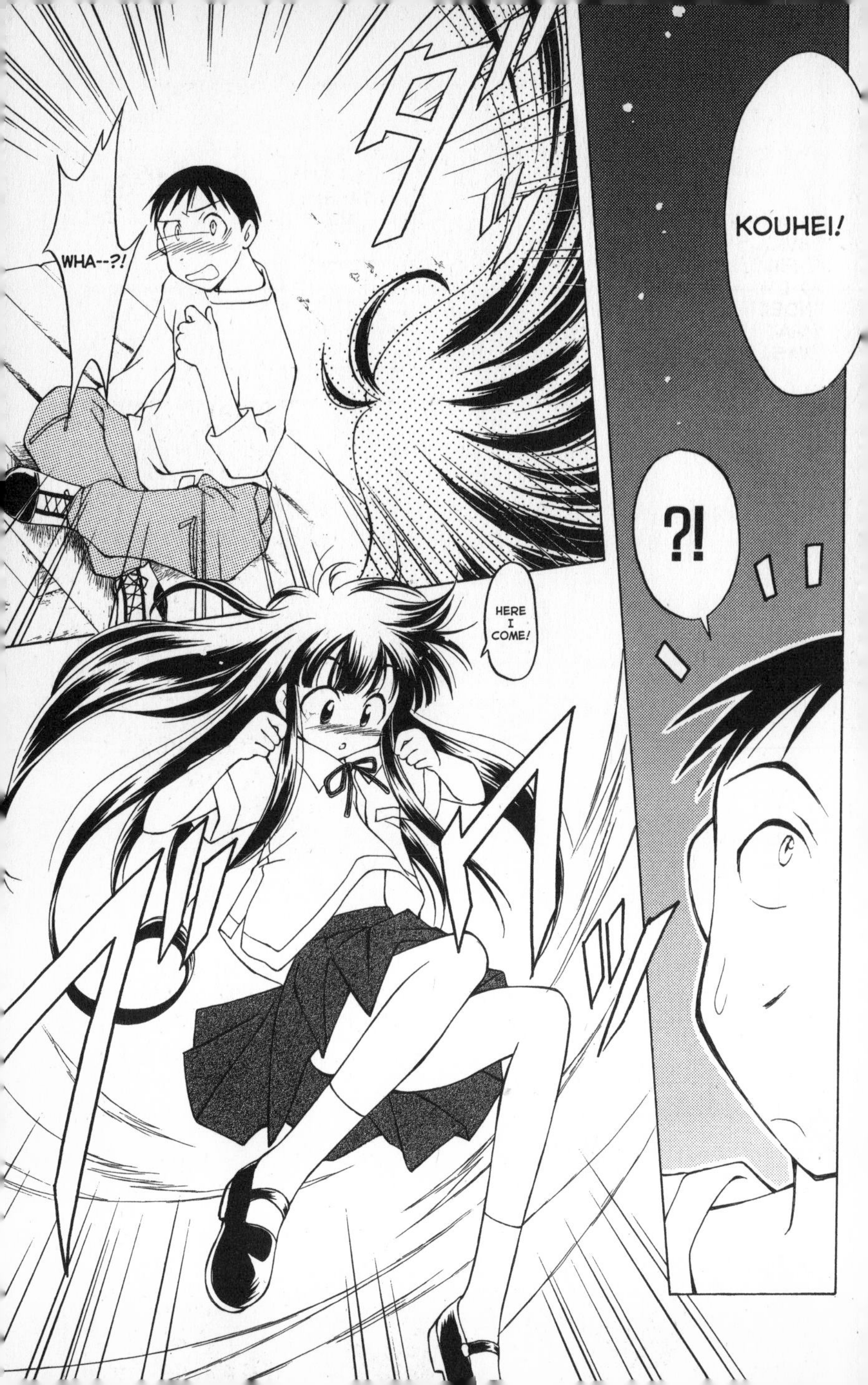
KOUHEI!
?!
HERE I COME!
WHA--?!

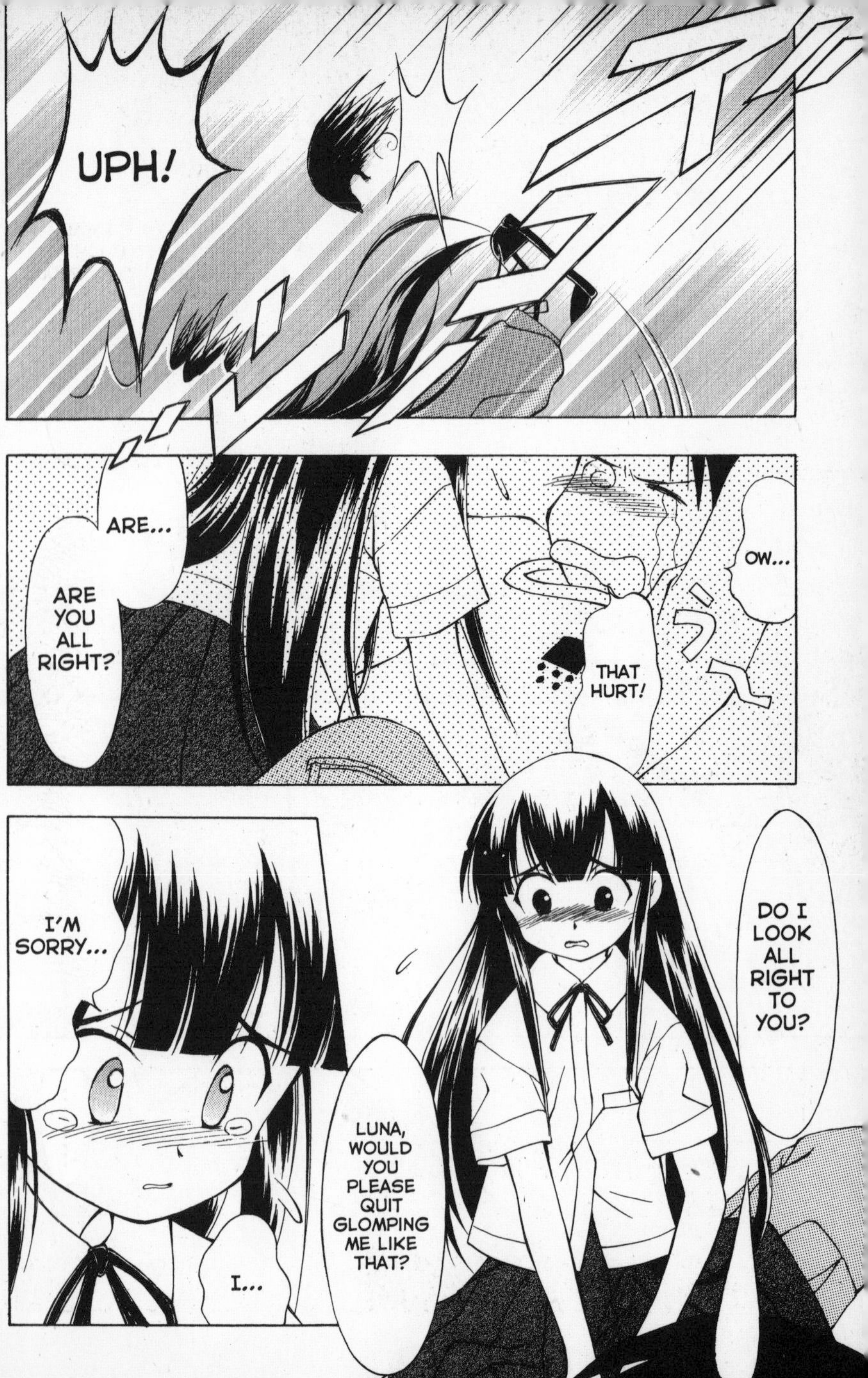
UPH!
OW...
THAT HURT!
ARE...
ARE YOU ALL RIGHT?
DO I LOOK ALL RIGHT TO YOU?
LUNA, WOULD YOU PLEASE QUIT GLOMPING ME LIKE THAT?
I'M SORRY...
I...

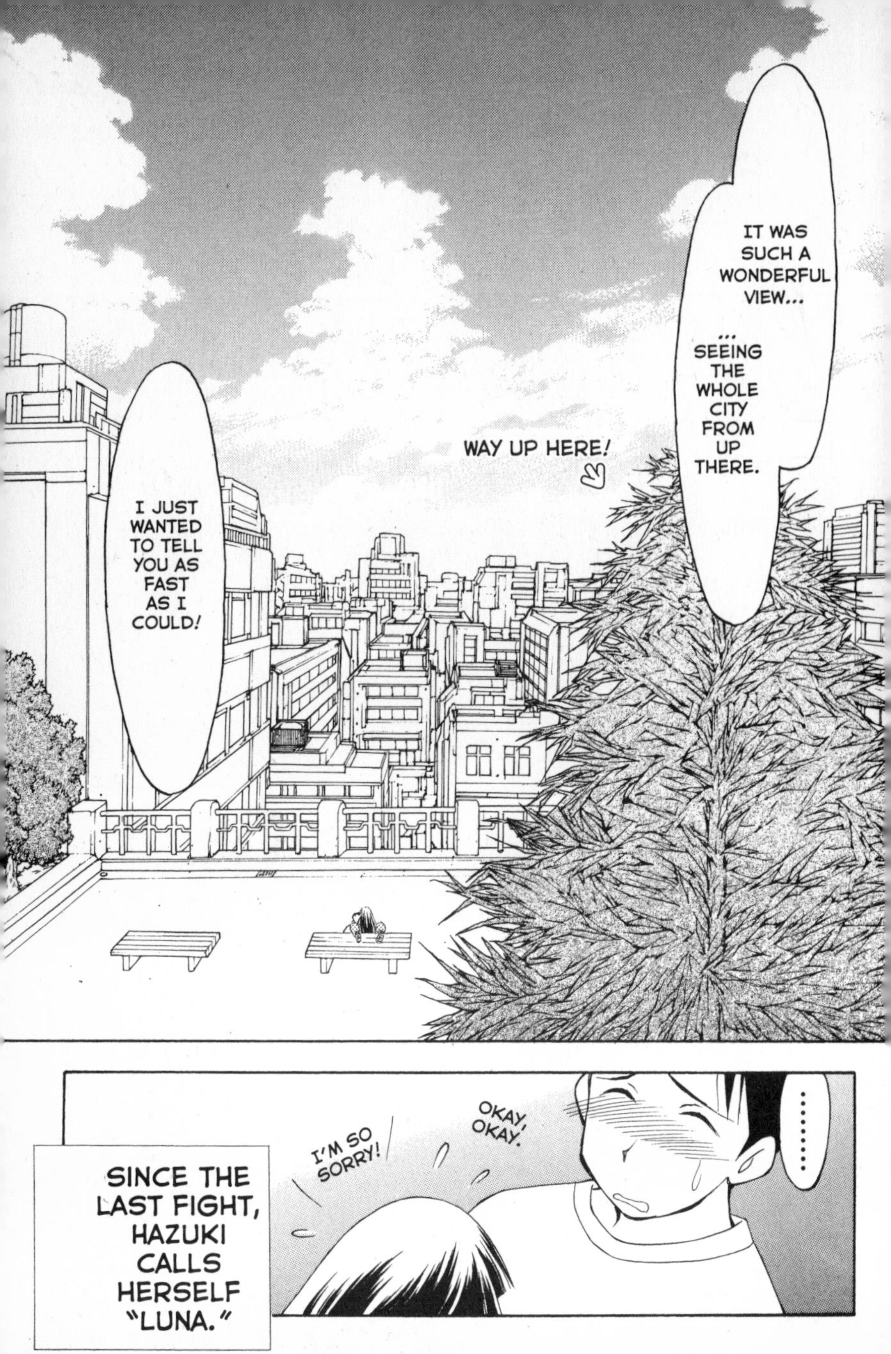
IT WAS SUCH A WONDERFUL VIEW...
...SEEING THE WHOLE CITY FROM UP THERE.
WAY UP HERE!
I JUST WANTED TO TELL YOU AS FAST AS I COULD!
....
OKAY, OKAY.
I'M SO SORRY!
SINCE THE LAST FIGHT, HAZUKI CALLS HERSELF "LUNA."

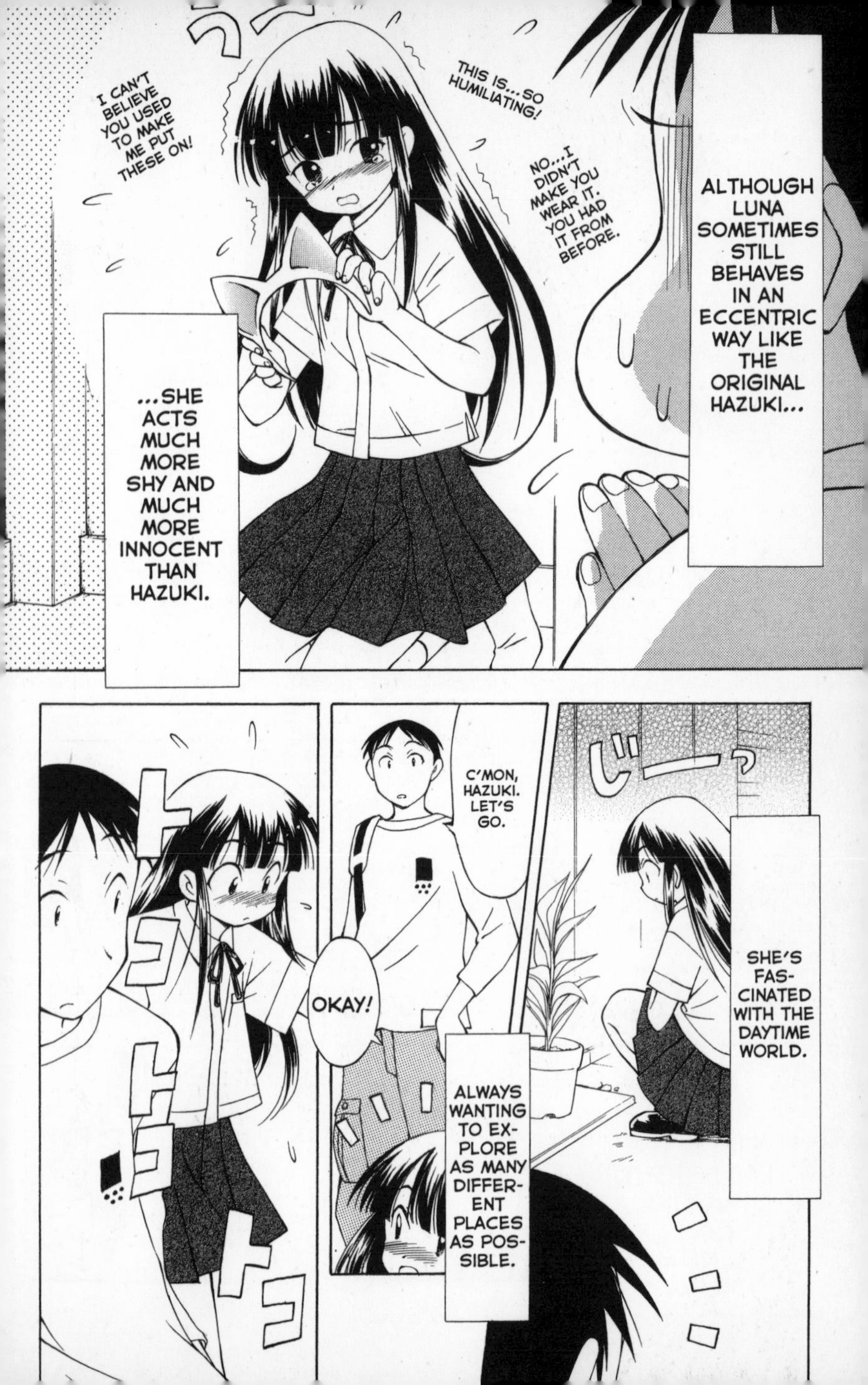

ALTHOUGH LUNA SOMETIMES STILL BEHAVES IN AN ECCENTRIC WAY LIKE THE ORIGINAL HAZUKI...
THIS IS... SO HUMILIATING!
NO... I DIDN'T MAKE YOU WEAR IT. YOU HAD IT FROM BEFORE.
I CAN'T BELIEVE YOU USED TO MAKE ME PUT THESE ON!
...SHE ACTS MUCH MORE SHY AND MUCH MORE INNOCENT THAN HAZUKI.
SHE'S FAS-CINATED WITH THE DAYTIME WORLD.
C'MON, HAZUKI. LET'S GO.
ALWAYS WANTING TO EX-PLORE AS MANY DIFFER-ENT PLACES AS POS-SIBLE.
OKAY!

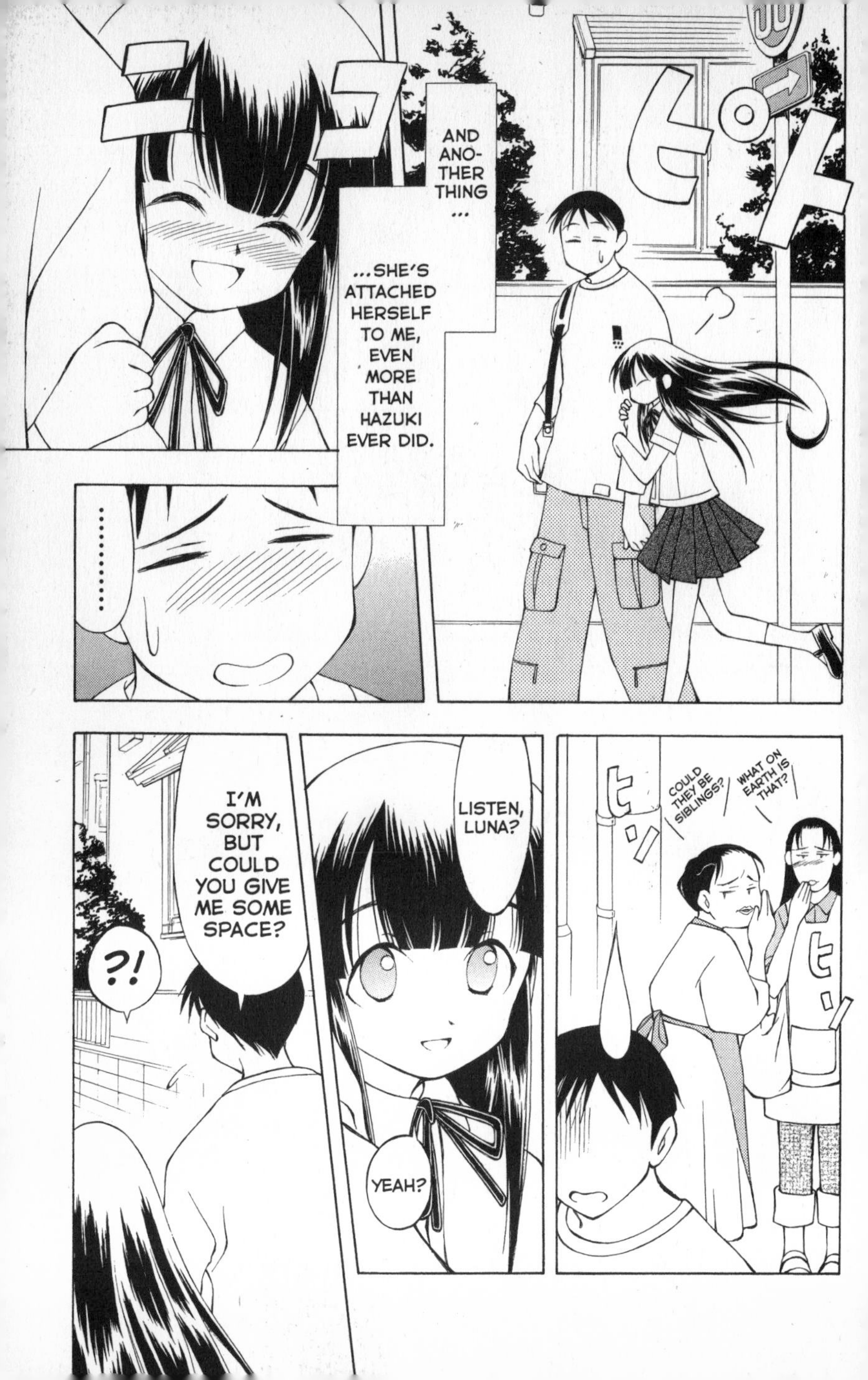
AND ANOTHER THING...
...SHE'S ATTACHED HERSELF TO ME, EVEN MORE THAN HAZUKI EVER DID.
......
CCOULD THEY BE SIBLINGS?
WHAT ON EARTH IS THAT?
LISTEN, LUNA?
YEAH?
I'M SORRY, BUT COULD YOU GIVE ME SOME SPACE?
?!

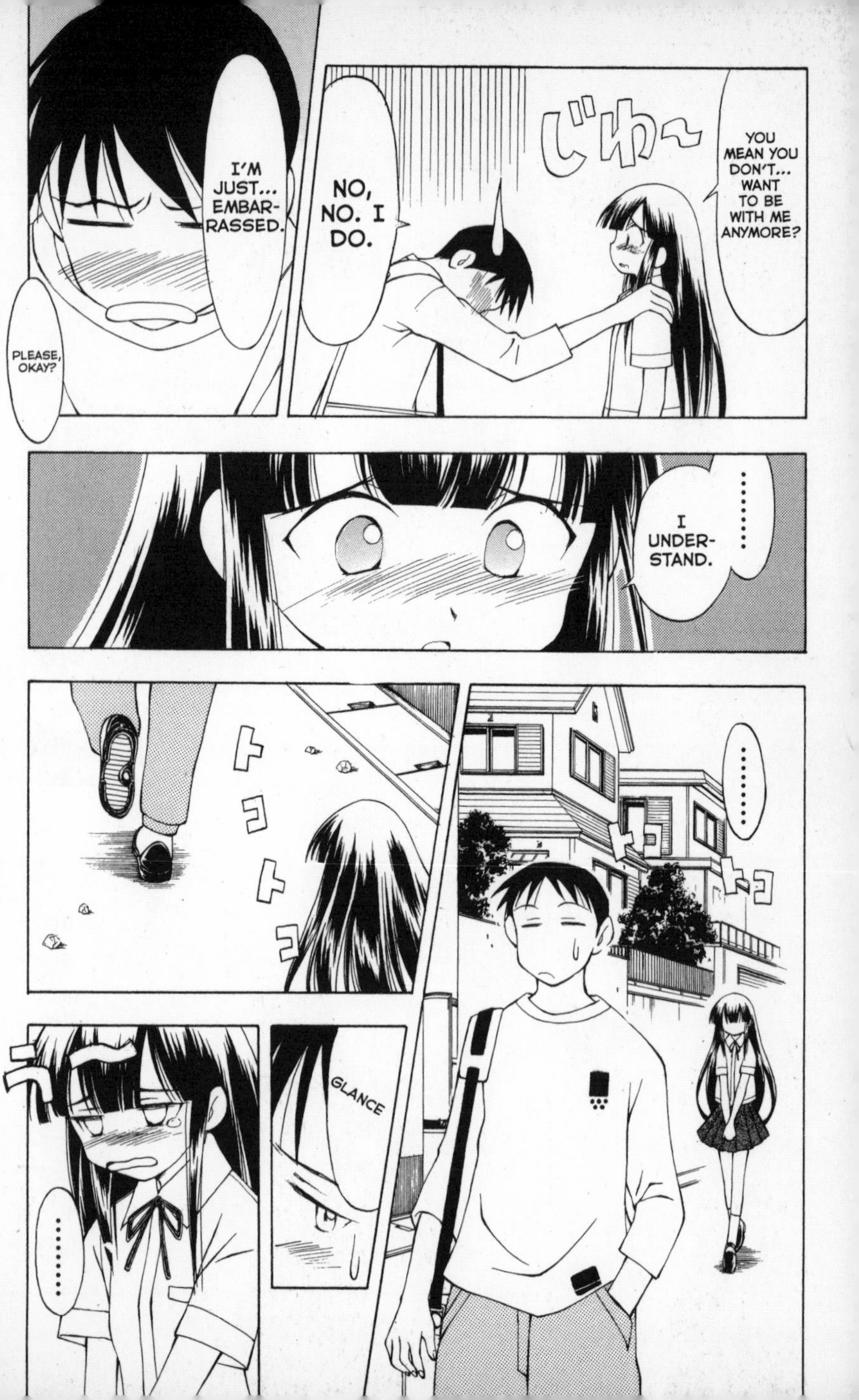
YOU MEAN YOU DON'T... WANT TO BE WITH ME ANYMORE?
じわ~
NO, NO. I DO.
I'M JUST... EMBARRASSED.
PLEASE, OKAY?
......
I UNDERSTAND.
......
トコ トコ
トコ トコ
GLANCE
......

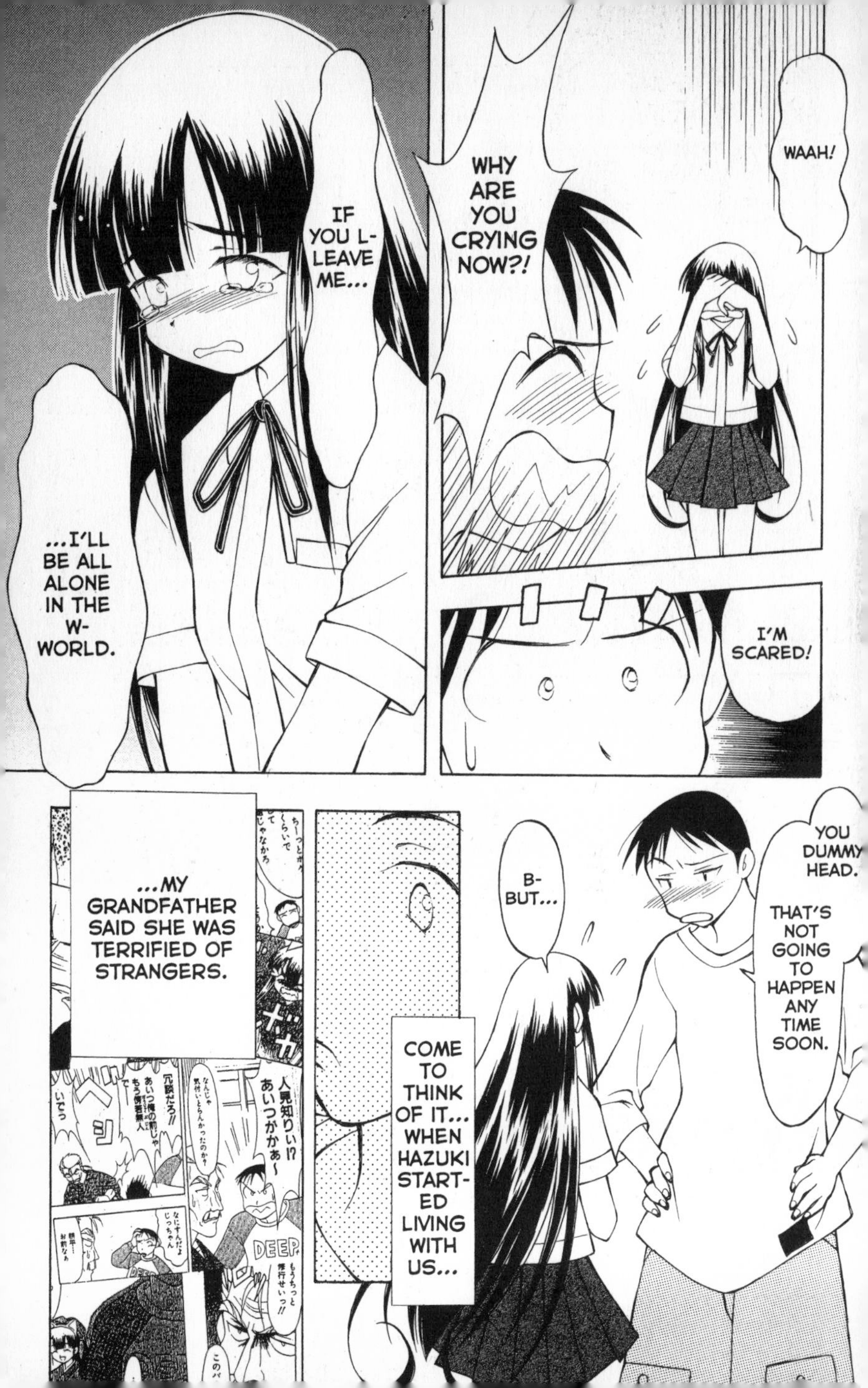
WAAH!
WHY ARE YOU CRYING NOW?!
I'M SCARED!
IF YOU L-LEAVE ME...
...I'LL BE ALL ALONE IN THE W-WORLD.
YOU DUMMY HEAD.
THAT'S NOT GOING TO HAPPEN ANY TIME SOON.
B-BUT...
COME TO THINK OF IT... WHEN HAZUKI START-ED LIVING WITH US...
...MY GRANDFATHER SAID SHE WAS TERRIFIED OF STRANGERS.

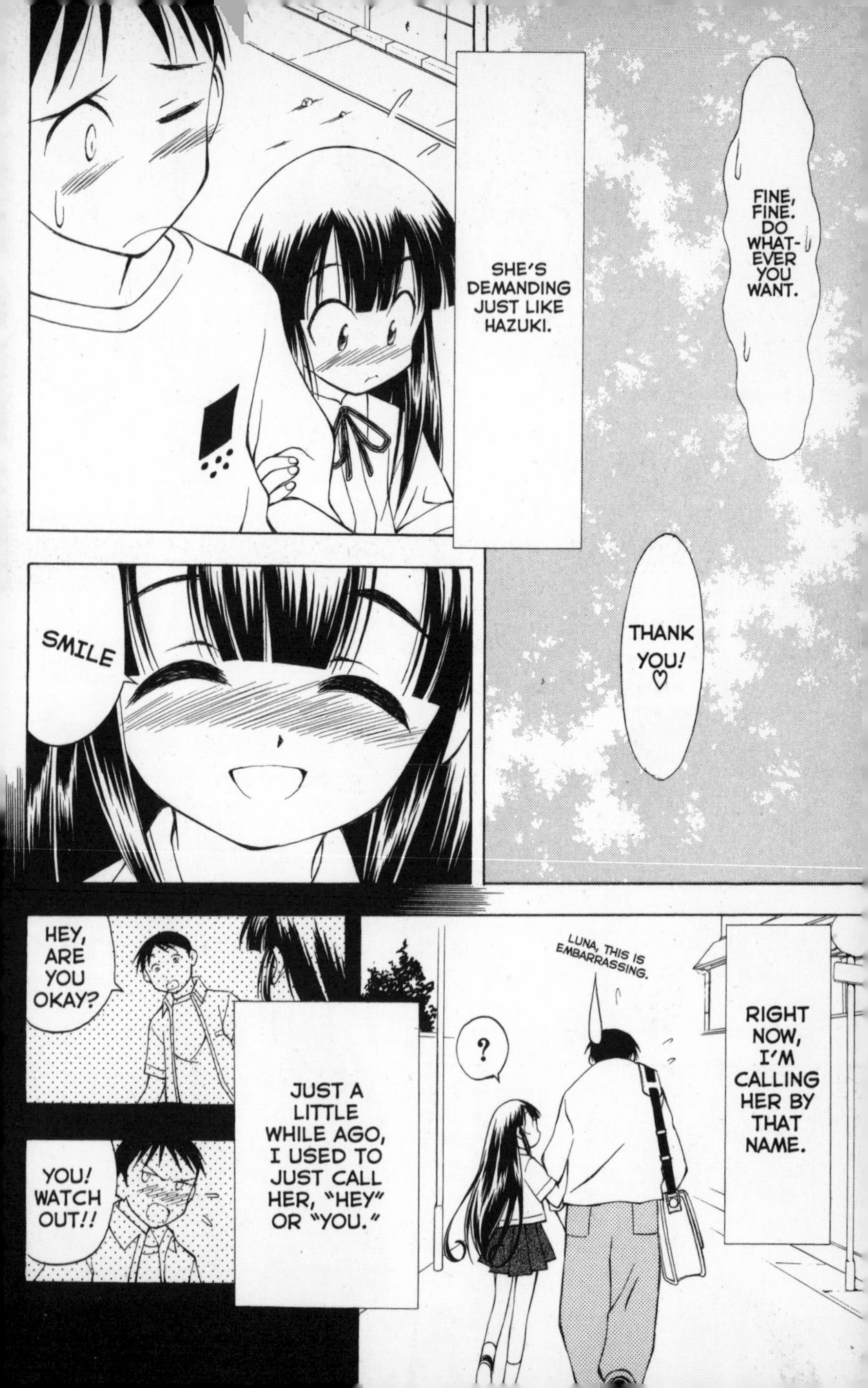
FINE, FINE. DO WHATEVER YOU WANT.
SHE'S DEMANDING JUST LIKE HAZUKI.
THANK YOU! ♡
SMILE
RIGHT NOW, I'M CALLING HER BY THAT NAME.
LUNA, THIS IS EMBARRASSING.
?
JUST A LITTLE WHILE AGO, I USED TO JUST CALL HER, "HEY" OR "YOU."
HEY, ARE YOU OKAY?
YOU! WATCH OUT!!

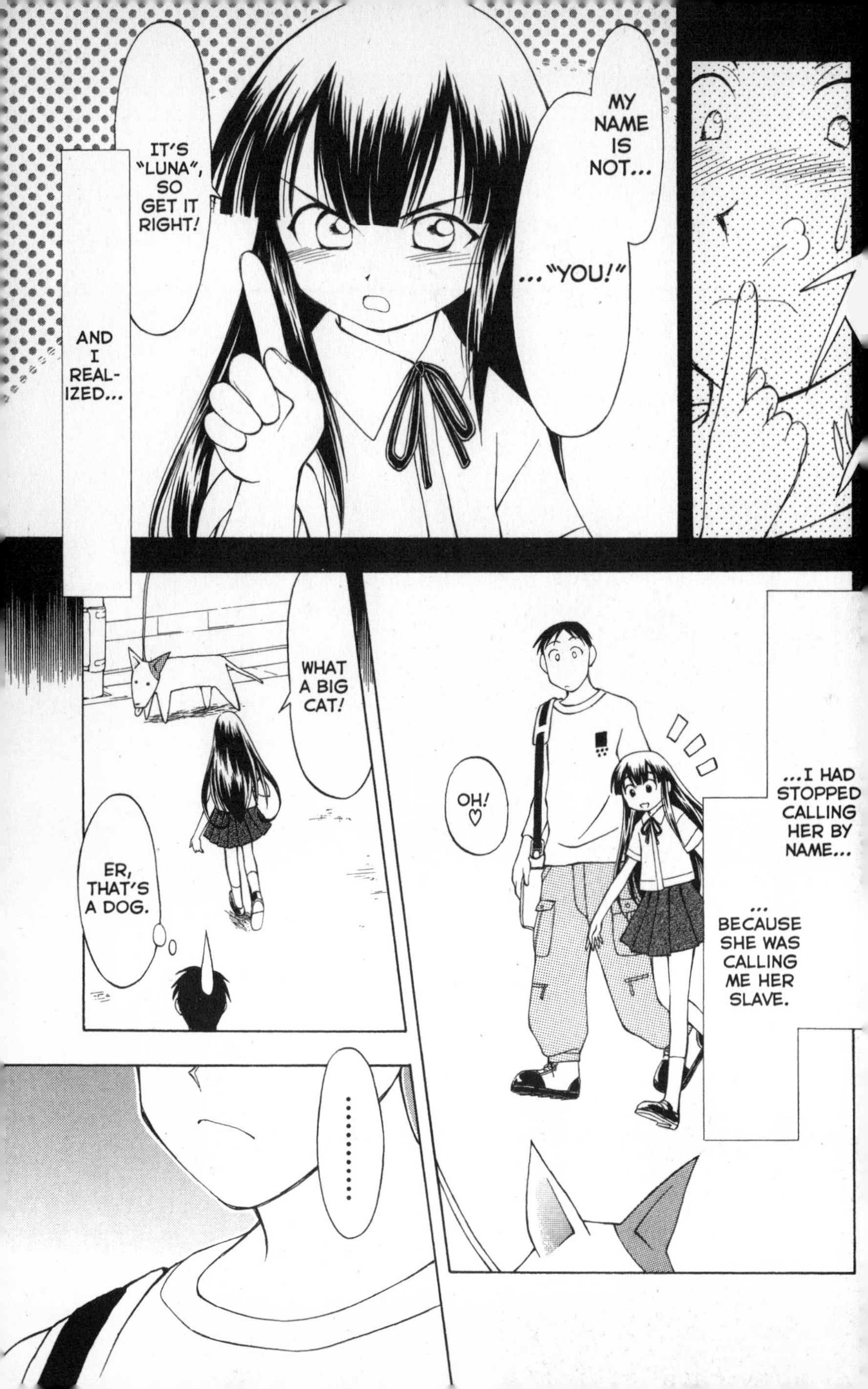
MY NAME IS NOT...
..."YOU!"
IT'S "LUNA", SO GET IT RIGHT!
AND I REALIZED...
WHAT A BIG CAT!
ER, THAT'S A DOG.
...I HAD STOPPED CALLING HER BY NAME...
... BECAUSE SHE WAS CALLING ME HER SLAVE.
OH! ♡
....

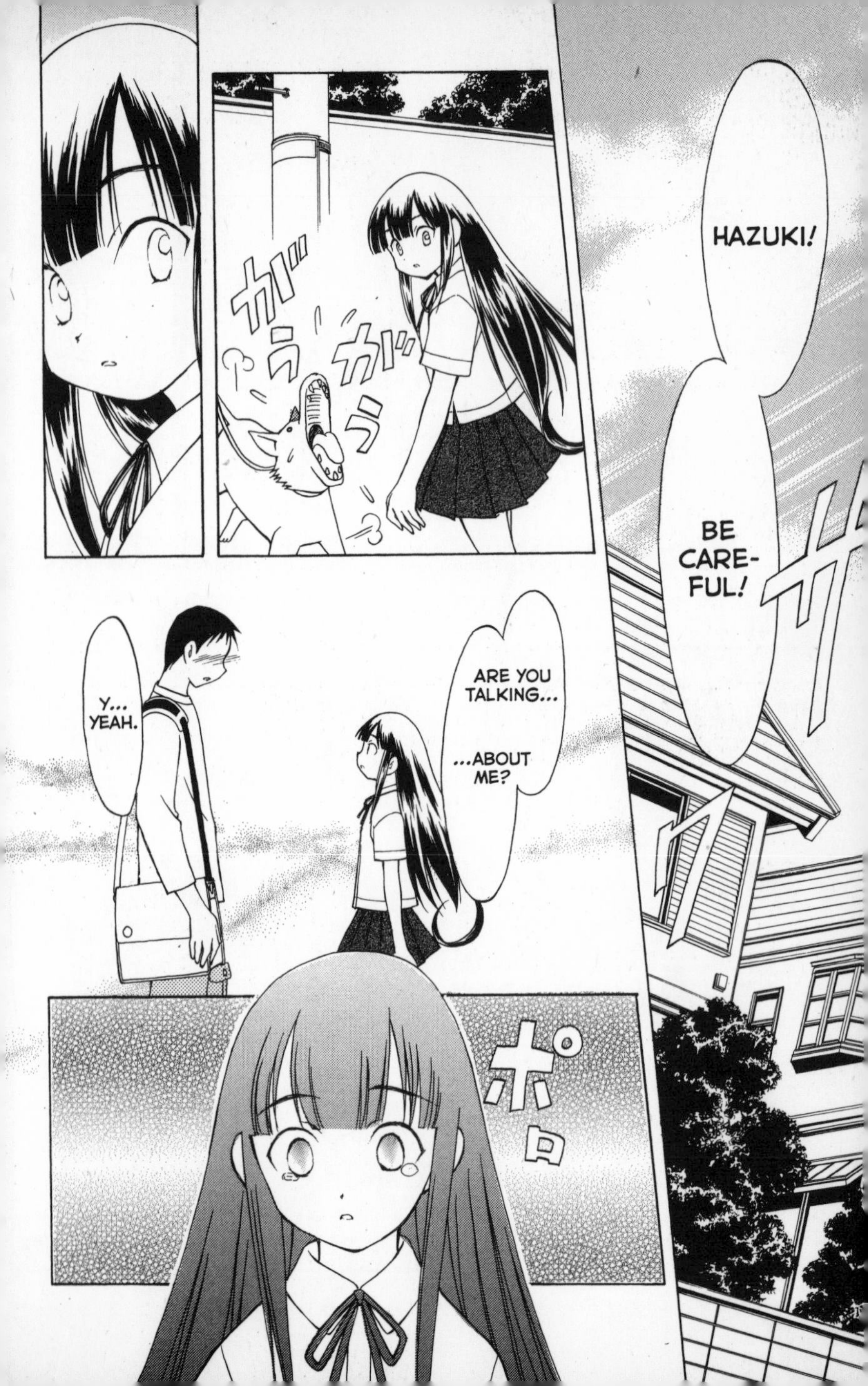

HAZUKI!
BE CARE-FUL!
ガう
ガう
ARE YOU TALKING...
...ABOUT ME?
Y... YEAH.
ポロ

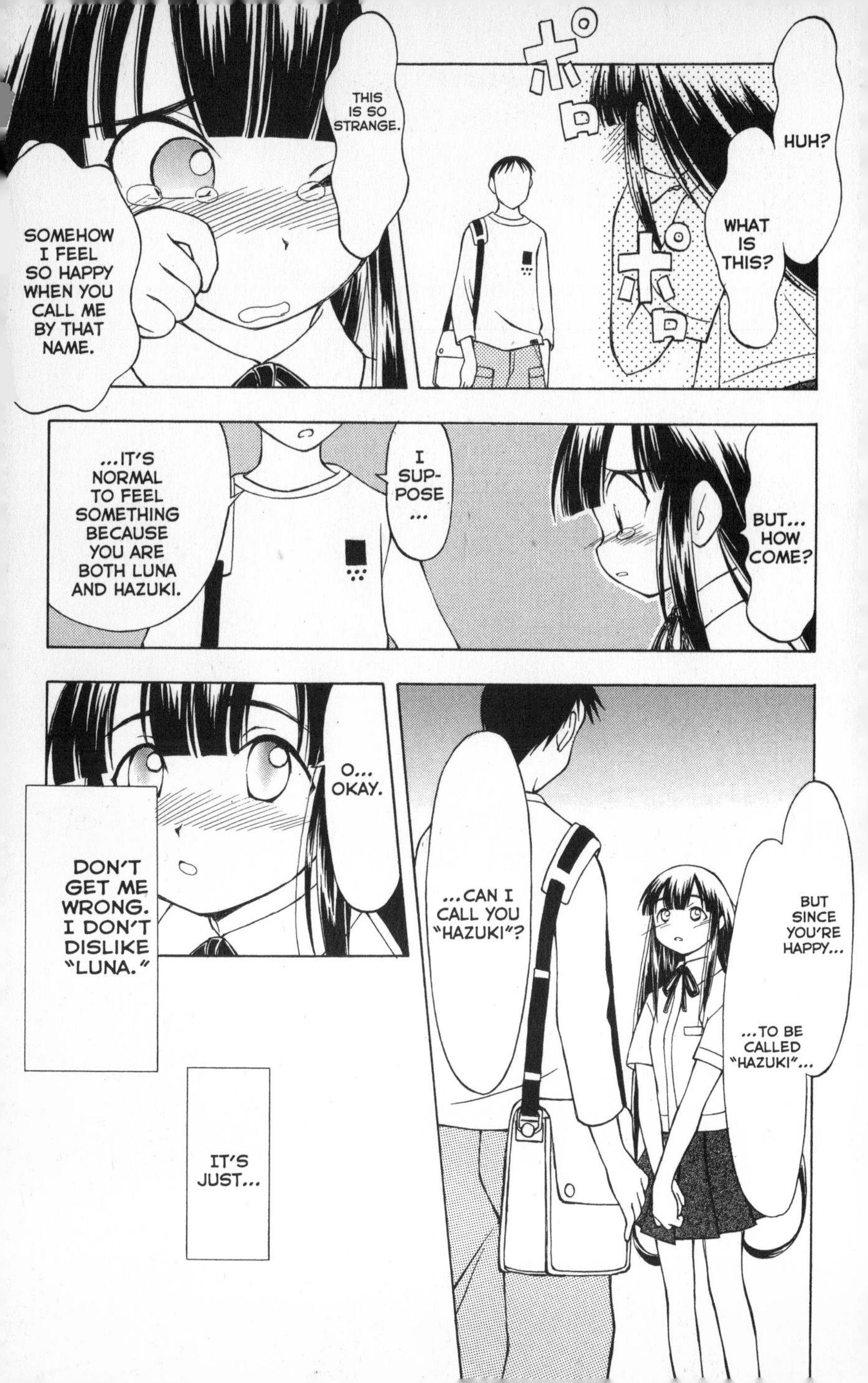
ポロ
HUH?
WHAT IS THIS?
ポロ
THIS IS SO STRANGE.
SOMEHOW I FEEL SO HAPPY WHEN YOU CALL ME BY THAT NAME.
BUT... HOW COME?
I SUP-POSE...
...IT'S NORMAL TO FEEL SOMETHING BECAUSE YOU ARE BOTH LUNA AND HAZUKI.
BUT SINCE YOU'RE HAPPY...
...TO BE CALLED "HAZUKI"...
...CAN I CALL YOU "HAZUKI"?
O... OKAY.
DON'T GET ME WRONG. I DON'T DISLIKE "LUNA."
IT'S JUST...

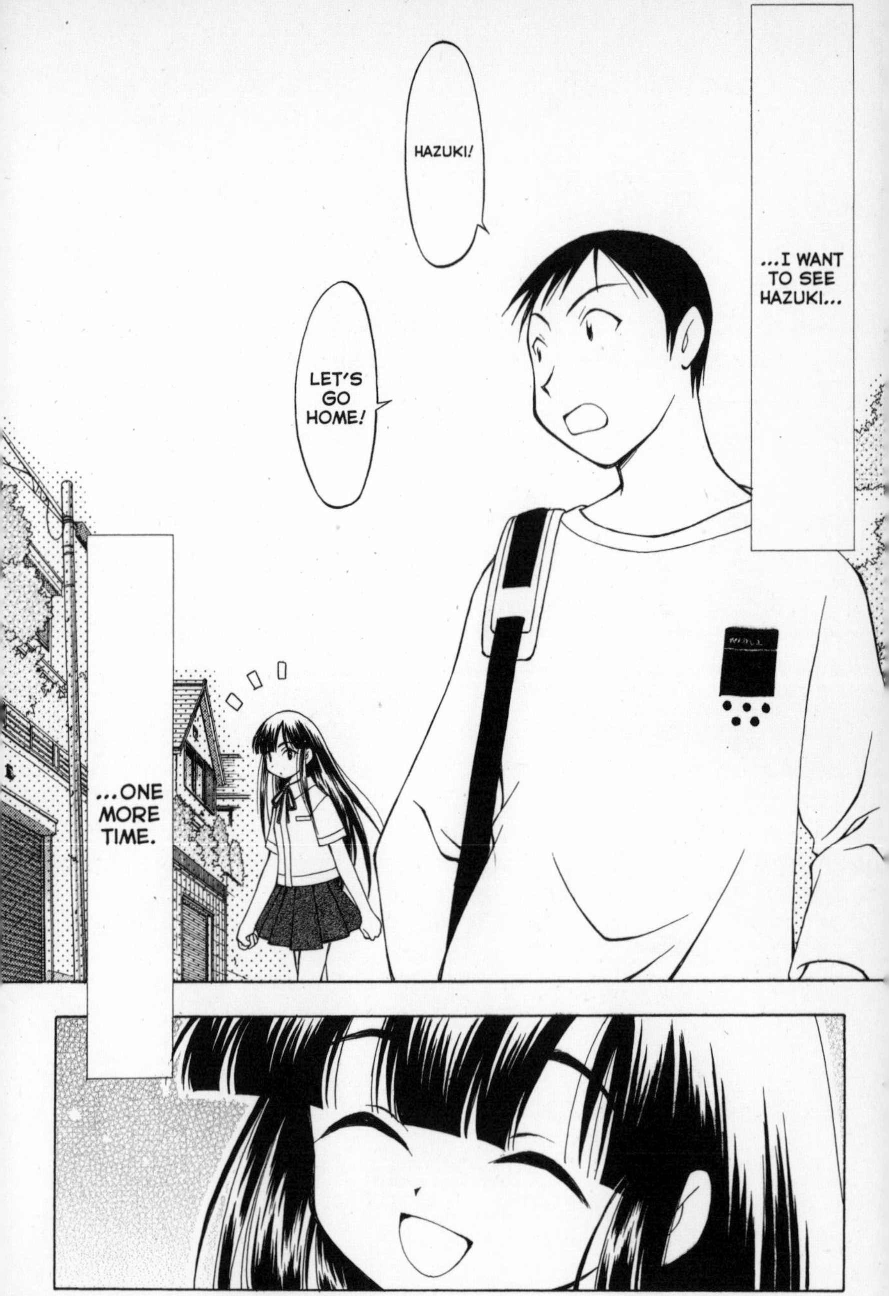
...I WANT TO SEE HAZUKI...
HAZUKI!
LET'S GO HOME!
...ONE MORE TIME.

MOON 月詠 PHASE

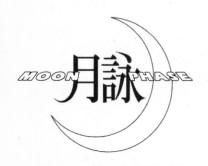

PART 1

MOON PHASE DOLL THEATER

☞ CONTINUED ON PAGE 50

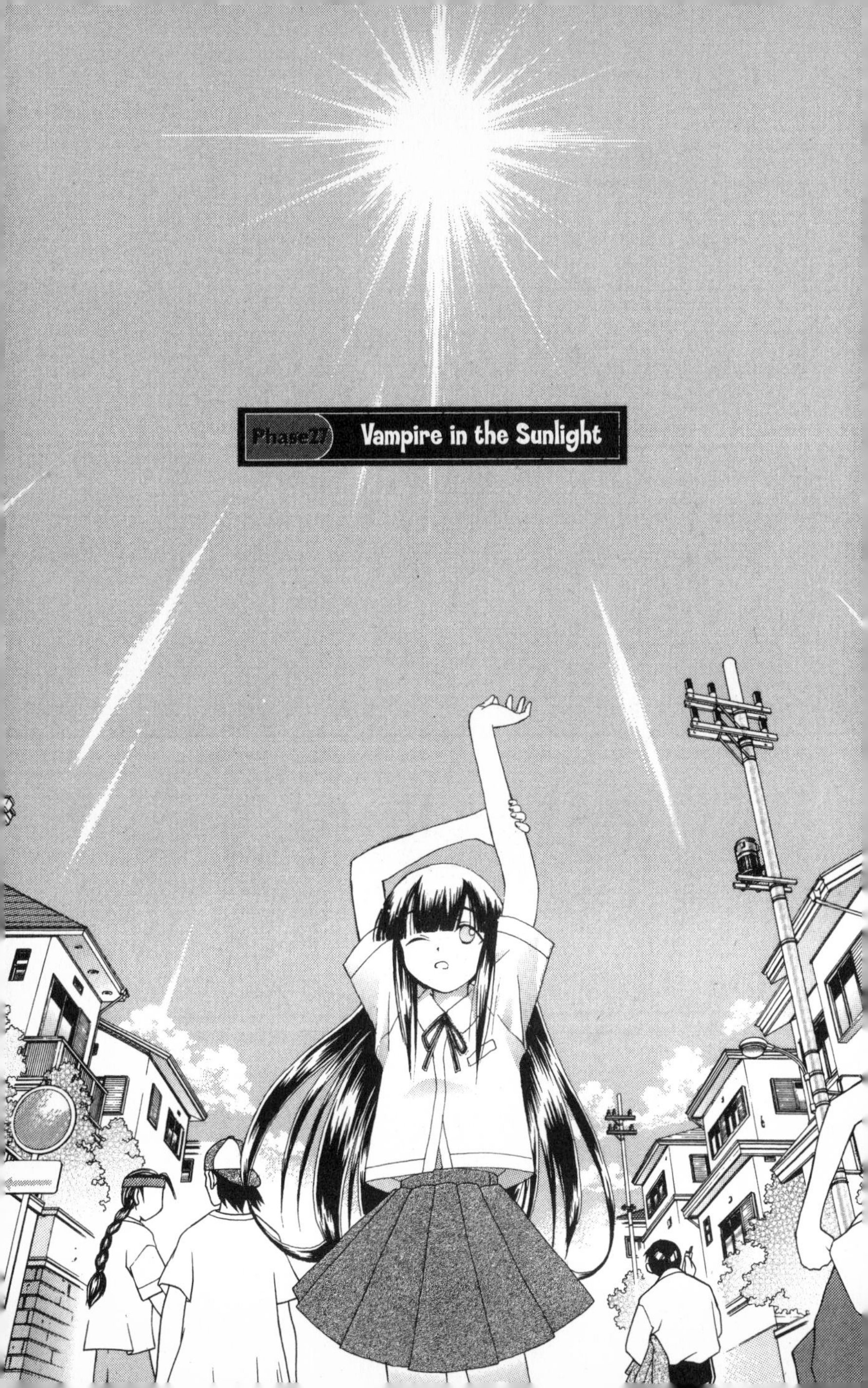
Phase27
Vampire in the Sunlight

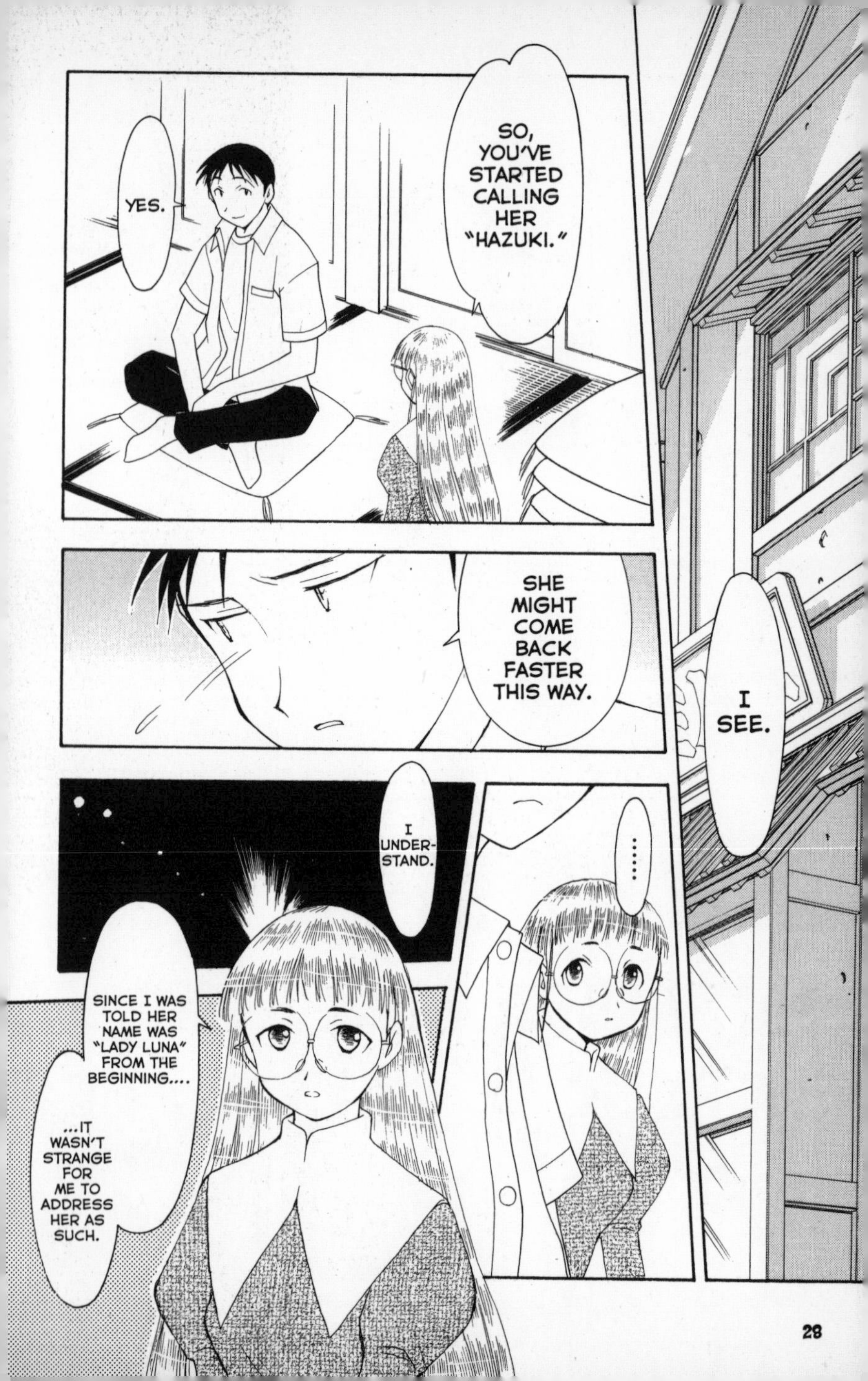

SO, YOU'VE STARTED CALLING HER "HAZUKI."
YES.
SHE MIGHT COME BACK FASTER THIS WAY.
I SEE.
......
I UNDER-STAND.
SINCE I WAS TOLD HER NAME WAS "LADY LUNA" FROM THE BEGINNING....
...IT WASN'T STRANGE FOR ME TO ADDRESS HER AS SUCH.

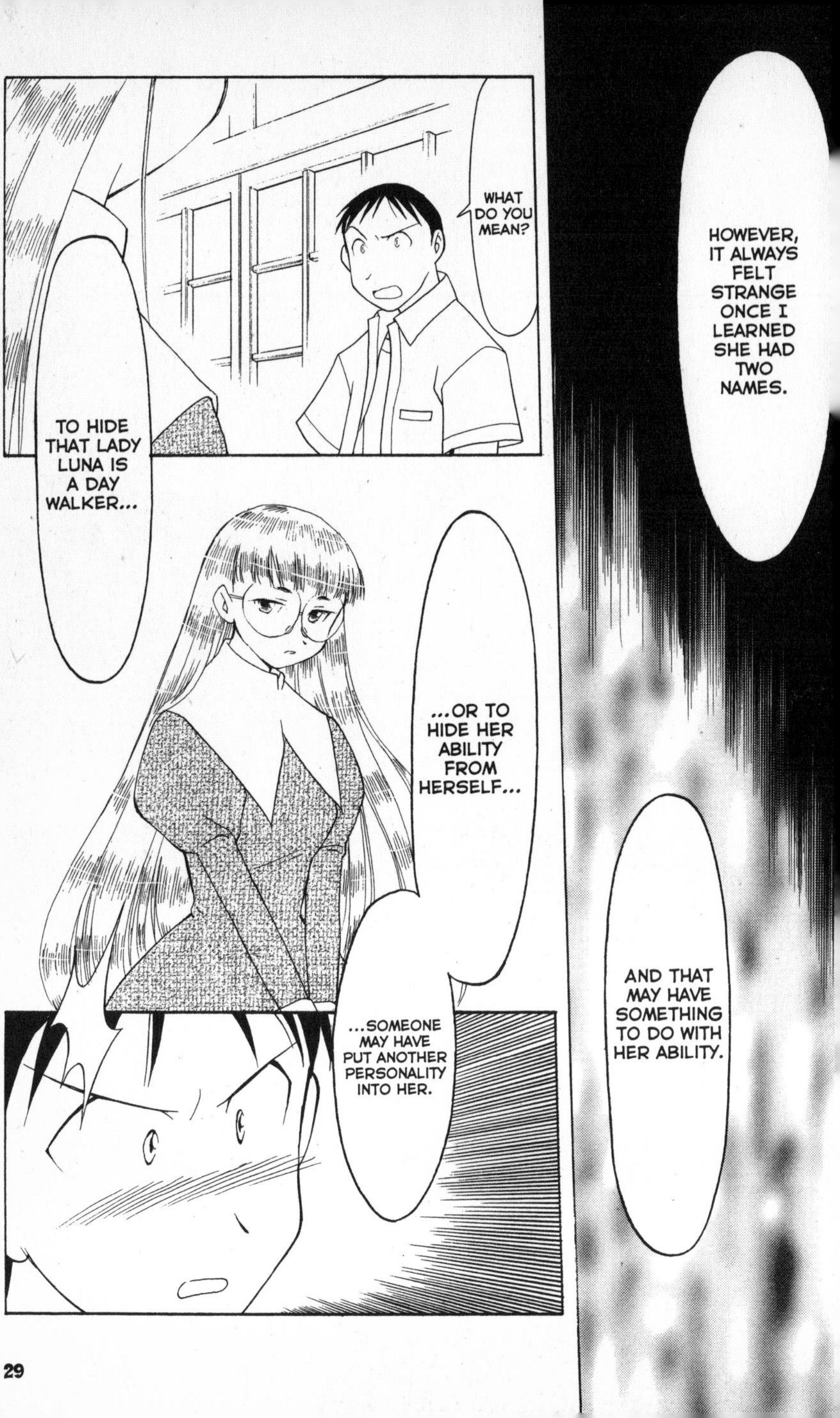
HOWEVER, IT ALWAYS FELT STRANGE ONCE I LEARNED SHE HAD TWO NAMES.
WHAT DO YOU MEAN?
TO HIDE THAT LADY LUNA IS A DAY WALKER...
...OR TO HIDE HER ABILITY FROM HERSELF...
AND THAT MAY HAVE SOMETHING TO DO WITH HER ABILITY.
...SOMEONE MAY HAVE PUT ANOTHER PERSONALITY INTO HER.

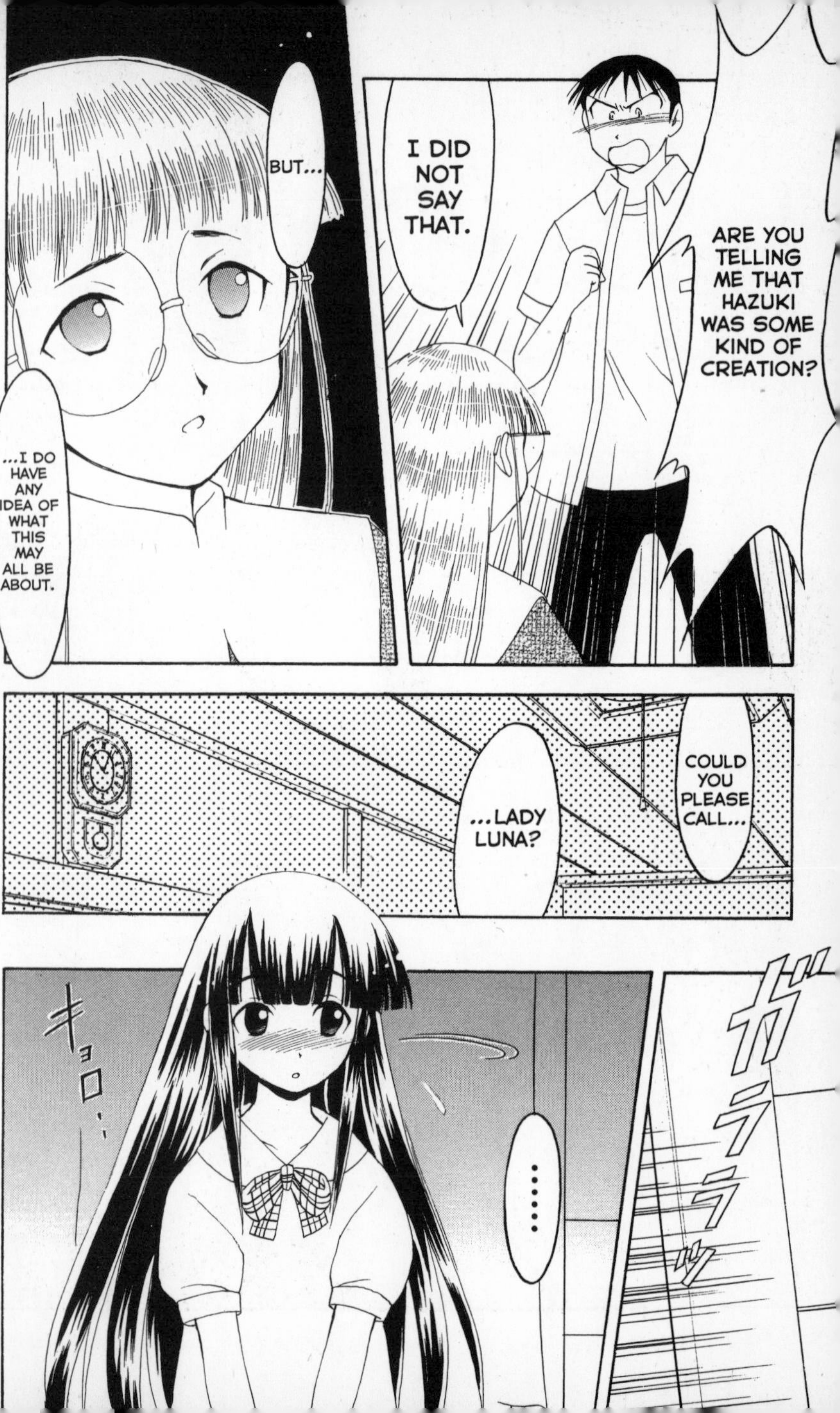
ARE YOU TELLING ME THAT HAZUKI WAS SOME KIND OF CREATION?
I DID NOT SAY THAT.
BUT...
...I DO HAVE ANY IDEA OF WHAT THIS MAY ALL BE ABOUT.
COULD YOU PLEASE CALL...
...LADY LUNA?
ガラララッ
......
キョロ

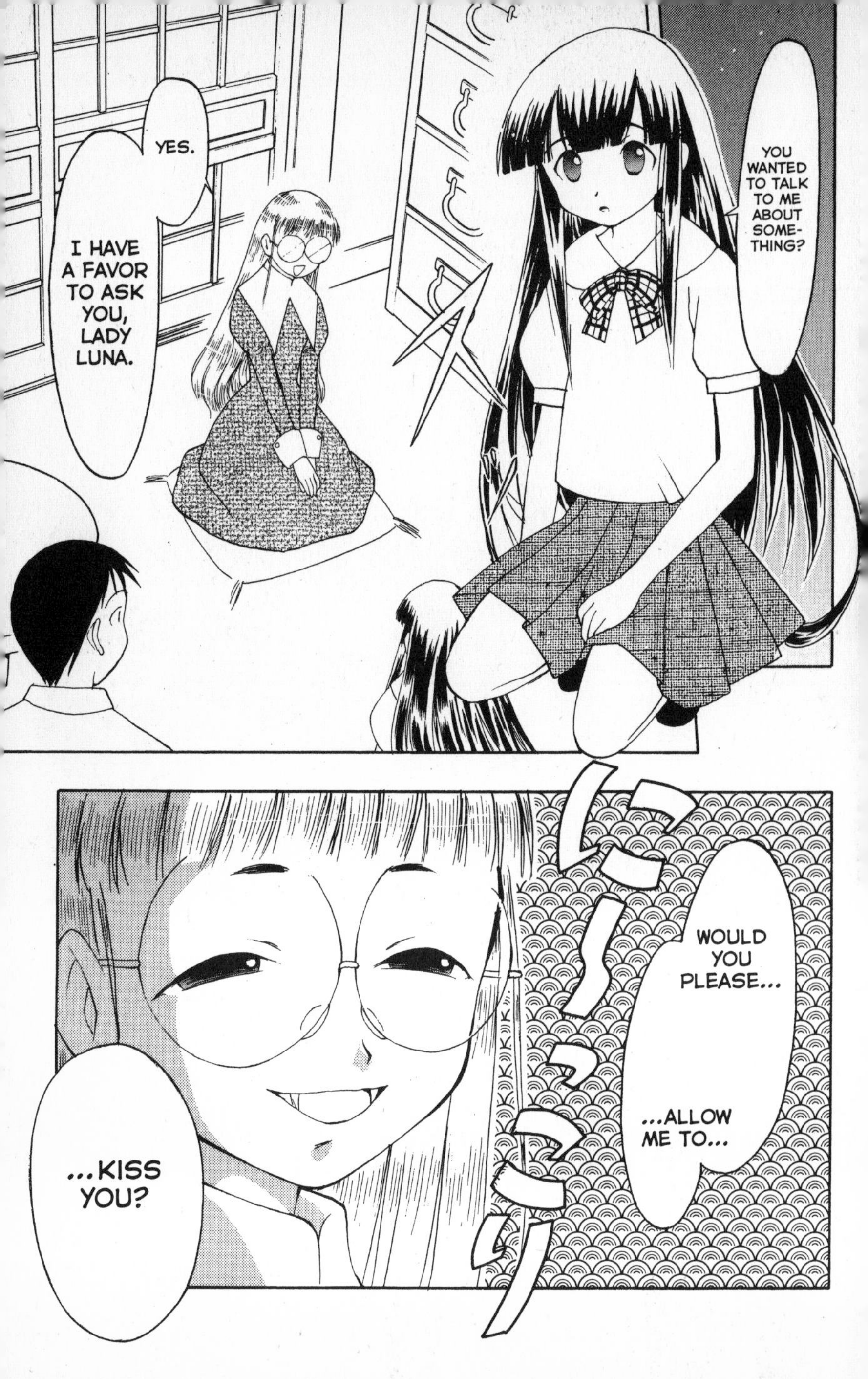
YOU WANTED TO TALK TO ME ABOUT SOME-THING?
YES.
I HAVE A FAVOR TO ASK YOU, LADY LUNA.
WOULD YOU PLEASE...
...ALLOW ME TO...
...KISS YOU?

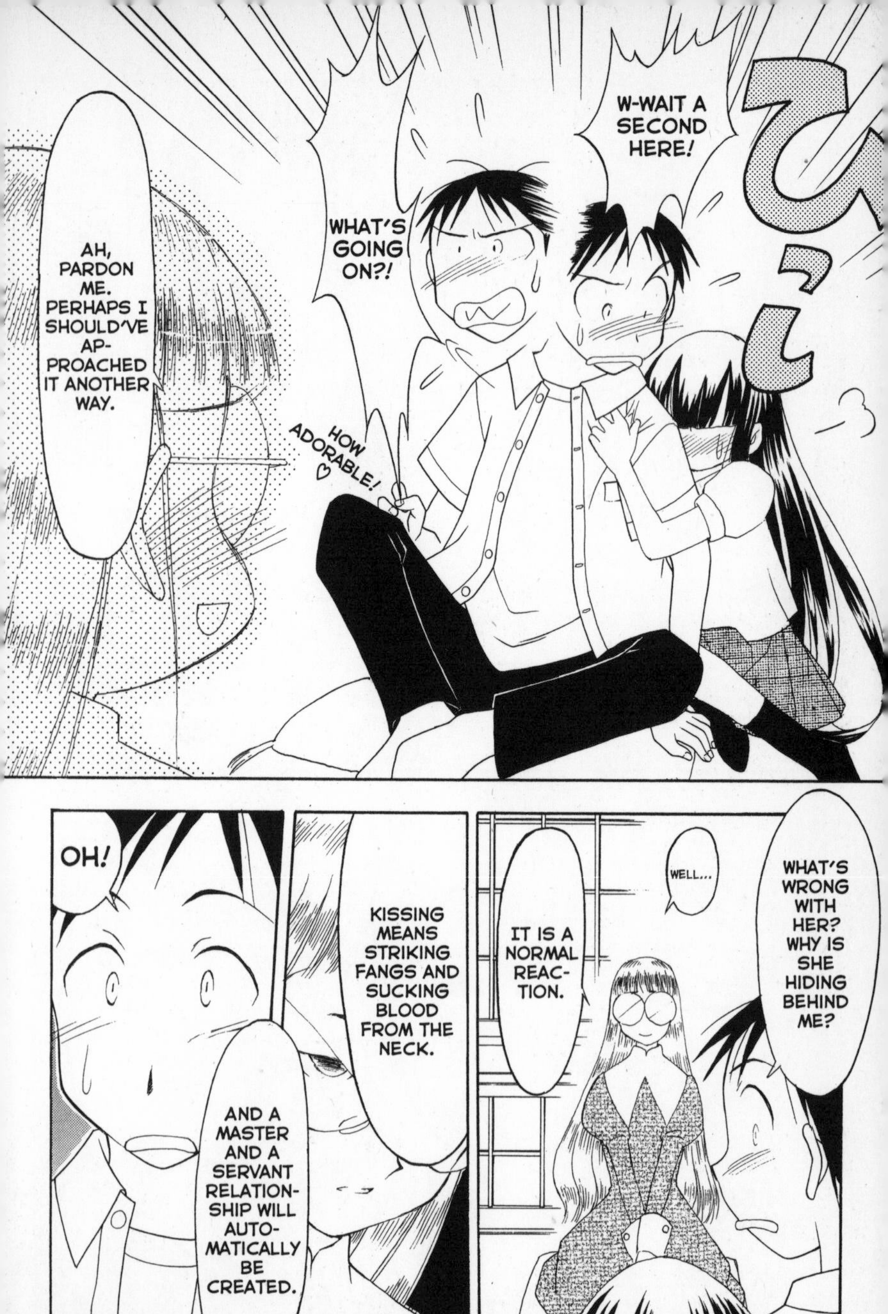
W-WAIT A SECOND HERE!
WHAT'S GOING ON?!
HOW ADORABLE! ♡
AH, PARDON ME. PERHAPS I SHOULD'VE AP-PROACHED IT ANOTHER WAY.
WHAT'S WRONG WITH HER? WHY IS SHE HIDING BEHIND ME?
WELL...
IT IS A NORMAL REAC-TION.
KISSING MEANS STRIKING FANGS AND SUCKING BLOOD FROM THE NECK.
OH!
AND A MASTER AND A SERVANT RELATION-SHIP WILL AUTO-MATICALLY BE CREATED.

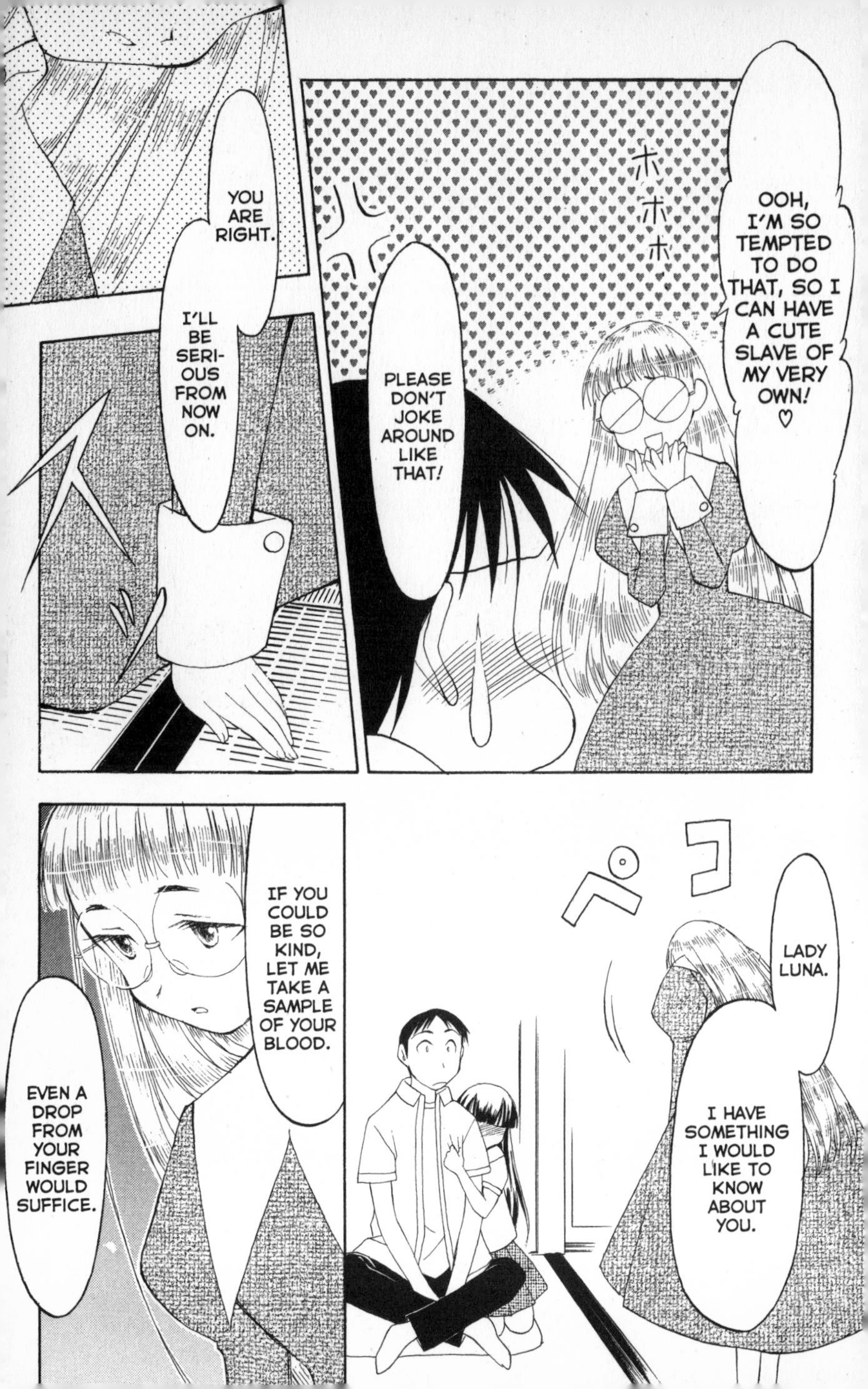
OOH, I'M SO TEMPTED TO DO THAT, SO I CAN HAVE A CUTE SLAVE OF MY VERY OWN! ♡
ホホホ
PLEASE DON'T JOKE AROUND LIKE THAT!
YOU ARE RIGHT.
I'LL BE SERI-OUS FROM NOW ON.
ペコ
LADY LUNA.
I HAVE SOMETHING I WOULD LIKE TO KNOW ABOUT YOU.
IF YOU COULD BE SO KIND, LET ME TAKE A SAMPLE OF YOUR BLOOD.
EVEN A DROP FROM YOUR FINGER WOULD SUFFICE.

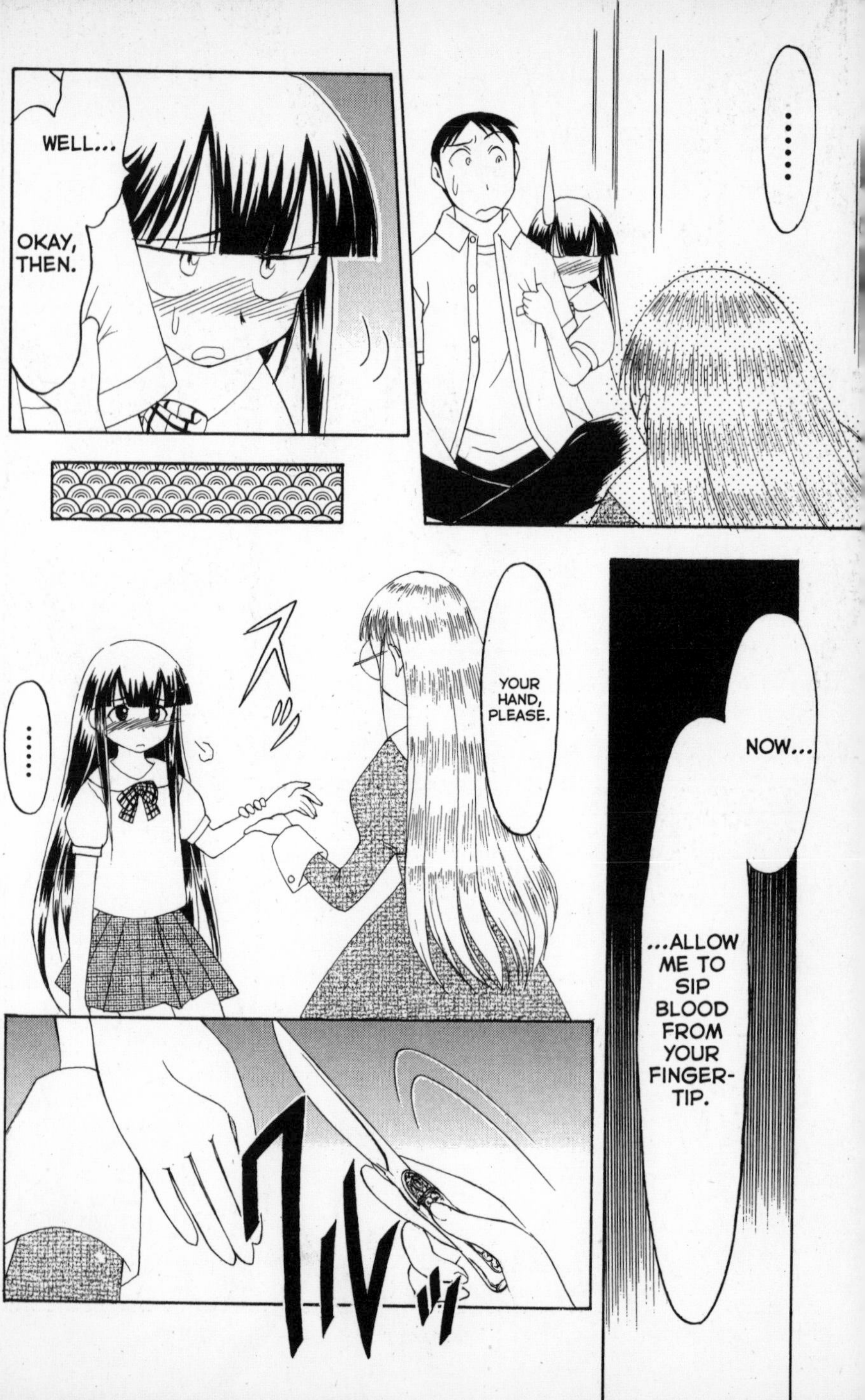
......
WELL...
OKAY, THEN.
NOW...
...ALLOW ME TO SIP BLOOD FROM YOUR FINGER-TIP.
YOUR HAND, PLEASE.
......

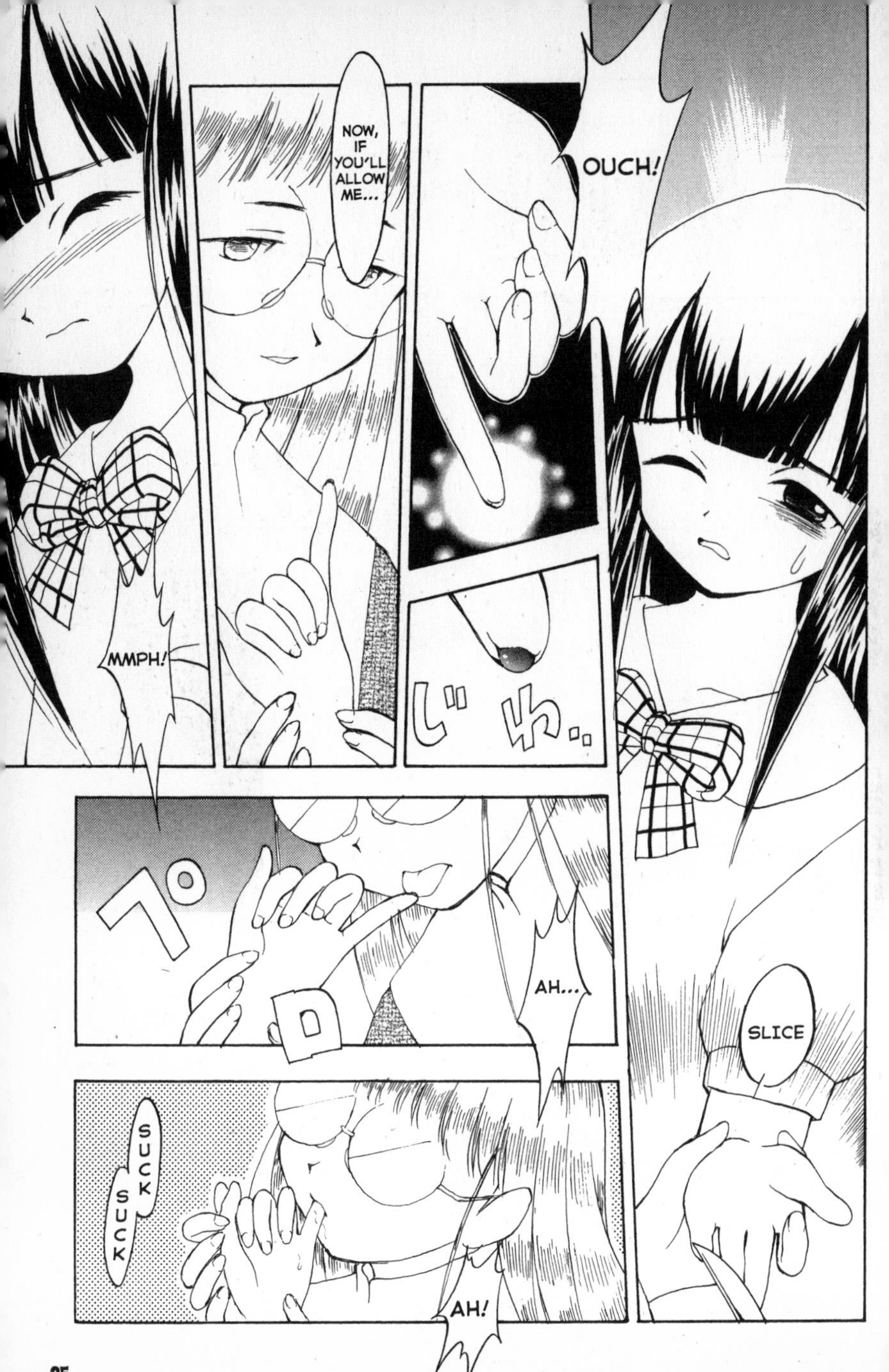
SLICE
OUCH!
じわ。。
NOW, IF YOU'LL ALLOW ME...
MMPH!
ペ
D
AH...
SUCK SUCK
AH!

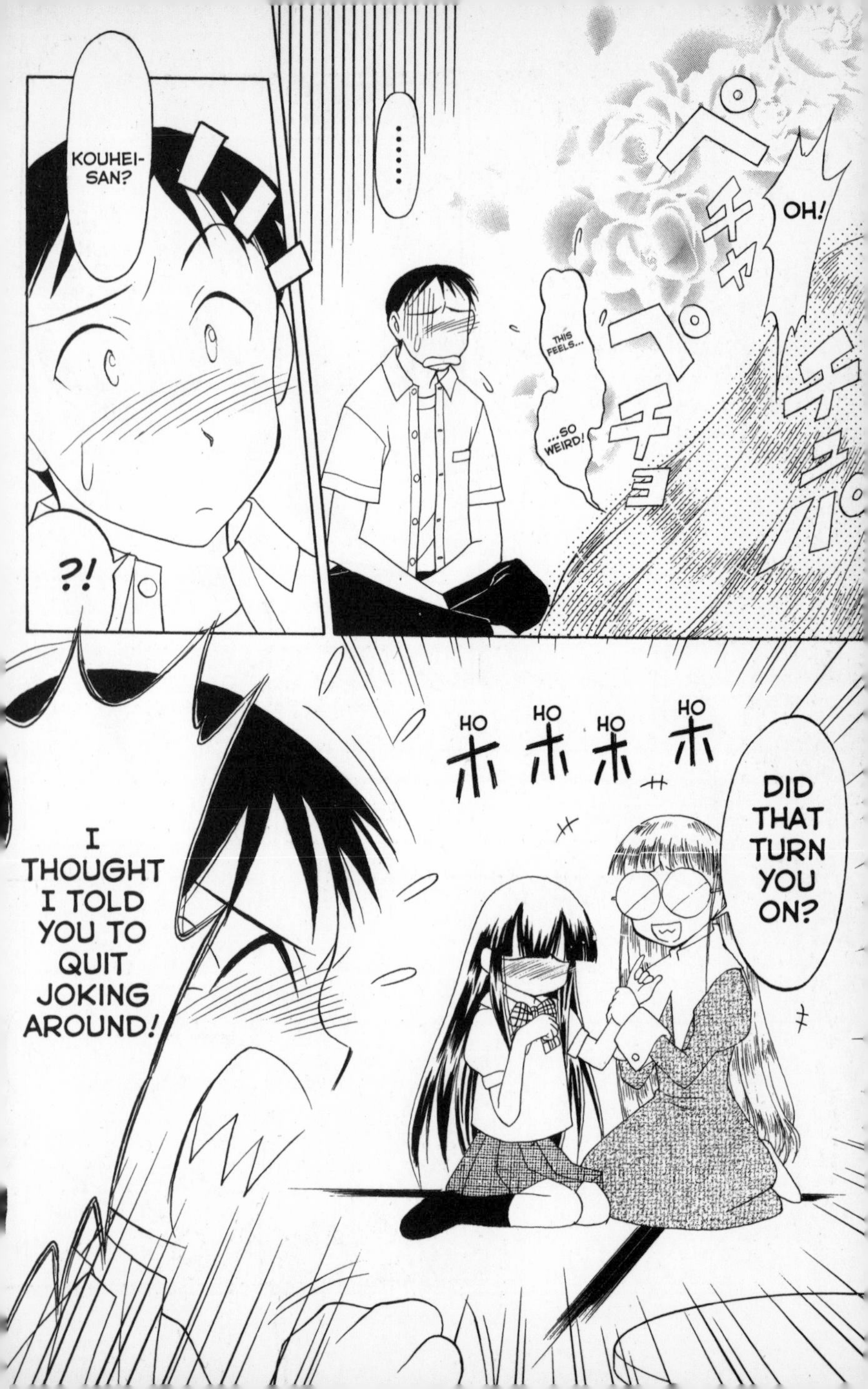
OH!
ペチャペチョ
チュパ
THIS FEELS...
...SO WEIRD!
......
KOUHEI-SAN?
?!
HO HO HO HO
ホホホホ
DID THAT TURN YOU ON?
I THOUGHT I TOLD YOU TO QUIT JOKING AROUND!

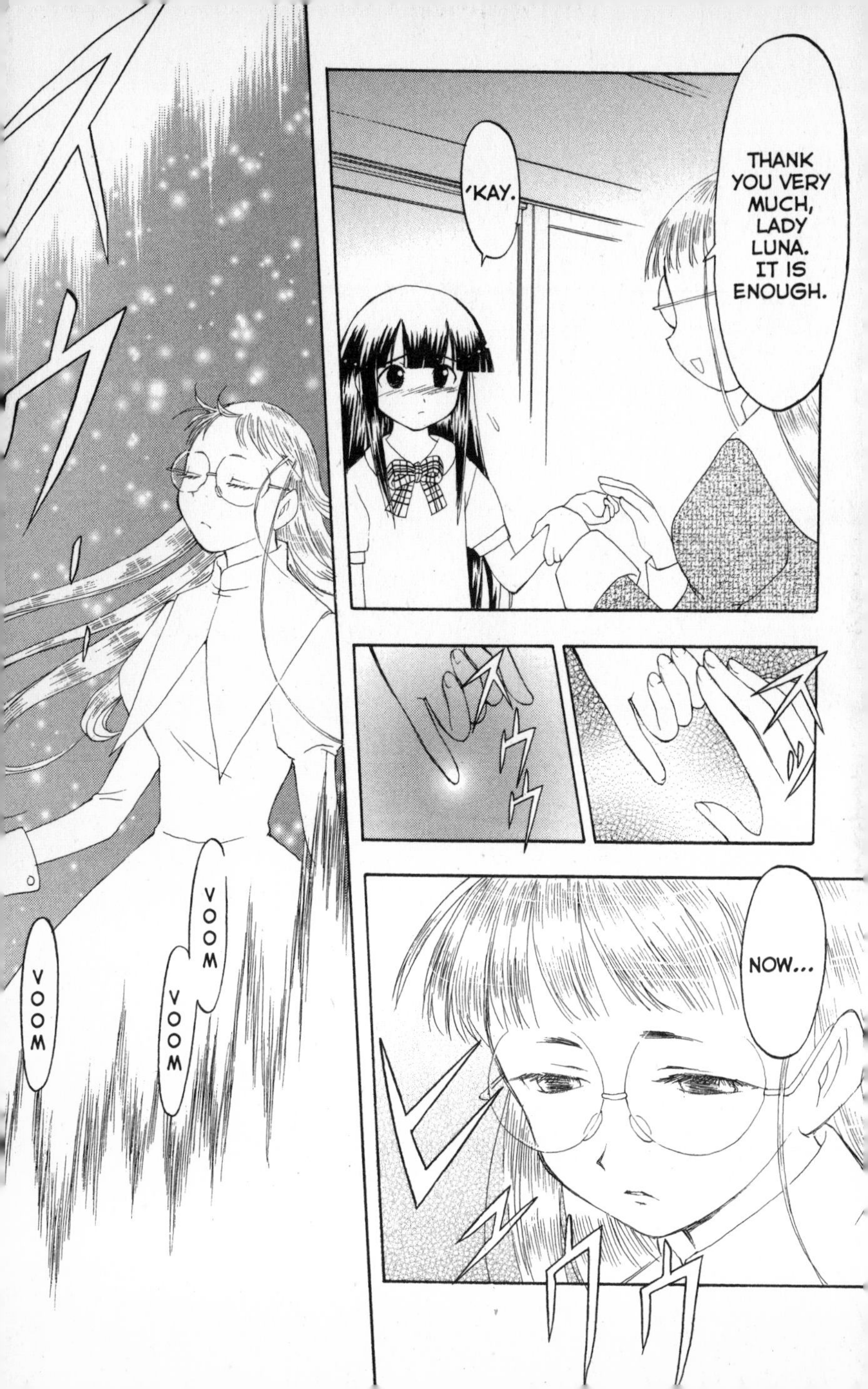
THANK YOU VERY MUCH, LADY LUNA. IT IS ENOUGH.
'KAY.
NOW...
VOOM
VOOM
VOOM

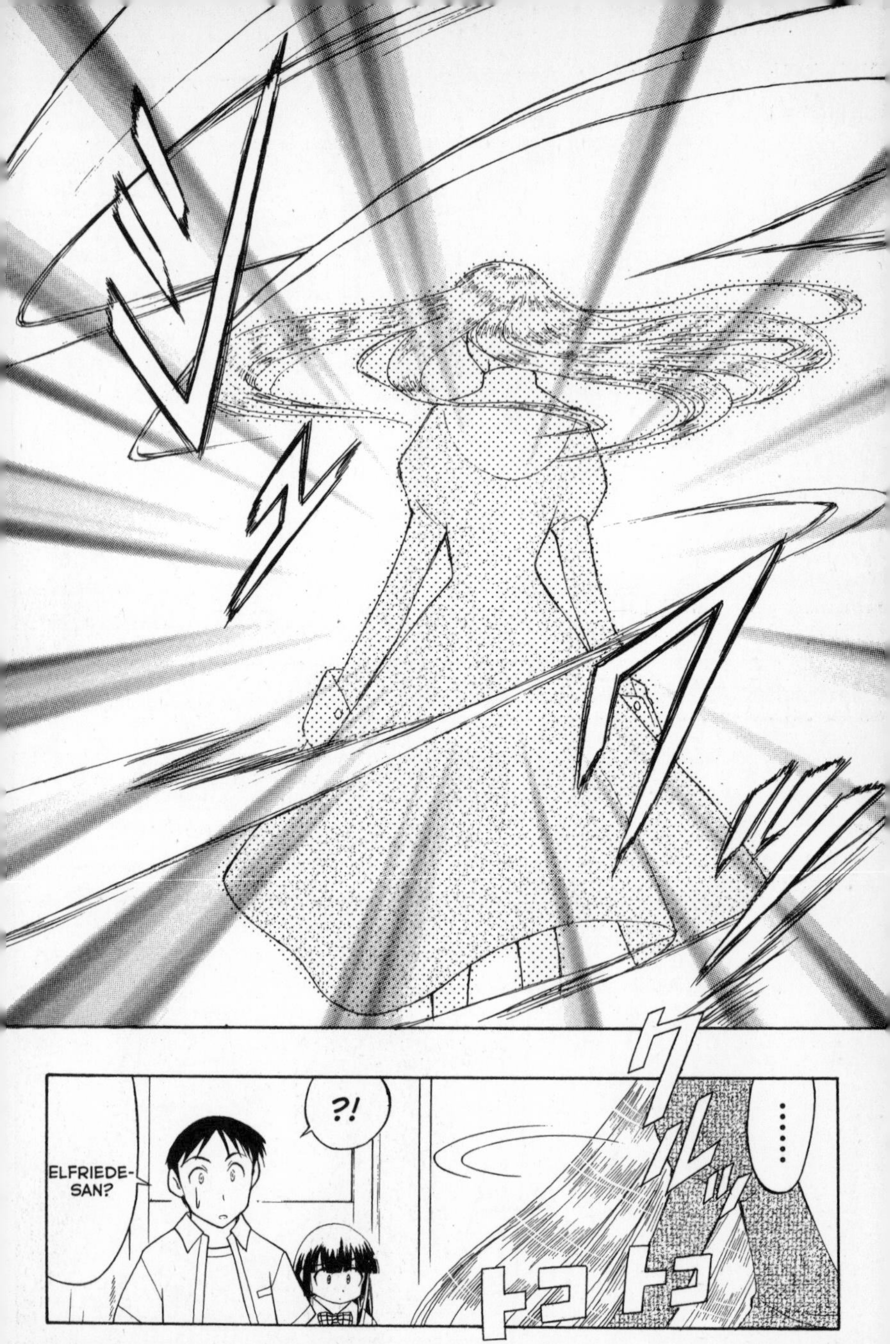
......
トコ トコ
?!
ELFRIEDE-SAN?

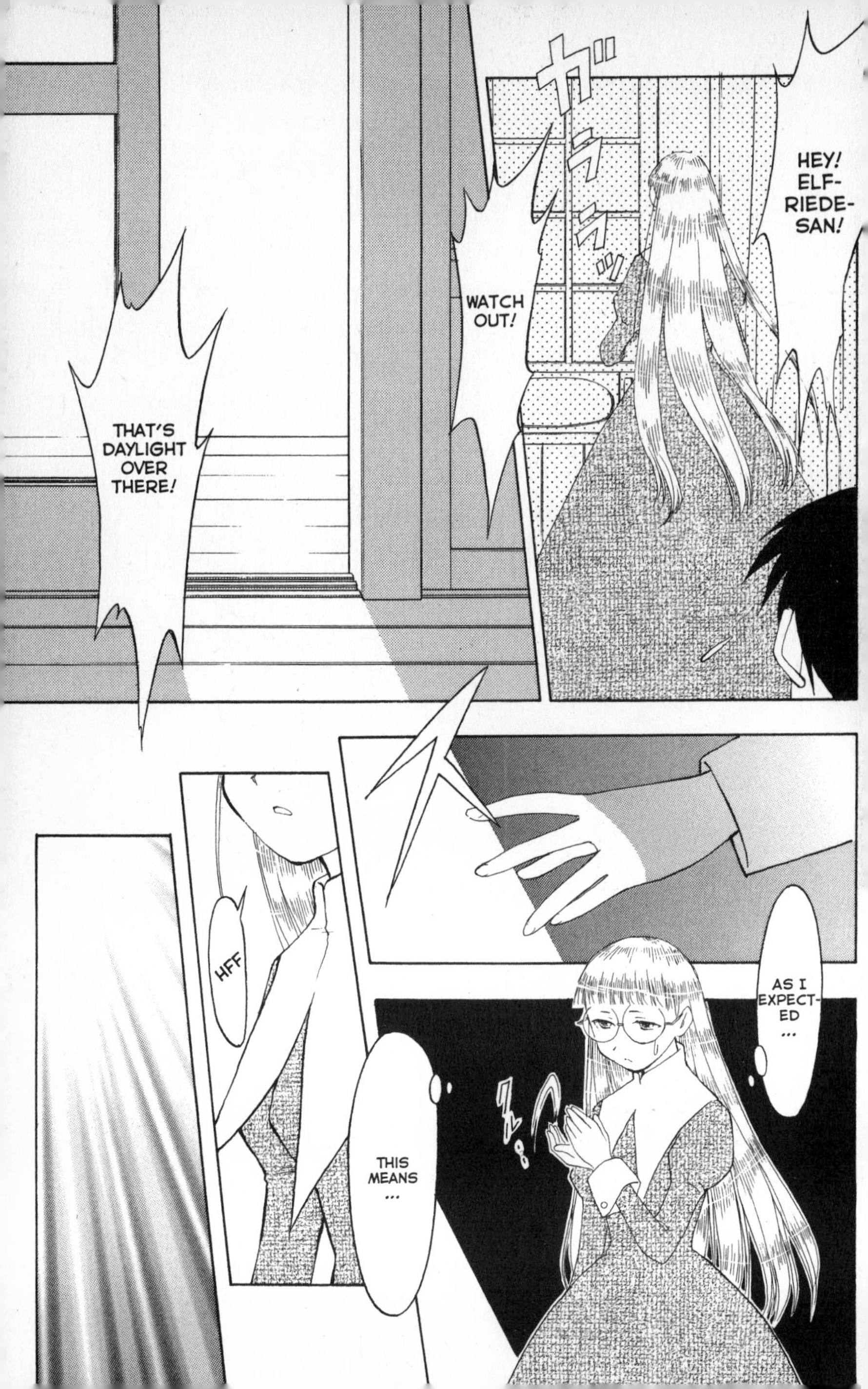
HEY! ELF-RIEDE-SAN!
WATCH OUT!
THAT'S DAYLIGHT OVER THERE!
HFF
AS I EXPECTED...
THIS MEANS...

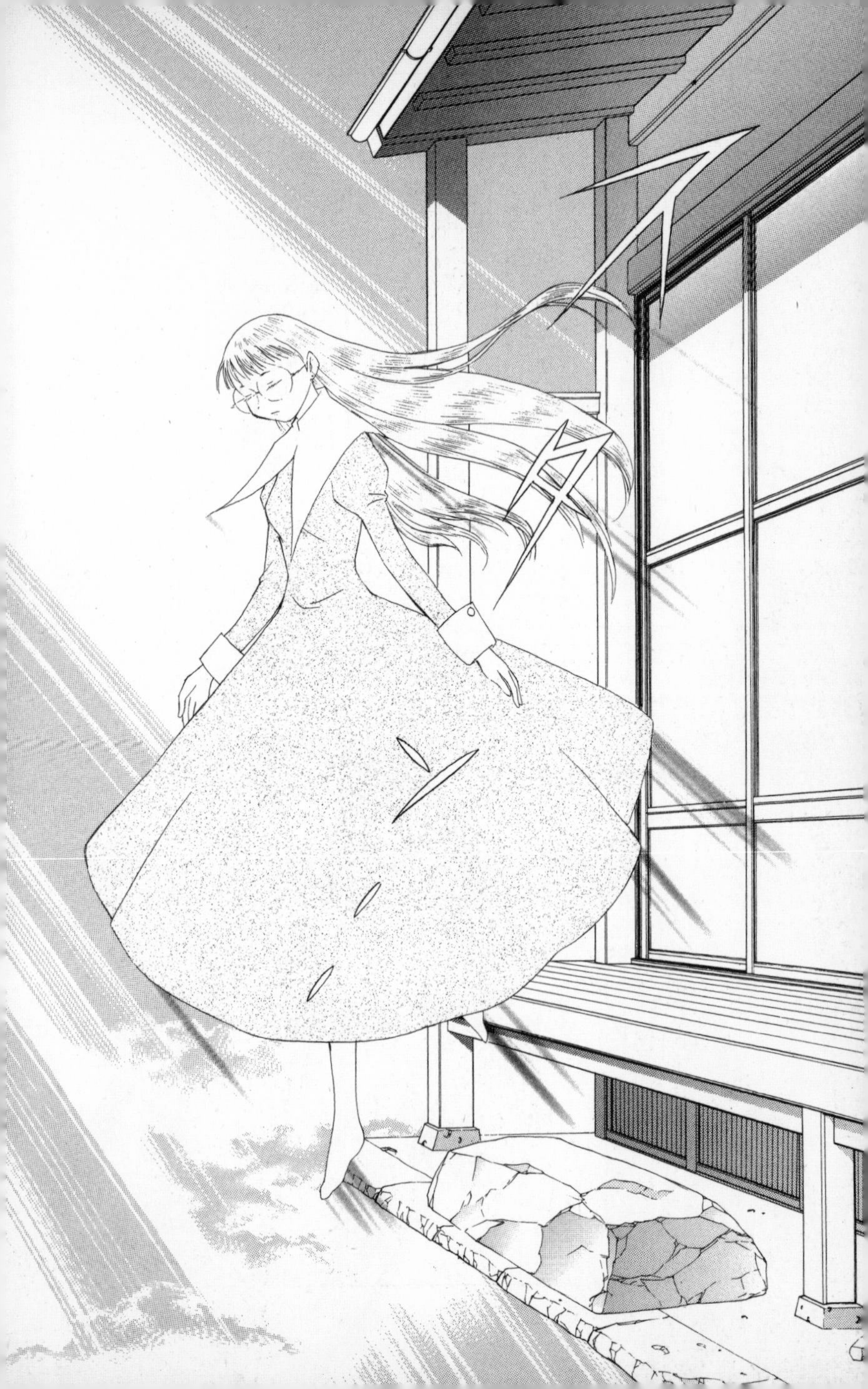

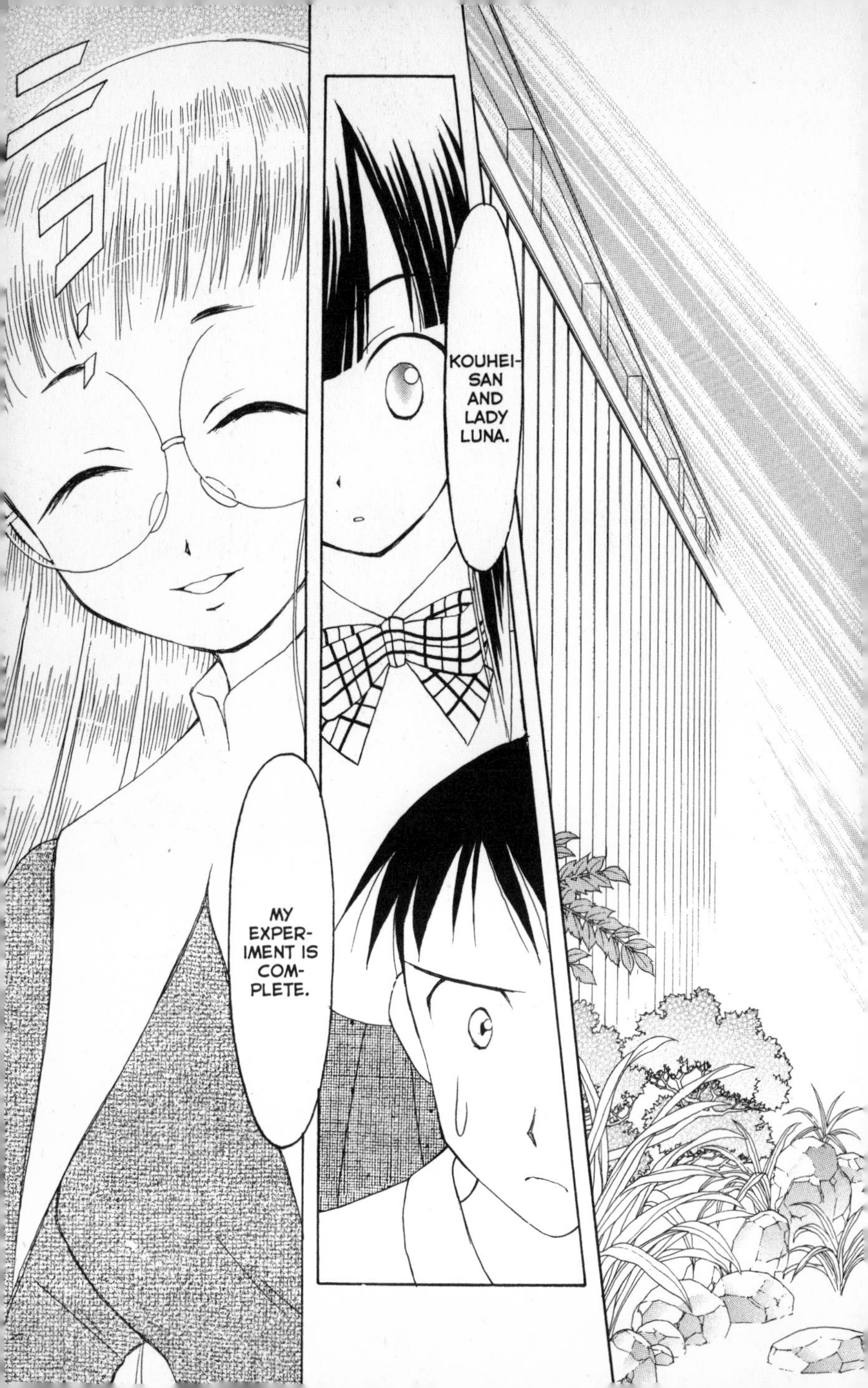
KOUHEI-SAN AND LADY LUNA.
MY EXPERIMENT IS COMPLETE.

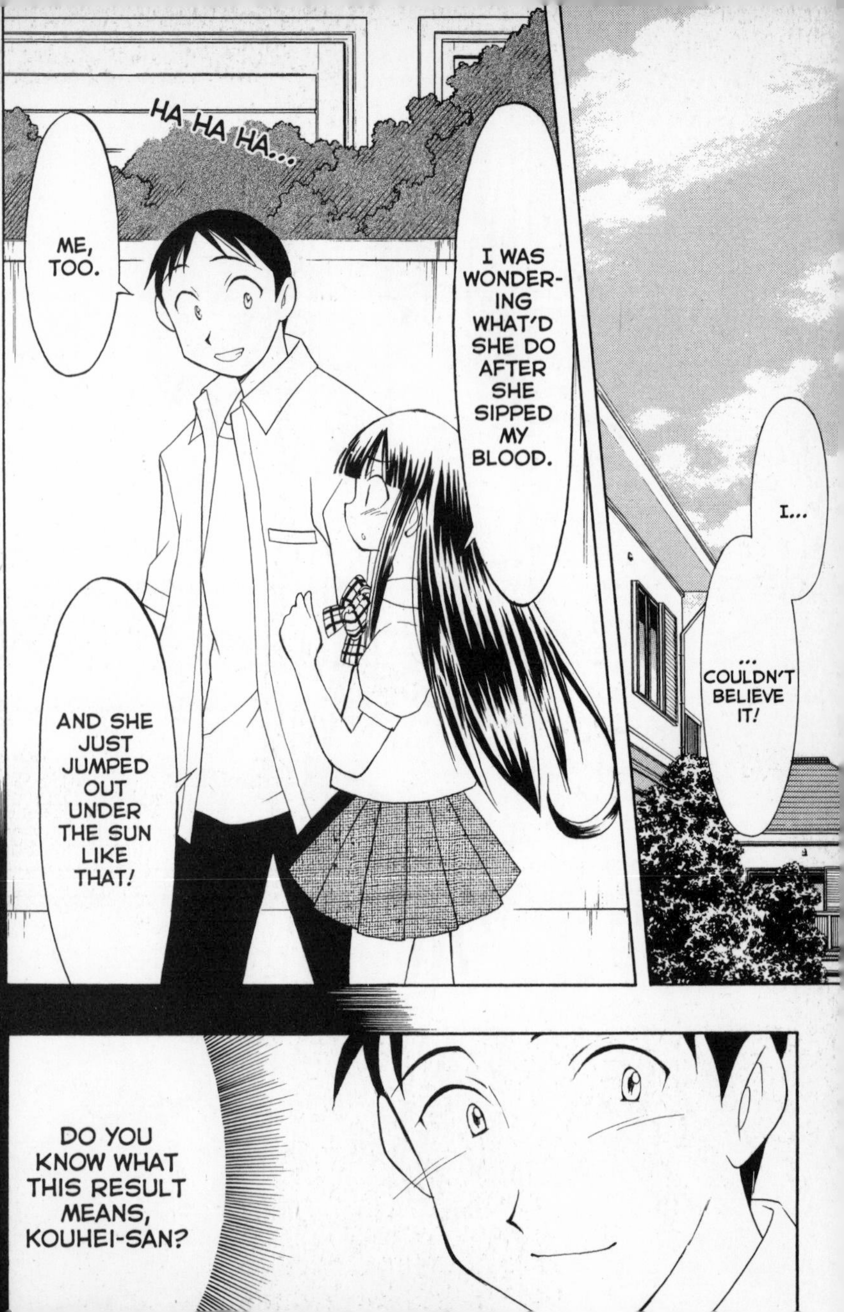
I WAS WONDERING WHAT'D SHE DO AFTER SHE SIPPED MY BLOOD.
HA HA HA...
ME, TOO.
I...
...COULDN'T BELIEVE IT!
AND SHE JUST JUMPED OUT UNDER THE SUN LIKE THAT!
DO YOU KNOW WHAT THIS RESULT MEANS, KOUHEI-SAN?

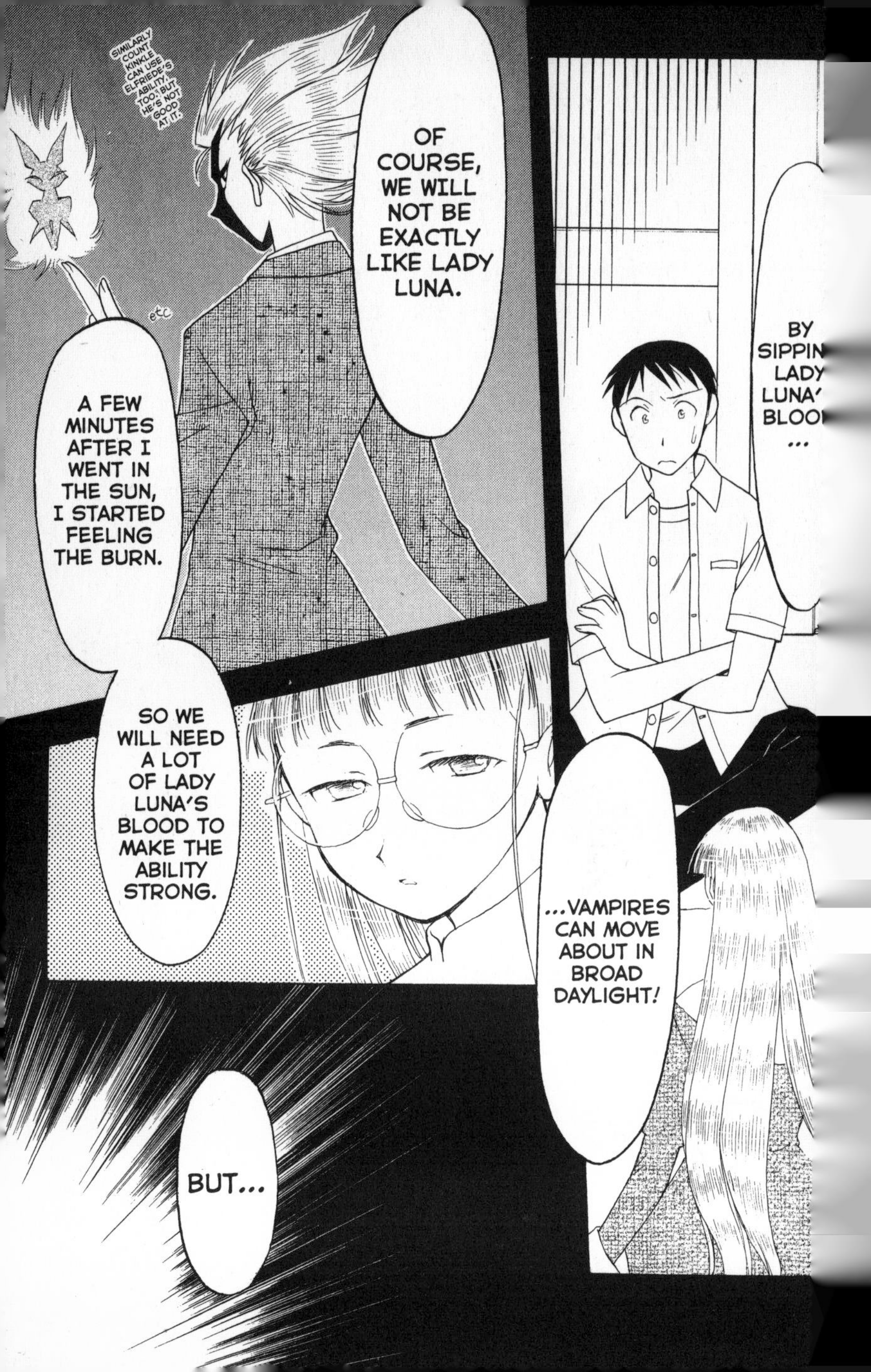

BY SIPPIN LADY LUNA' BLOO ...
...VAMPIRES CAN MOVE ABOUT IN BROAD DAYLIGHT!
OF COURSE, WE WILL NOT BE EXACTLY LIKE LADY LUNA.
SIMILARLY COUNT KINKLE CAN USE ELFRIEDE'S ABILITY, TOO. BUT HE'S NOT GOOD AT IT.
etc
A FEW MINUTES AFTER I WENT IN THE SUN, I STARTED FEELING THE BURN.
SO WE WILL NEED A LOT OF LADY LUNA'S BLOOD TO MAKE THE ABILITY STRONG.
BUT...

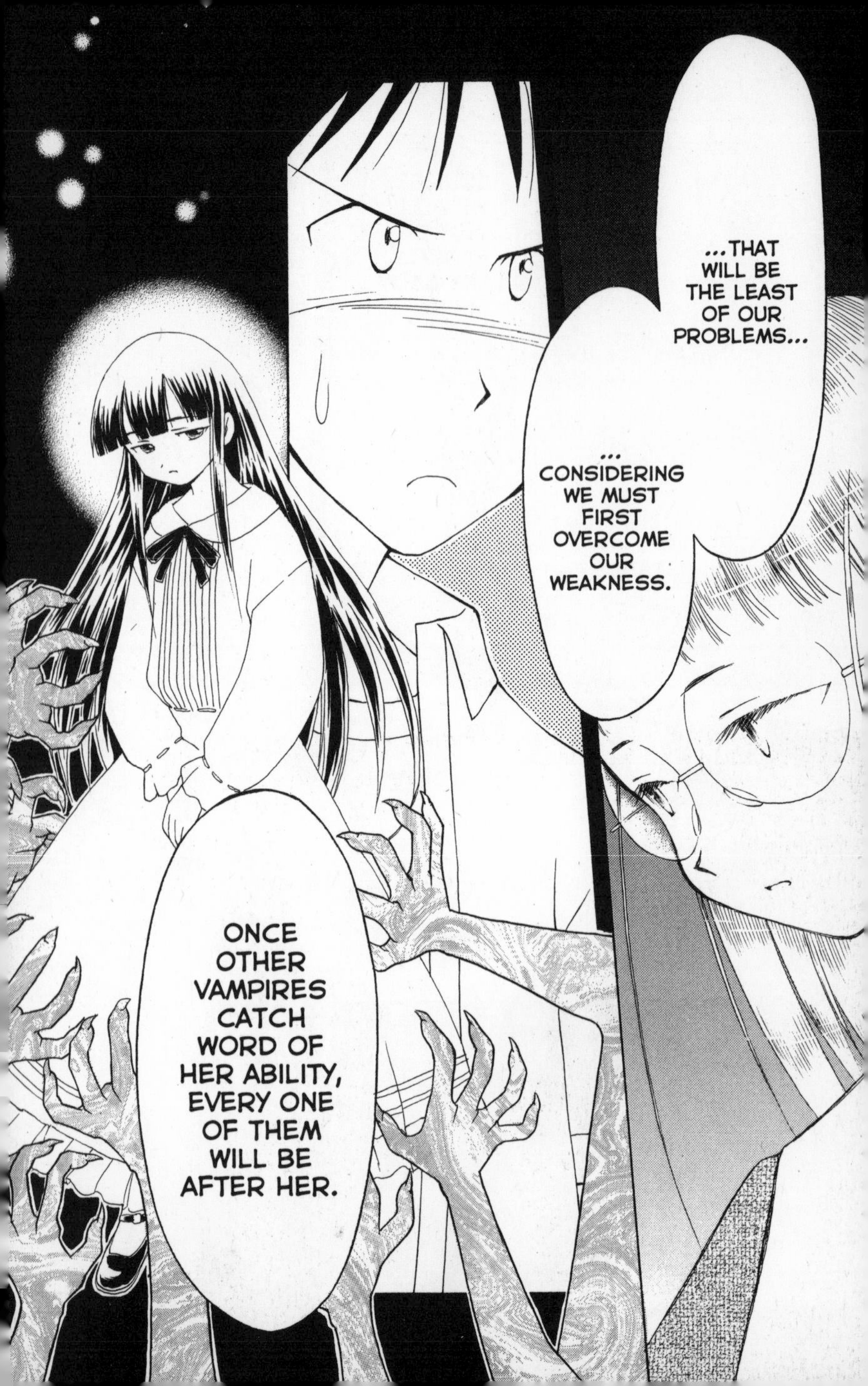
...THAT WILL BE THE LEAST OF OUR PROBLEMS...
...CONSIDERING WE MUST FIRST OVERCOME OUR WEAKNESS.
ONCE OTHER VAMPIRES CATCH WORD OF HER ABILITY, EVERY ONE OF THEM WILL BE AFTER HER.

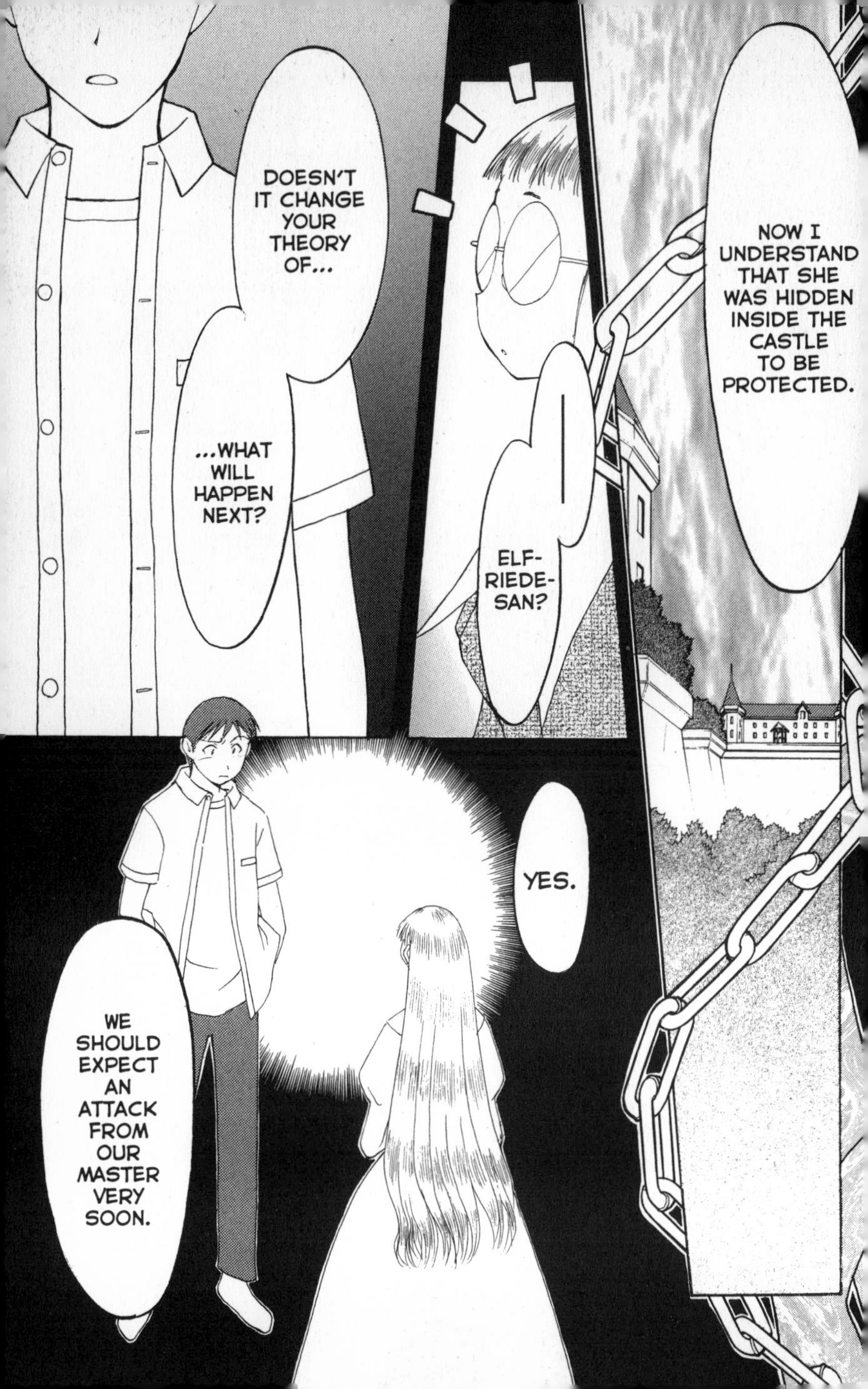
NOW I UNDERSTAND THAT SHE WAS HIDDEN INSIDE THE CASTLE TO BE PROTECTED.
ELF-RIEDE-SAN?
DOESN'T IT CHANGE YOUR THEORY OF...
...WHAT WILL HAPPEN NEXT?
YES.
WE SHOULD EXPECT AN ATTACK FROM OUR MASTER VERY SOON.

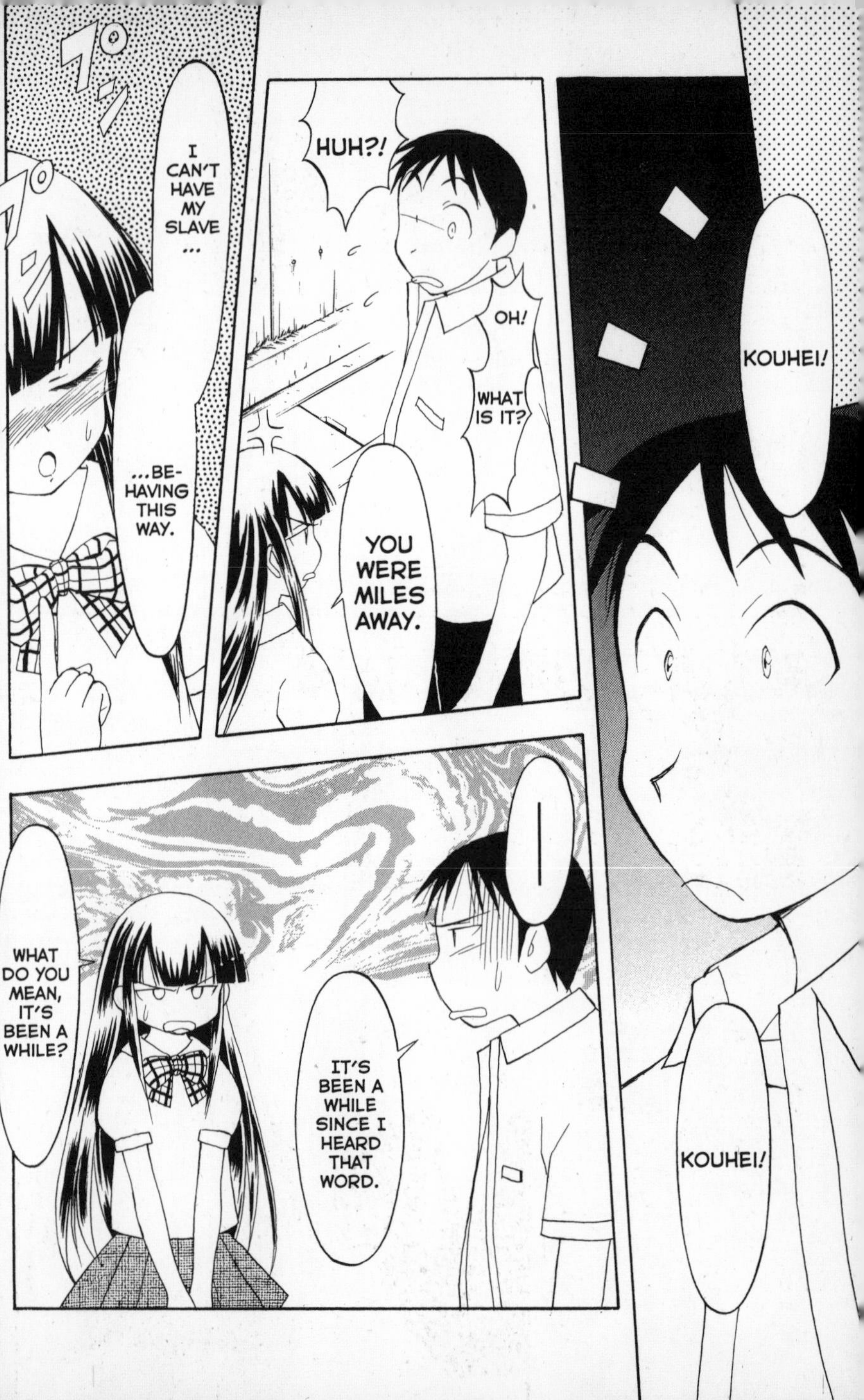
KOUHEI!
KOUHEI!
HUH?!
OH! WHAT IS IT?
YOU WERE MILES AWAY.
I CAN'T HAVE MY SLAVE...
...BE-HAVING THIS WAY.
IT'S BEEN A WHILE SINCE I HEARD THAT WORD.
WHAT DO YOU MEAN, IT'S BEEN A WHILE?

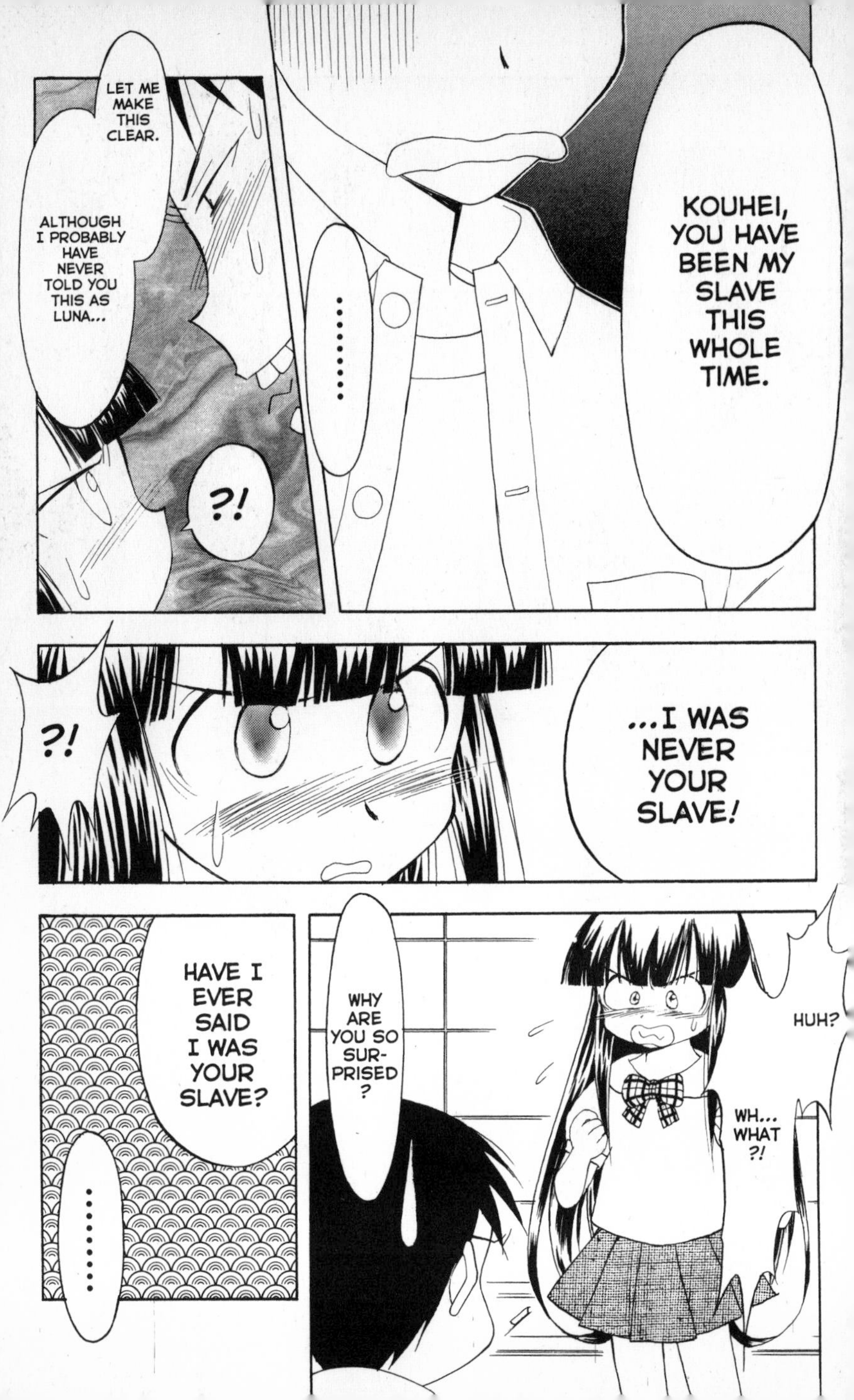
KOUHEI, YOU HAVE BEEN MY SLAVE THIS WHOLE TIME.
....
LET ME MAKE THIS CLEAR.
ALTHOUGH I PROBABLY HAVE NEVER TOLD YOU THIS AS LUNA...
?!
...I WAS NEVER YOUR SLAVE!
?!
HUH?
WH... WHAT?!
WHY ARE YOU SO SUR-PRISED?
HAVE I EVER SAID I WAS YOUR SLAVE?
....

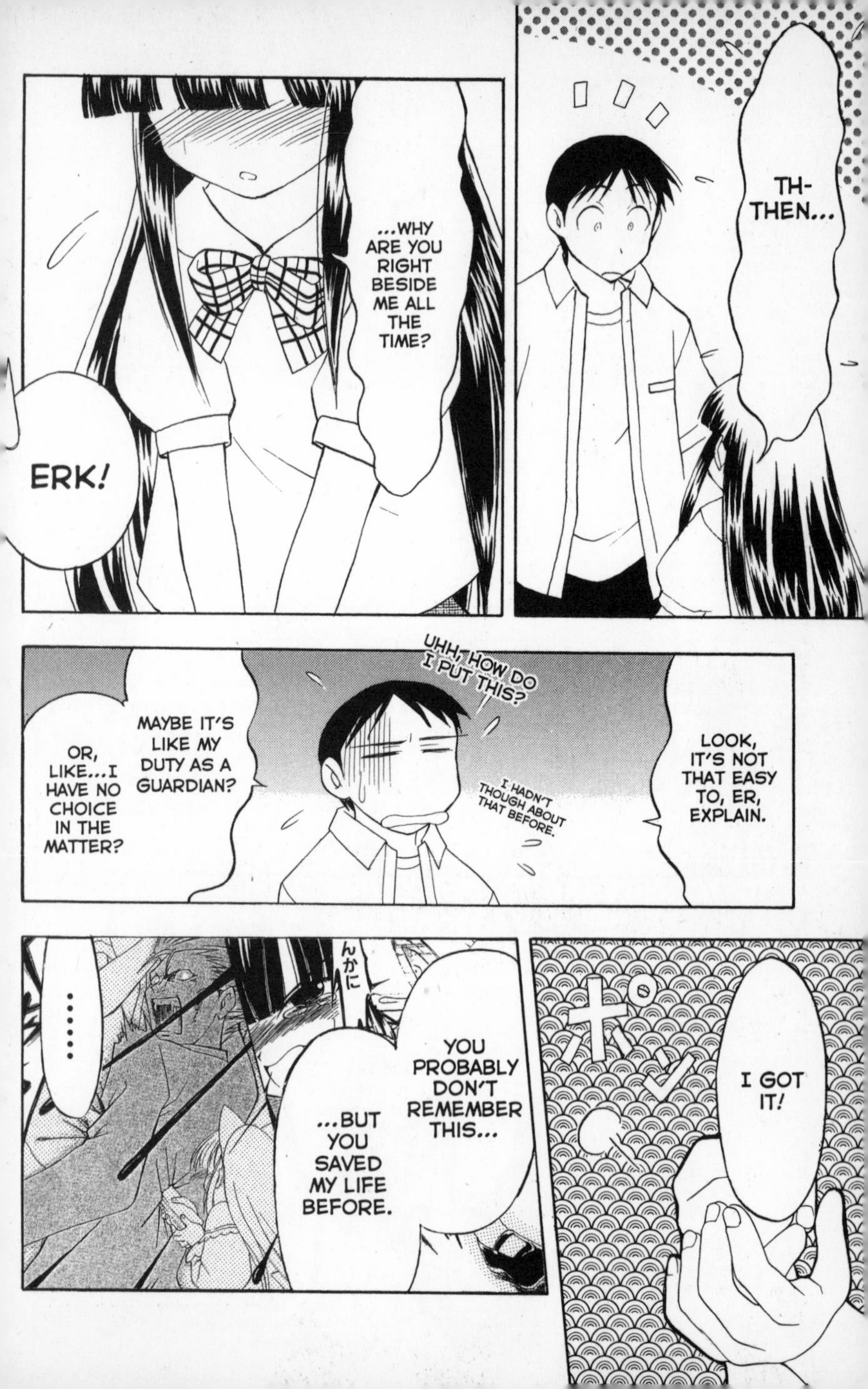
TH- THEN...
...WHY ARE YOU RIGHT BESIDE ME ALL THE TIME?
ERK!
LOOK, IT'S NOT THAT EASY TO, ER, EXPLAIN.
UHH, HOW DO I PUT THIS?
I HADN'T THOUGH ABOUT THAT BEFORE.
MAYBE IT'S LIKE MY DUTY AS A GUARDIAN?
OR, LIKE...I HAVE NO CHOICE IN THE MATTER?
ポン
I GOT IT!
んかに
YOU PROBABLY DON'T REMEMBER THIS...
...BUT YOU SAVED MY LIFE BEFORE.
......

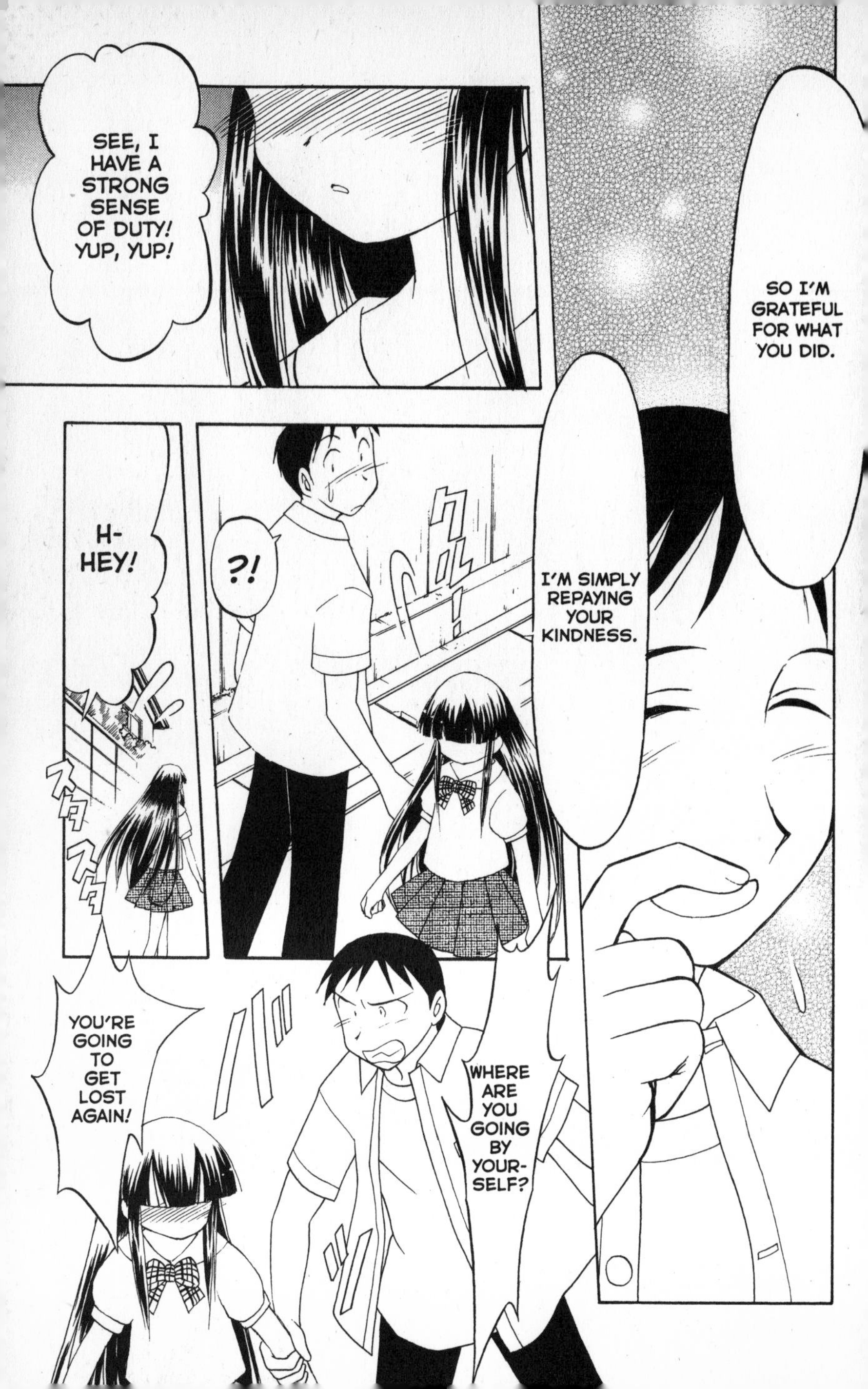
SO I'M GRATEFUL FOR WHAT YOU DID.
I'M SIMPLY REPAYING YOUR KINDNESS.
SEE, I HAVE A STRONG SENSE OF DUTY! YUP, YUP!
?!
H- HEY!
WHERE ARE YOU GOING BY YOUR-SELF?
YOU'RE GOING TO GET LOST AGAIN!

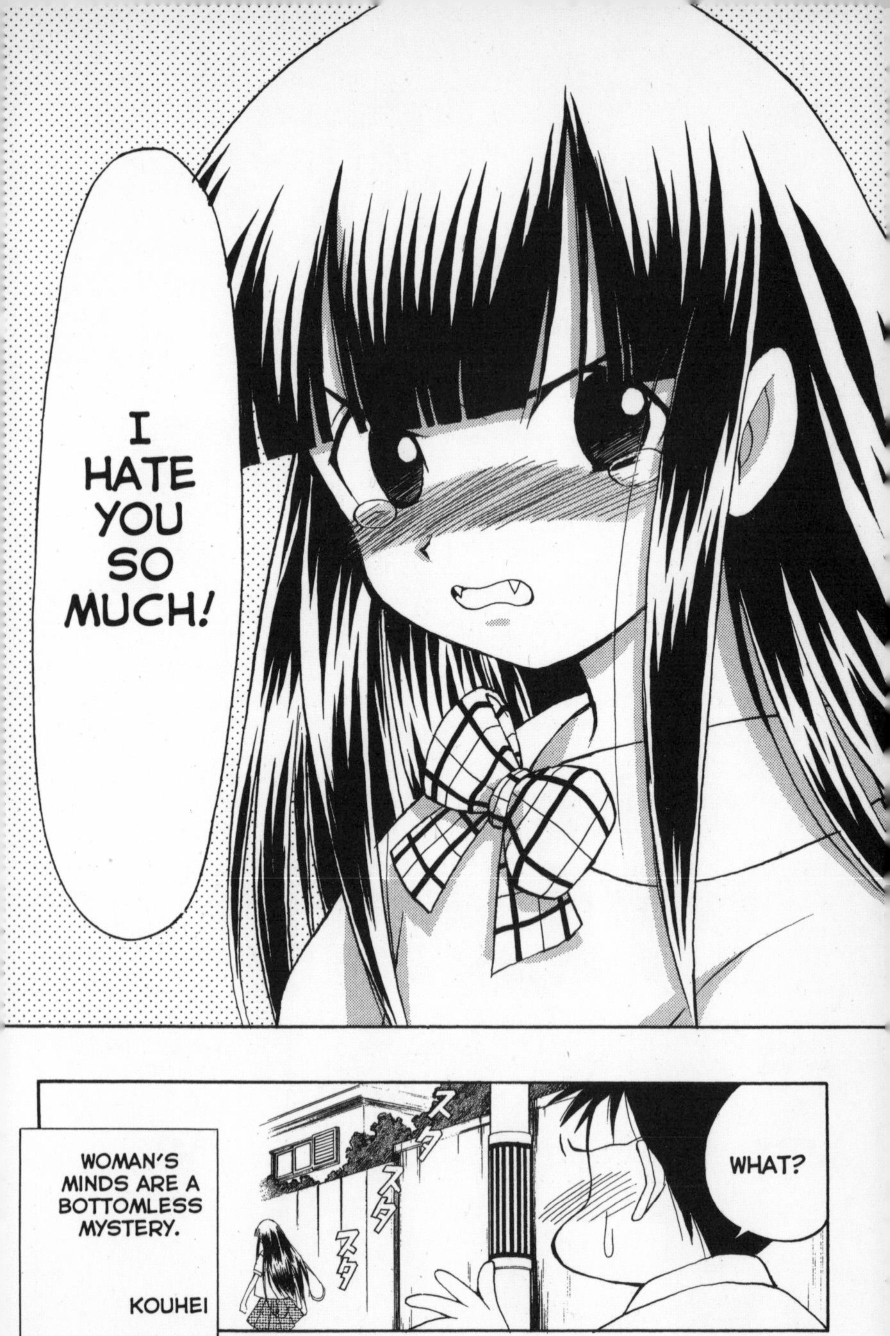

I HATE YOU SO MUCH!
WHAT?
スタ
スタ
スタ
WOMAN'S MINDS ARE A BOTTOMLESS MYSTERY.
KOUHEI

MOON 月詠 PHASE

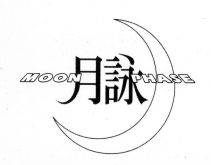

PART 2

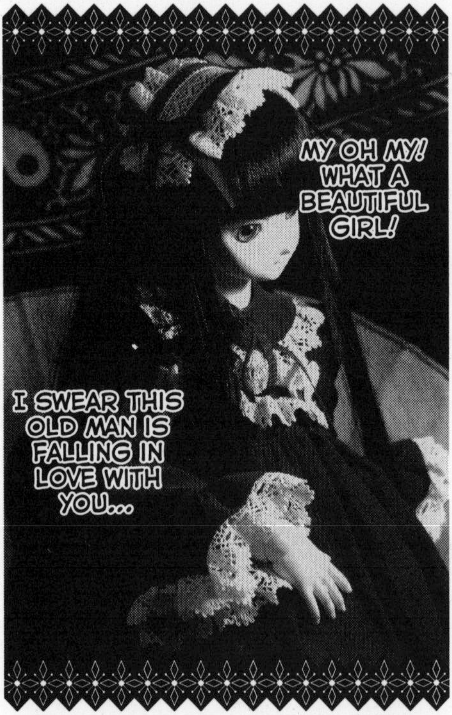
MY OH MY! WHAT A BEAUTIFUL GIRL!
I SWEAR THIS OLD MAN IS FALLING IN LOVE WITH YOU...

CONTINUED ON PAGE 74

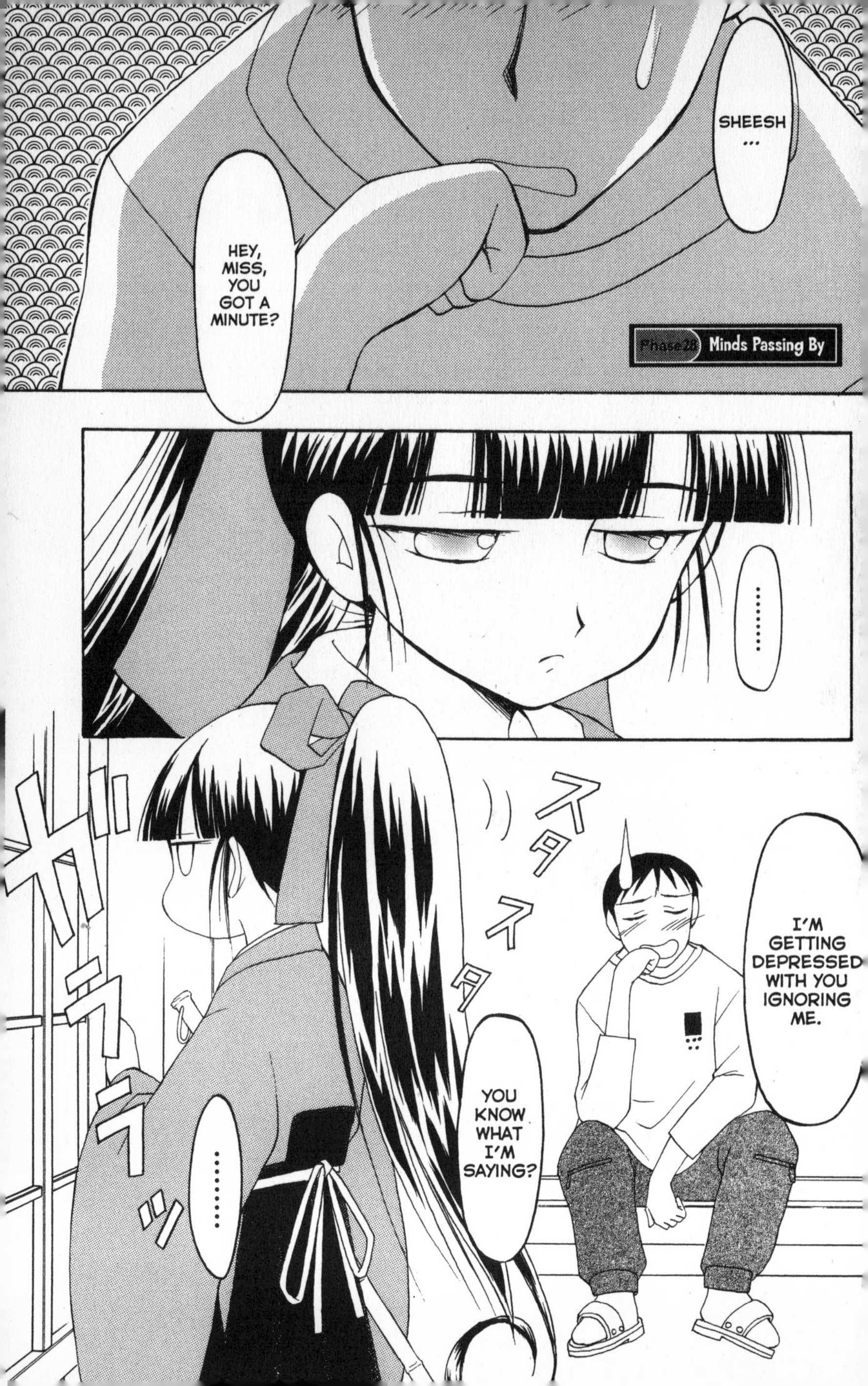
SHEESH...
HEY, MISS, YOU GOT A MINUTE?
Phase28 Minds Passing By
....
スタスタ
I'M GETTING DEPRESSED WITH YOU IGNORING ME.
YOU KNOW WHAT I'M SAYING?
......

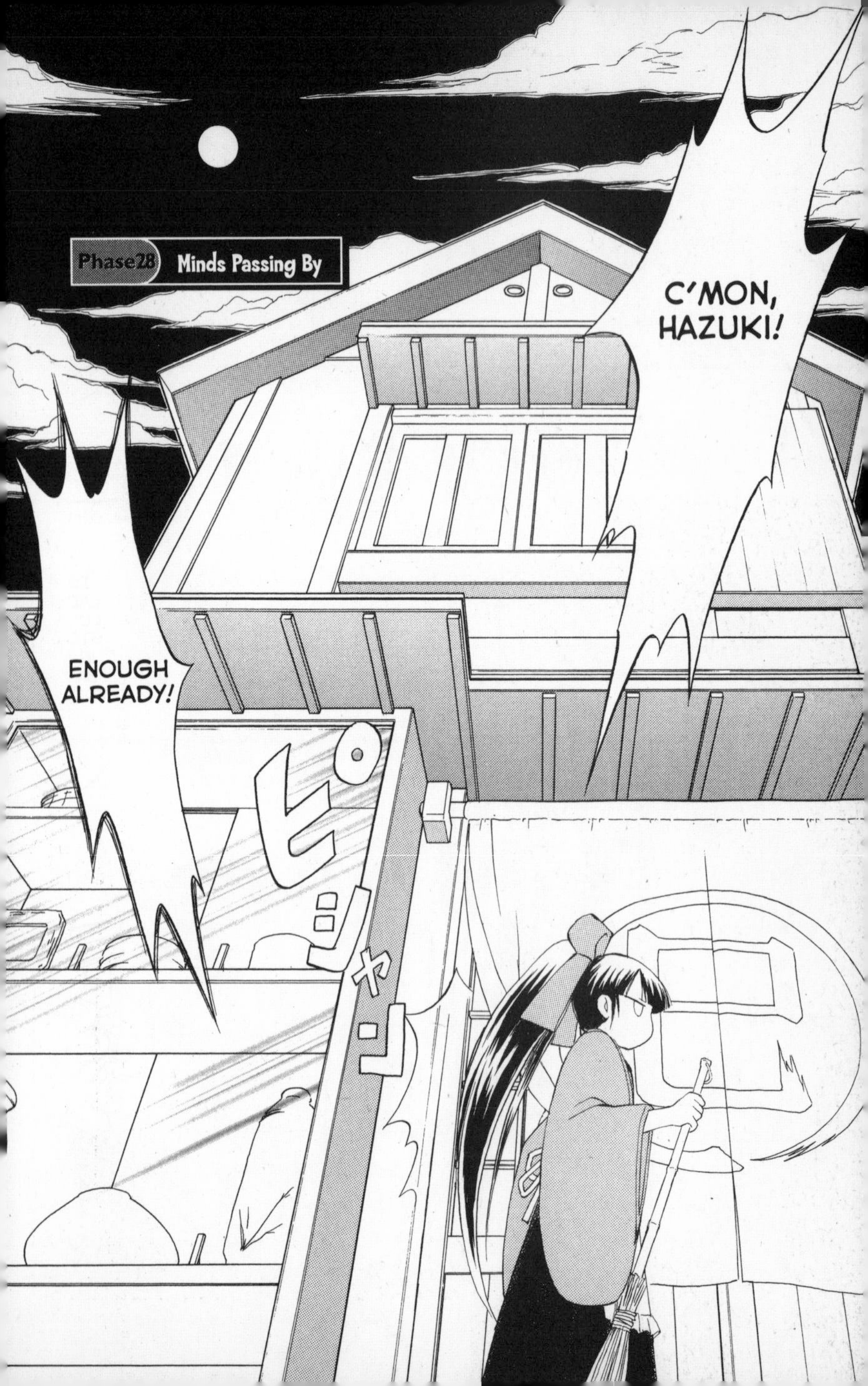
Phase28 Minds Passing By
C'MON, HAZUKI!
ENOUGH ALREADY!
ピシャン

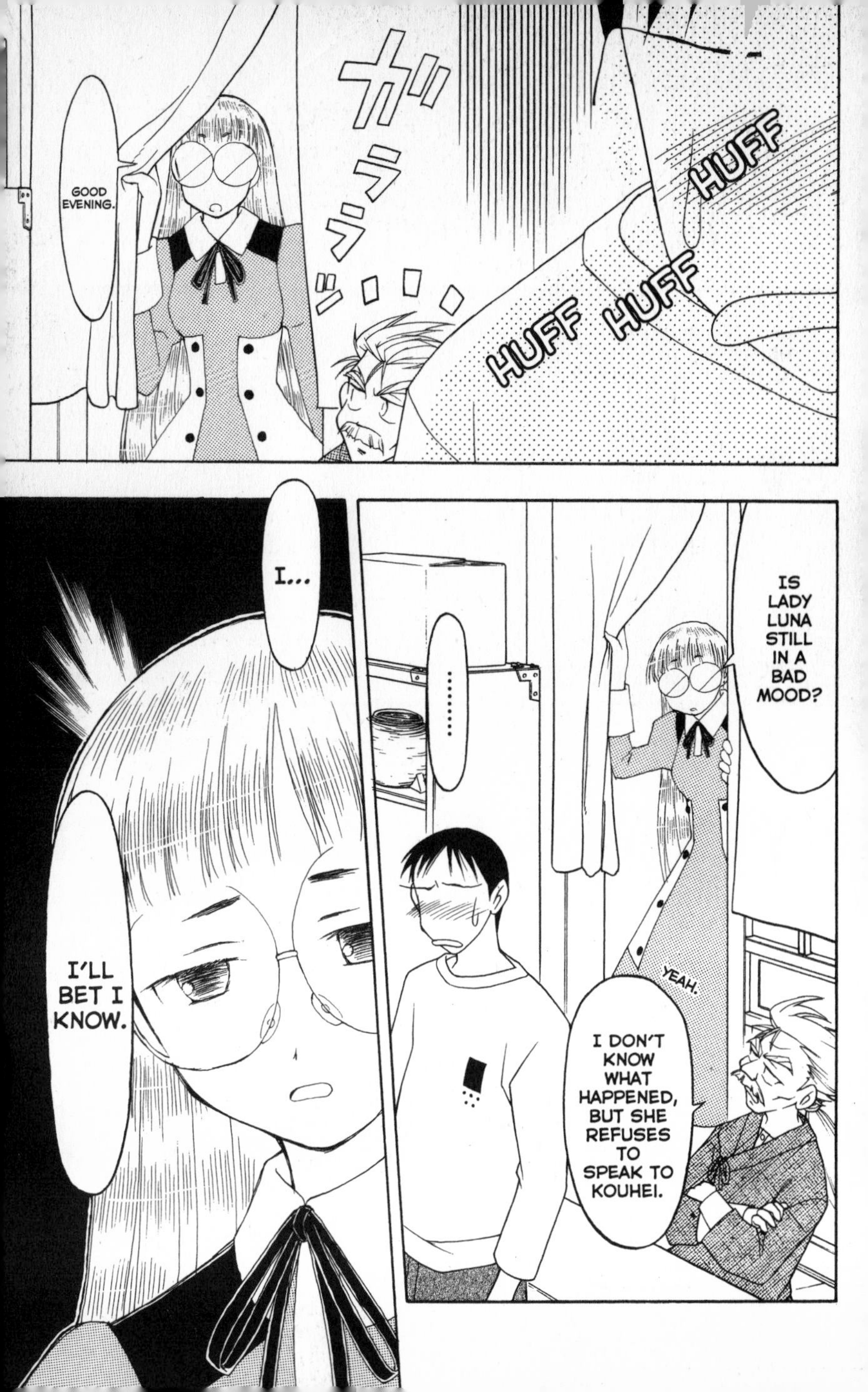
HUFF HUFF HUFF
ガララ
GOOD EVENING.
IS LADY LUNA STILL IN A BAD MOOD?
YEAH.
I DON'T KNOW WHAT HAPPENED, BUT SHE REFUSES TO SPEAK TO KOUHEI.
....
I...
I'LL BET I KNOW.

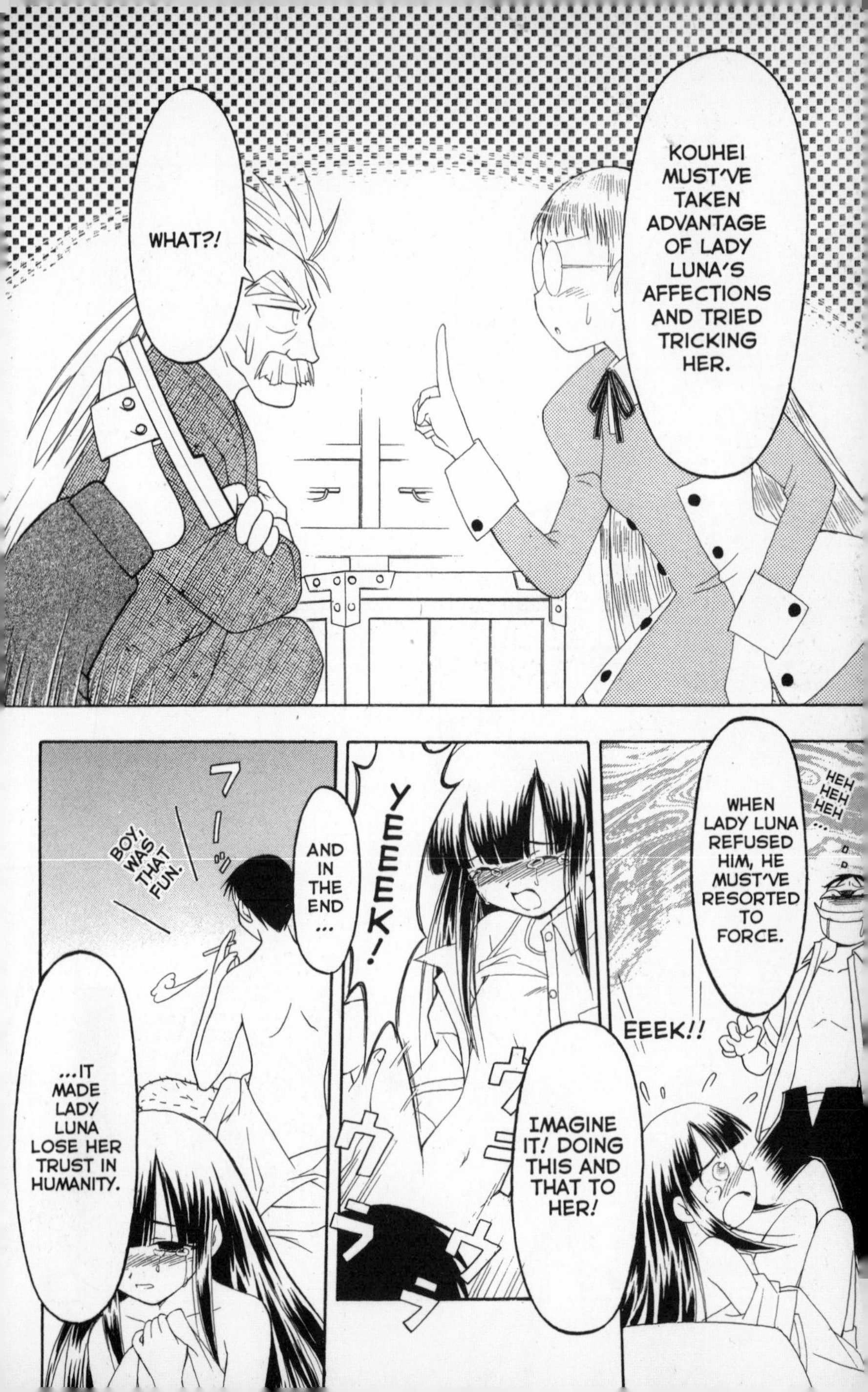

KOUHEI MUST'VE TAKEN ADVANTAGE OF LADY LUNA'S AFFECTIONS AND TRIED TRICKING HER.
WHAT?!
HEH HEH HEH ...
WHEN LADY LUNA REFUSED HIM, HE MUST'VE RESORTED TO FORCE.
EEEK!!
IMAGINE IT! DOING THIS AND THAT TO HER!
YEEEK!
AND IN THE END ...
BOY, WAS THAT FUN.
...IT MADE LADY LUNA LOSE HER TRUST IN HUMANITY.

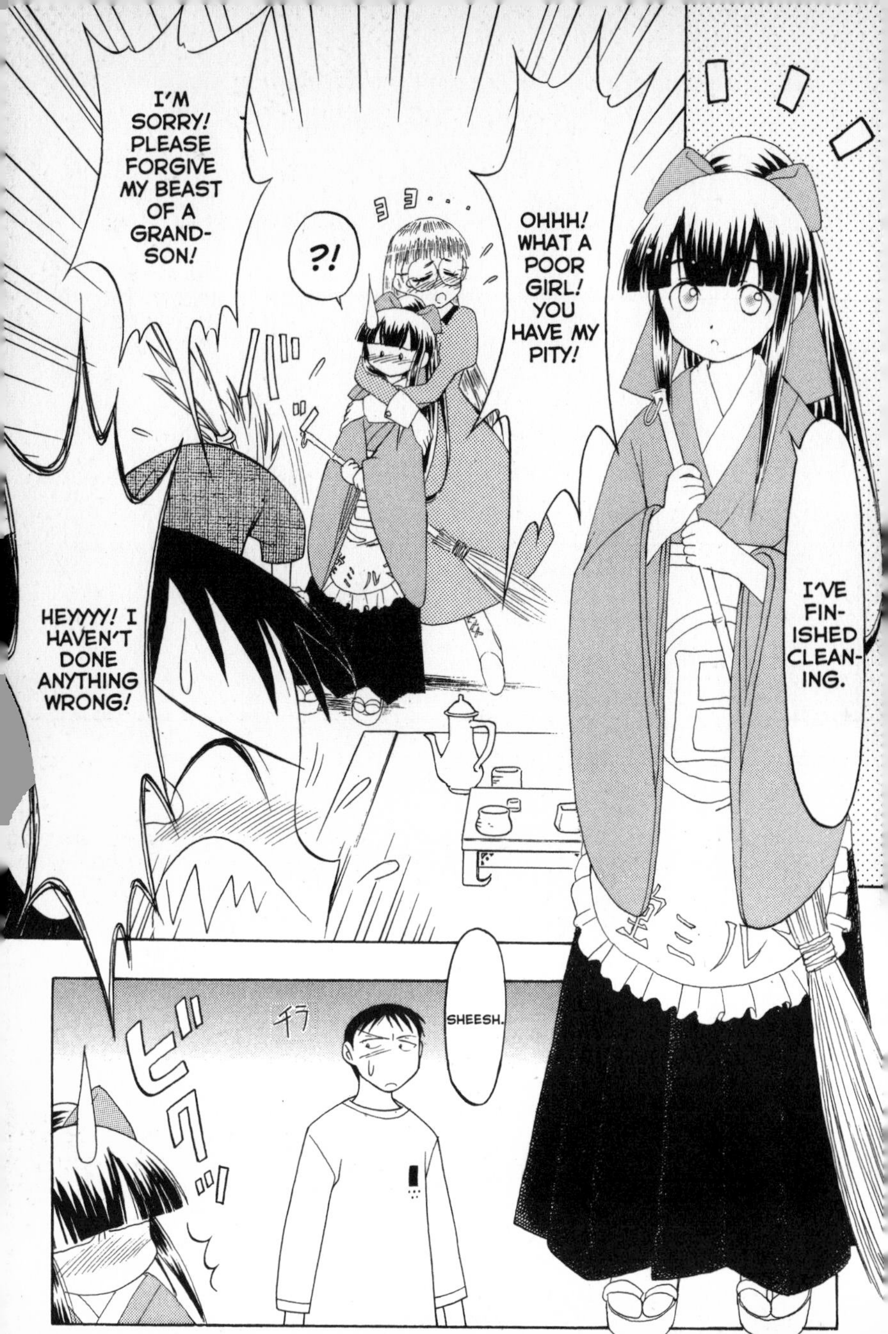
I'VE FIN-ISHED CLEAN-ING.
OHHH! WHAT A POOR GIRL! YOU HAVE MY PITY!
?!
I'M SORRY! PLEASE FORGIVE MY BEAST OF A GRAND-SON!
HEYYYY! I HAVEN'T DONE ANYTHING WRONG!
SHEESH.

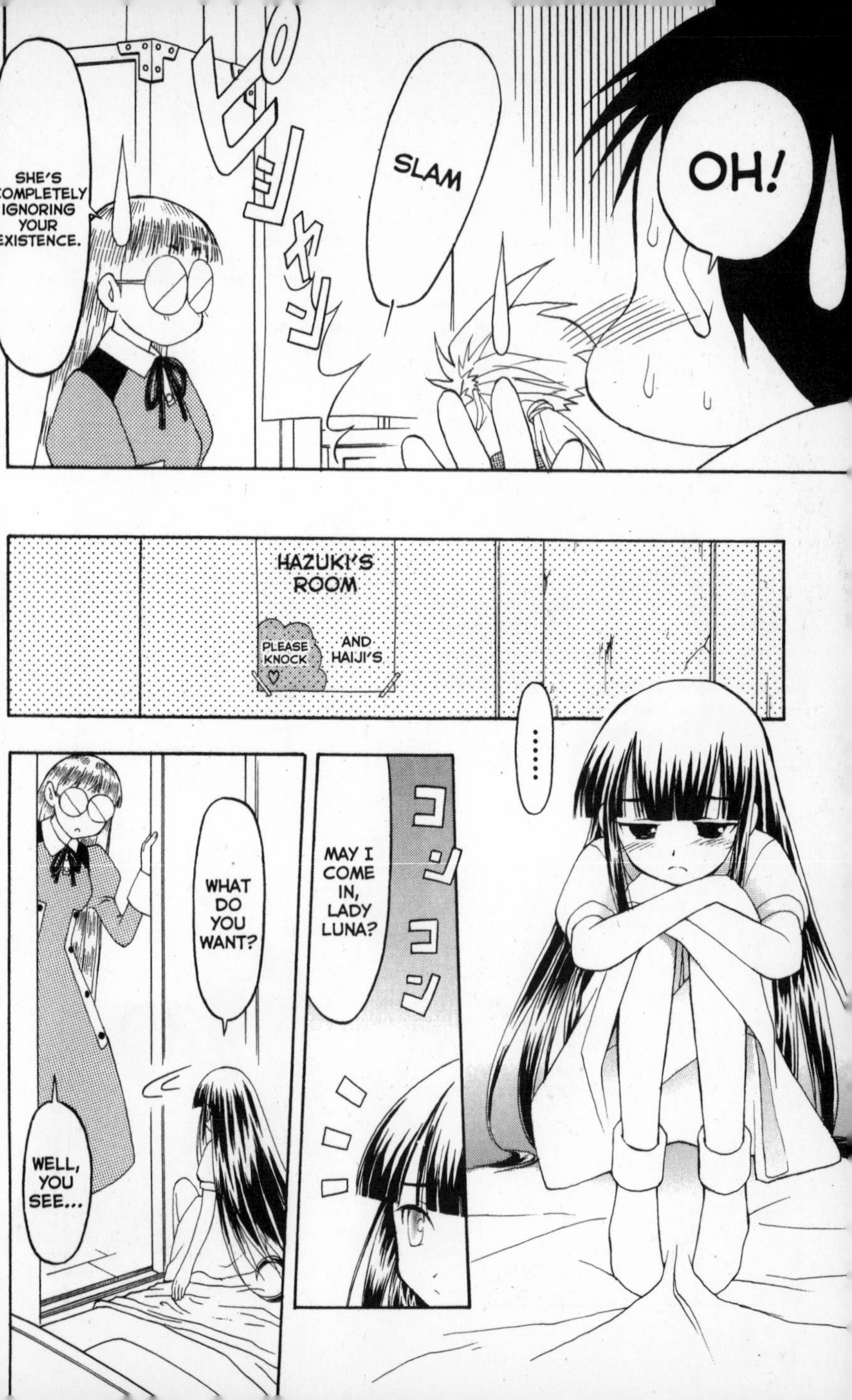
OH!
SLAM
SHE'S COMPLETELY IGNORING YOUR EXISTENCE.
HAZUKI'S ROOM
AND HAIJI'S
PLEASE KNOCK ♥
......
MAY I COME IN, LADY LUNA?
WHAT DO YOU WANT?
WELL, YOU SEE...

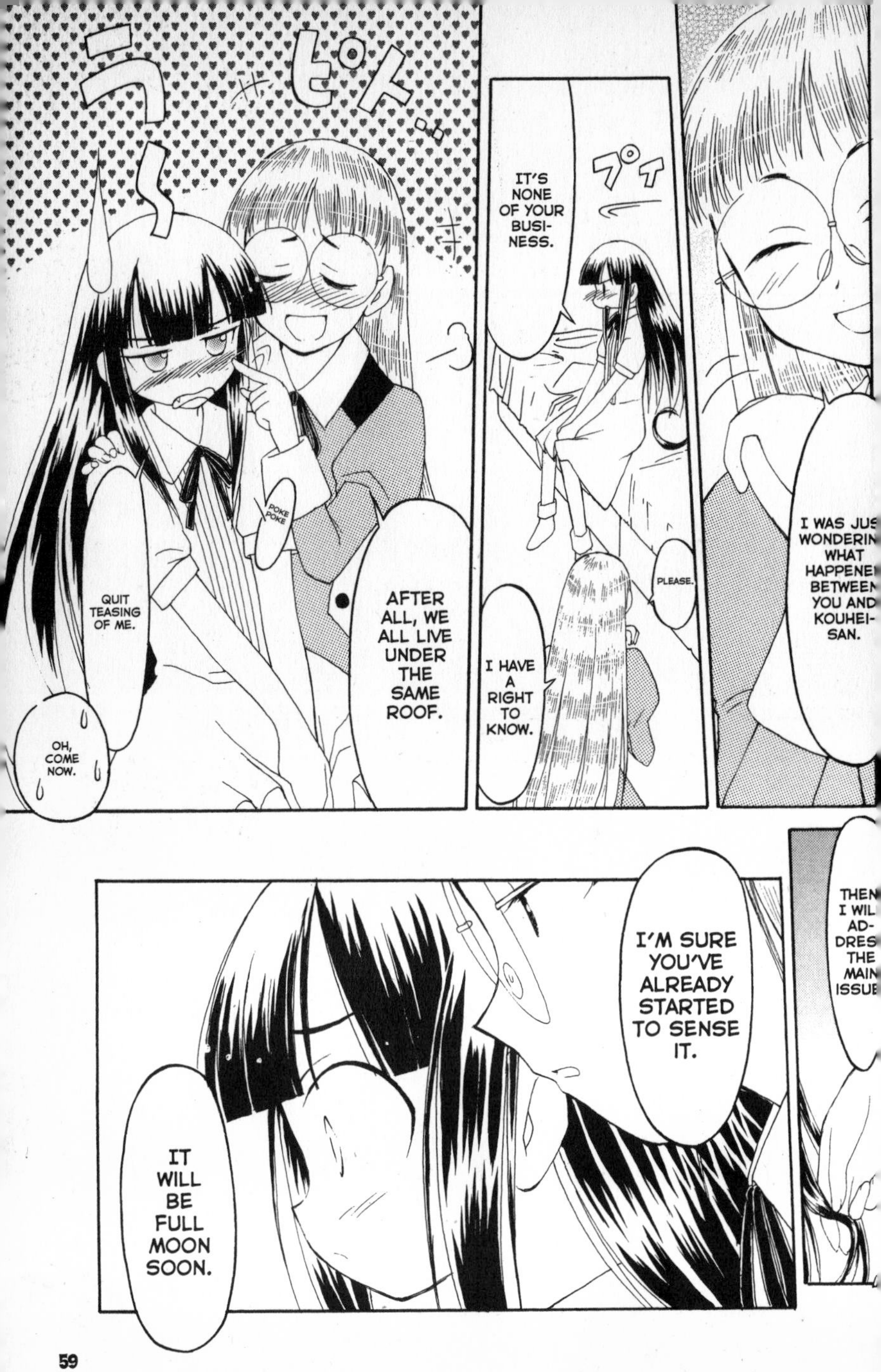
I WAS JUS WONDERIN WHAT HAPPENE BETWEEN YOU AND KOUHEI-SAN.
プイ
IT'S NONE OF YOUR BUSI-NESS.
PLEASE.
I HAVE A RIGHT TO KNOW.
AFTER ALL, WE ALL LIVE UNDER THE SAME ROOF.
POKE POKE
QUIT TEASING OF ME.
OH, COME NOW.
THEN I WIL AD-DRES THE MAIN ISSUE
I'M SURE YOU'VE ALREADY STARTED TO SENSE IT.
IT WILL BE FULL MOON SOON.

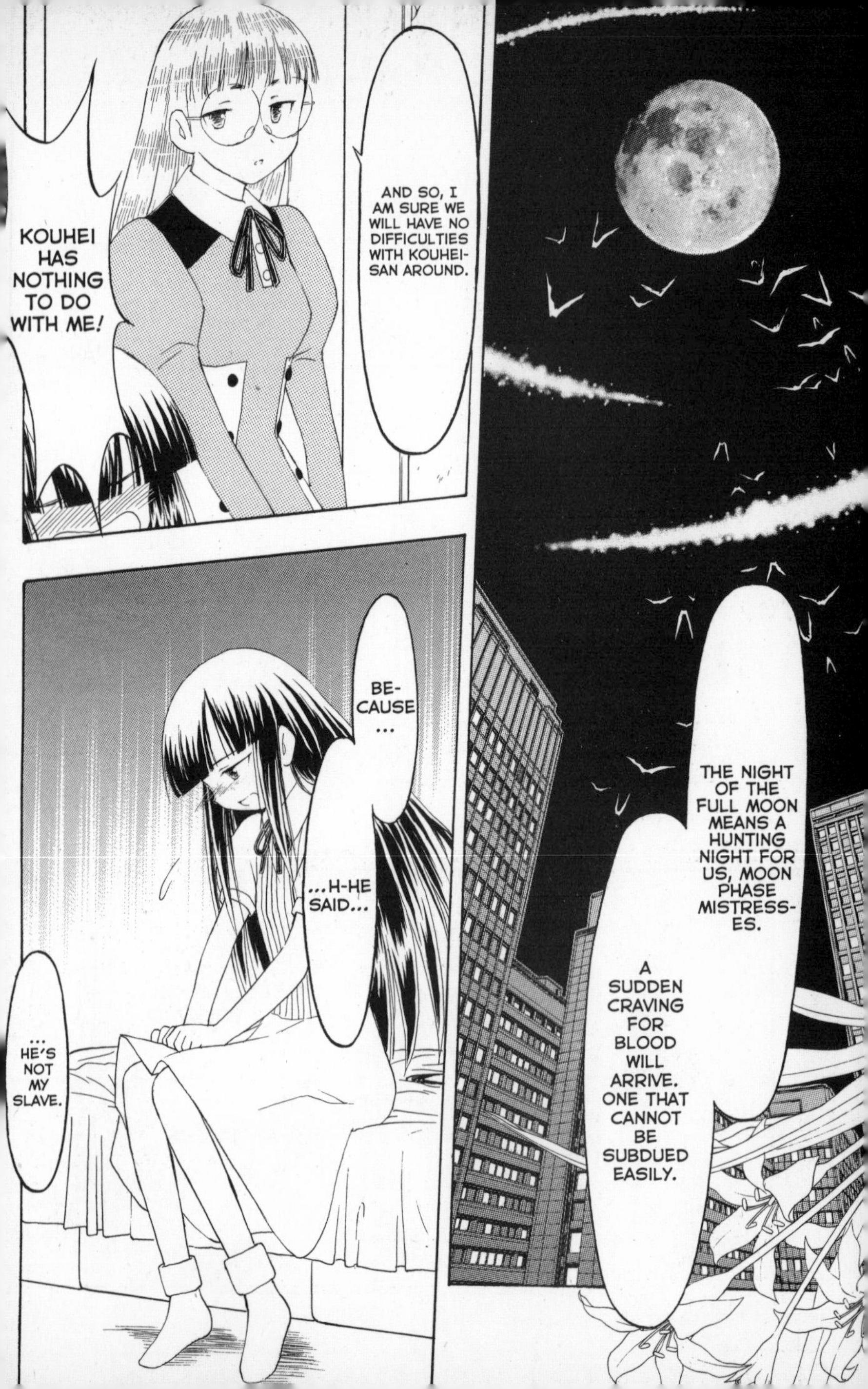
THE NIGHT OF THE FULL MOON MEANS A HUNTING NIGHT FOR US, MOON PHASE MISTRESS-ES.
A SUDDEN CRAVING FOR BLOOD WILL ARRIVE. ONE THAT CANNOT BE SUBDUED EASILY.
AND SO, I AM SURE WE WILL HAVE NO DIFFICULTIES WITH KOUHEI-SAN AROUND.
KOUHEI HAS NOTHING TO DO WITH ME!
BE-CAUSE...
...H-HE SAID...
...HE'S NOT MY SLAVE.

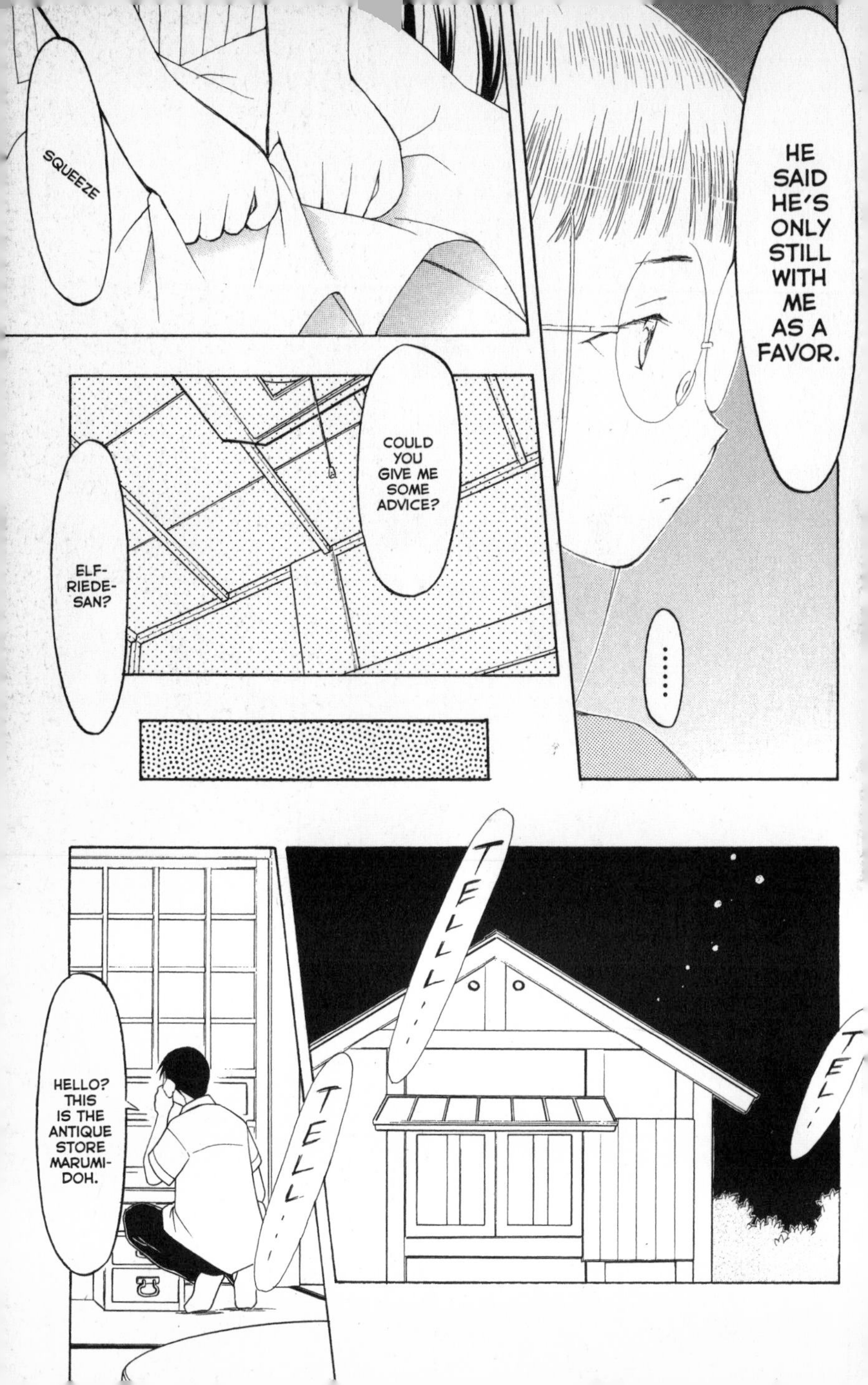
HE SAID HE'S ONLY STILL WITH ME AS A FAVOR.
SQUEEZE
......
COULD YOU GIVE ME SOME ADVICE?
ELF-RIEDE-SAN?
TEL...
TELL...
TELL...
HELLO? THIS IS THE ANTIQUE STORE MARUMI-DOH.

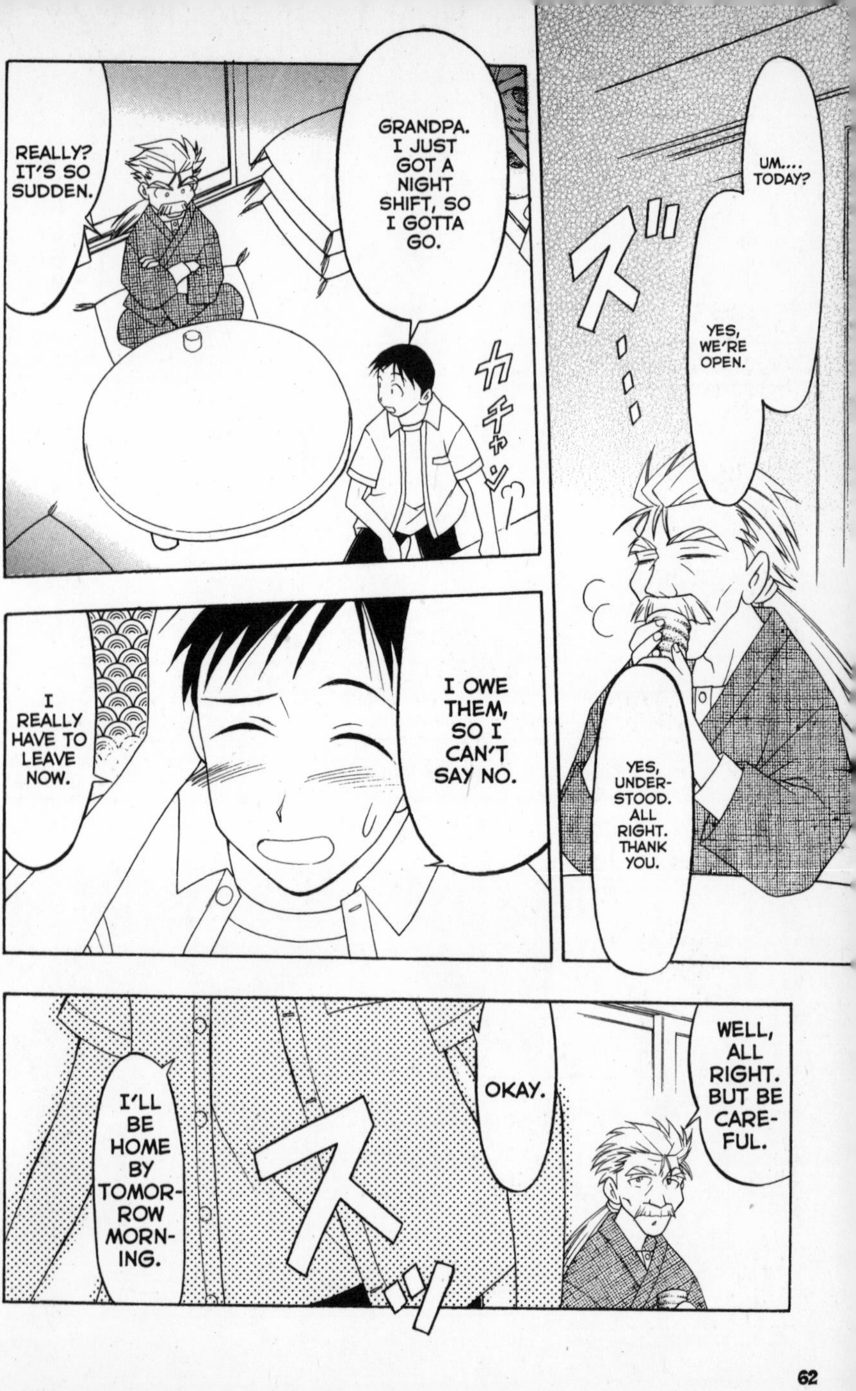
UM.... TODAY?
ズ...
YES, WE'RE OPEN.
YES, UNDERSTOOD. ALL RIGHT. THANK YOU.
GRANDPA. I JUST GOT A NIGHT SHIFT, SO I GOTTA GO.
カチャン
REALLY? IT'S SO SUDDEN.
I OWE THEM, SO I CAN'T SAY NO.
I REALLY HAVE TO LEAVE NOW.
WELL, ALL RIGHT. BUT BE CAREFUL.
OKAY.
ズッ
I'LL BE HOME BY TOMORROW MORNING.

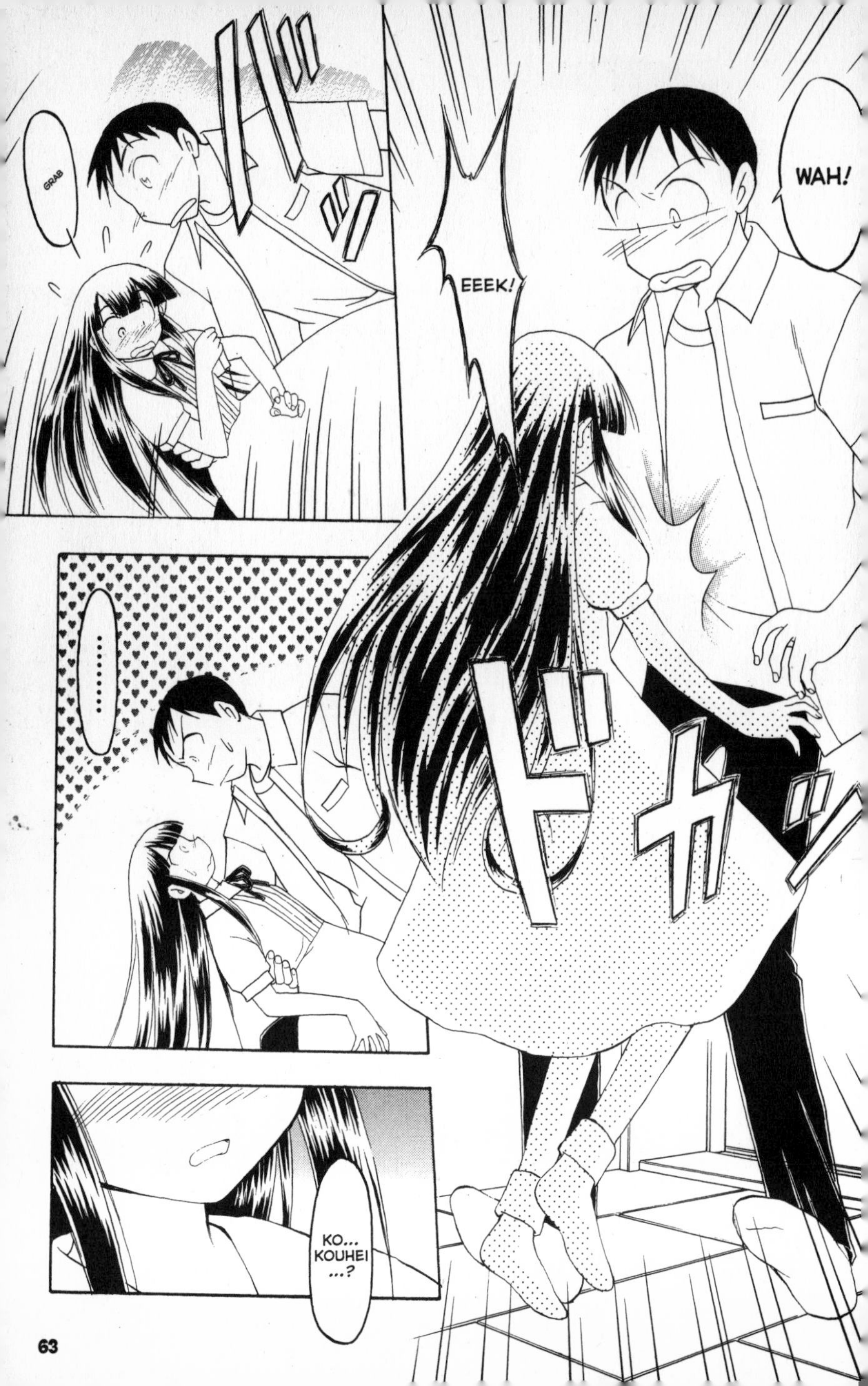
WAH!
EEEK!
GRAB
......
KO... KOUHEI ...?

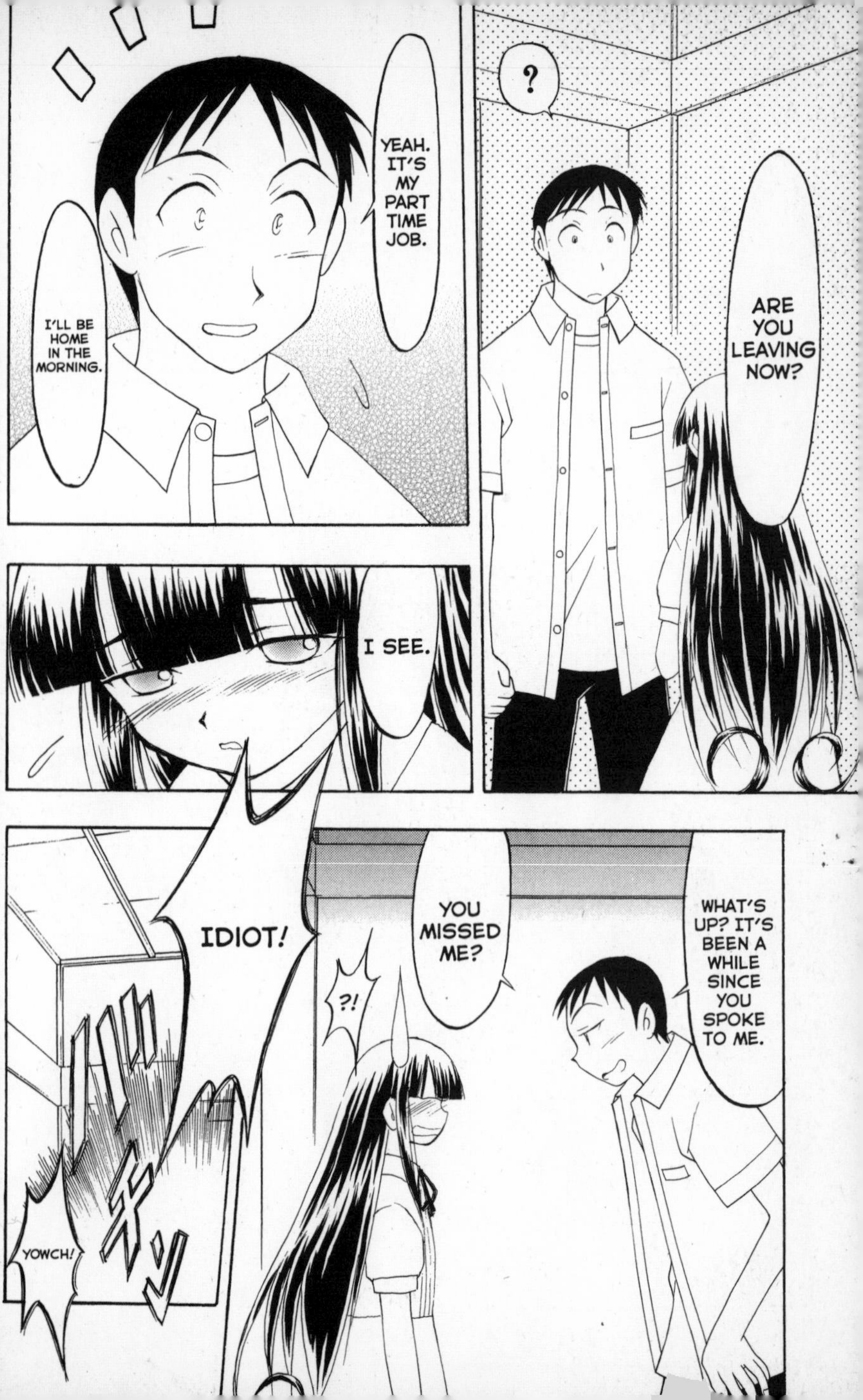
?
ARE YOU LEAVING NOW?
YEAH. IT'S MY PART TIME JOB.
I'LL BE HOME IN THE MORNING.
I SEE.
WHAT'S UP? IT'S BEEN A WHILE SINCE YOU SPOKE TO ME.
YOU MISSED ME?
?!
IDIOT!
YOWCH!

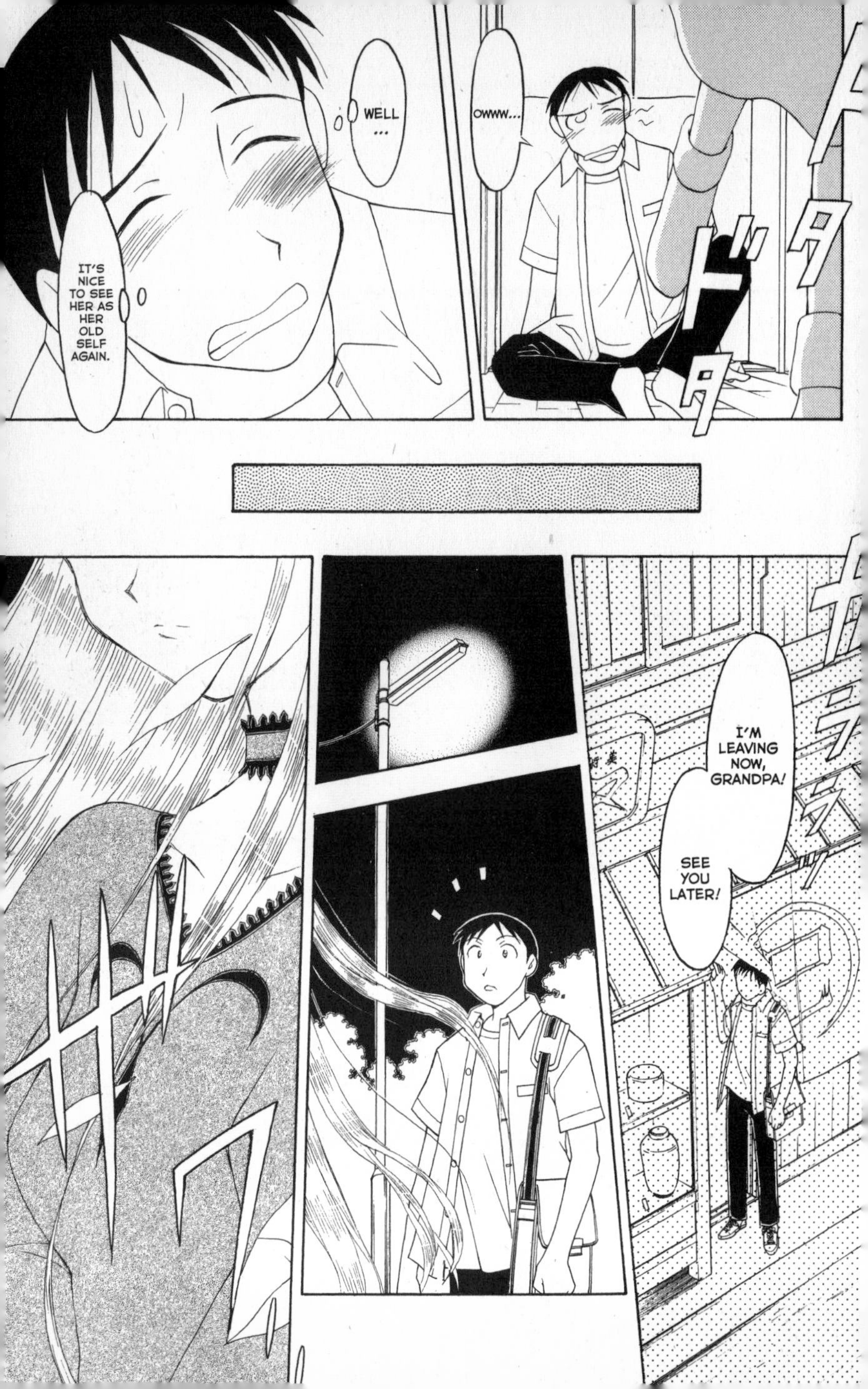
OWWW...
WELL ...
IT'S NICE TO SEE HER AS HER OLD SELF AGAIN.
I'M LEAVING NOW, GRANDPA!
SEE YOU LATER!

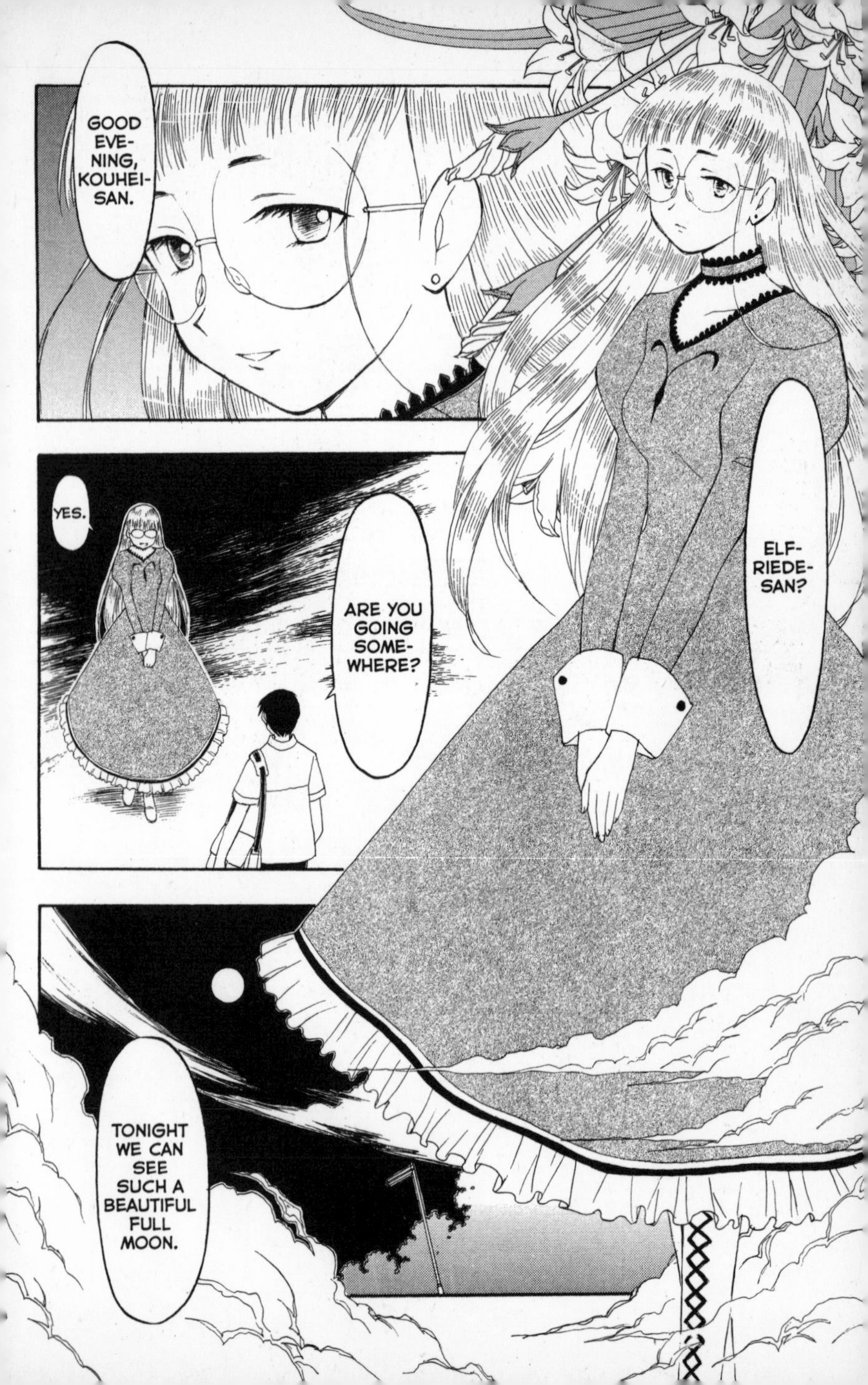
GOOD EVE-NING, KOUHEI-SAN.
ELF-RIEDE-SAN?
ARE YOU GOING SOME-WHERE?
YES.
TONIGHT WE CAN SEE SUCH A BEAUTIFUL FULL MOON.

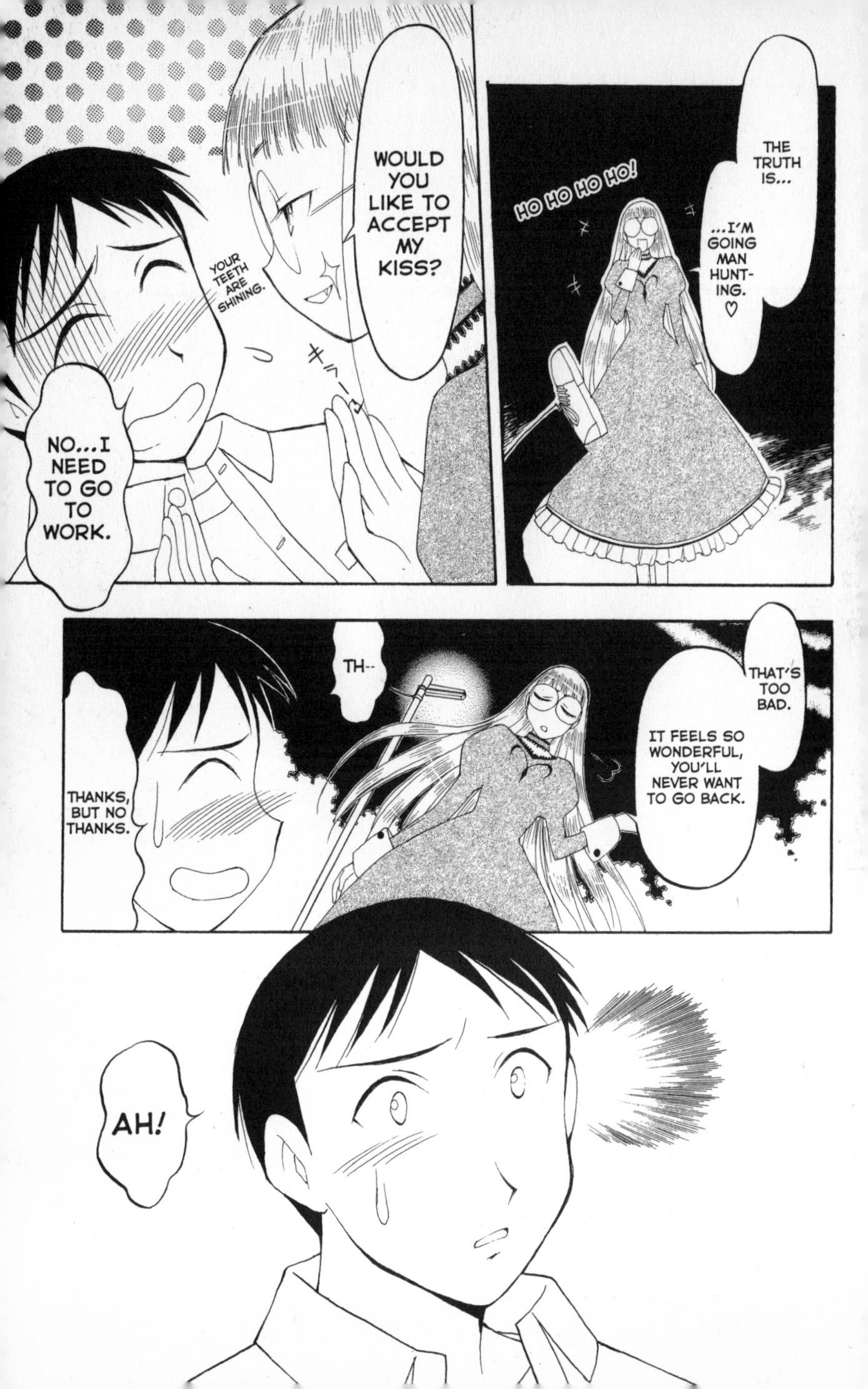
THE TRUTH IS...
...I'M GOING MAN HUNT-ING. ♡
HO HO HO HO!
WOULD YOU LIKE TO ACCEPT MY KISS?
YOUR TEETH ARE SHINING.
NO...I NEED TO GO TO WORK.
THAT'S TOO BAD.
IT FEELS SO WONDERFUL, YOU'LL NEVER WANT TO GO BACK.
TH--
THANKS, BUT NO THANKS.
AH!

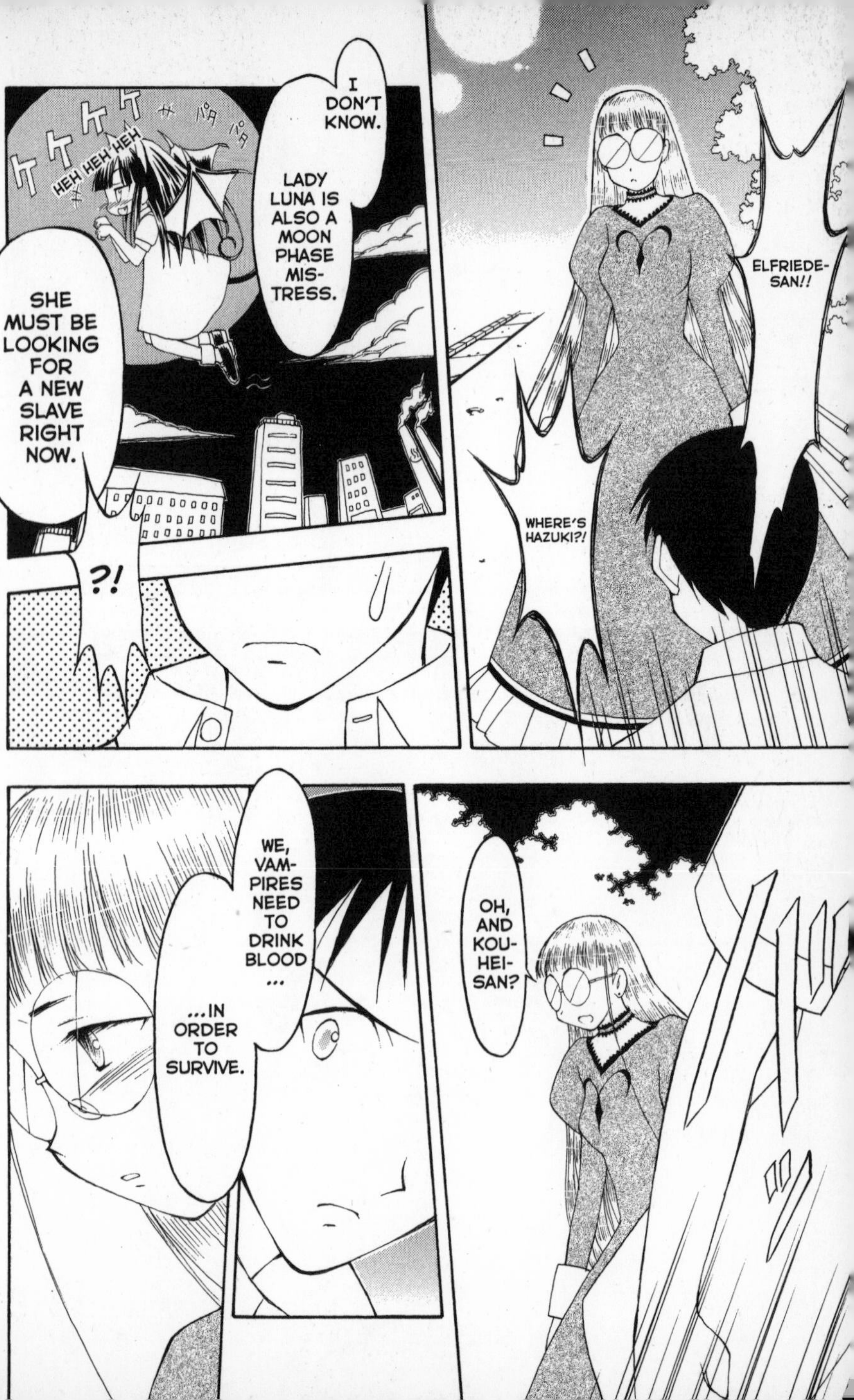
ELFRIEDE-SAN!!
WHERE'S HAZUKI?!
I DON'T KNOW.
LADY LUNA IS ALSO A MOON PHASE MISTRESS.
HEH HEH HEH
SHE MUST BE LOOKING FOR A NEW SLAVE RIGHT NOW.
?!
OH, AND KOUHEI-SAN?
WE, VAMPIRES NEED TO DRINK BLOOD...
...IN ORDER TO SURVIVE.

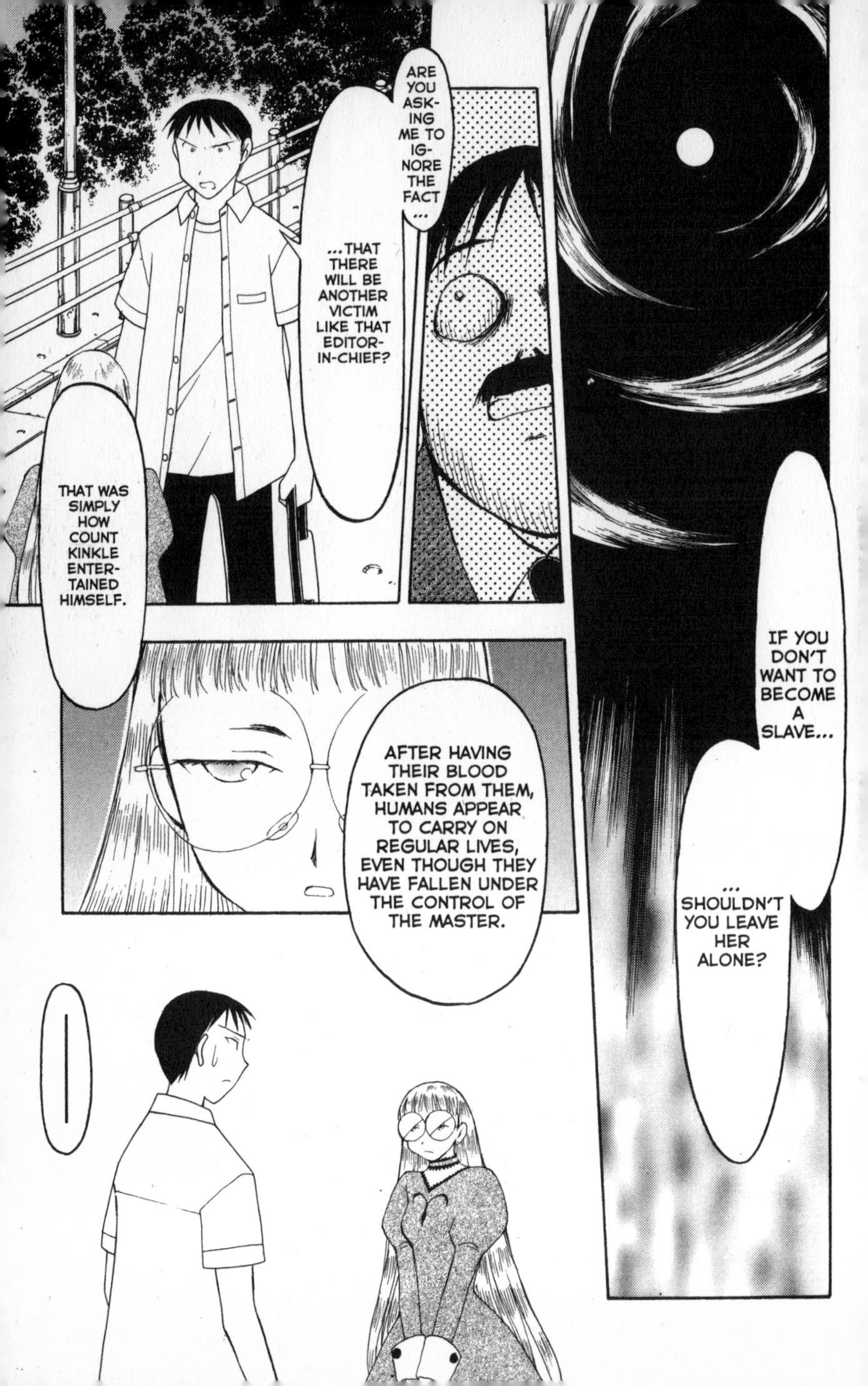
ARE YOU ASKING ME TO IGNORE THE FACT...
...THAT THERE WILL BE ANOTHER VICTIM LIKE THAT EDITOR-IN-CHIEF?
THAT WAS SIMPLY HOW COUNT KINKLE ENTERTAINED HIMSELF.
AFTER HAVING THEIR BLOOD TAKEN FROM THEM, HUMANS APPEAR TO CARRY ON REGULAR LIVES, EVEN THOUGH THEY HAVE FALLEN UNDER THE CONTROL OF THE MASTER.
IF YOU DON'T WANT TO BECOME A SLAVE...
...SHOULDN'T YOU LEAVE HER ALONE?
—

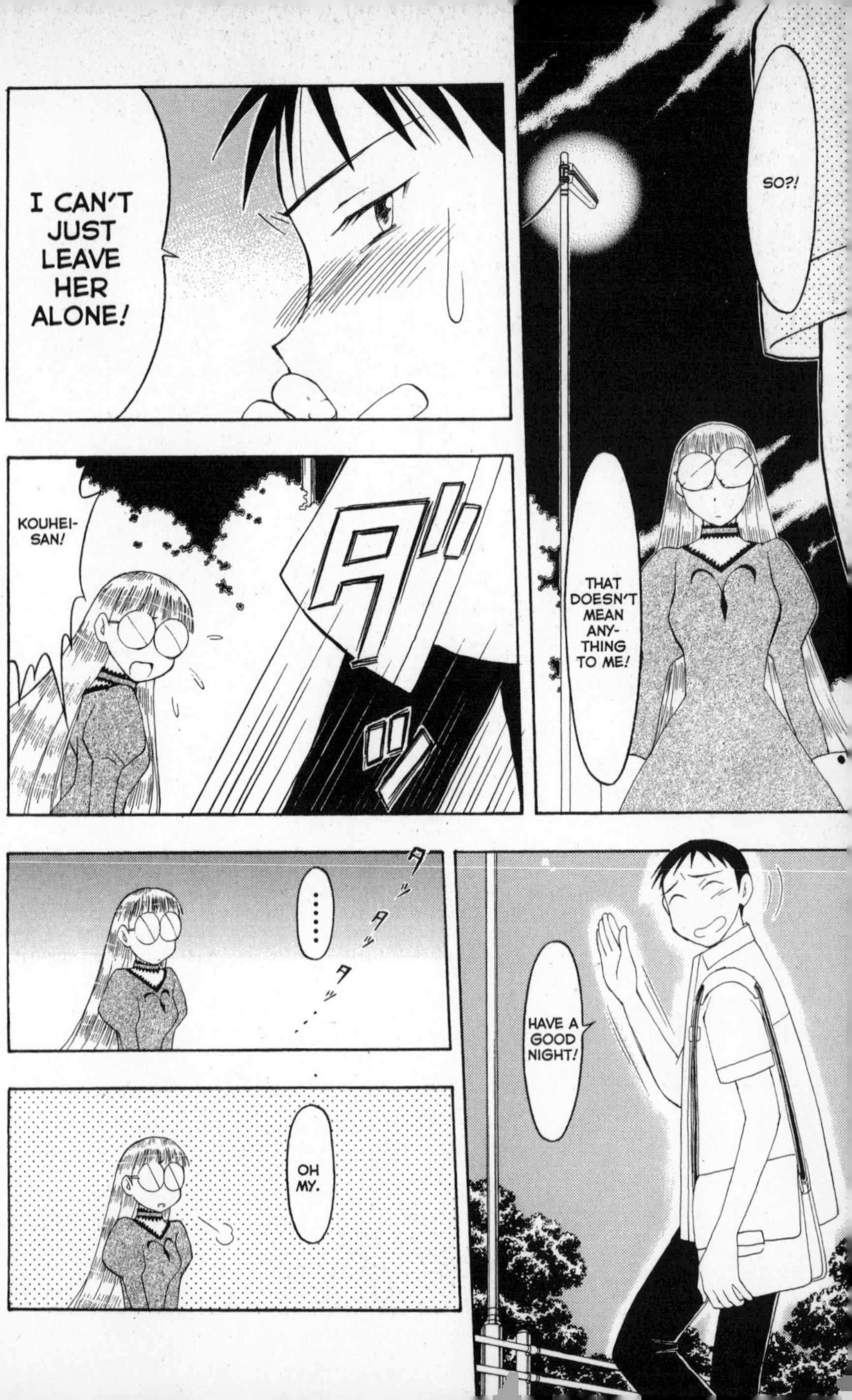
SO?!
THAT DOESN'T MEAN ANY-THING TO ME!
I CAN'T JUST LEAVE HER ALONE!
KOUHEI-SAN!
HAVE A GOOD NIGHT!
......
OH MY.

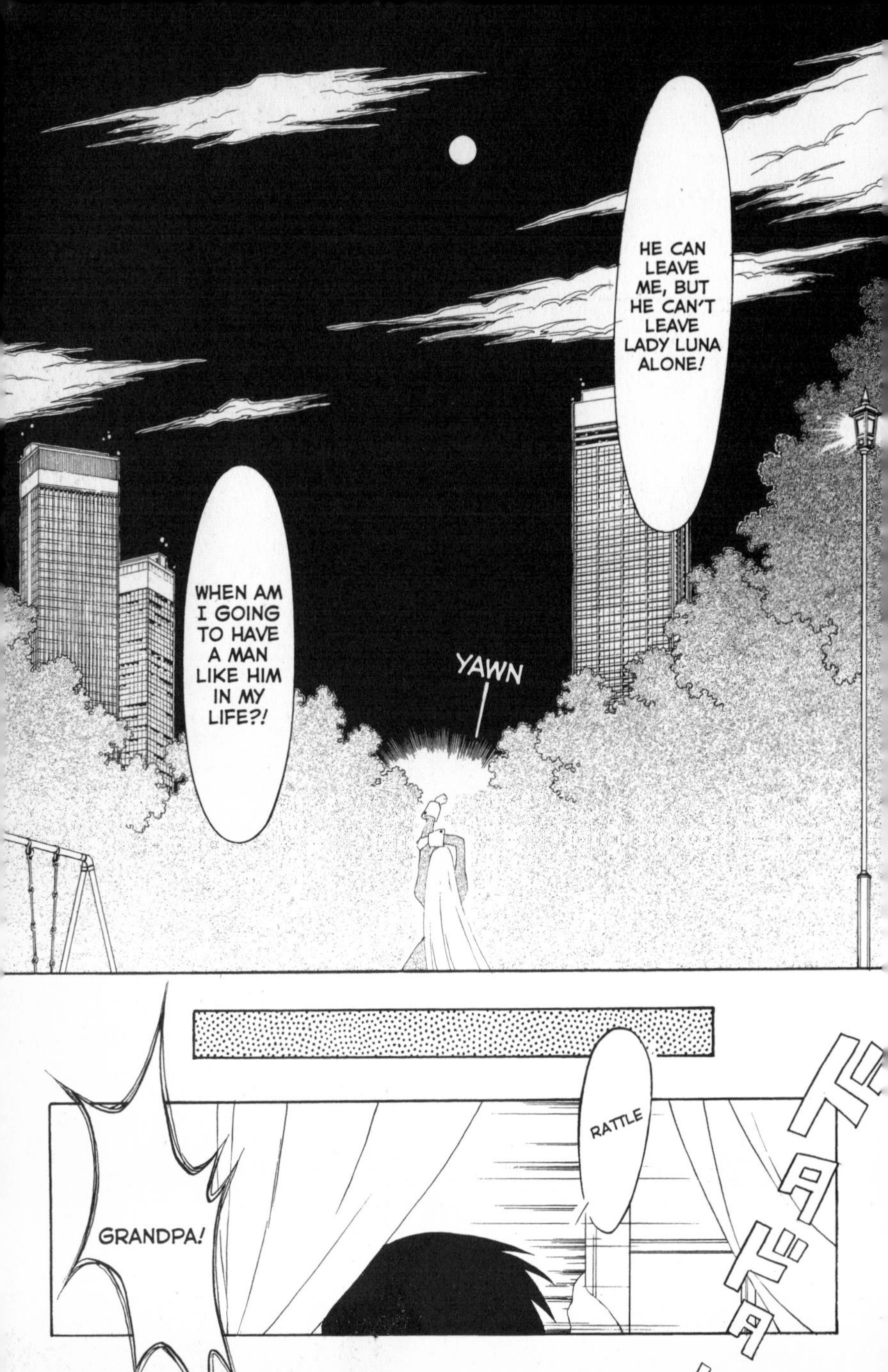
HE CAN LEAVE ME, BUT HE CAN'T LEAVE LADY LUNA ALONE!
YAWN
WHEN AM I GOING TO HAVE A MAN LIKE HIM IN MY LIFE?!
ドタドタ
RATTLE
GRANDPA!

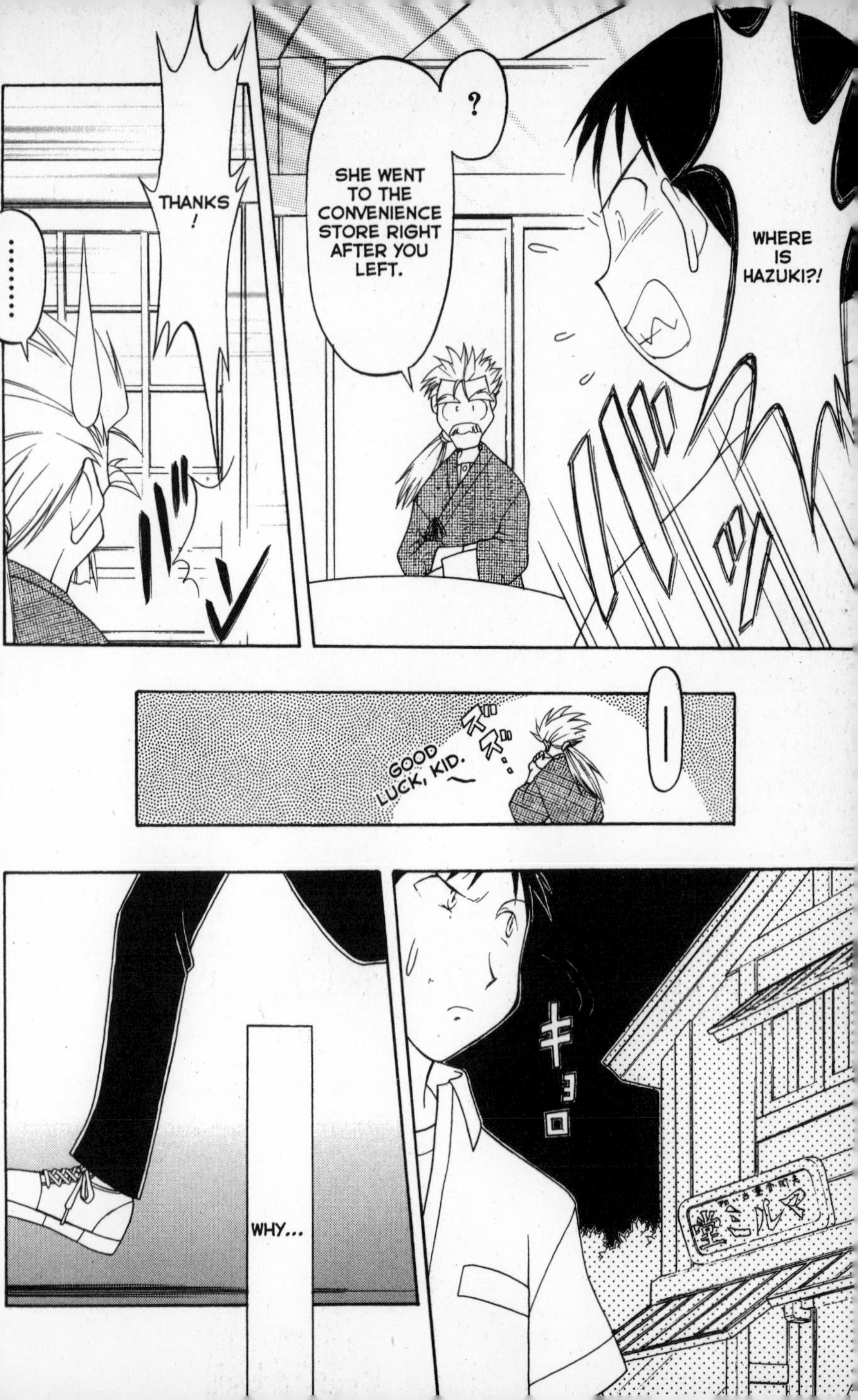
WHERE IS HAZUKI?!
?
SHE WENT TO THE CONVENIENCE STORE RIGHT AFTER YOU LEFT.
THANKS!
....
GOOD LUCK, KID.
WHY...

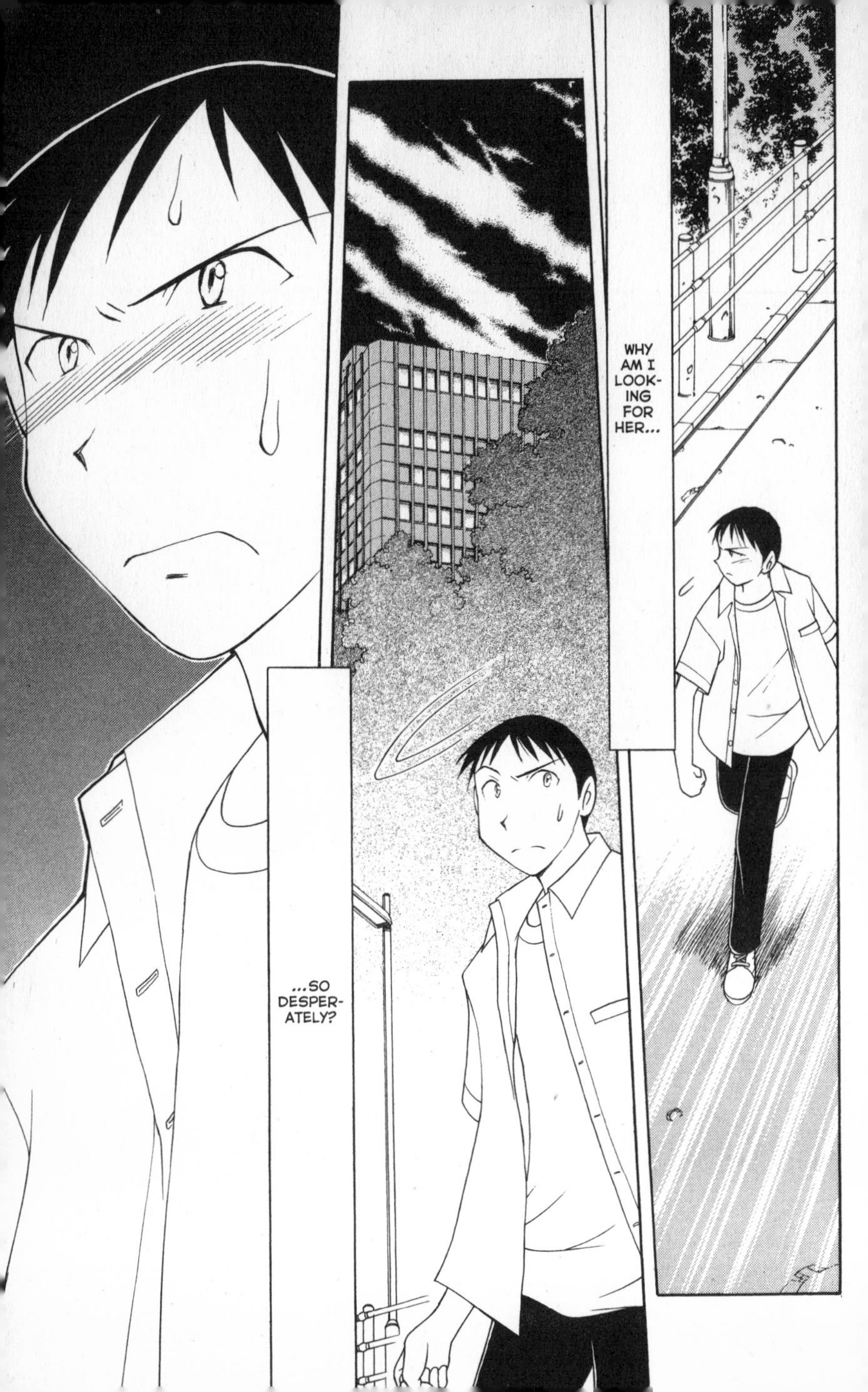
WHY AM I LOOKING FOR HER...
...SO DESPERATELY?

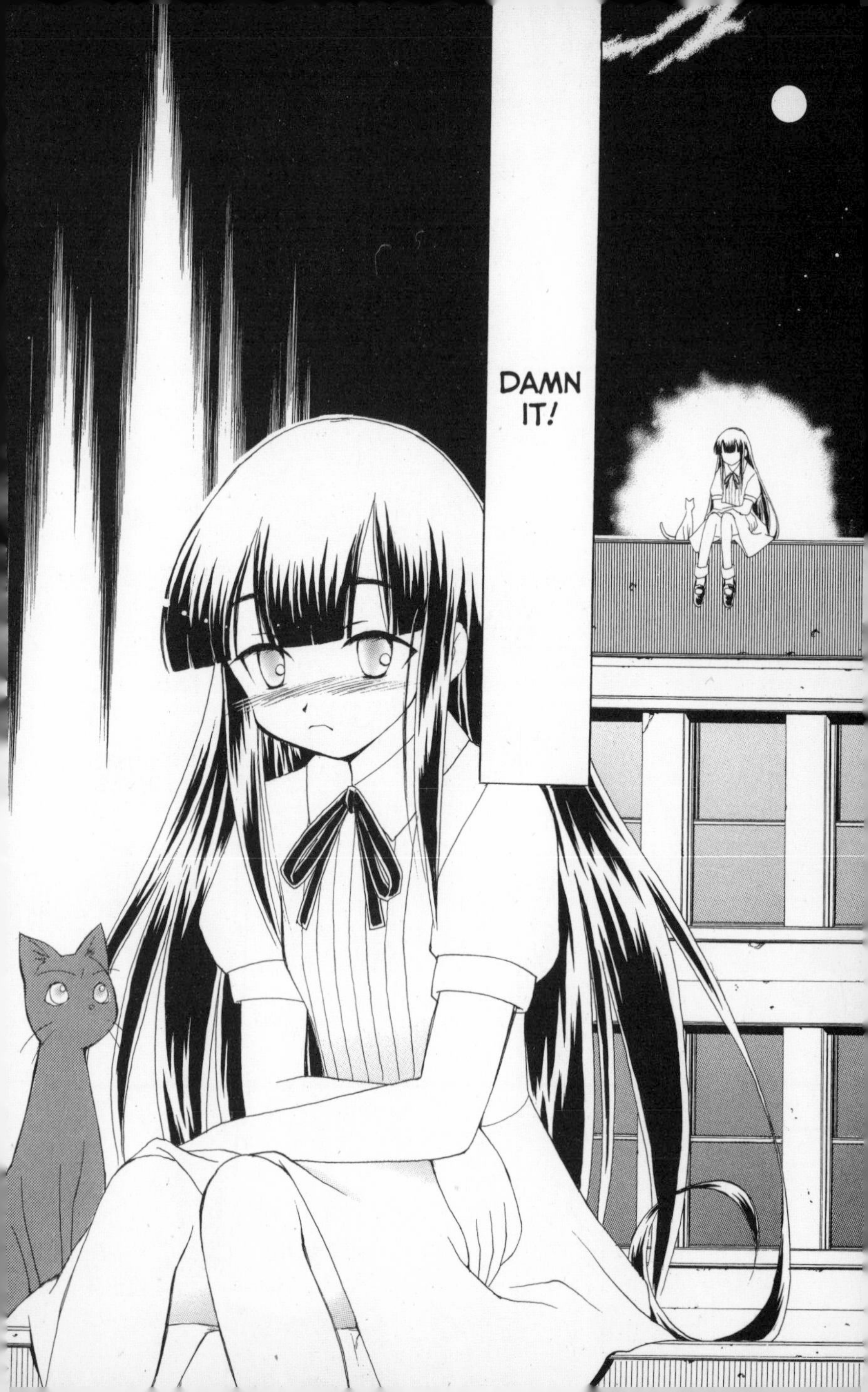
DAMN IT!

MOON 月詠 PHASE

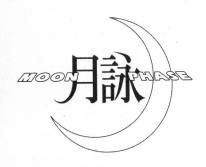

PART 3

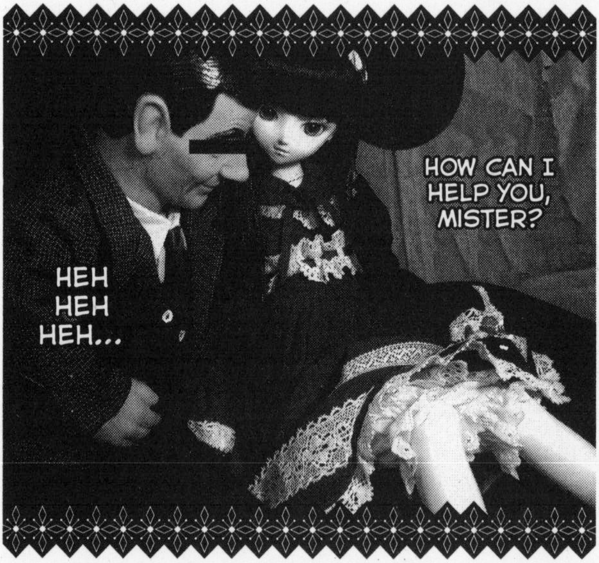
HOW CAN I HELP YOU, MISTER?
HEH HEH HEH...

☞ CONTINUED ON PAGE 104

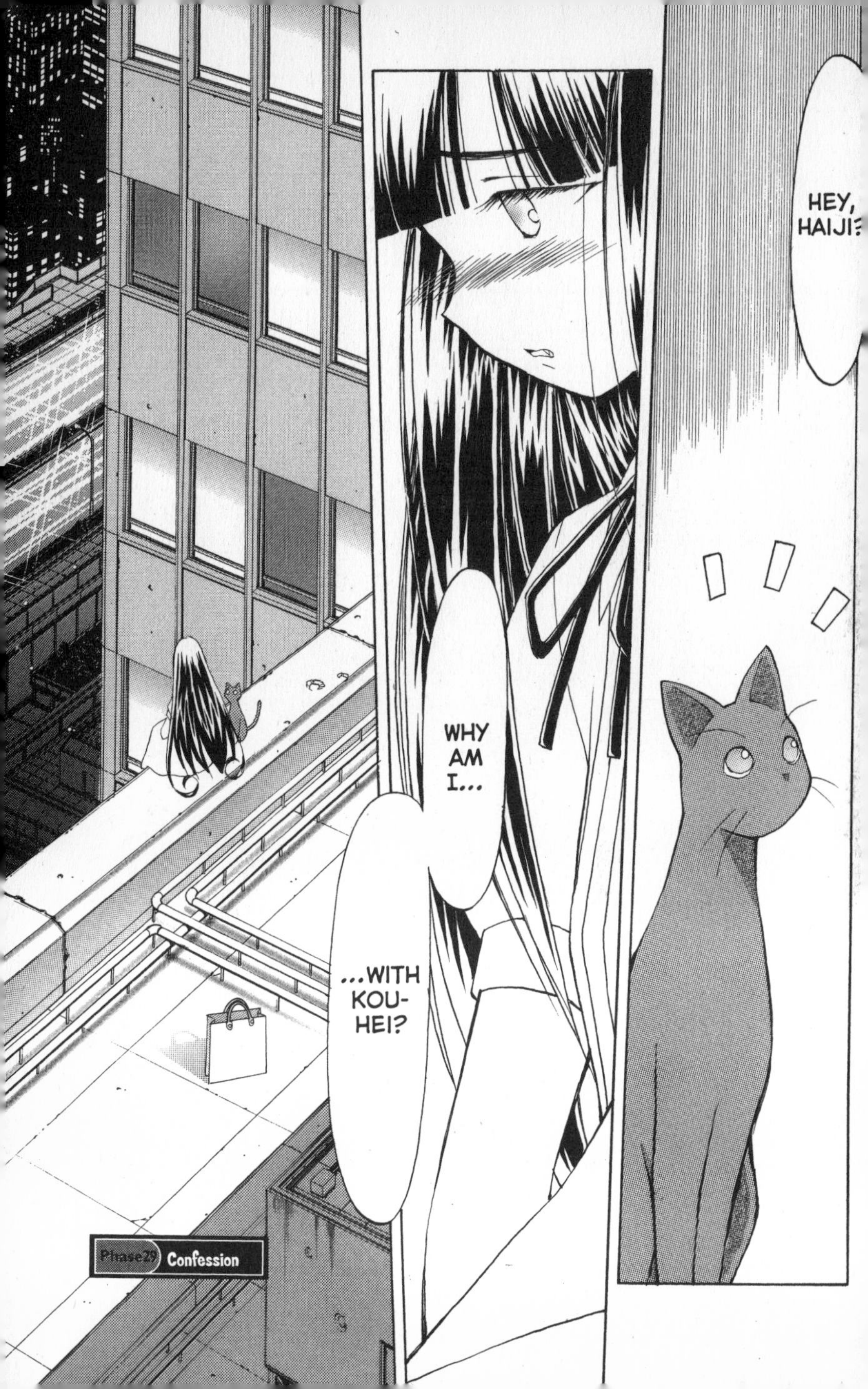
HEY, HAIJI?
WHY AM I...
...WITH KOU-HEI?
Phase 29 Confession

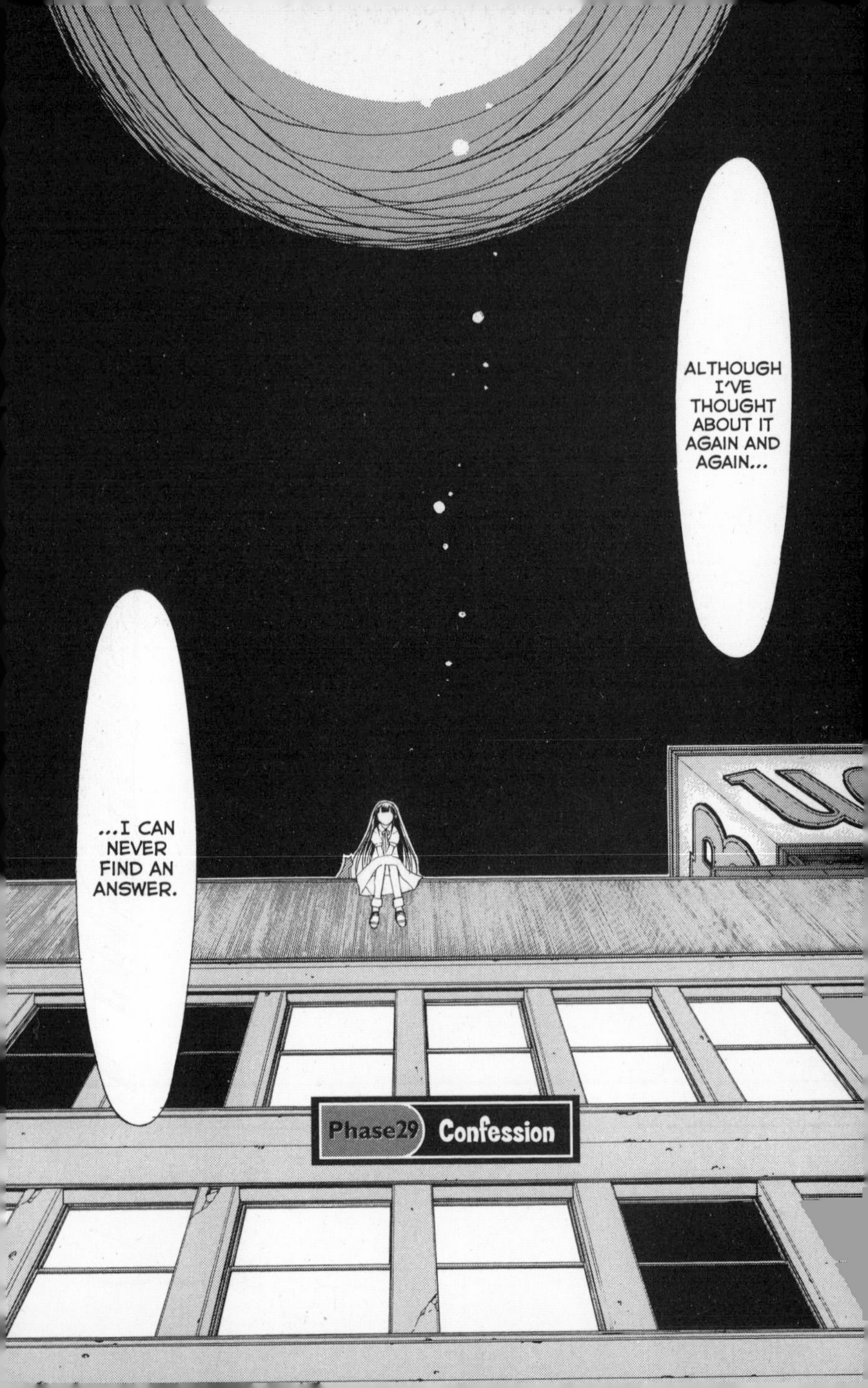
ALTHOUGH I'VE THOUGHT ABOUT IT AGAIN AND AGAIN...
...I CAN NEVER FIND AN ANSWER.
Phase29 Confession

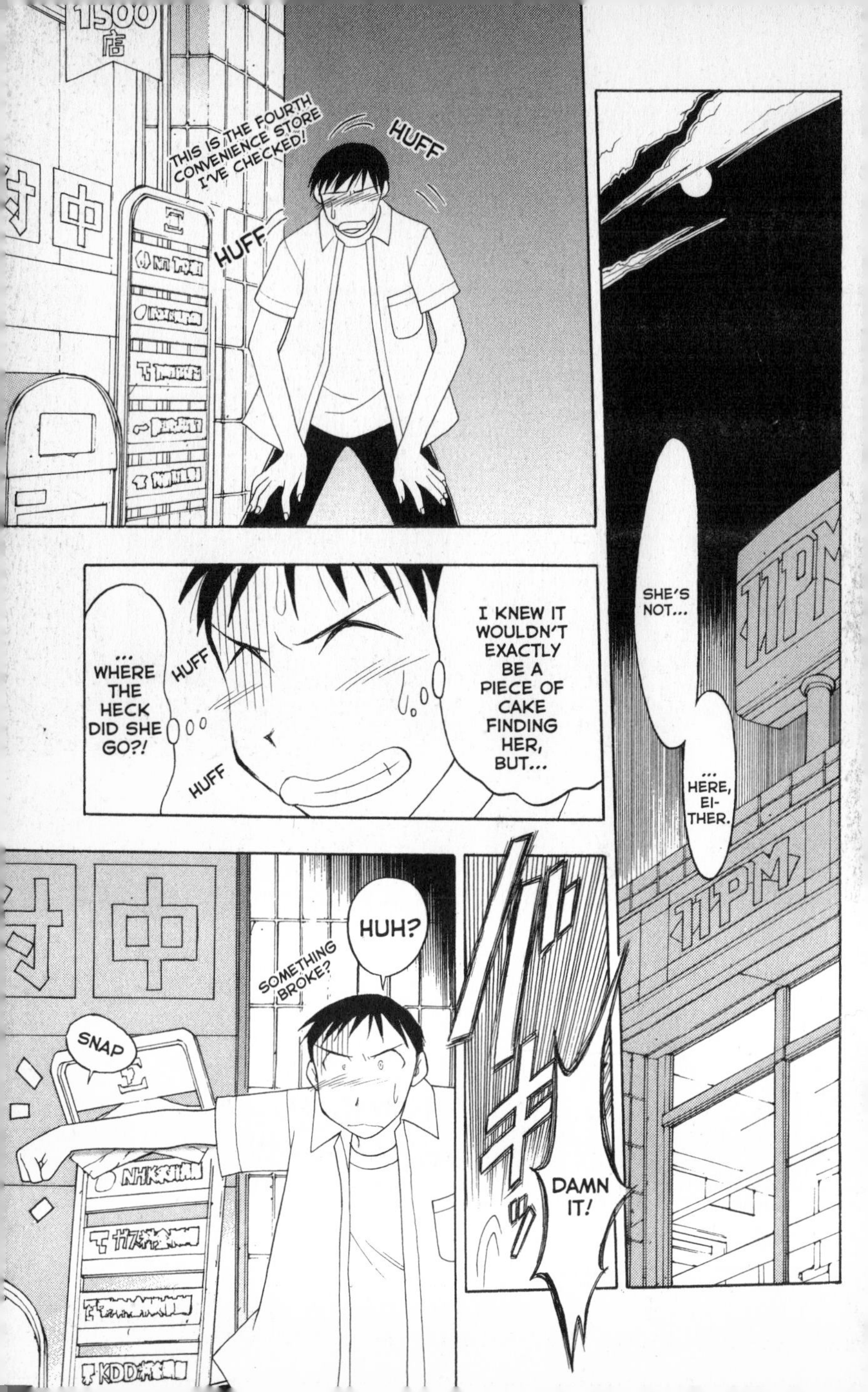

SHE'S NOT...
...HERE, EI-THER.
11PM
1500 店
THIS IS THE FOURTH CONVENIENCE STORE I'VE CHECKED!
HUFF
HUFF
I KNEW IT WOULDN'T EXACTLY BE A PIECE OF CAKE FINDING HER, BUT...
... WHERE THE HECK DID SHE GO?!
HUFF
HUFF
DAMN IT!
HUH?
SOMETHING BROKE?
SNAP

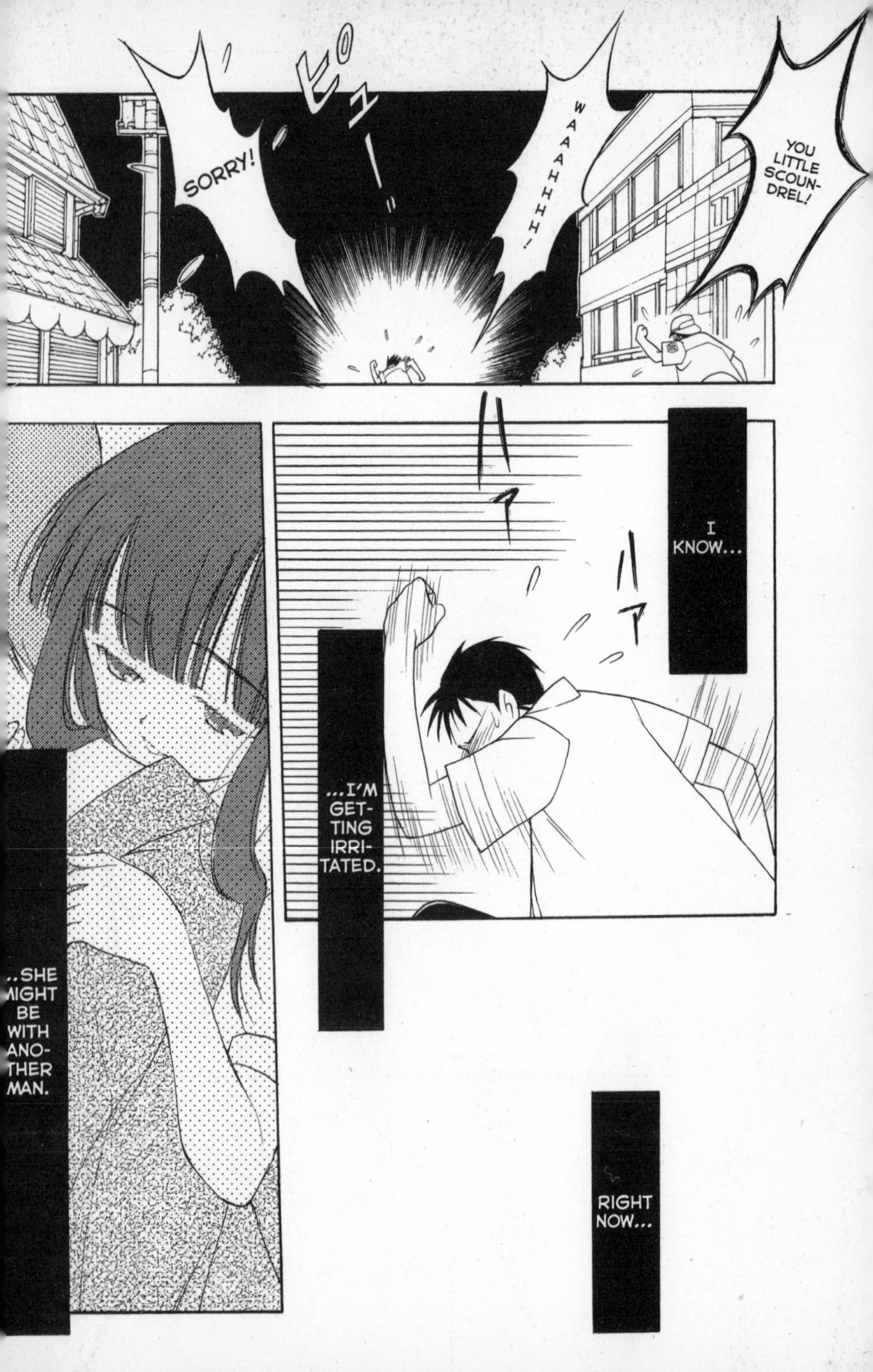
YOU LITTLE SCOUN-DREL!
WAAAHHHHH!
ヒュー！
SORRY!
I KNOW...
ハァ
ハァ
...I'M GET-TING IRRI-TATED.
RIGHT NOW...
..SHE MIGHT BE WITH ANO-THER MAN.

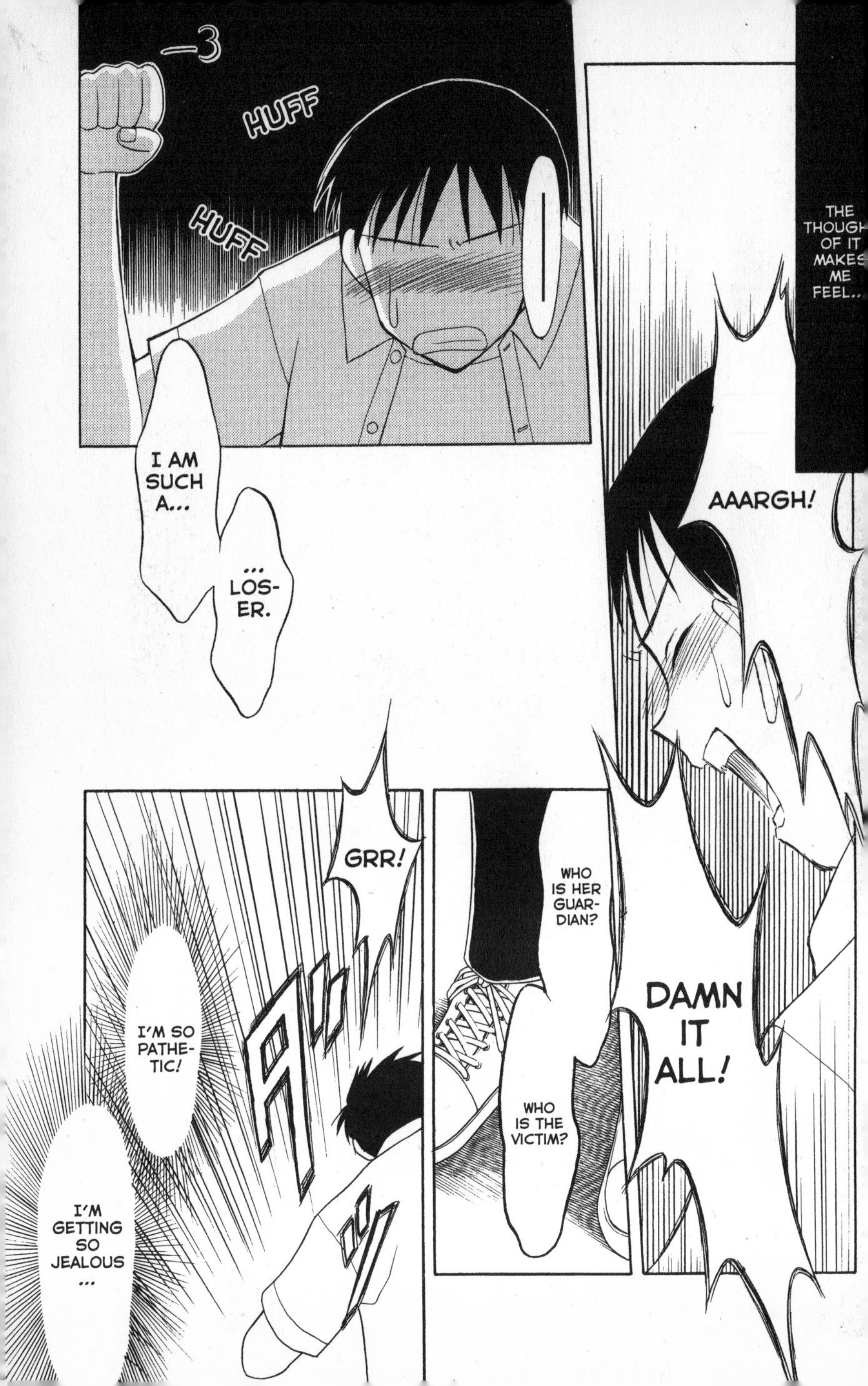
THE THOUGH OF IT MAKES ME FEEL..
HUFF
HUFF
I AM SUCH A...
... LOS-ER.
AAARGH!
DAMN IT ALL!
WHO IS HER GUAR-DIAN?
WHO IS THE VICTIM?
GRR!
I'M SO PATHE-TIC!
I'M GETTING SO JEALOUS ...

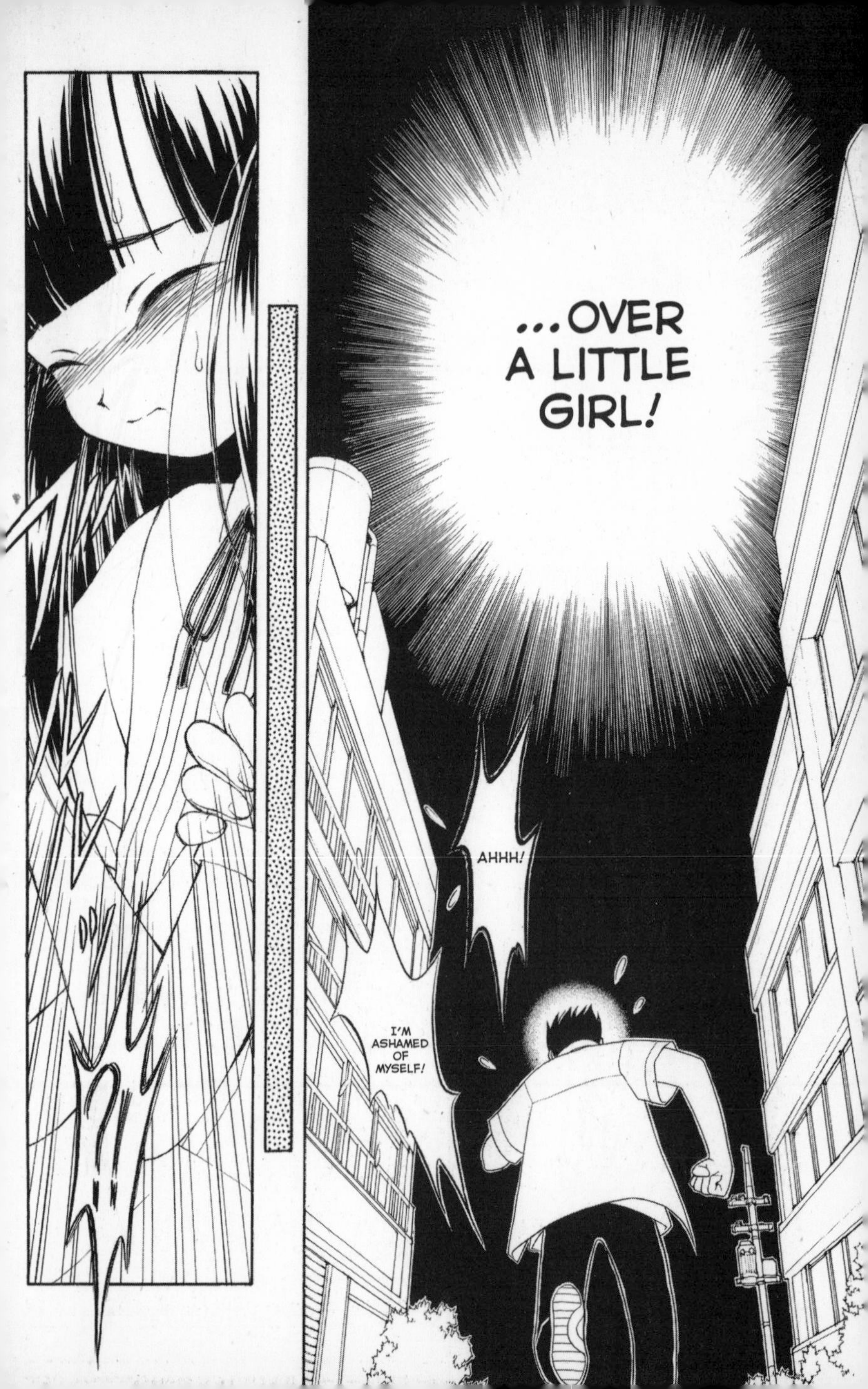
...OVER A LITTLE GIRL!
AHHH!
I'M ASHAMED OF MYSELF!

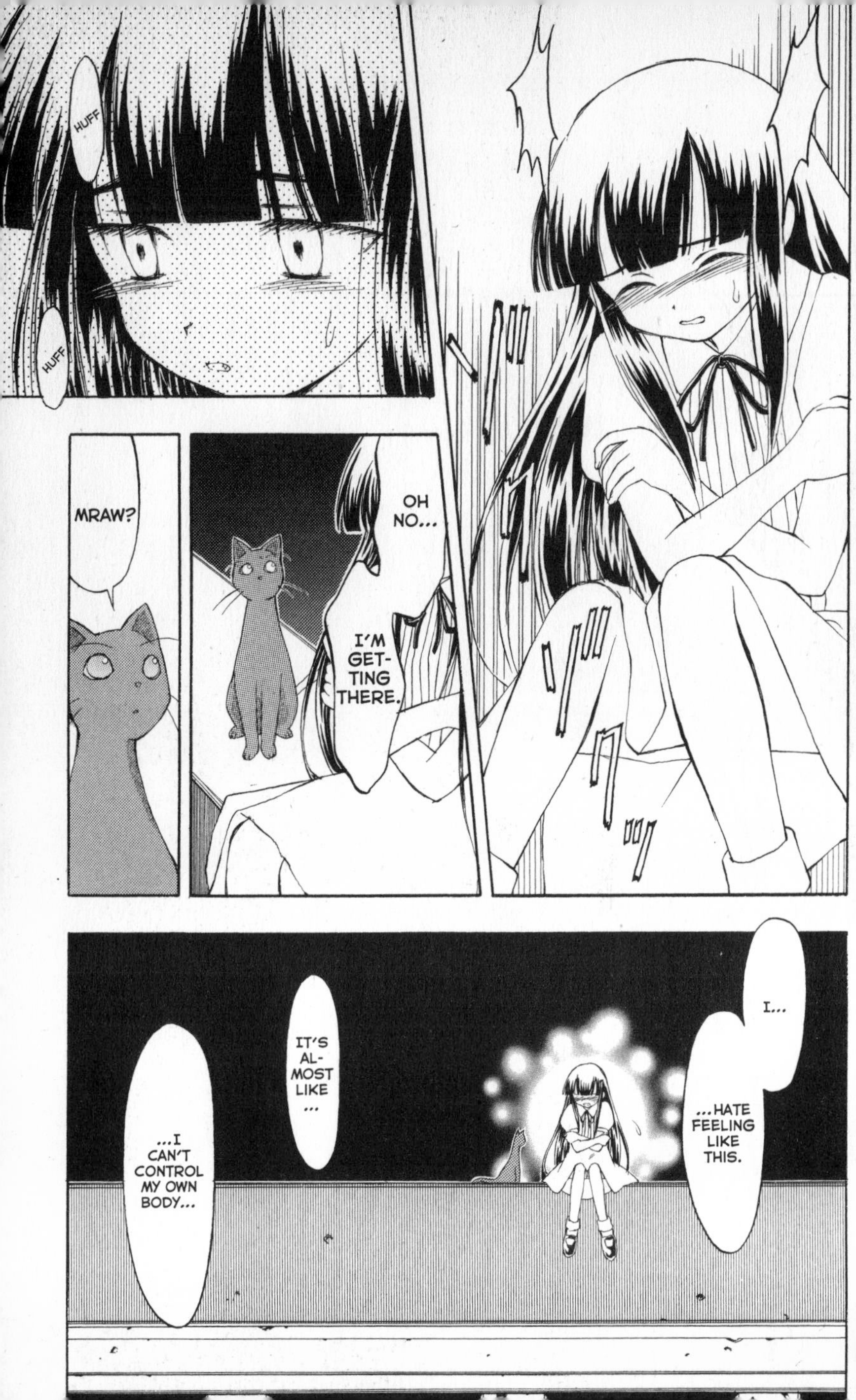
HUFF
HUFF
OH NO...
I'M GETTING THERE.
MRAW?
I...
...HATE FEELING LIKE THIS.
IT'S ALMOST LIKE...
...I CAN'T CONTROL MY OWN BODY...

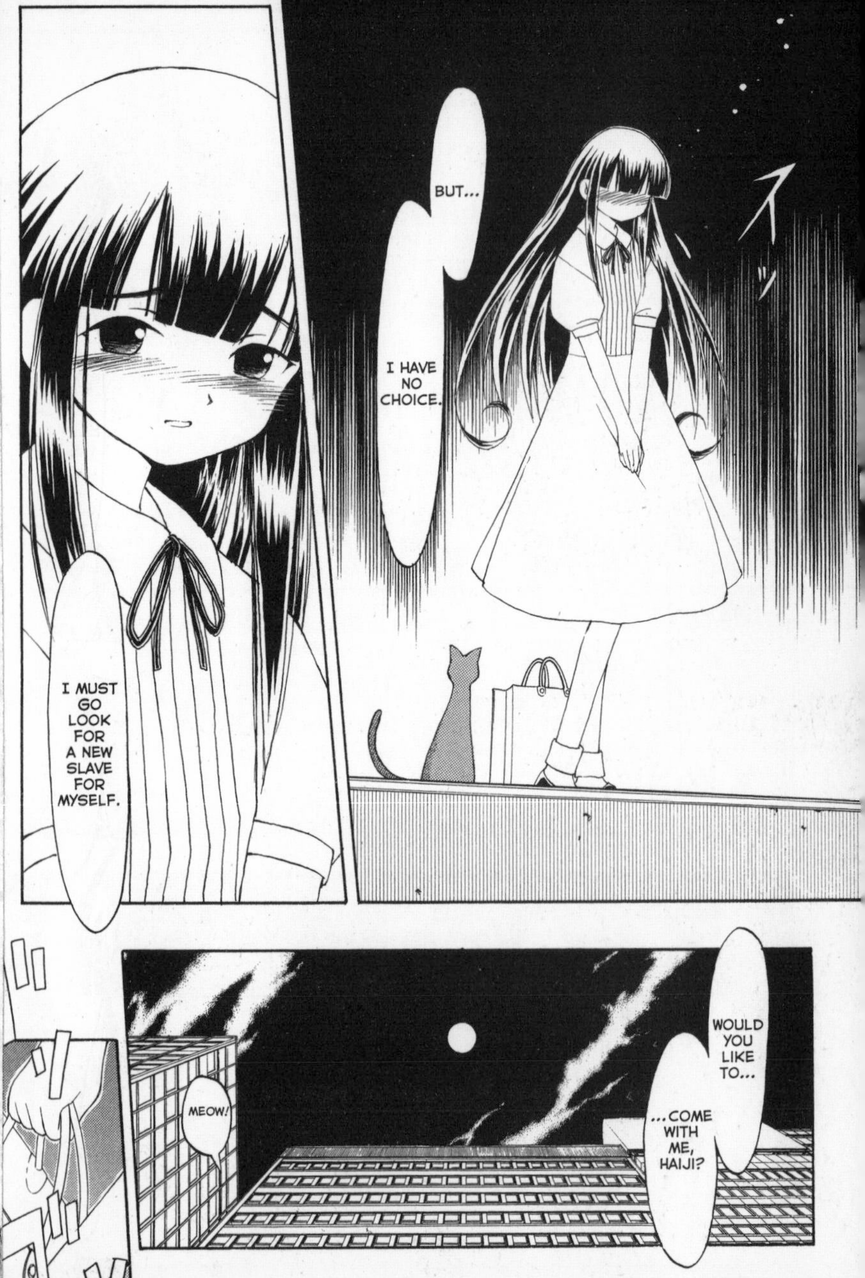
BUT...
I HAVE NO CHOICE.
I MUST GO LOOK FOR A NEW SLAVE FOR MYSELF.
WOULD YOU LIKE TO...
...COME WITH ME, HAIJI?
MEOW!

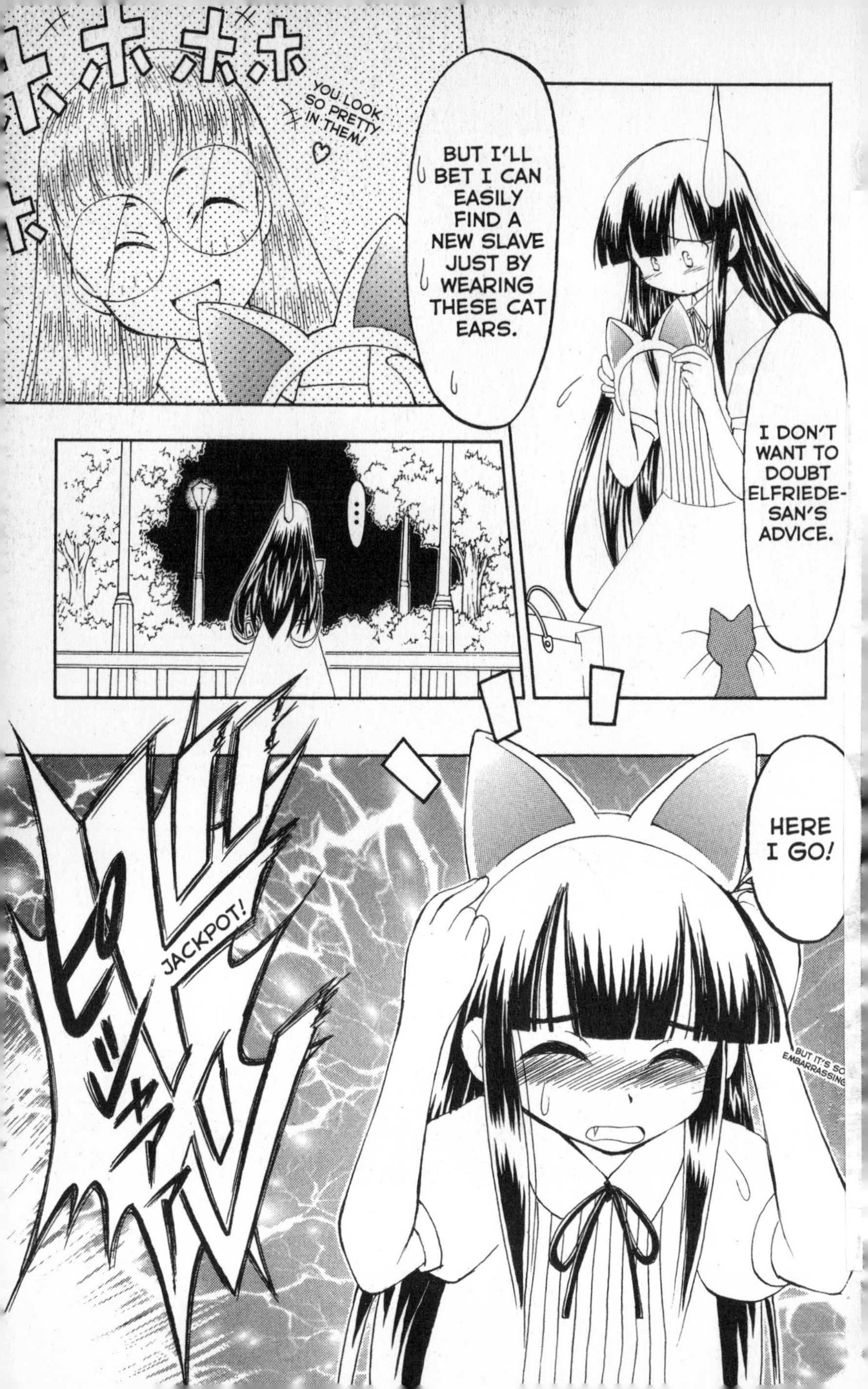
YOU LOOK SO PRETTY IN THEM! ♥
BUT I'LL BET I CAN EASILY FIND A NEW SLAVE JUST BY WEARING THESE CAT EARS.
I DON'T WANT TO DOUBT ELFRIEDE-SAN'S ADVICE.
...
HERE I GO!
BUT IT'S SO EMBARRASSING
JACKPOT!

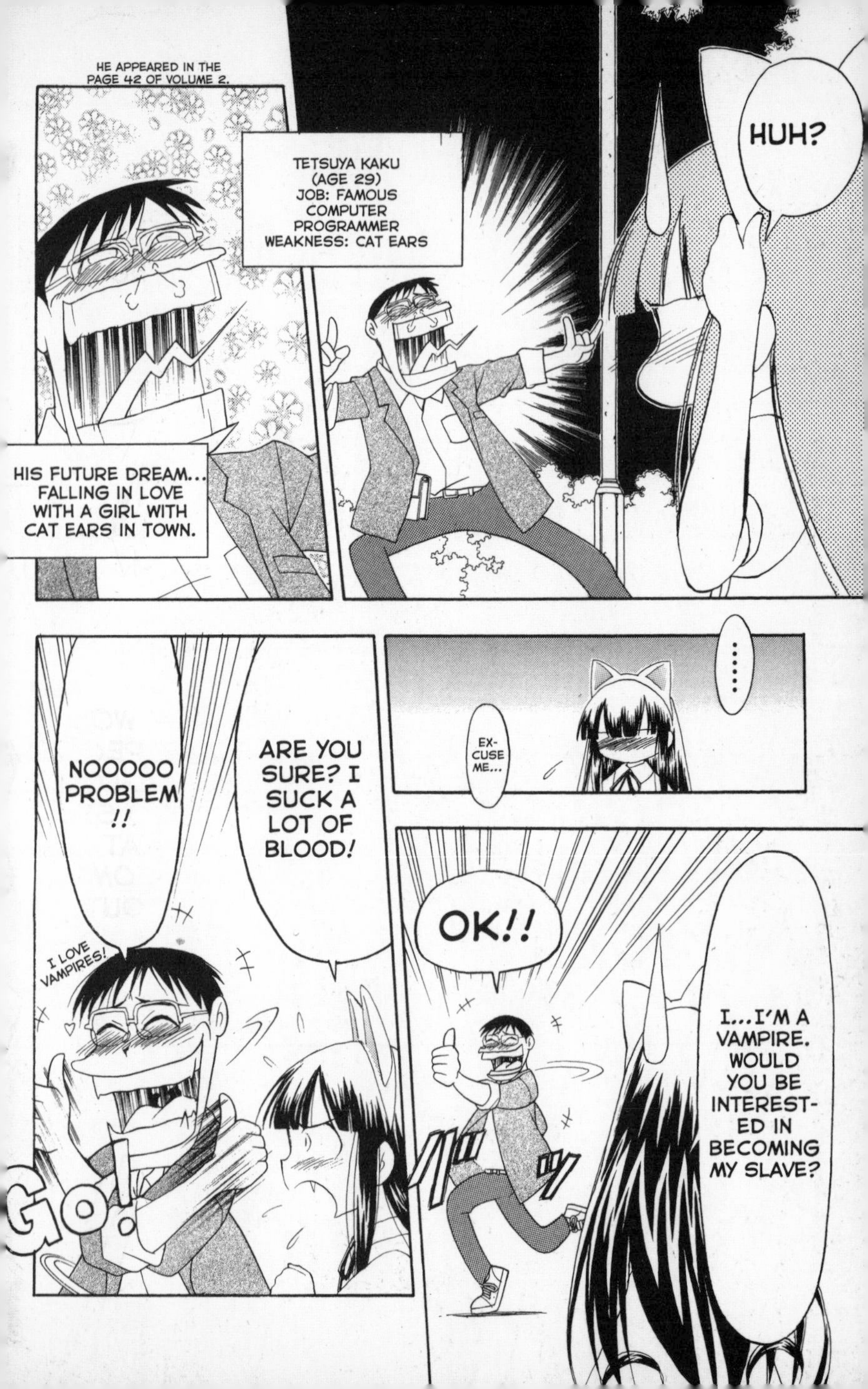
HUH?
HE APPEARED IN THE PAGE 42 OF VOLUME 2.
TETSUYA KAKU (AGE 29) JOB: FAMOUS COMPUTER PROGRAMMER WEAKNESS: CAT EARS
HIS FUTURE DREAM... FALLING IN LOVE WITH A GIRL WITH CAT EARS IN TOWN.
......
EX-CUSE ME...
I...I'M A VAMPIRE. WOULD YOU BE INTEREST-ED IN BECOMING MY SLAVE?
OK!!
ARE YOU SURE? I SUCK A LOT OF BLOOD!
NOOOOO PROBLEM!!
I LOVE VAMPIRES!
GO!

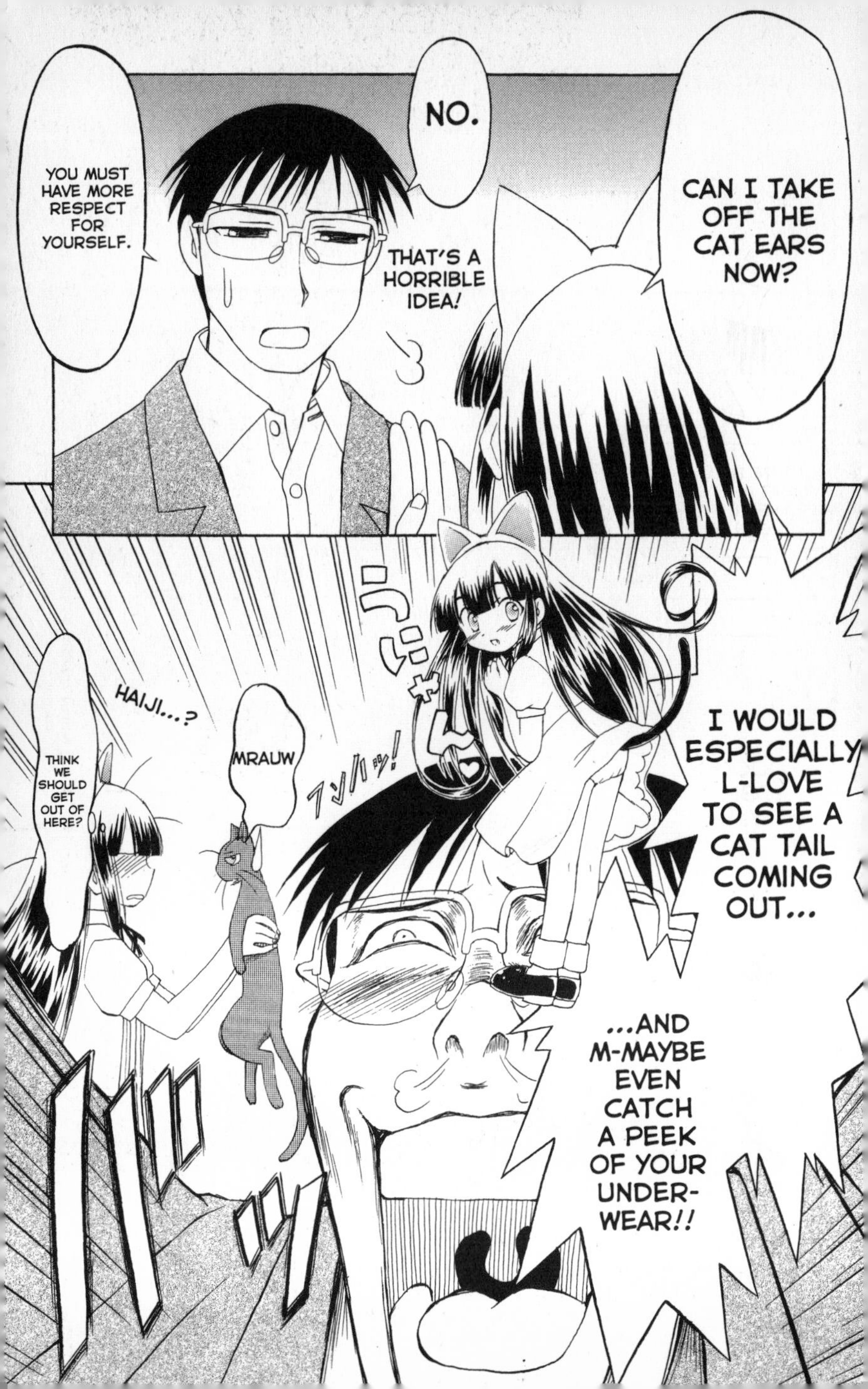
CAN I TAKE OFF THE CAT EARS NOW?
NO.
THAT'S A HORRIBLE IDEA!
YOU MUST HAVE MORE RESPECT FOR YOURSELF.
I WOULD ESPECIALLY L-LOVE TO SEE A CAT TAIL COMING OUT...
...AND M-MAYBE EVEN CATCH A PEEK OF YOUR UNDER-WEAR!!
HAIJI...?
MRAUW
THINK WE SHOULD GET OUT OF HERE?

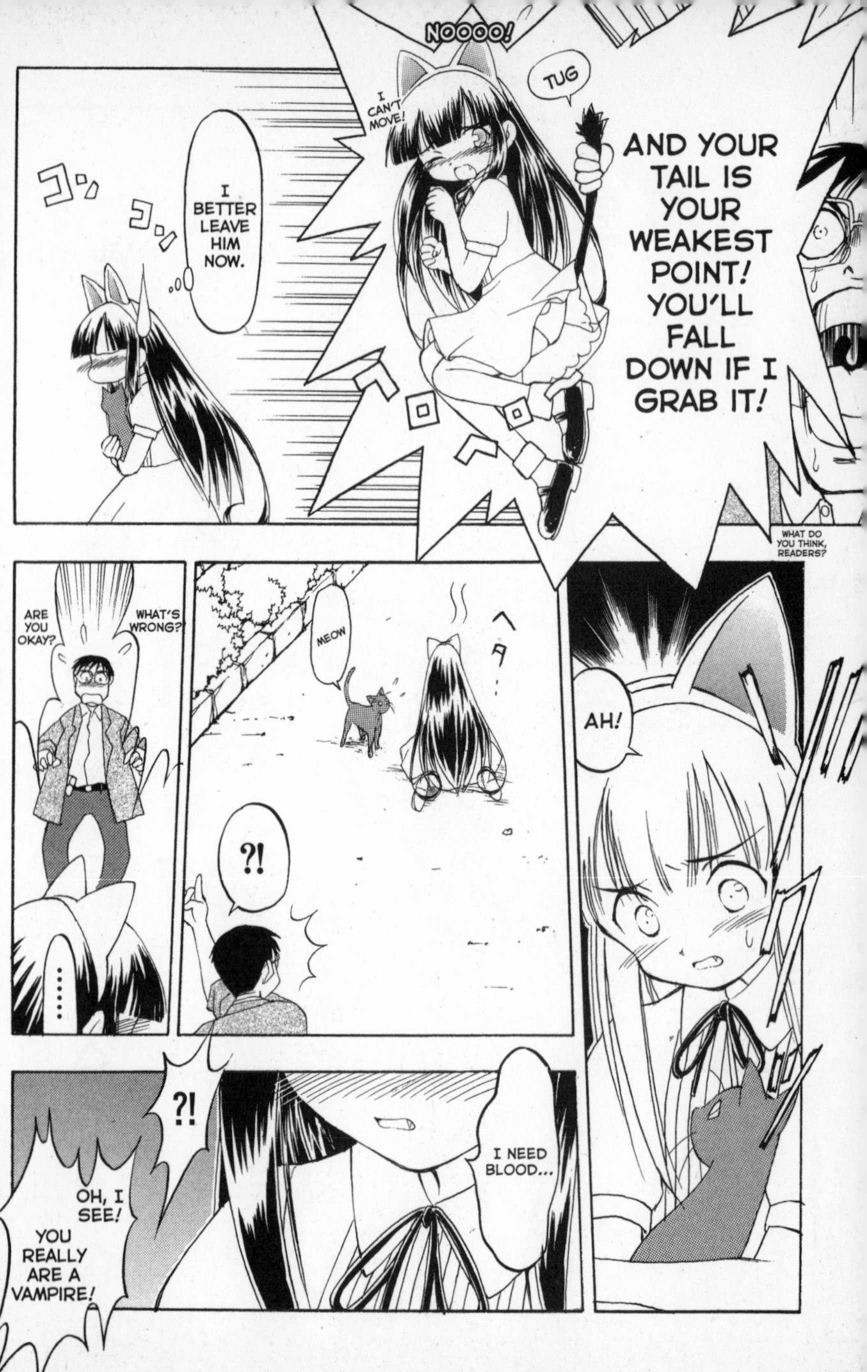
NOOOO!
TUG
AND YOUR TAIL IS YOUR WEAKEST POINT! YOU'LL FALL DOWN IF I GRAB IT!
I CAN'T MOVE!
WHAT DO YOU THINK, READERS?
I BETTER LEAVE HIM NOW.
AH!
MEOW
?!
WHAT'S WRONG?
ARE YOU OKAY?
......
I NEED BLOOD...
?!
OH, I SEE! YOU REALLY ARE A VAMPIRE!

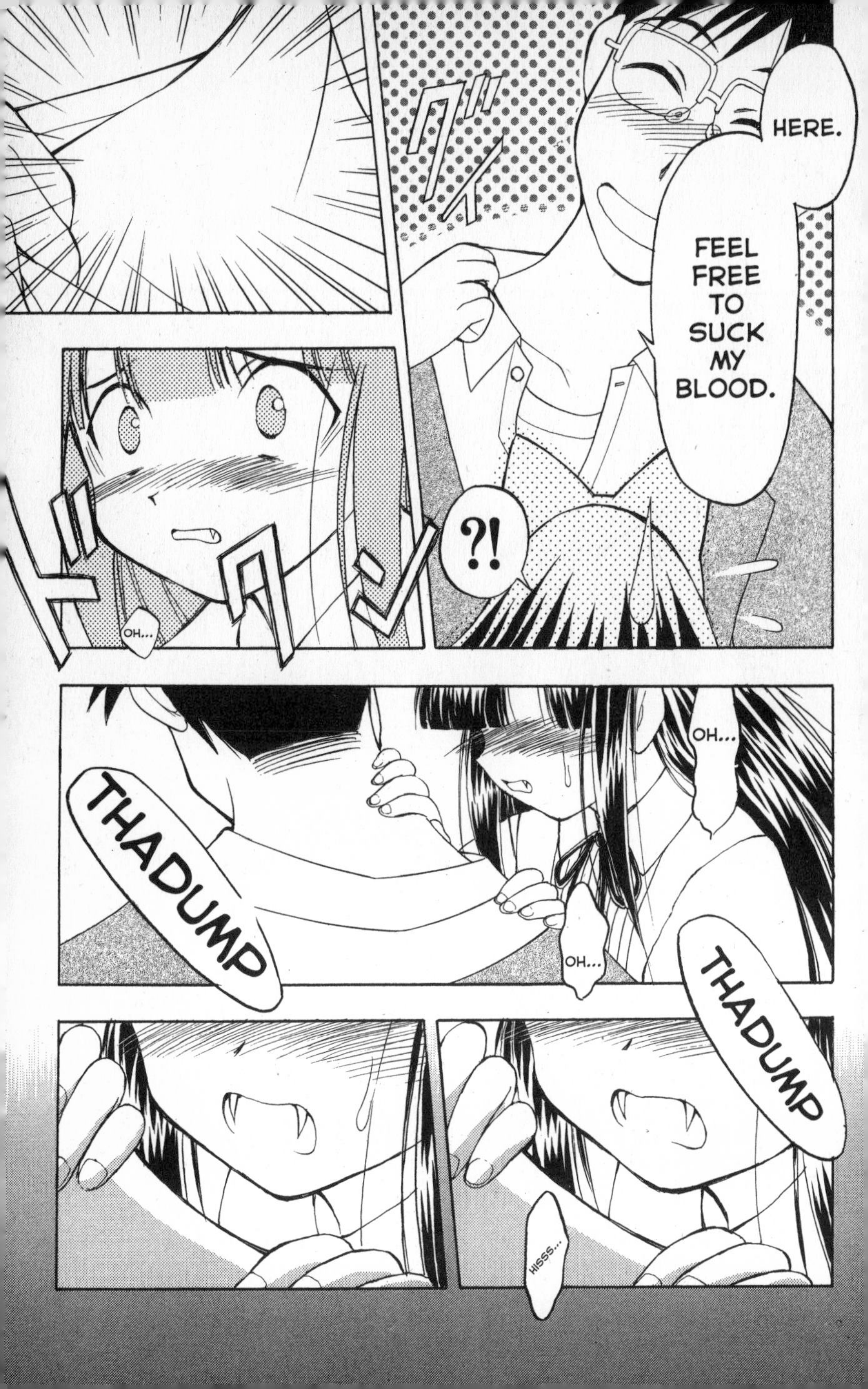
HERE.
FEEL FREE TO SUCK MY BLOOD.
?!
OH...
OH...
THADUMP
OH...
THADUMP
HISSS...

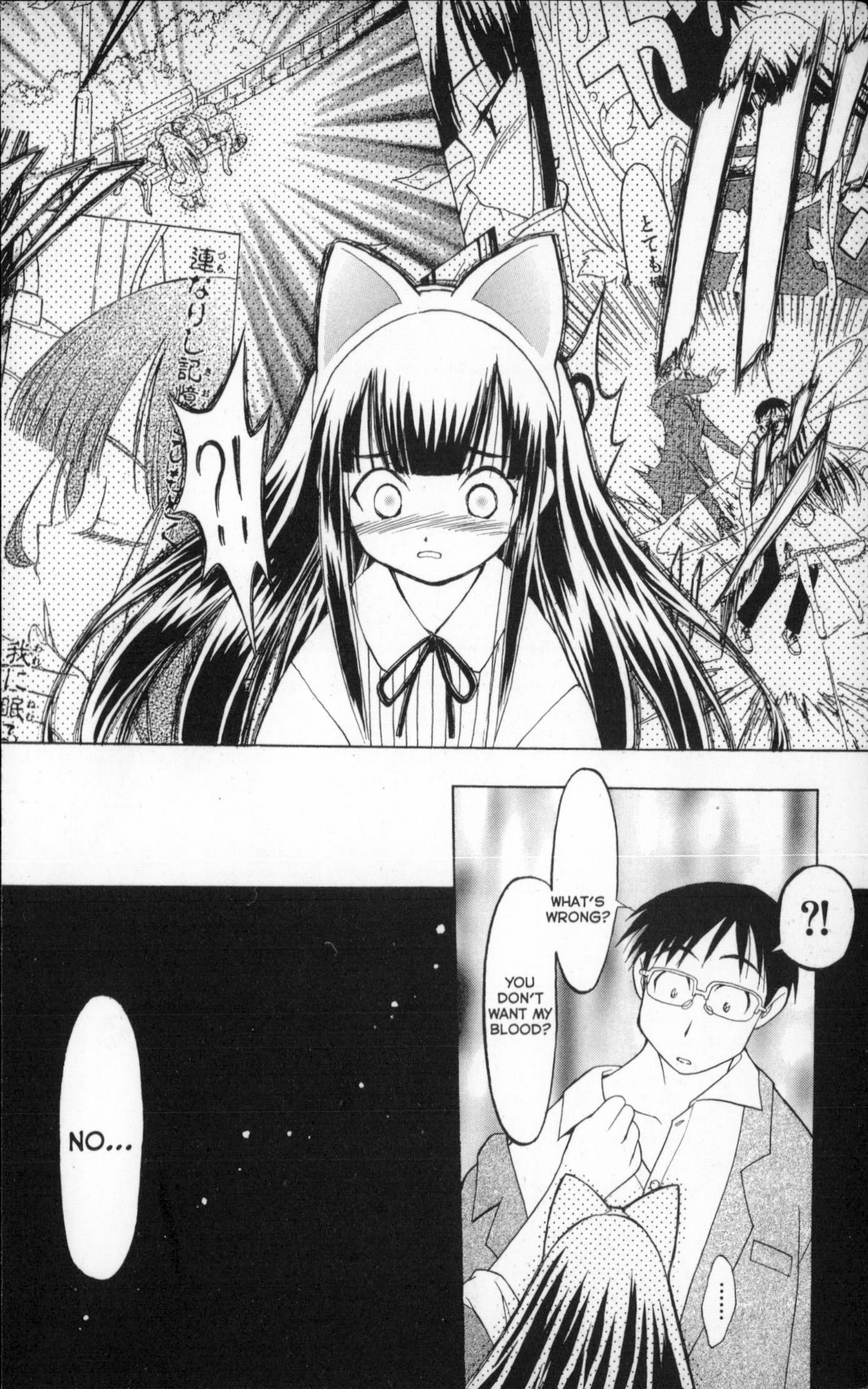
連なりし記憶
?!
?!
WHAT'S WRONG?
YOU DON'T WANT MY BLOOD?
......
NO...

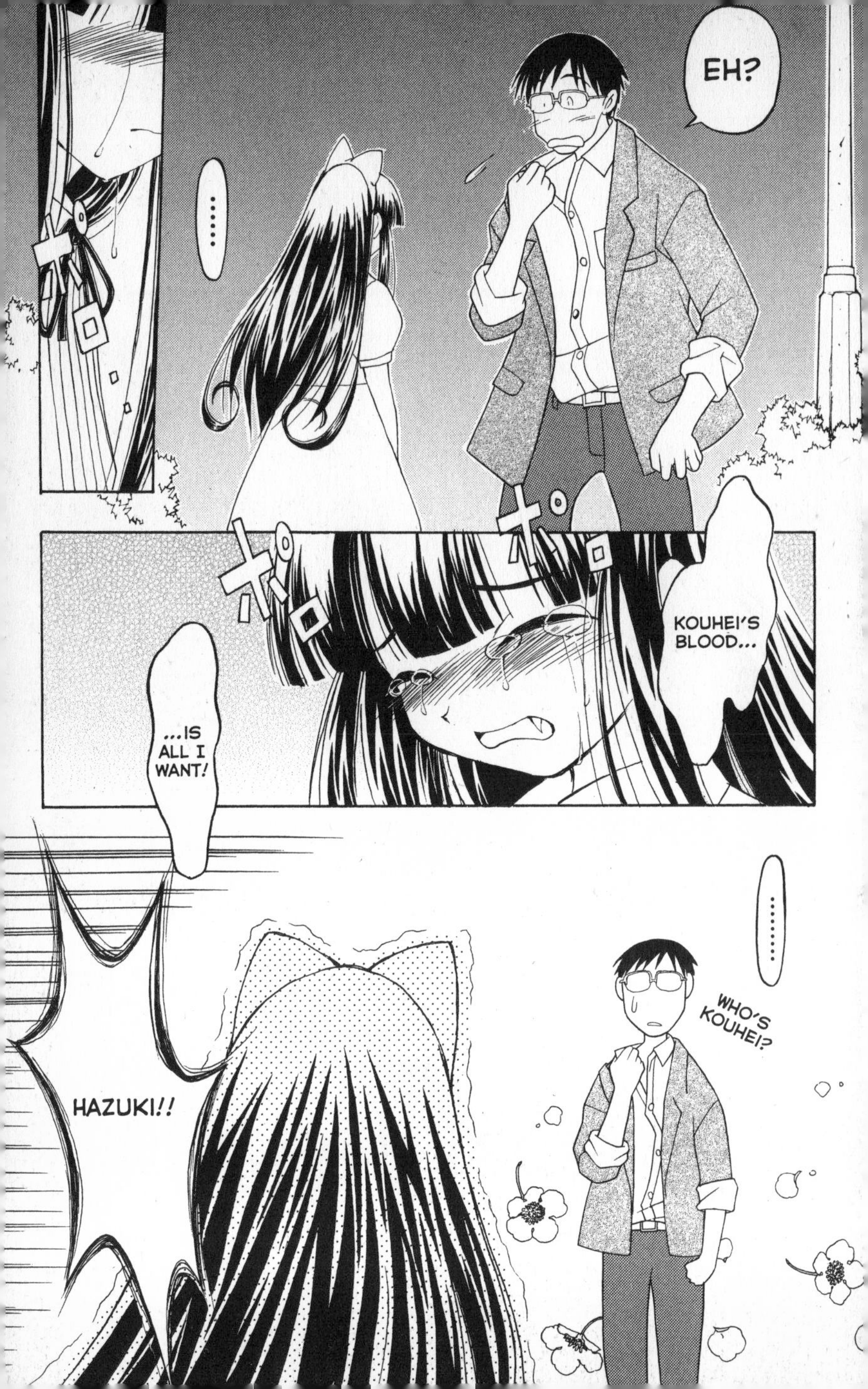
EH?
......
KOUHEI'S BLOOD...
...IS ALL I WANT!
......
WHO'S KOUHEI?
HAZUKI!!

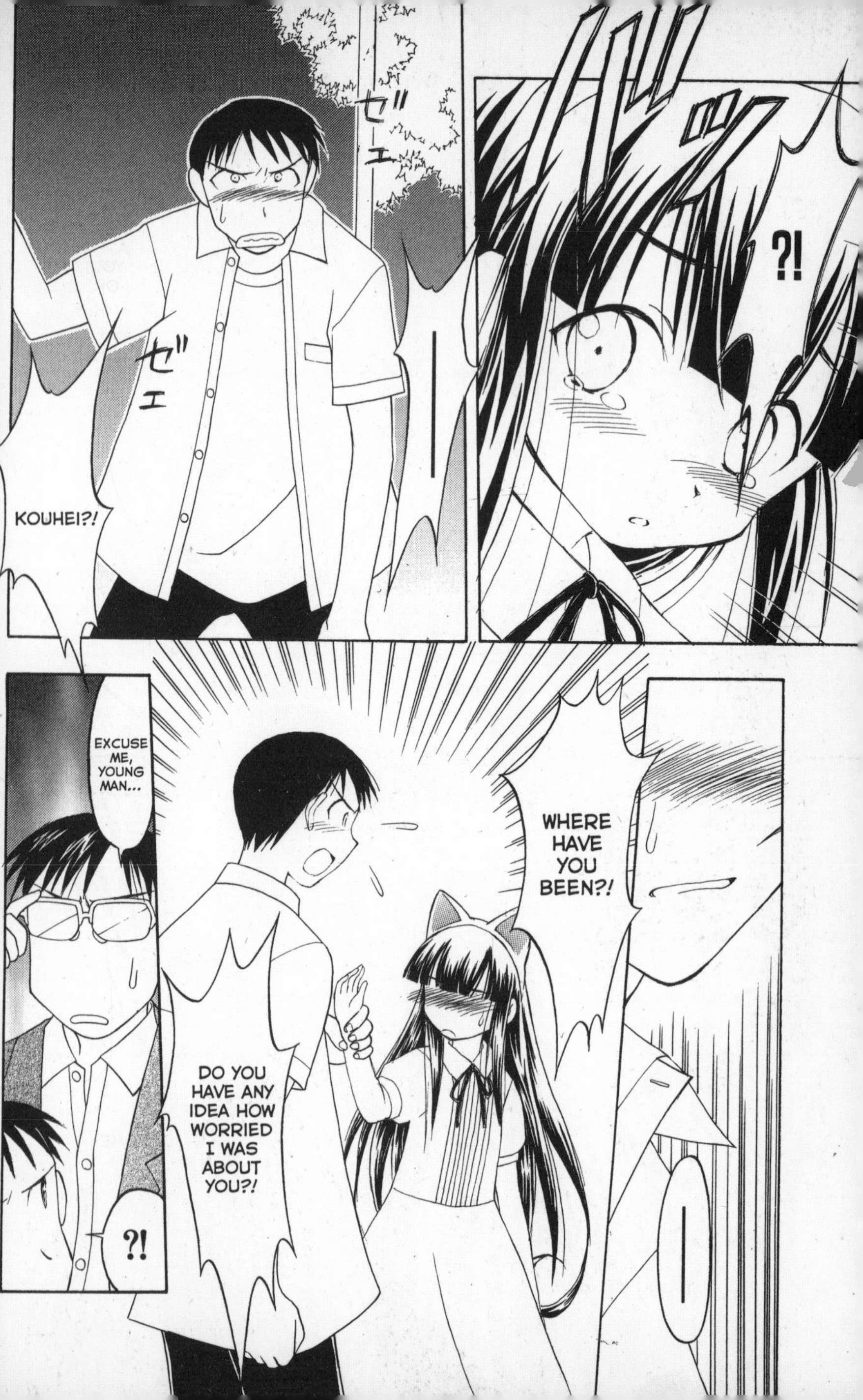
?!
ゼェ
ゼェ
KOUHEI?!
WHERE HAVE YOU BEEN?!
DO YOU HAVE ANY IDEA HOW WORRIED I WAS ABOUT YOU?!
EXCUSE ME, YOUNG MAN...
?!

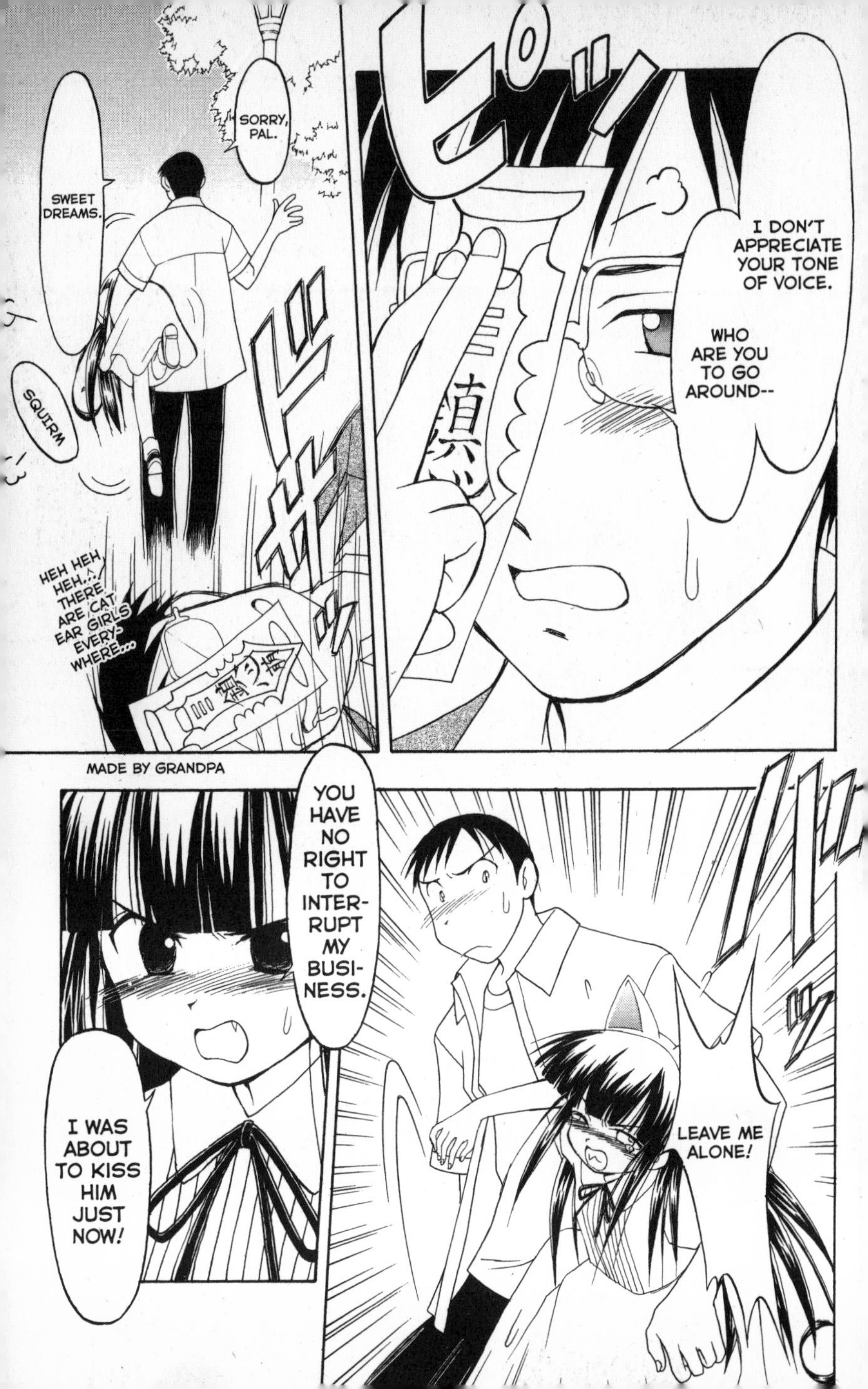
I DON'T APPRECIATE YOUR TONE OF VOICE.
WHO ARE YOU TO GO AROUND--
SORRY, PAL.
SWEET DREAMS.
SQUIRM
HEH HEH HEH... THERE ARE CAT EAR GIRLS EVERYWHERE...
MADE BY GRANDPA
LEAVE ME ALONE!
YOU HAVE NO RIGHT TO INTERRUPT MY BUSINESS.
I WAS ABOUT TO KISS HIM JUST NOW!

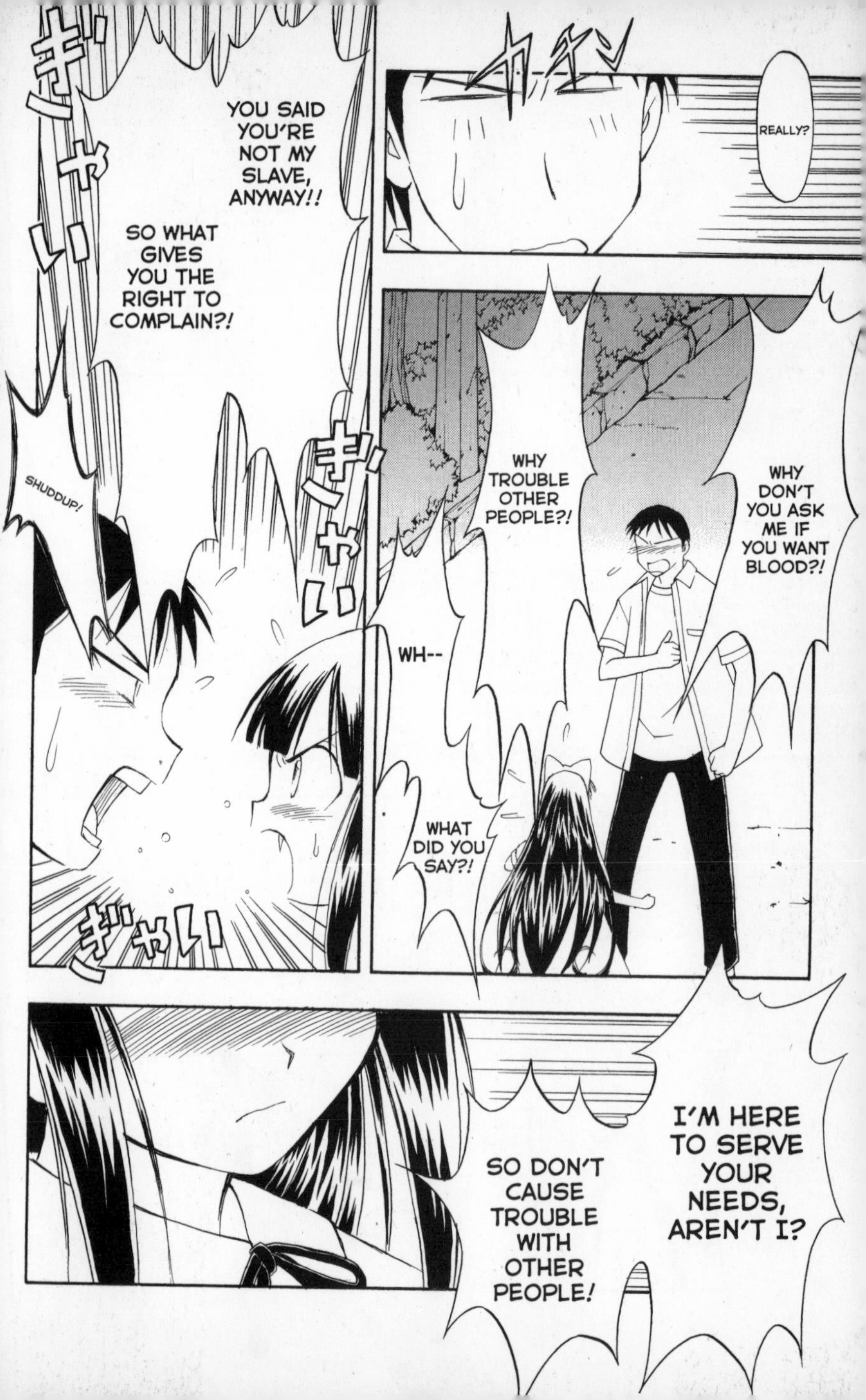
REALLY?
WHY DON'T YOU ASK ME IF YOU WANT BLOOD?!
WHY TROUBLE OTHER PEOPLE?!
WH--
WHAT DID YOU SAY?!
YOU SAID YOU'RE NOT MY SLAVE, ANYWAY!!
SO WHAT GIVES YOU THE RIGHT TO COMPLAIN?!
SHUDDUP!
I'M HERE TO SERVE YOUR NEEDS, AREN'T I?
SO DON'T CAUSE TROUBLE WITH OTHER PEOPLE!

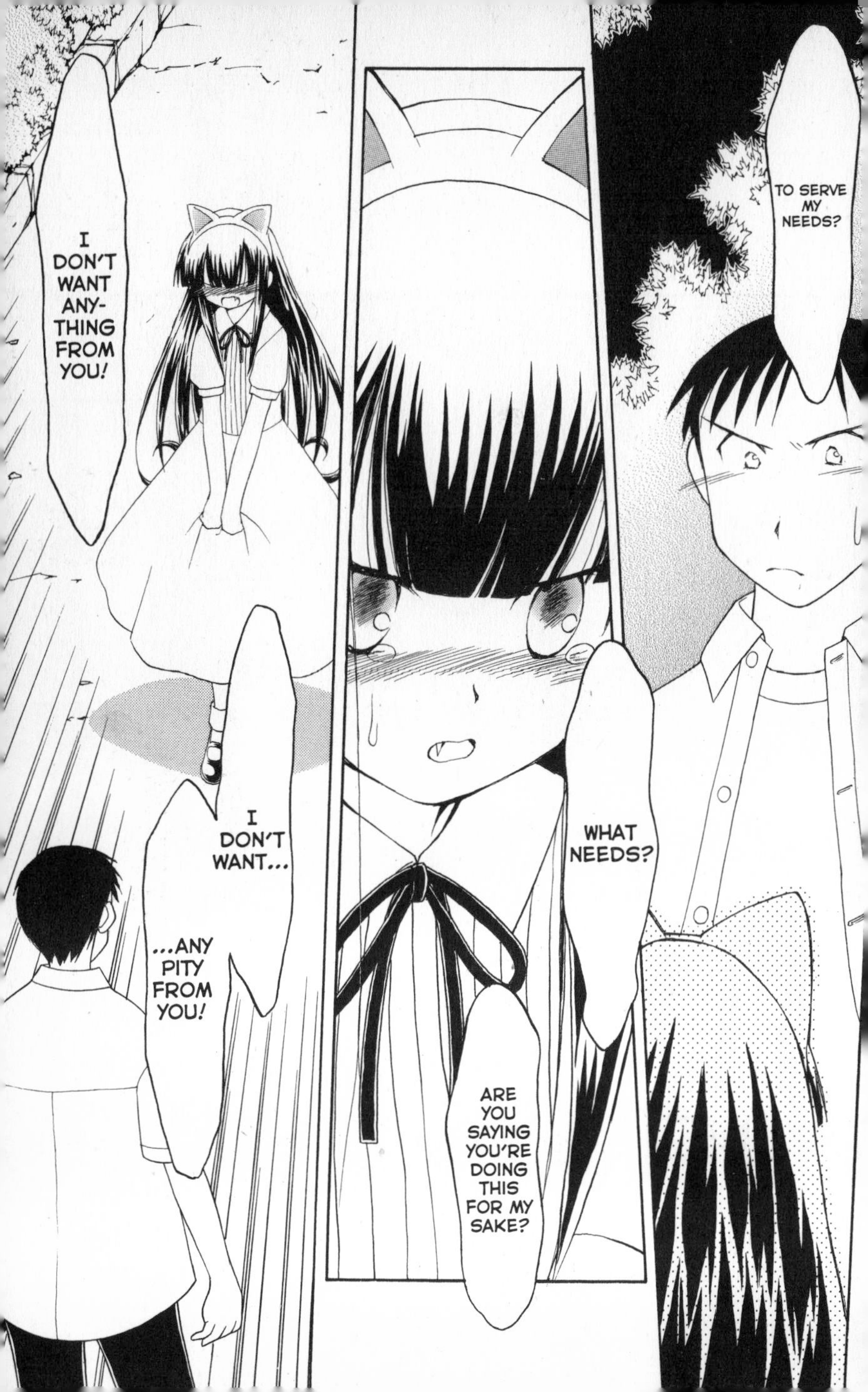

TO SERVE MY NEEDS?
WHAT NEEDS?
ARE YOU SAYING YOU'RE DOING THIS FOR MY SAKE?
I DON'T WANT ANY-THING FROM YOU!
I DON'T WANT...
...ANY PITY FROM YOU!

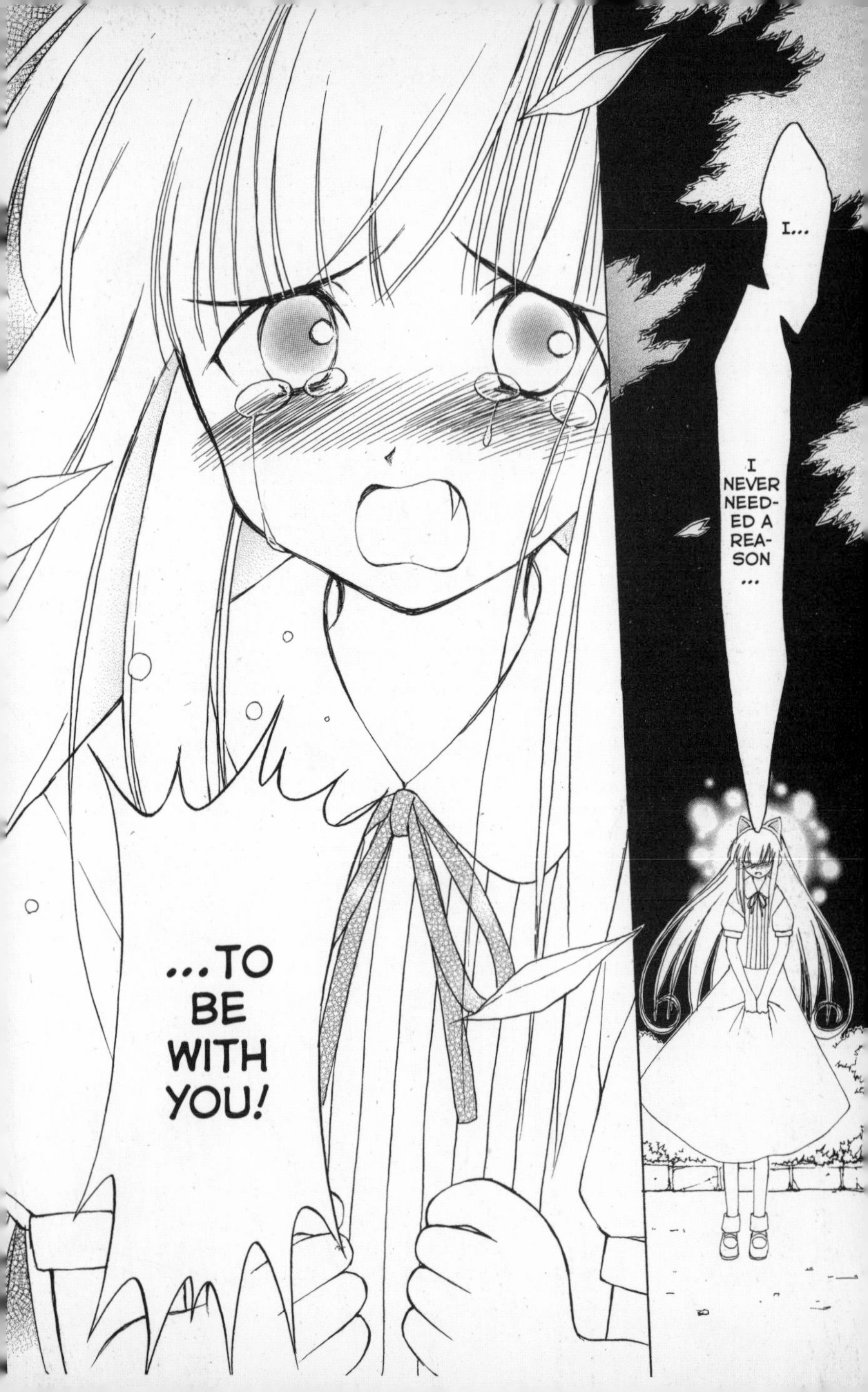
I...
I NEVER NEED-ED A REA-SON ...
...TO BE WITH YOU!

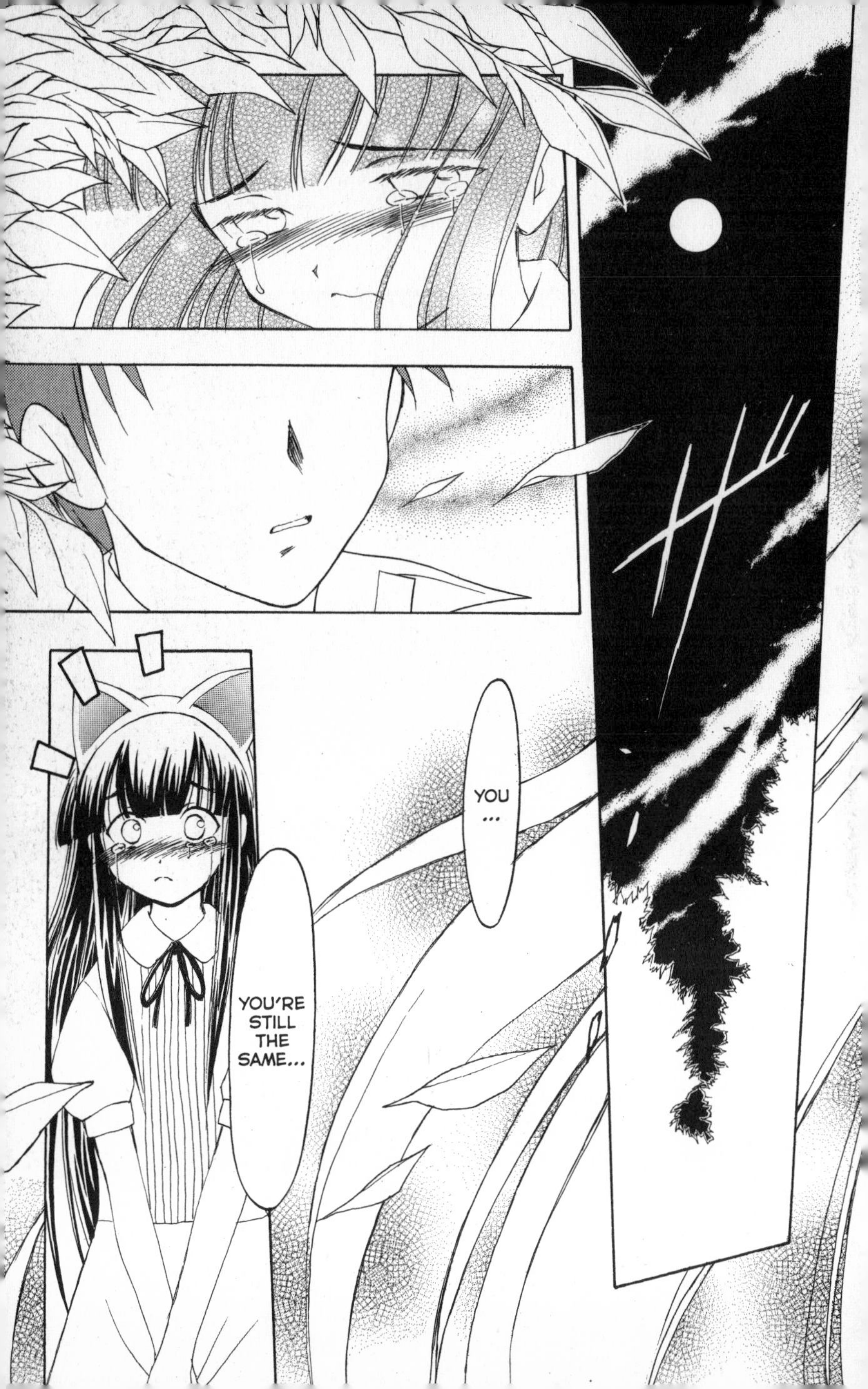
YOU...
YOU'RE STILL THE SAME...

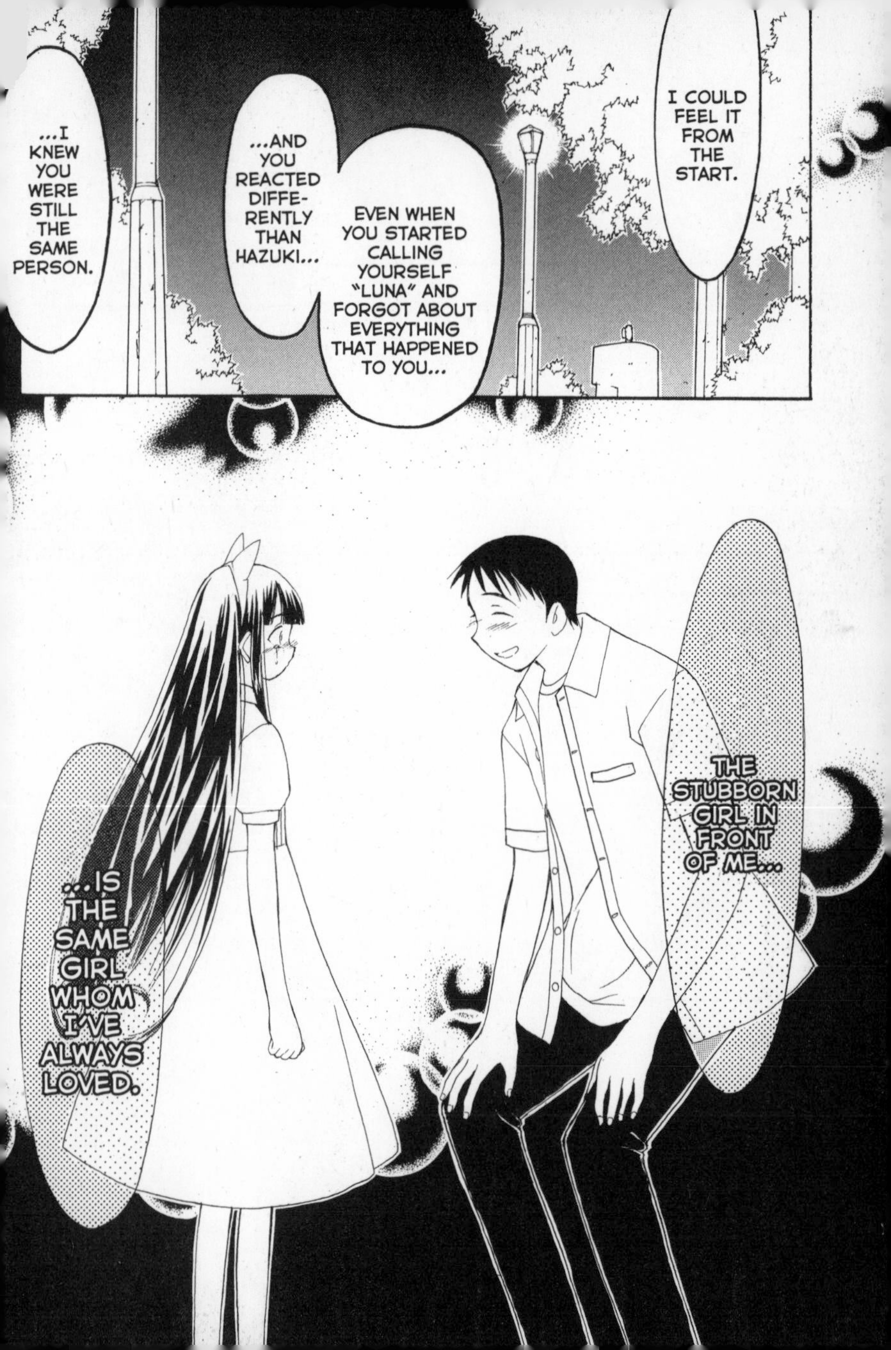
I COULD FEEL IT FROM THE START.
EVEN WHEN YOU STARTED CALLING YOURSELF "LUNA" AND FORGOT ABOUT EVERYTHING THAT HAPPENED TO YOU...
...AND YOU REACTED DIFFE-RENTLY THAN HAZUKI...
...I KNEW YOU WERE STILL THE SAME PERSON.
THE STUBBORN GIRL IN FRONT OF ME...
...IS THE SAME GIRL WHOM I'VE ALWAYS LOVED.

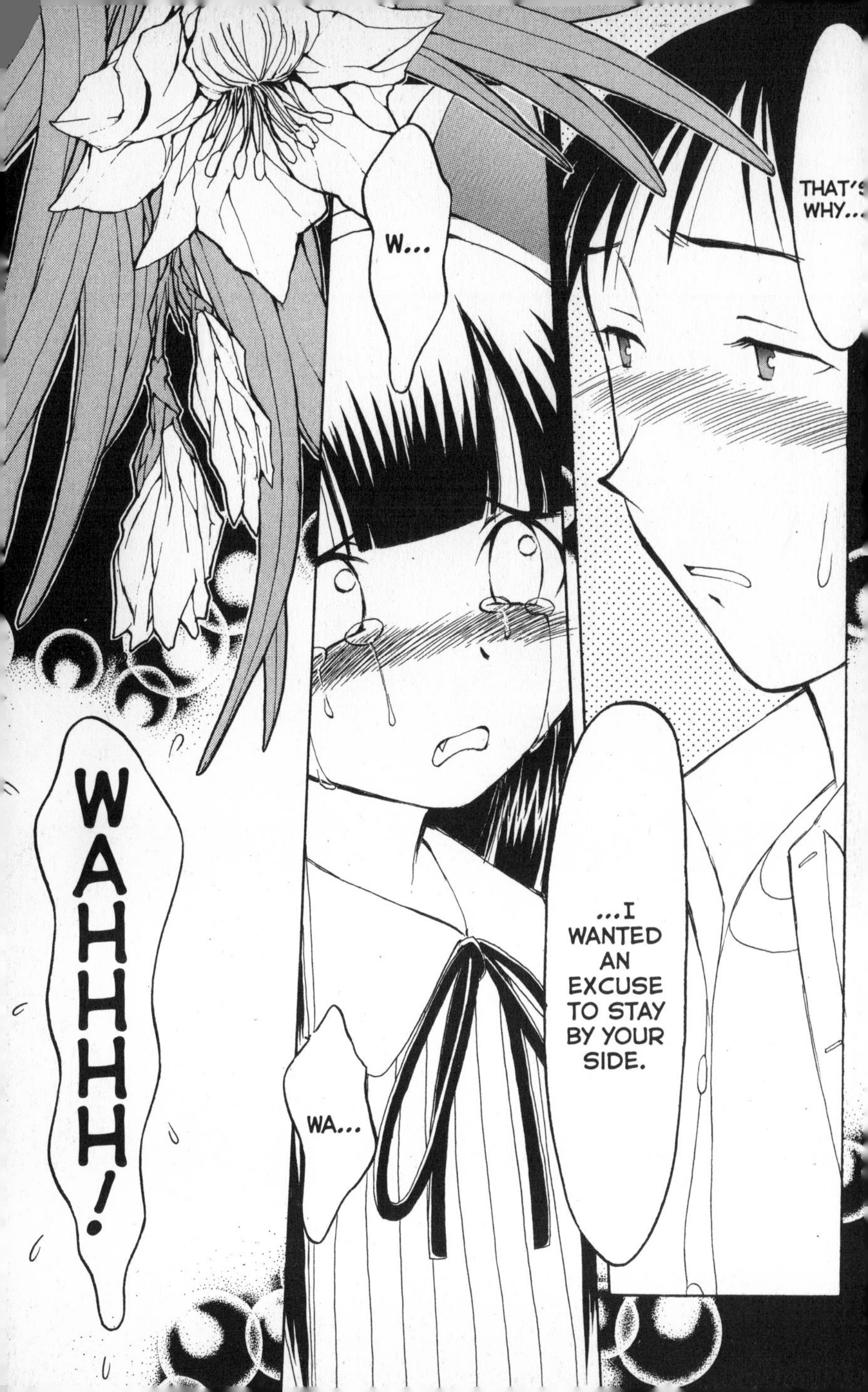
THAT'S WHY...
W...
...I WANTED AN EXCUSE TO STAY BY YOUR SIDE.
WA...
WAHHH!

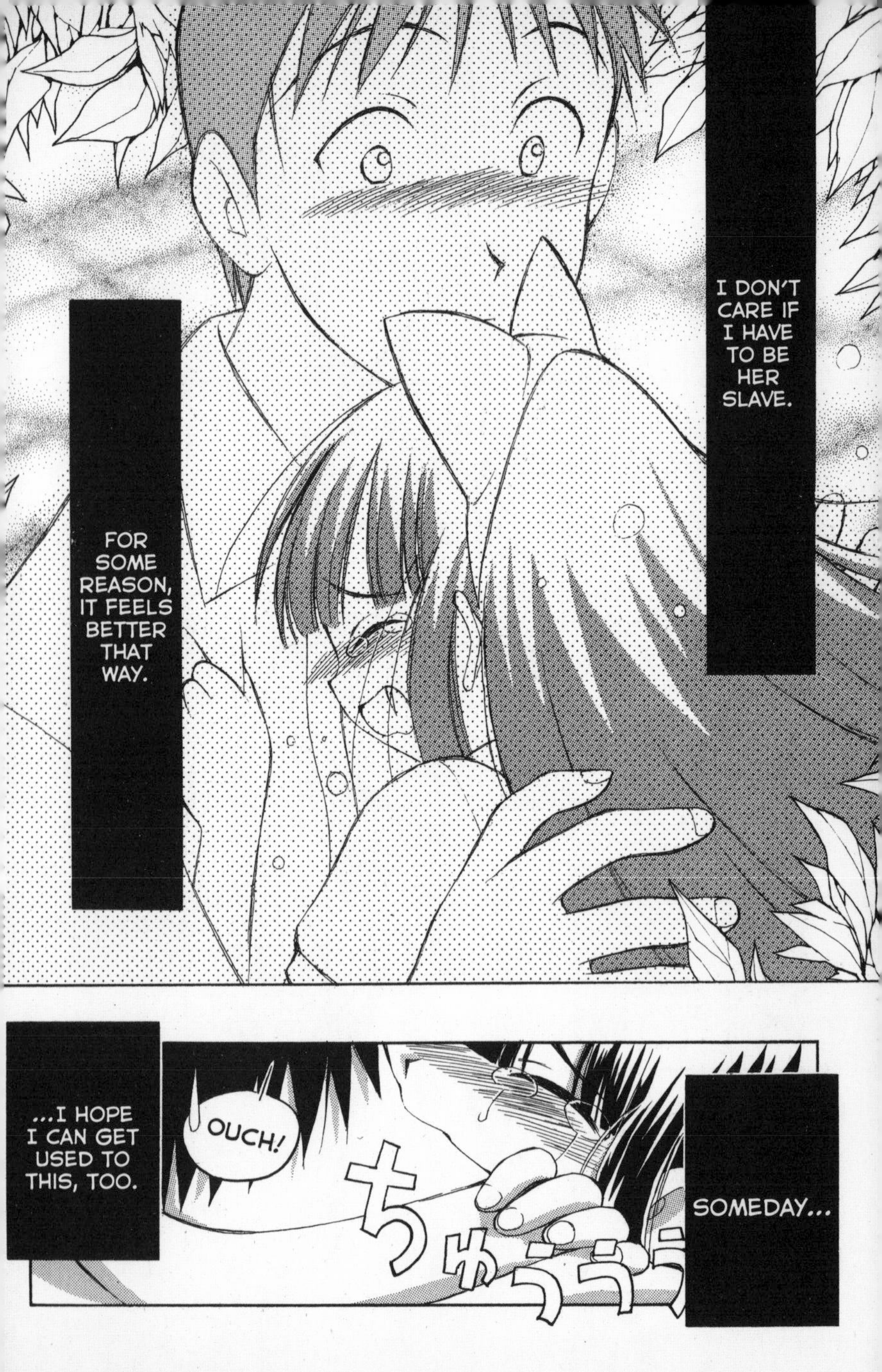

I DON'T CARE IF I HAVE TO BE HER SLAVE.
FOR SOME REASON, IT FEELS BETTER THAT WAY.
SOMEDAY...
OUCH!
ちゅううう
...I HOPE I CAN GET USED TO THIS, TOO.

MOON

PHASE

BONUS

THEATER

STARTING
NOW!

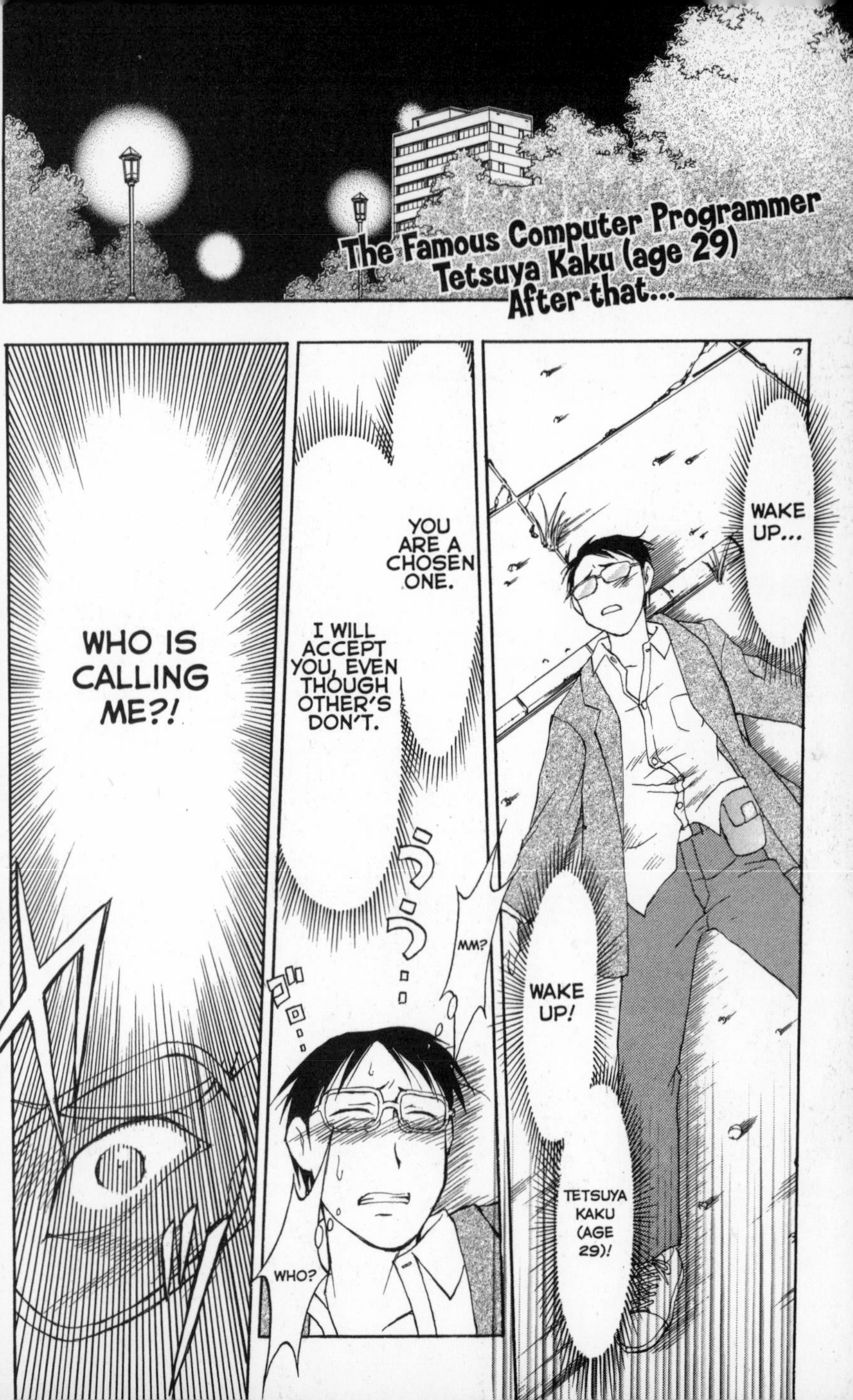
The Famous Computer Programmer
Tetsuya Kaku (age 29)
After that...
WAKE UP...
WAKE UP!
TETSUYA KAKU (AGE 29)!
YOU ARE A CHOSEN ONE.
I WILL ACCEPT YOU, EVEN THOUGH OTHER'S DON'T.
MM?
WHO?
WHO IS CALLING ME?!

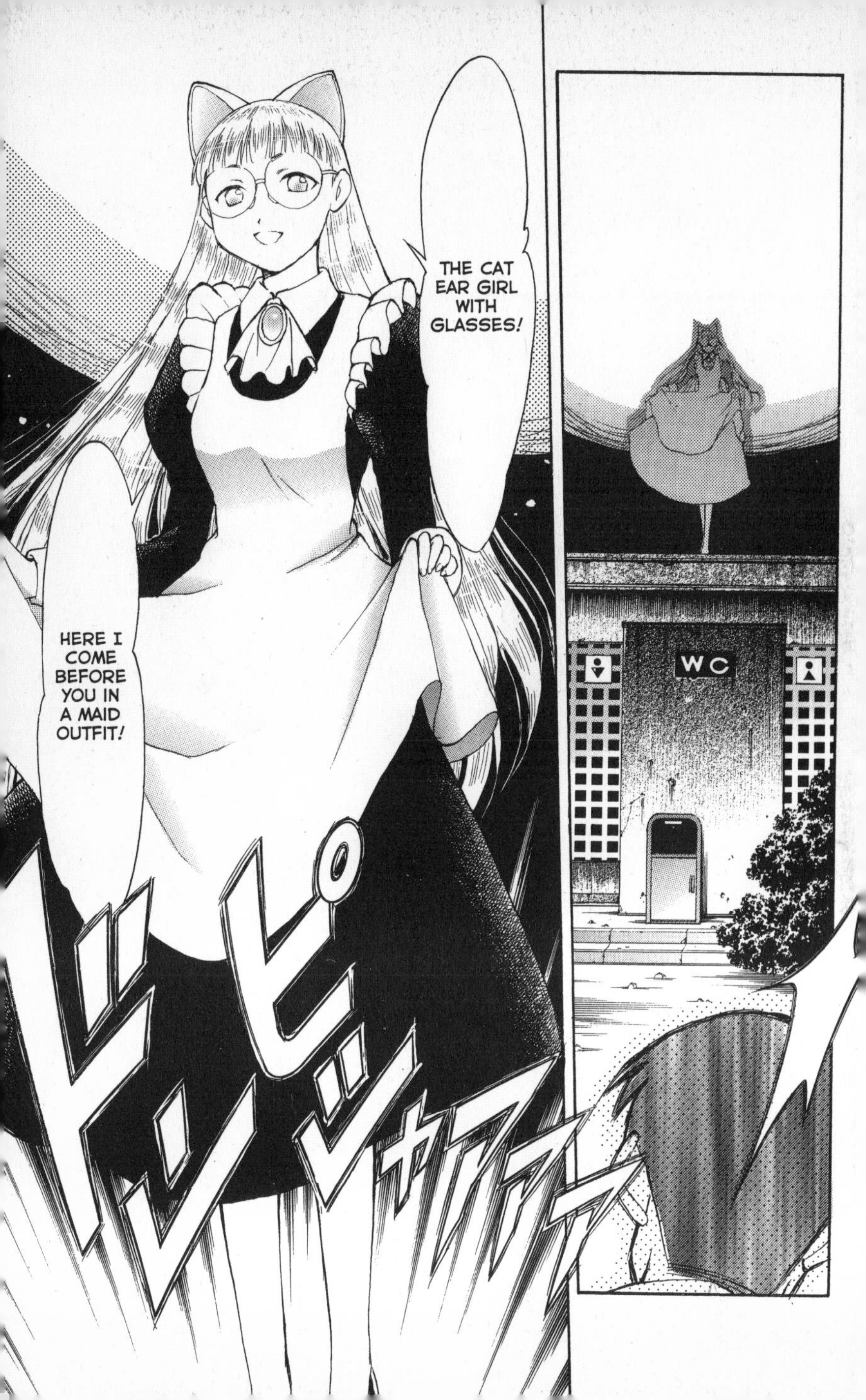
THE CAT EAR GIRL WITH GLASSES!
HERE I COME BEFORE YOU IN A MAID OUTFIT!
WC

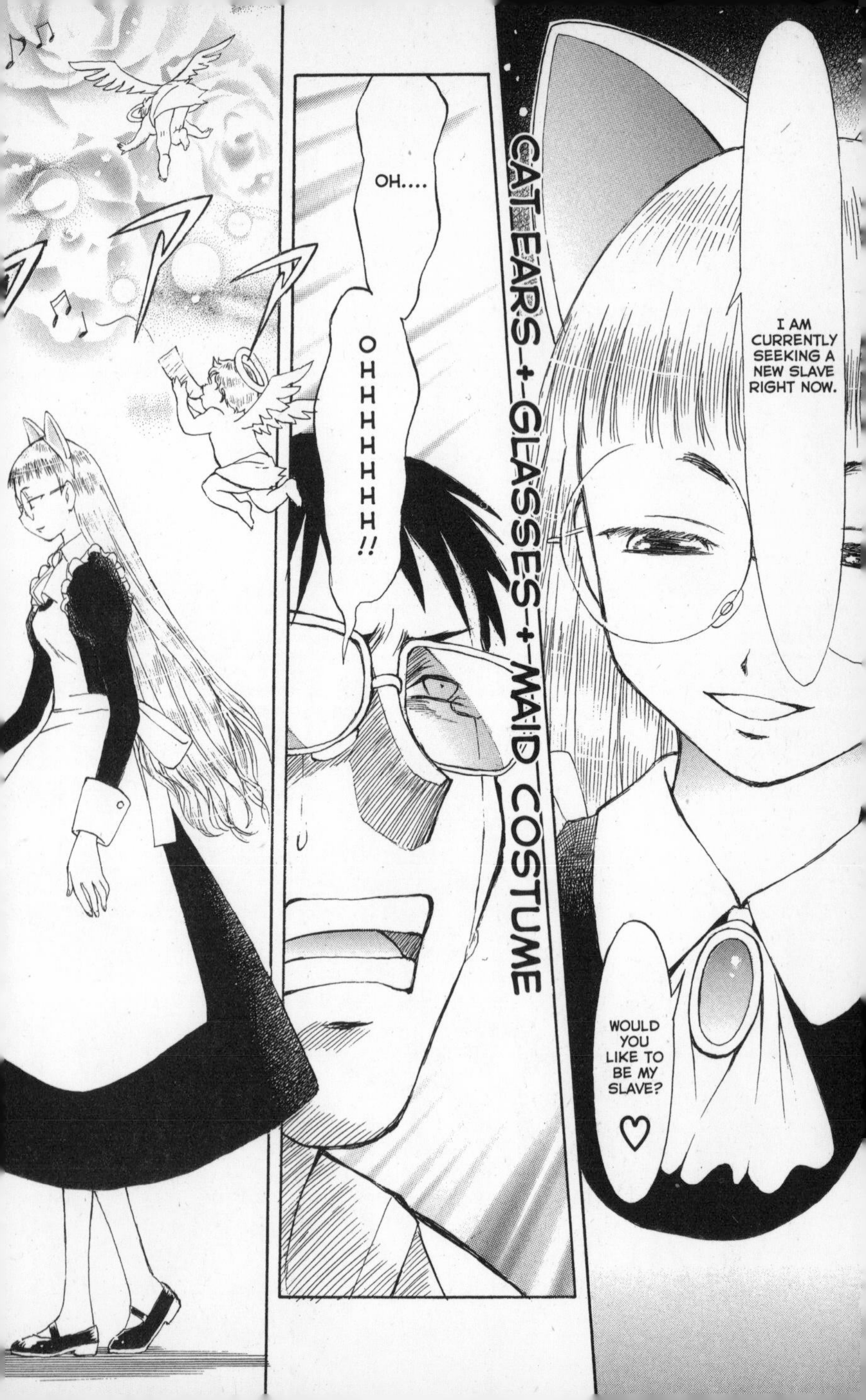

I AM CURRENTLY SEEKING A NEW SLAVE RIGHT NOW.
WOULD YOU LIKE TO BE MY SLAVE? ♡
CAT EARS + GLASSES + MAID COSTUME
OH....
OHHHHHHH!!

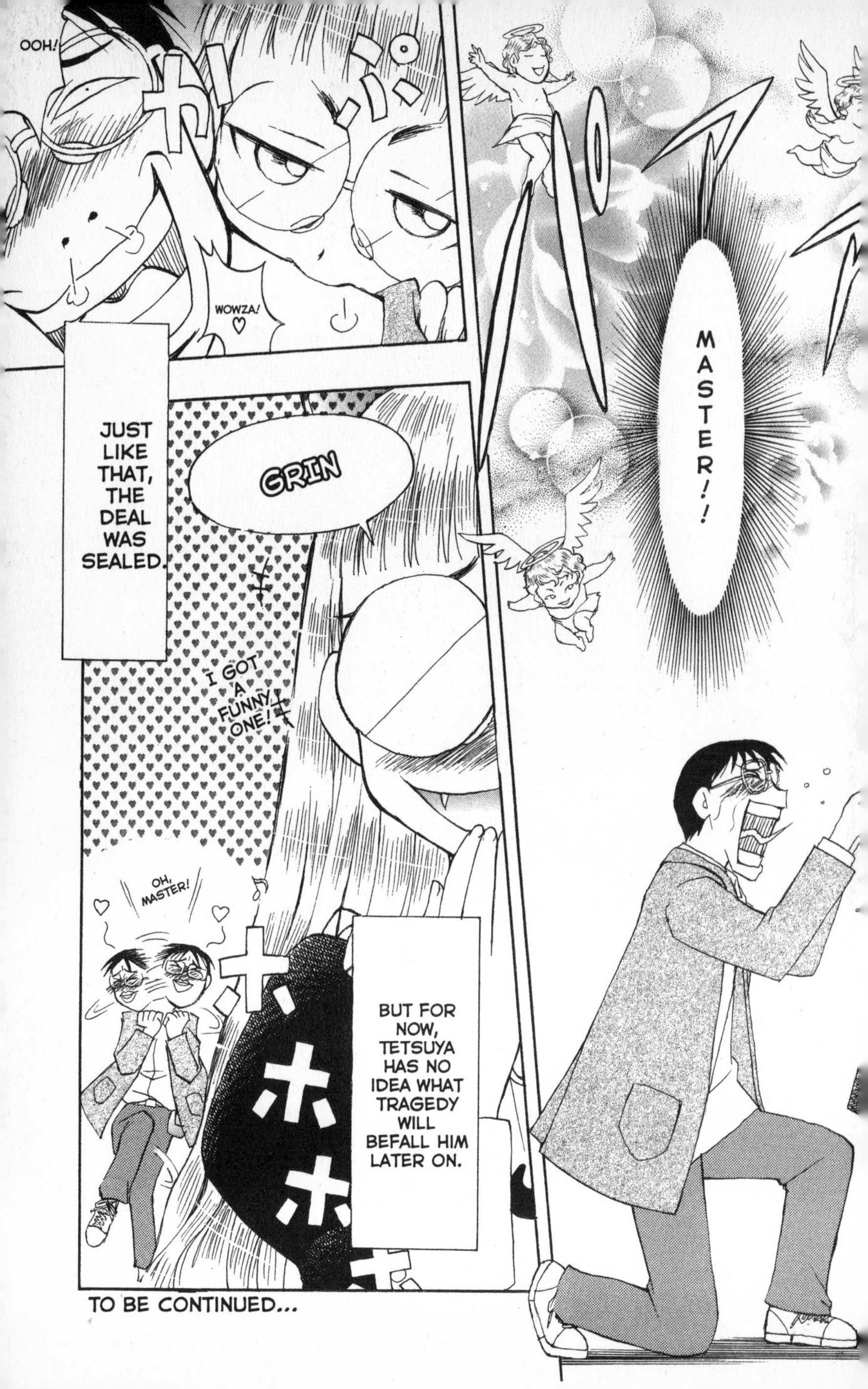
OOH!
WOWZA! ♡
MASTER!!
JUST LIKE THAT, THE DEAL WAS SEALED.
GRIN
I GOT A FUNNY ONE!
OH, MASTER!
BUT FOR NOW, TETSUYA HAS NO IDEA WHAT TRAGEDY WILL BEFALL HIM LATER ON.

TO BE CONTINUED...

PART 4

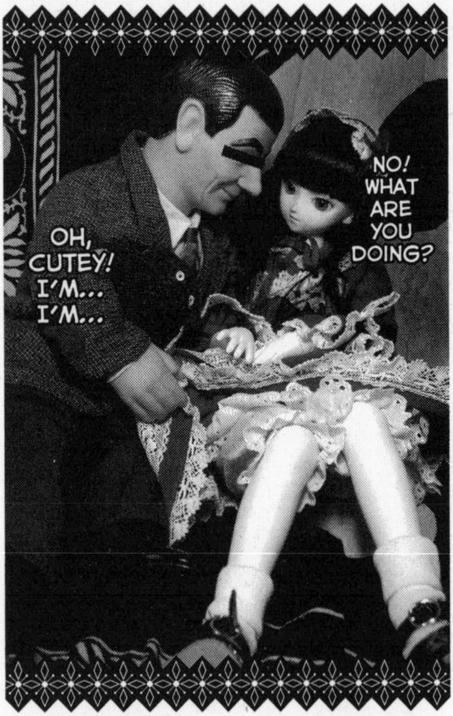
NO! WHAT ARE YOU DOING?
OH, CUTEY! I'M... I'M...

CONTINUED ON PAGE 130

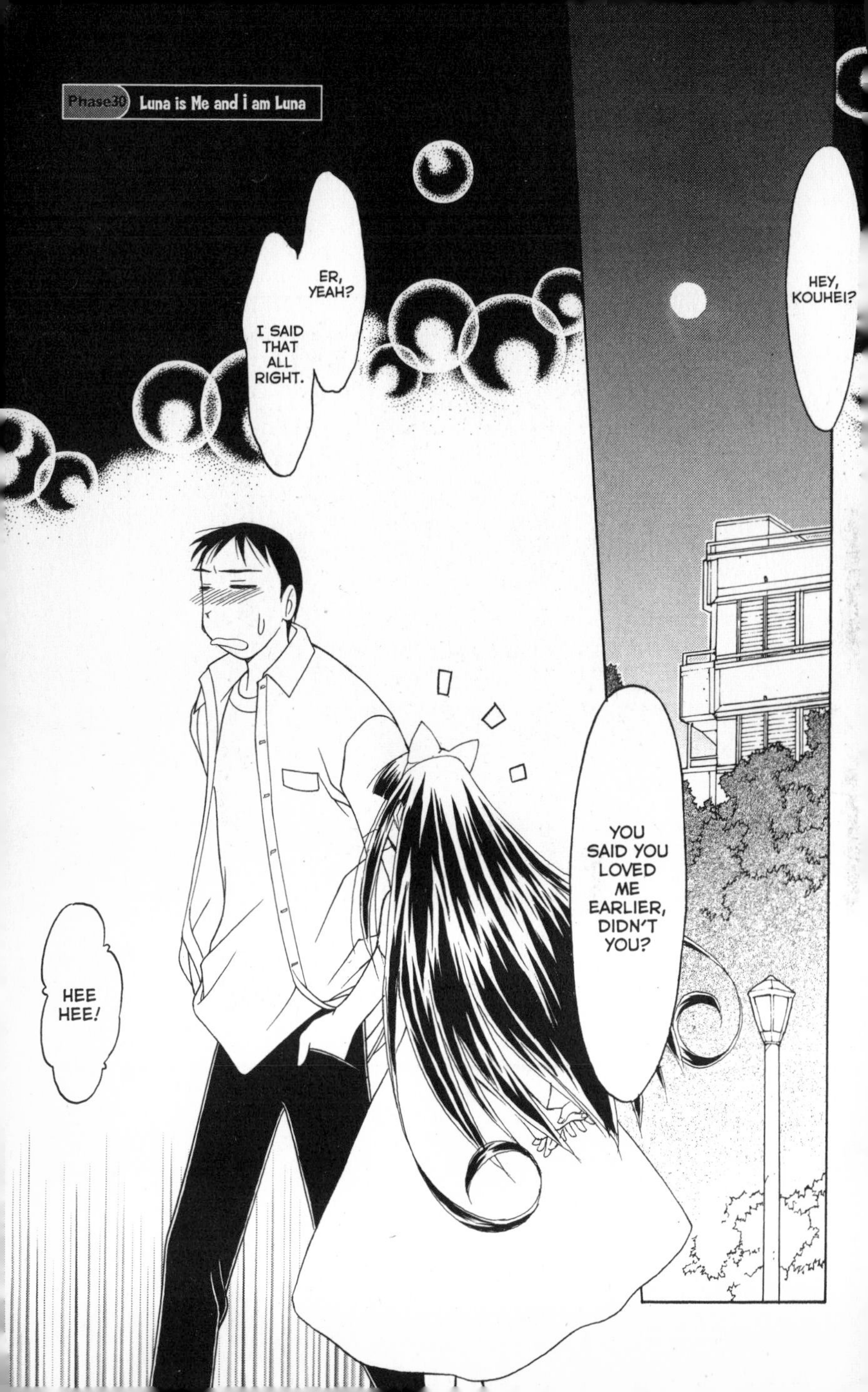
Phase30 Luna is Me and i am Luna
HEY, KOUHEI?
YOU SAID YOU LOVED ME EARLIER, DIDN'T YOU?
ER, YEAH?
I SAID THAT ALL RIGHT.
HEE HEE!

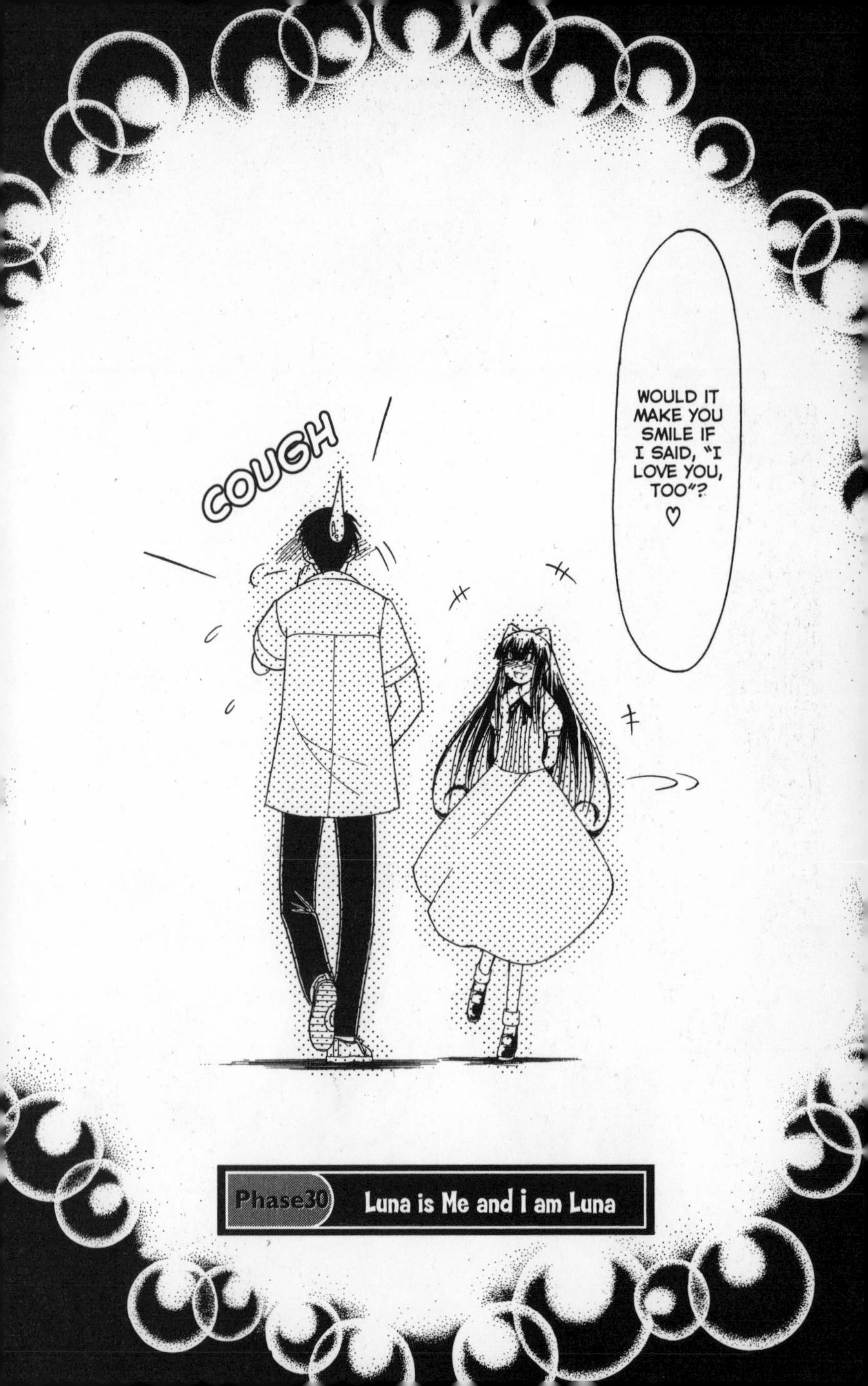
WOULD IT MAKE YOU SMILE IF I SAID, "I LOVE YOU, TOO"? ♡
COUGH
Phase30 Luna is Me and i am Luna

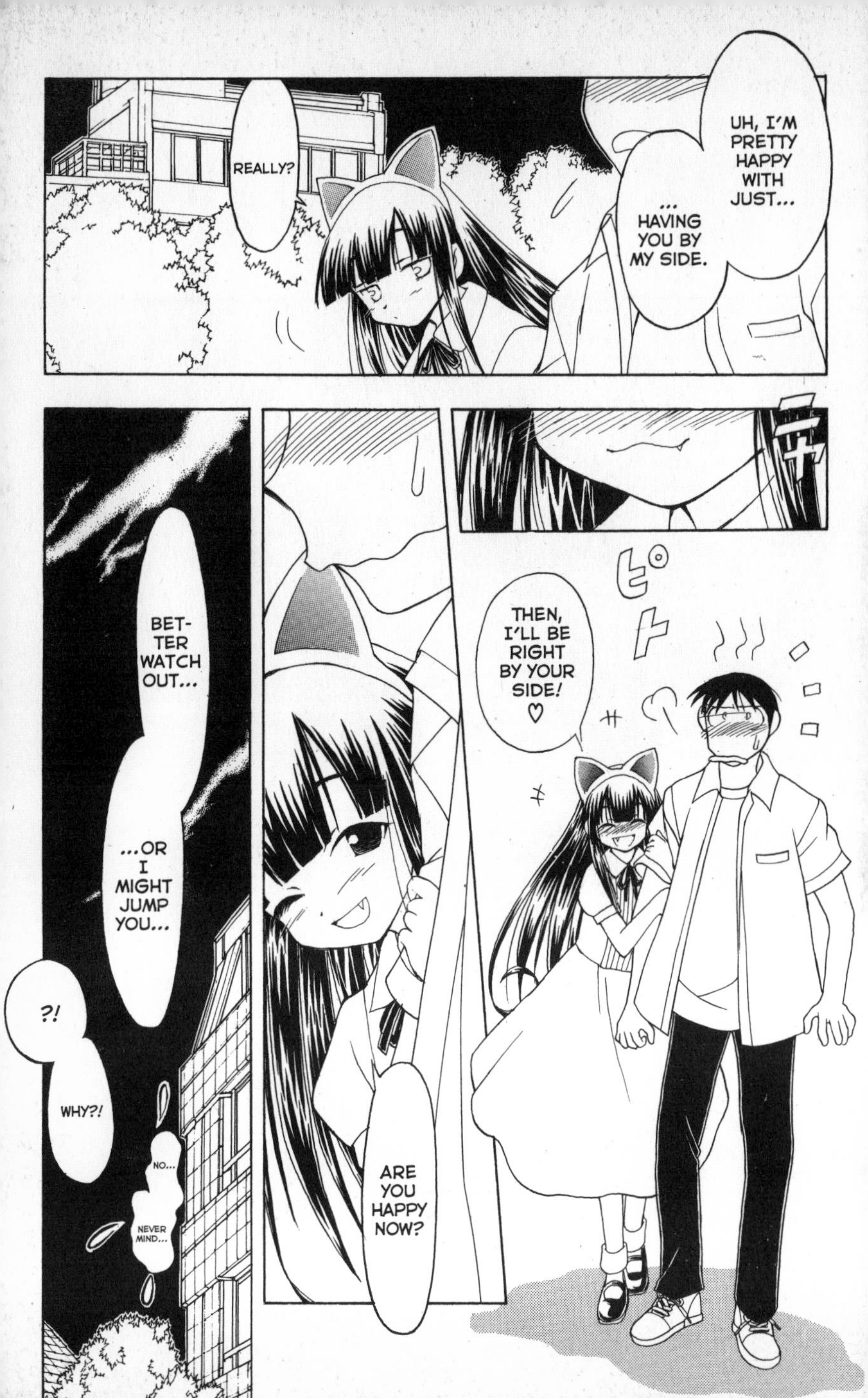
UH, I'M PRETTY HAPPY WITH JUST...
...HAVING YOU BY MY SIDE.
REALLY?
ピト
THEN, I'LL BE RIGHT BY YOUR SIDE! ♡
ARE YOU HAPPY NOW?
BET-TER WATCH OUT...
...OR I MIGHT JUMP YOU...
?!
WHY?!
NO...
NEVER MIND...

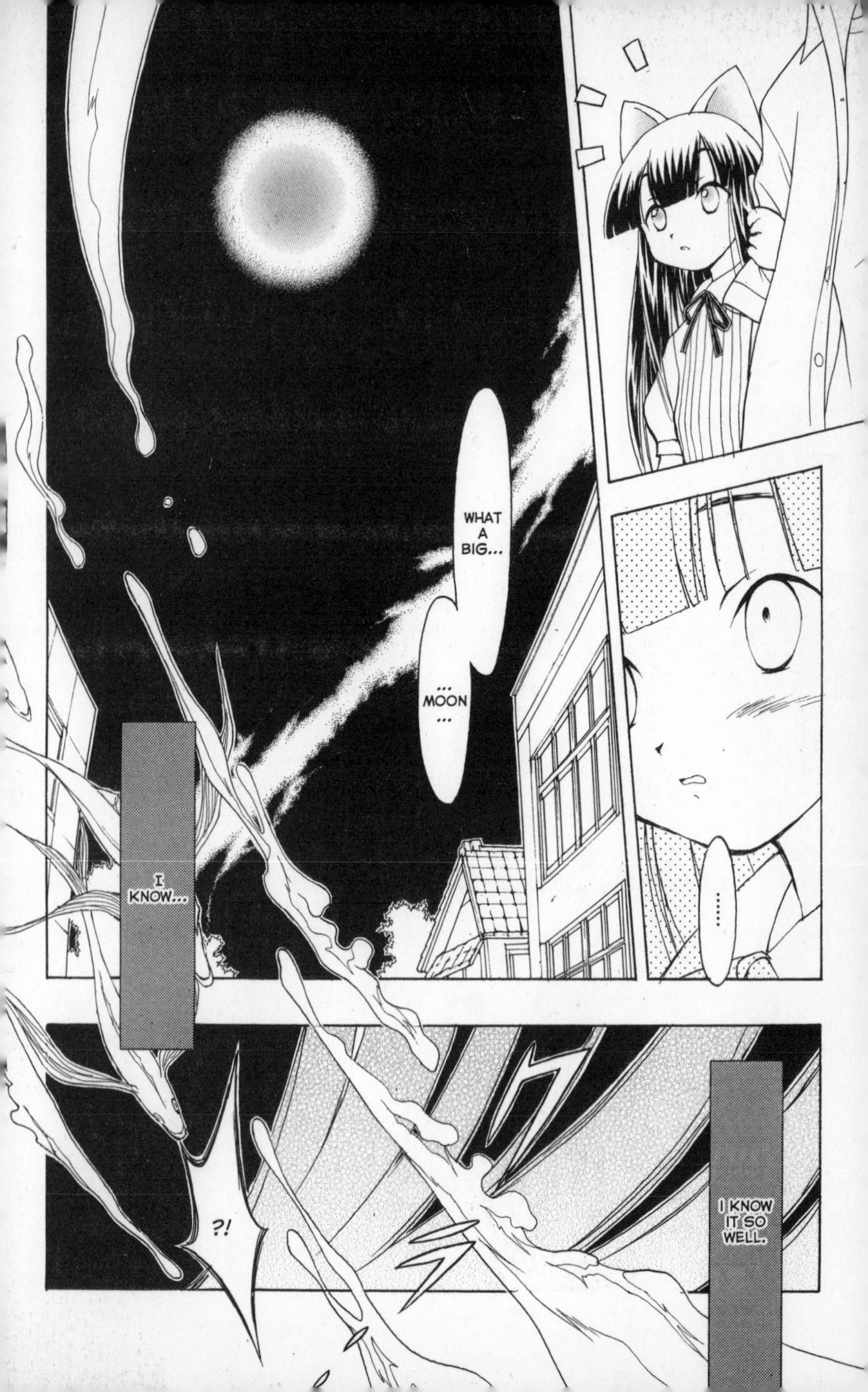
WHAT A BIG...
...MOON...
......
I KNOW...
I KNOW IT SO WELL.
?!

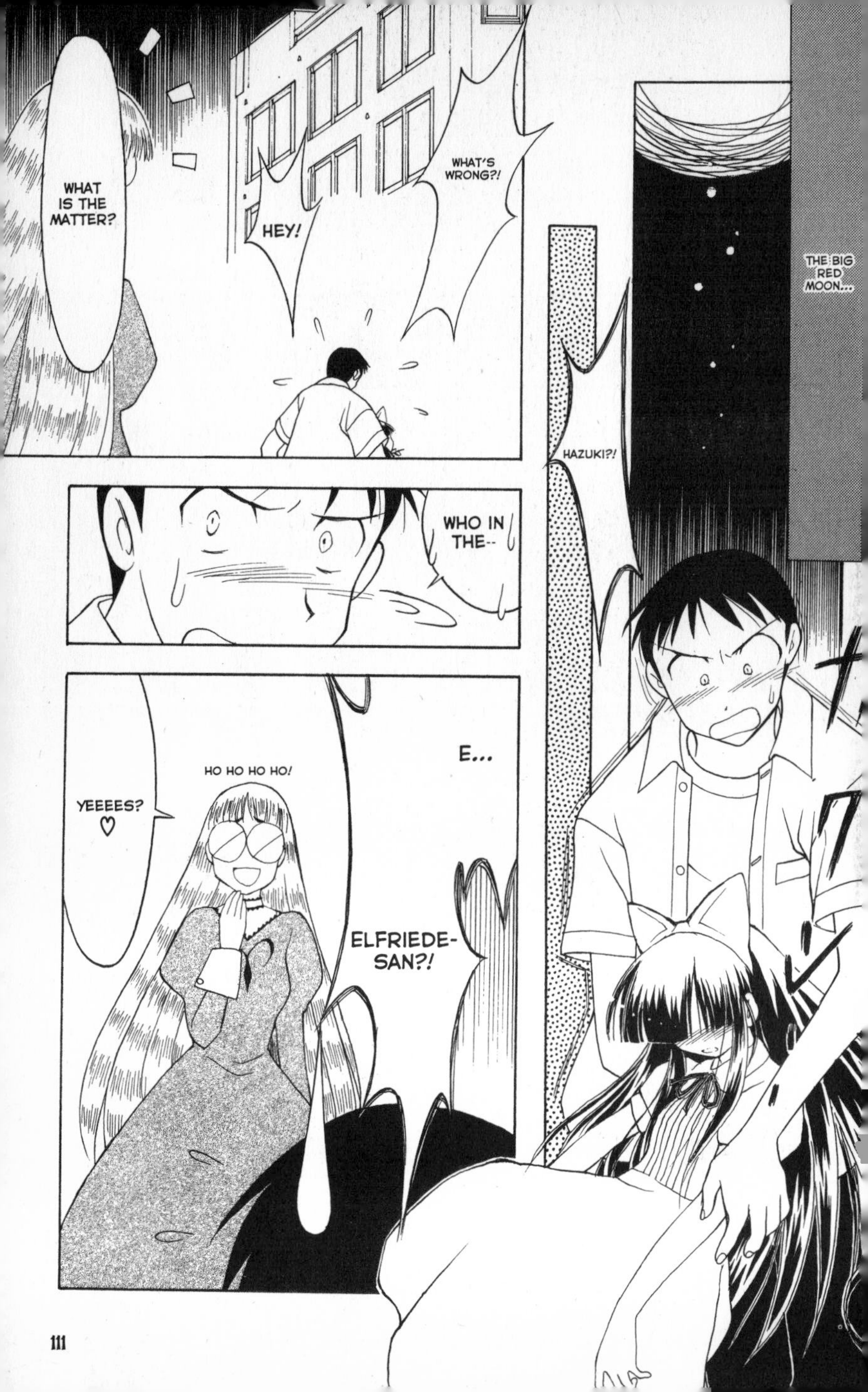
THE BIG RED MOON...
HAZUKI?!
WHAT'S WRONG?!
HEY!
WHAT IS THE MATTER?
WHO IN THE--
E...
ELFRIEDE-SAN?!
HO HO HO HO!
YEEEES? ♡

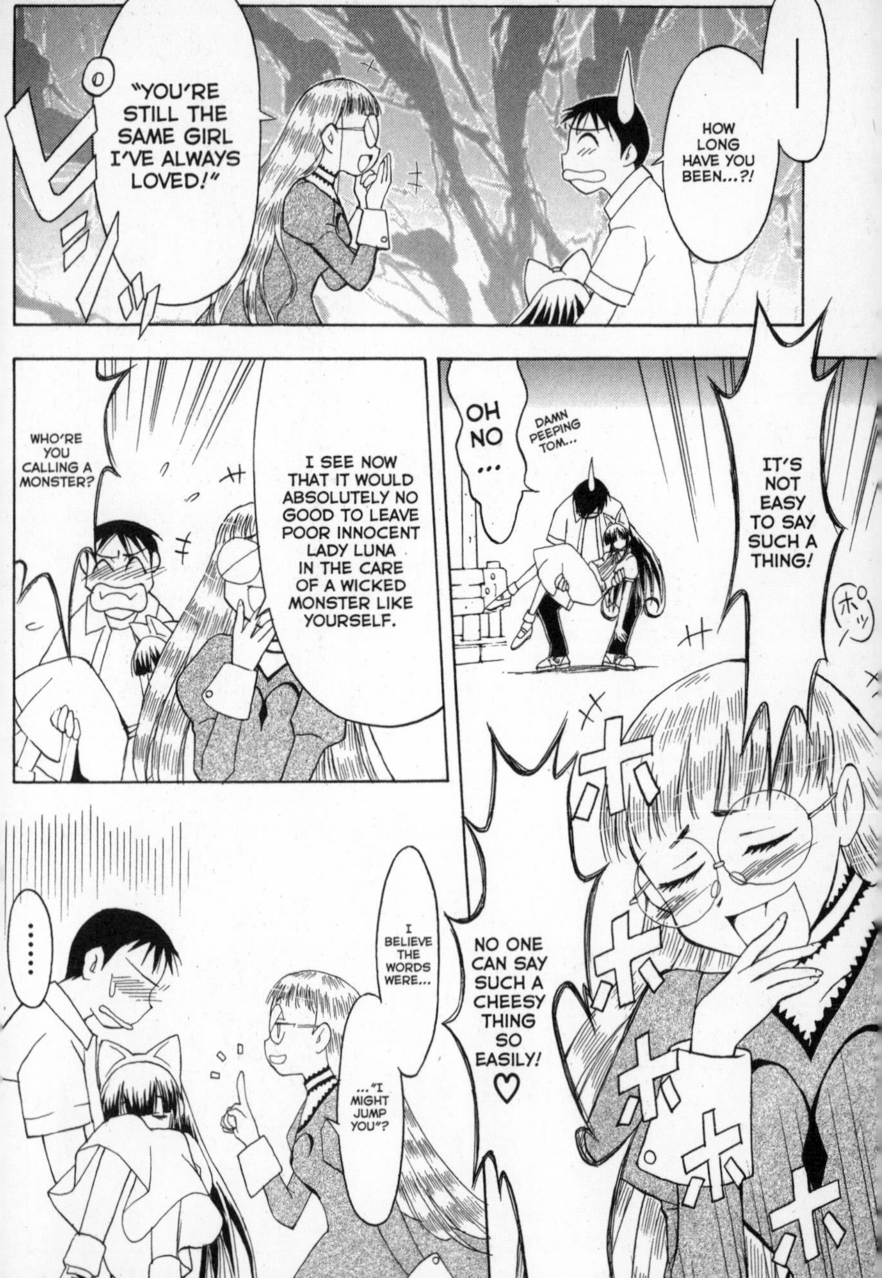
HOW LONG HAVE YOU BEEN...?!
"YOU'RE STILL THE SAME GIRL I'VE ALWAYS LOVED!"
IT'S NOT EASY TO SAY SUCH A THING!
OH NO ...
DAMN PEEPING TOM...
I SEE NOW THAT IT WOULD ABSOLUTELY NO GOOD TO LEAVE POOR INNOCENT LADY LUNA IN THE CARE OF A WICKED MONSTER LIKE YOURSELF.
WHO'RE YOU CALLING A MONSTER?
NO ONE CAN SAY SUCH A CHEESY THING SO EASILY! ♡
I BELIEVE THE WORDS WERE...
..."I MIGHT JUMP YOU"?
......

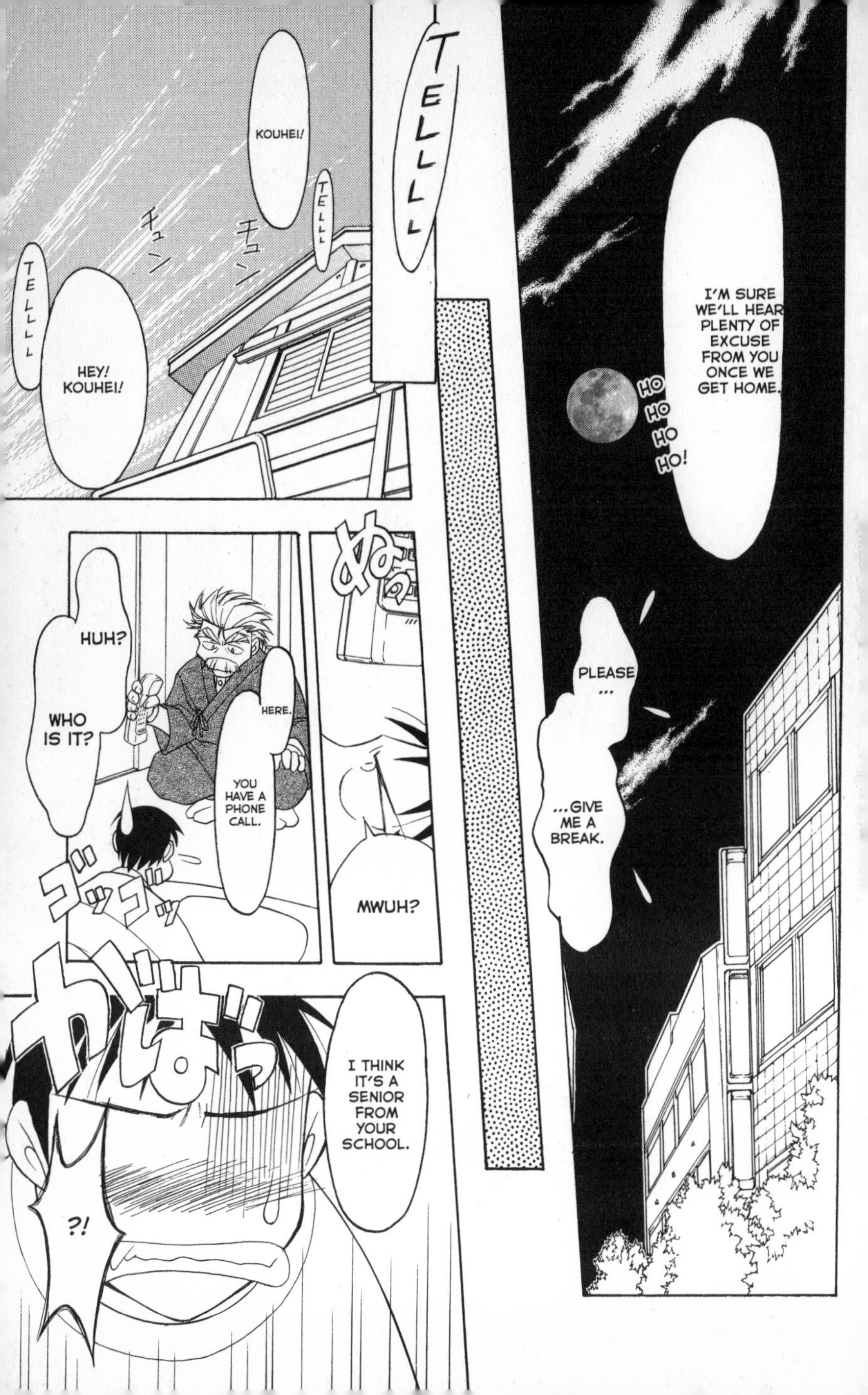
I'M SURE WE'LL HEAR PLENTY OF EXCUSE FROM YOU ONCE WE GET HOME.
HO HO HO HO!
PLEASE...
...GIVE ME A BREAK.
TELLLLL
KOUHEI!
TELLL
チュン
チュン
HEY! KOUHEI!
TELLLL
ぬっ
MWUH?
HERE.
YOU HAVE A PHONE CALL.
HUH?
WHO IS IT?
I THINK IT'S A SENIOR FROM YOUR SCHOOL.
?!

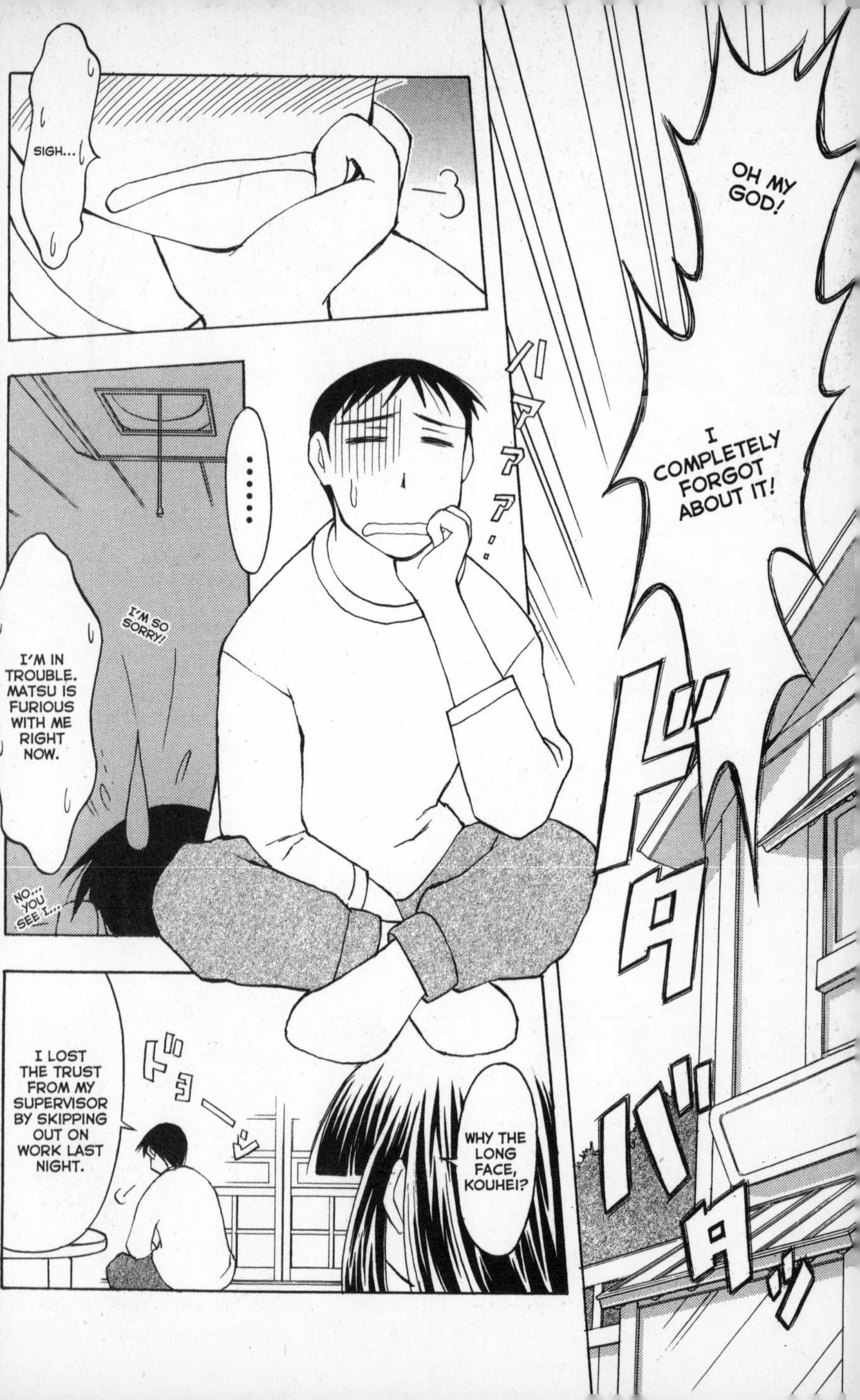

OH MY GOD!
I COMPLETELY FORGOT ABOUT IT!
SIGH...
......
I'M IN TROUBLE. MATSU IS FURIOUS WITH ME RIGHT NOW.
I'M SO SORRY!
NO... YOU SEE I...
WHY THE LONG FACE, KOUHEI?
I LOST THE TRUST FROM MY SUPERVISOR BY SKIPPING OUT ON WORK LAST NIGHT.

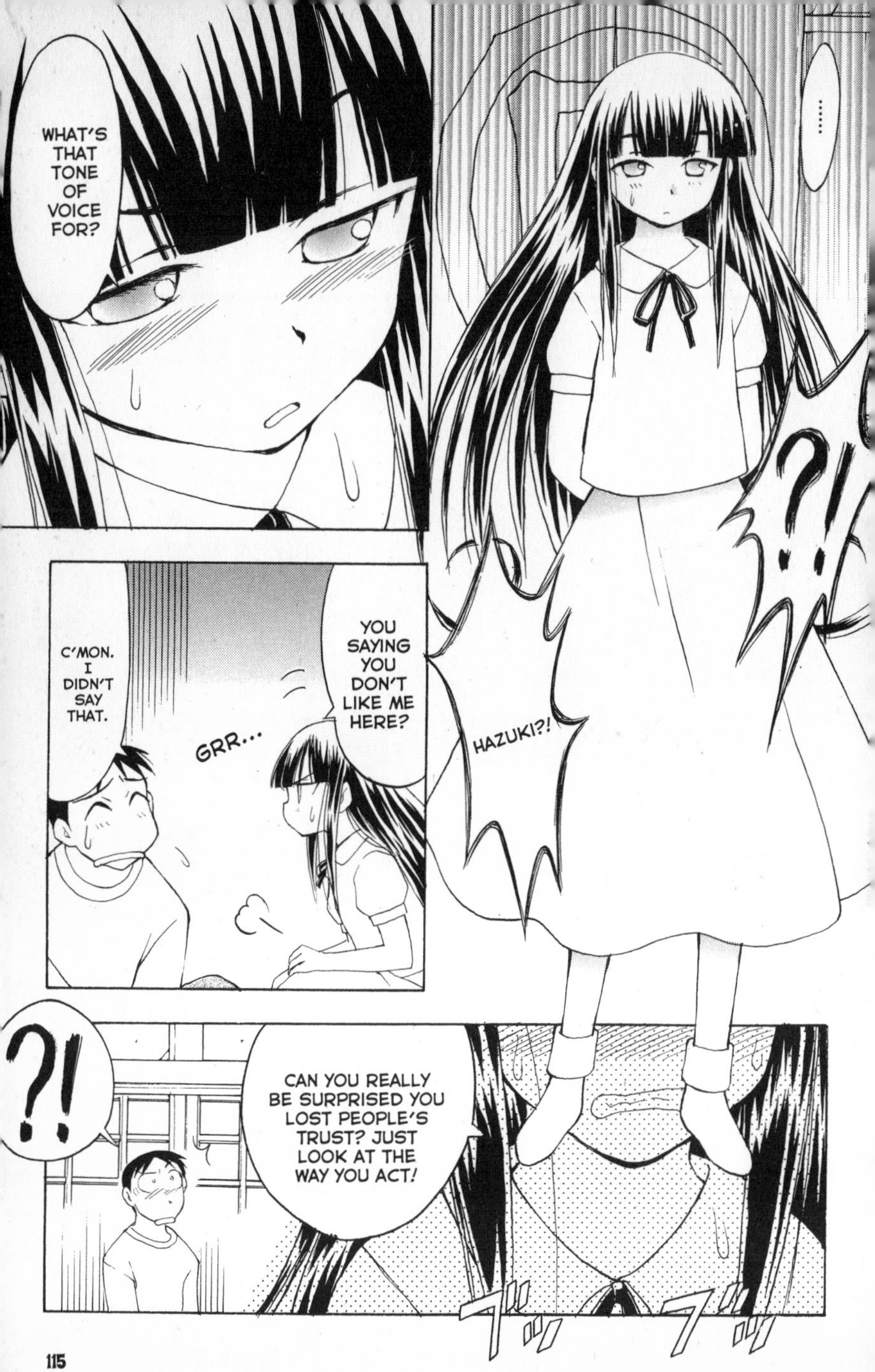
WHAT'S THAT TONE OF VOICE FOR?
YOU SAYING YOU DON'T LIKE ME HERE?
C'MON. I DIDN'T SAY THAT.
GRR...
?!
CAN YOU REALLY BE SURPRISED YOU LOST PEOPLE'S TRUST? JUST LOOK AT THE WAY YOU ACT!
......
?!
HAZUKI?!

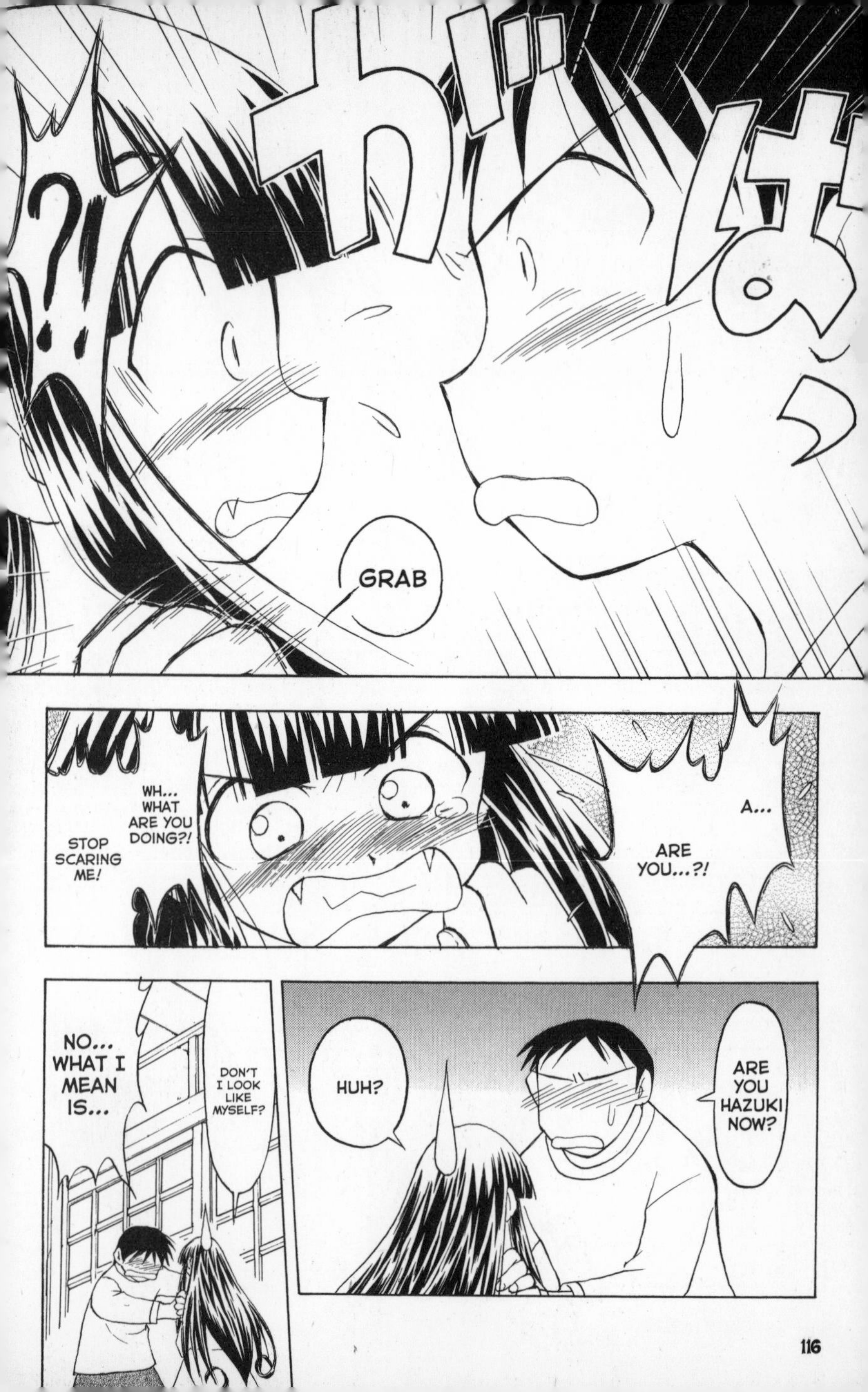
GRAB
A...
ARE YOU...?!
WH... WHAT ARE YOU DOING?!
STOP SCARING ME!
ARE YOU HAZUKI NOW?
HUH?
DON'T I LOOK LIKE MYSELF?
NO... WHAT I MEAN IS...

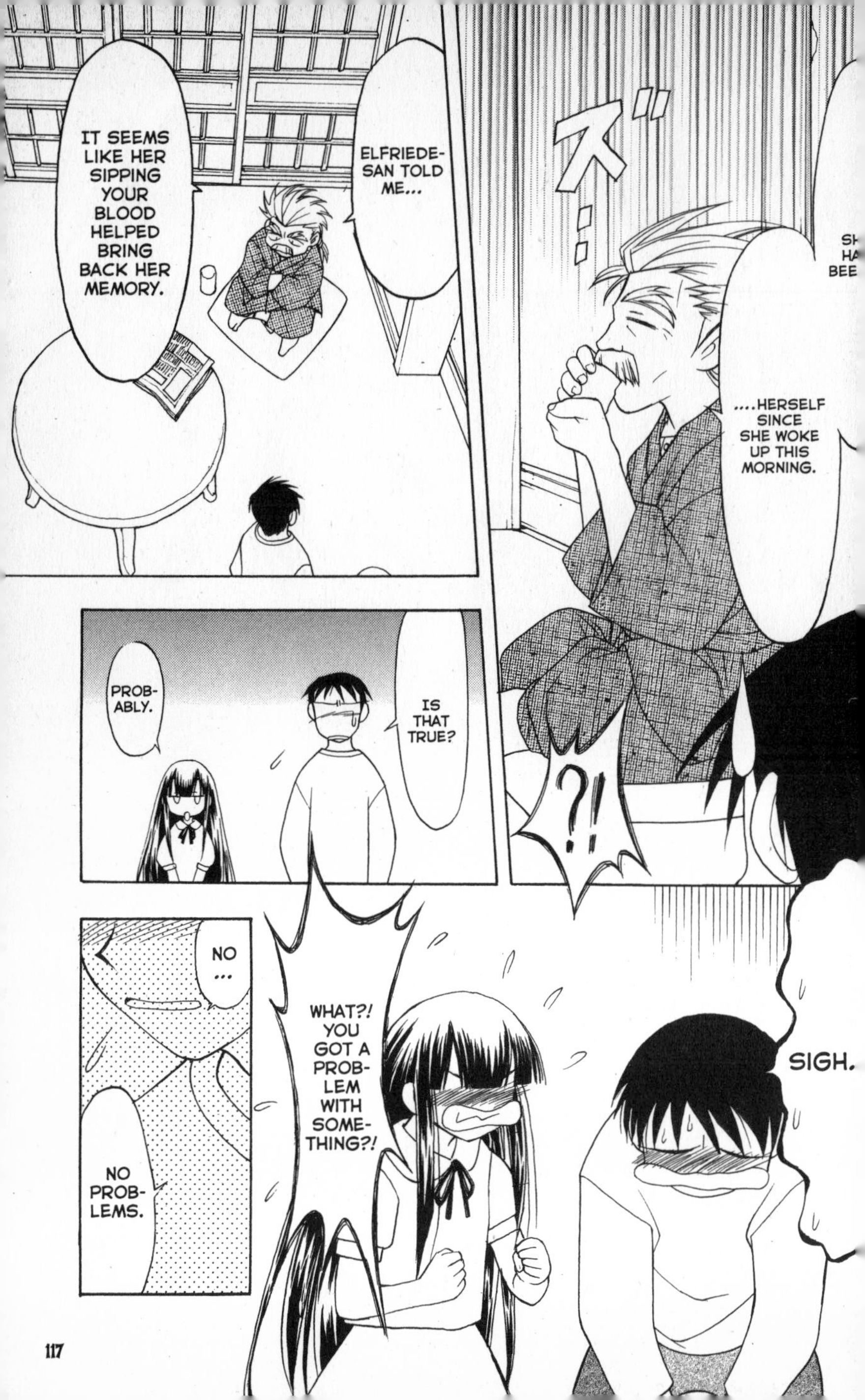
ズ
....HERSELF SINCE SHE WOKE UP THIS MORNING.
ELFRIEDE-SAN TOLD ME...
IT SEEMS LIKE HER SIPPING YOUR BLOOD HELPED BRING BACK HER MEMORY.
?!
IS THAT TRUE?
PROB-ABLY.
SIGH.
WHAT?! YOU GOT A PROB-LEM WITH SOME-THING?!
NO...
NO PROB-LEMS.

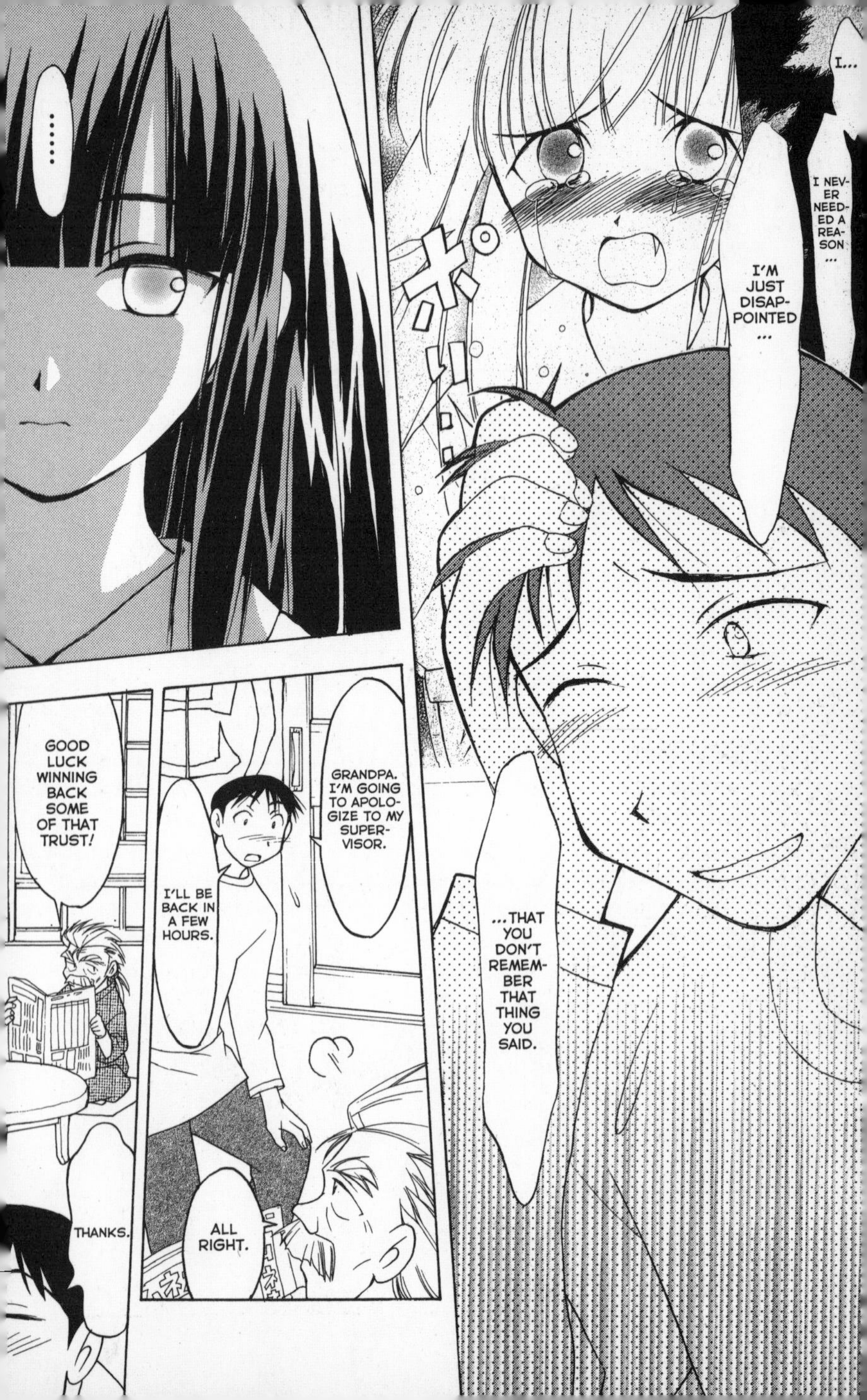
I...
I NEVER NEEDED A REASON...
I'M JUST DISAPPOINTED...
...THAT YOU DON'T REMEMBER THAT THING YOU SAID.
......
GRANDPA. I'M GOING TO APOLOGIZE TO MY SUPERVISOR.
I'LL BE BACK IN A FEW HOURS.
ALL RIGHT.
GOOD LUCK WINNING BACK SOME OF THAT TRUST!
THANKS.

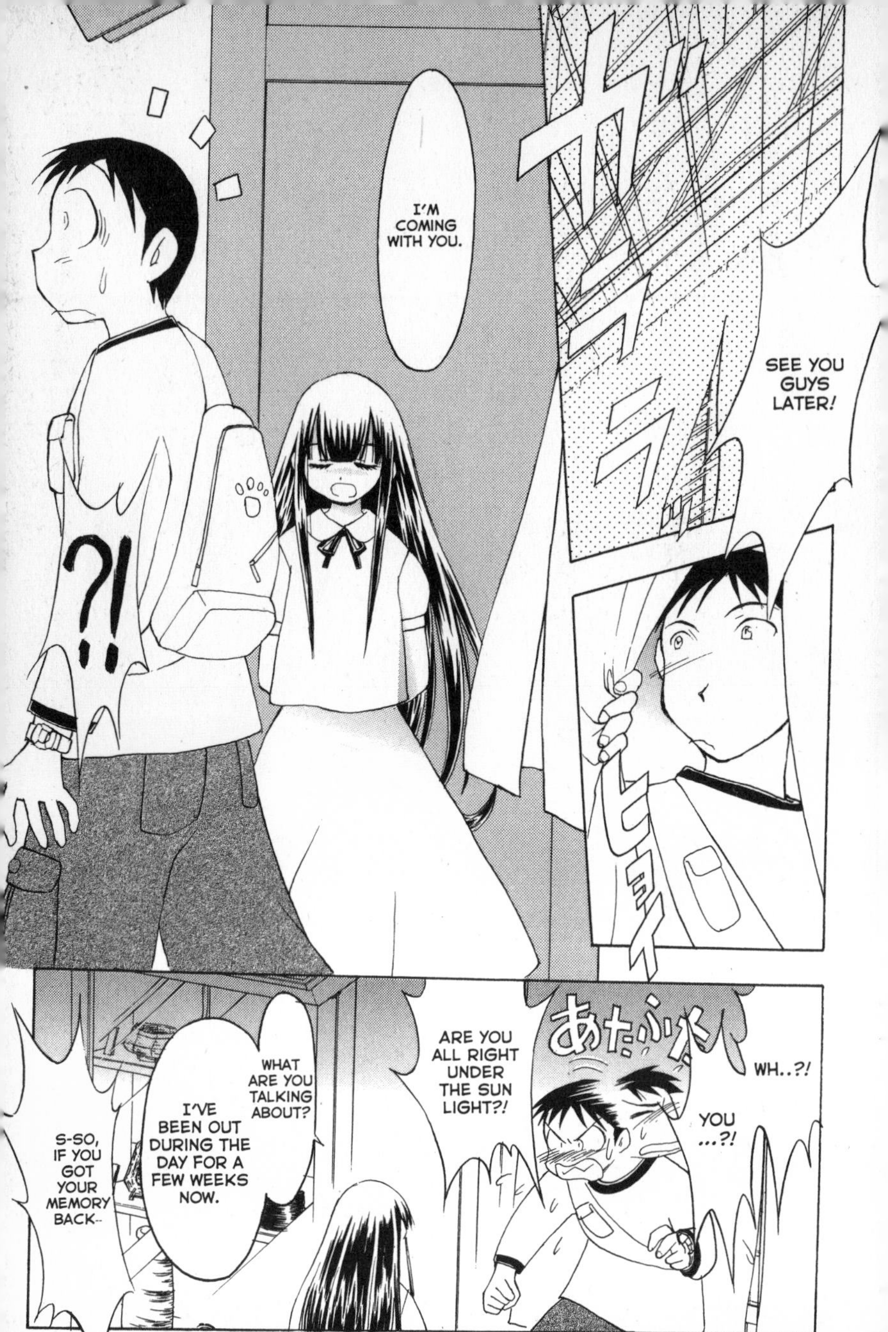
SEE YOU GUYS LATER!
I'M COMING WITH YOU.
WH..?!
YOU ...?!
ARE YOU ALL RIGHT UNDER THE SUN LIGHT?!
WHAT ARE YOU TALKING ABOUT?
I'VE BEEN OUT DURING THE DAY FOR A FEW WEEKS NOW.
S-SO, IF YOU GOT YOUR MEMORY BACK--

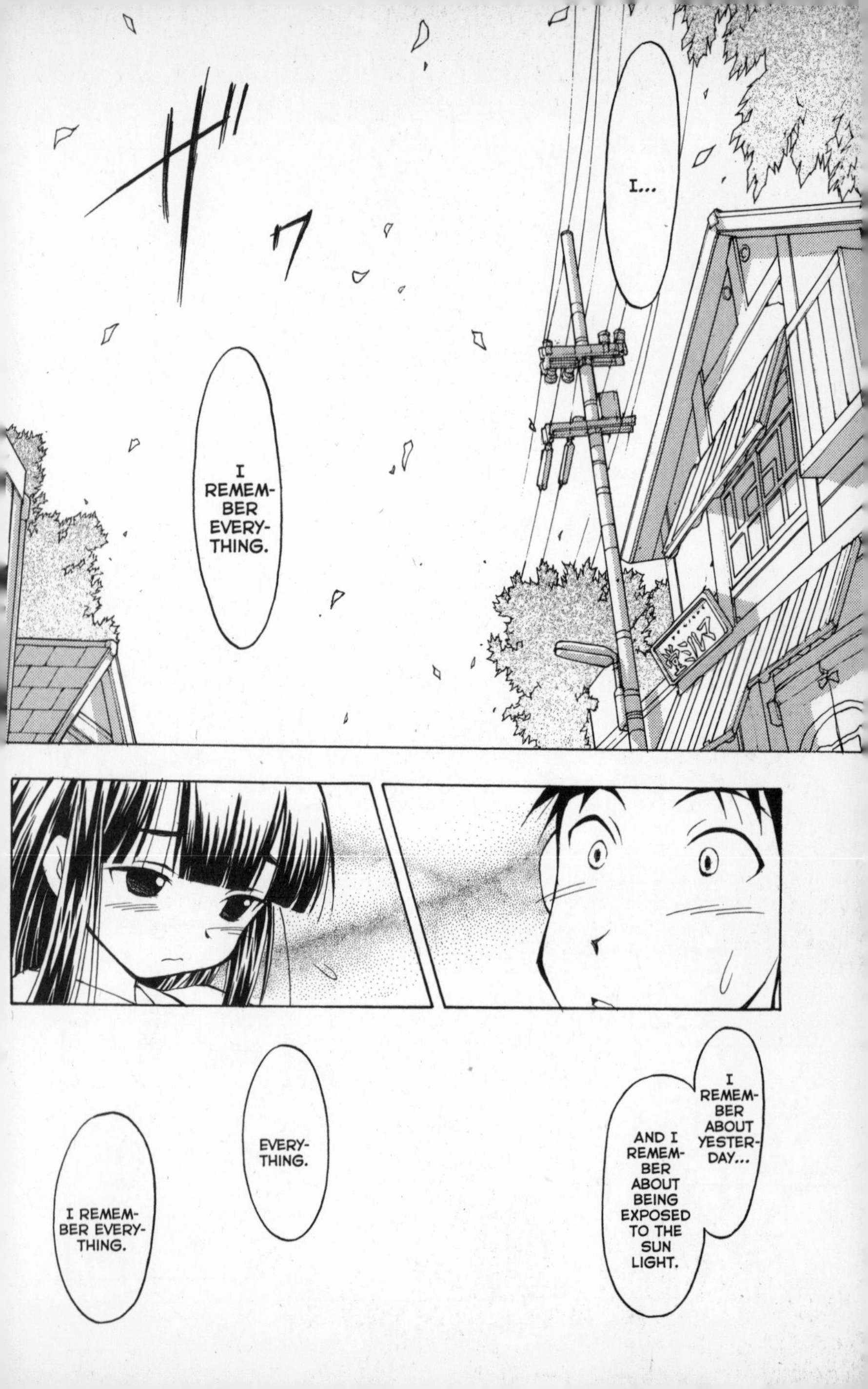
I...
I REMEMBER EVERYTHING.
I REMEMBER ABOUT YESTERDAY...
AND I REMEMBER ABOUT BEING EXPOSED TO THE SUN LIGHT.
EVERYTHING.
I REMEMBER EVERYTHING.

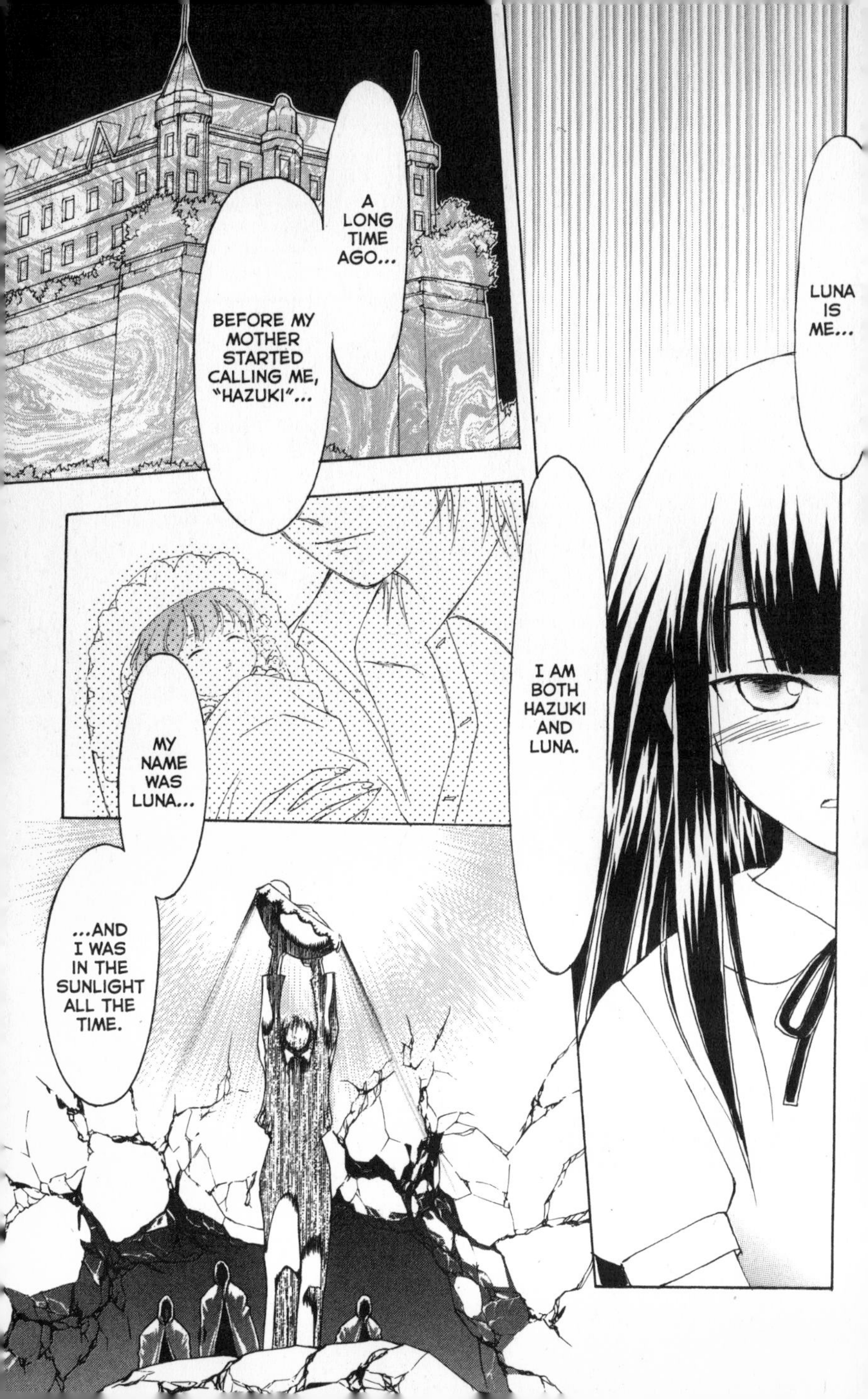
LUNA IS ME...
A LONG TIME AGO...
BEFORE MY MOTHER STARTED CALLING ME, "HAZUKI"...
I AM BOTH HAZUKI AND LUNA.
MY NAME WAS LUNA...
...AND I WAS IN THE SUNLIGHT ALL THE TIME.

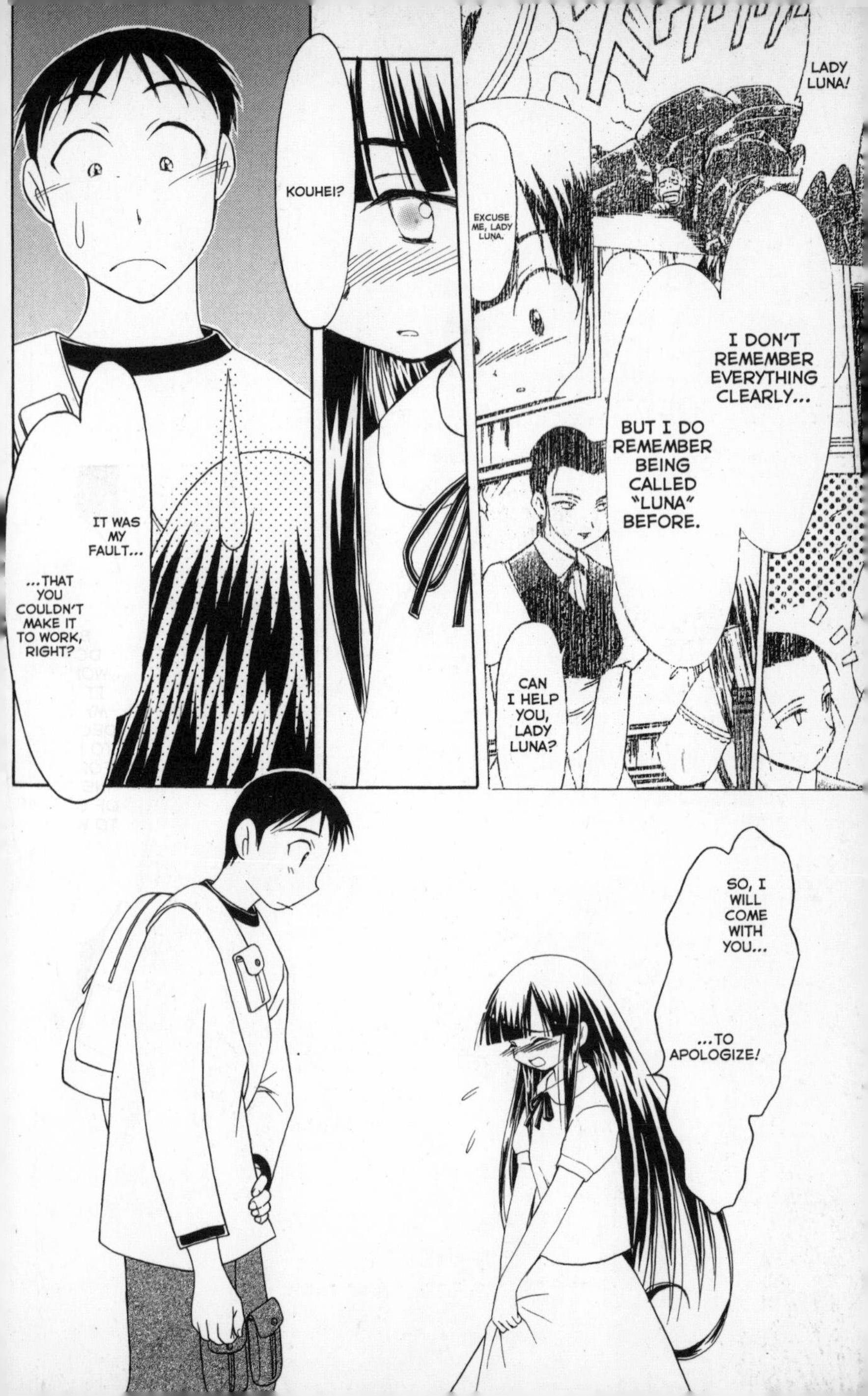
LADY LUNA!
EXCUSE ME, LADY LUNA.
CAN I HELP YOU, LADY LUNA?
I DON'T REMEMBER EVERYTHING CLEARLY...
BUT I DO REMEMBER BEING CALLED "LUNA" BEFORE.
KOUHEI?
IT WAS MY FAULT...
...THAT YOU COULDN'T MAKE IT TO WORK, RIGHT?
SO, I WILL COME WITH YOU...
...TO APOLOGIZE!

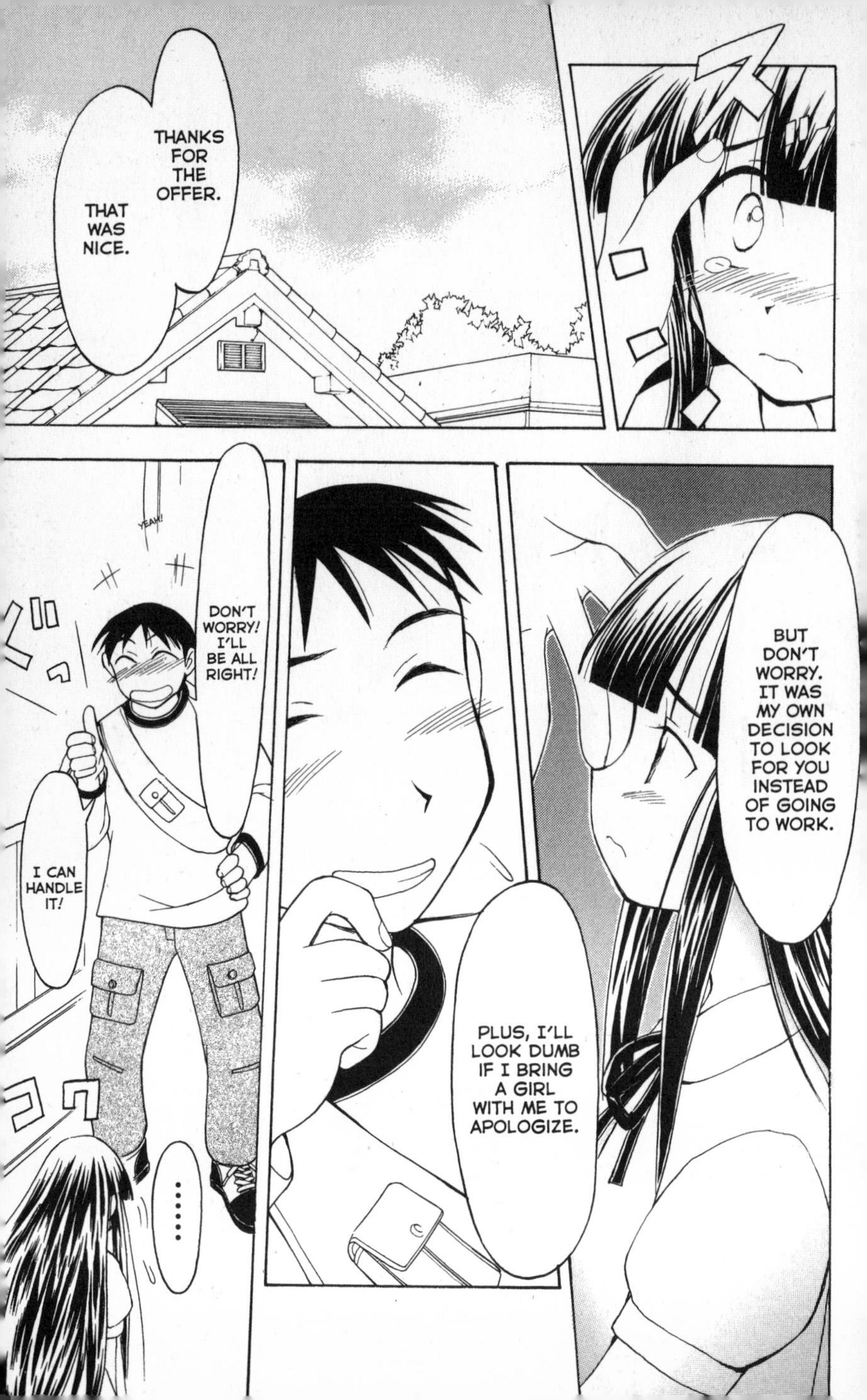
THANKS FOR THE OFFER.
THAT WAS NICE.
BUT DON'T WORRY. IT WAS MY OWN DECISION TO LOOK FOR YOU INSTEAD OF GOING TO WORK.
PLUS, I'LL LOOK DUMB IF I BRING A GIRL WITH ME TO APOLOGIZE.
YEAH!
DON'T WORRY! I'LL BE ALL RIGHT!
I CAN HANDLE IT!
......

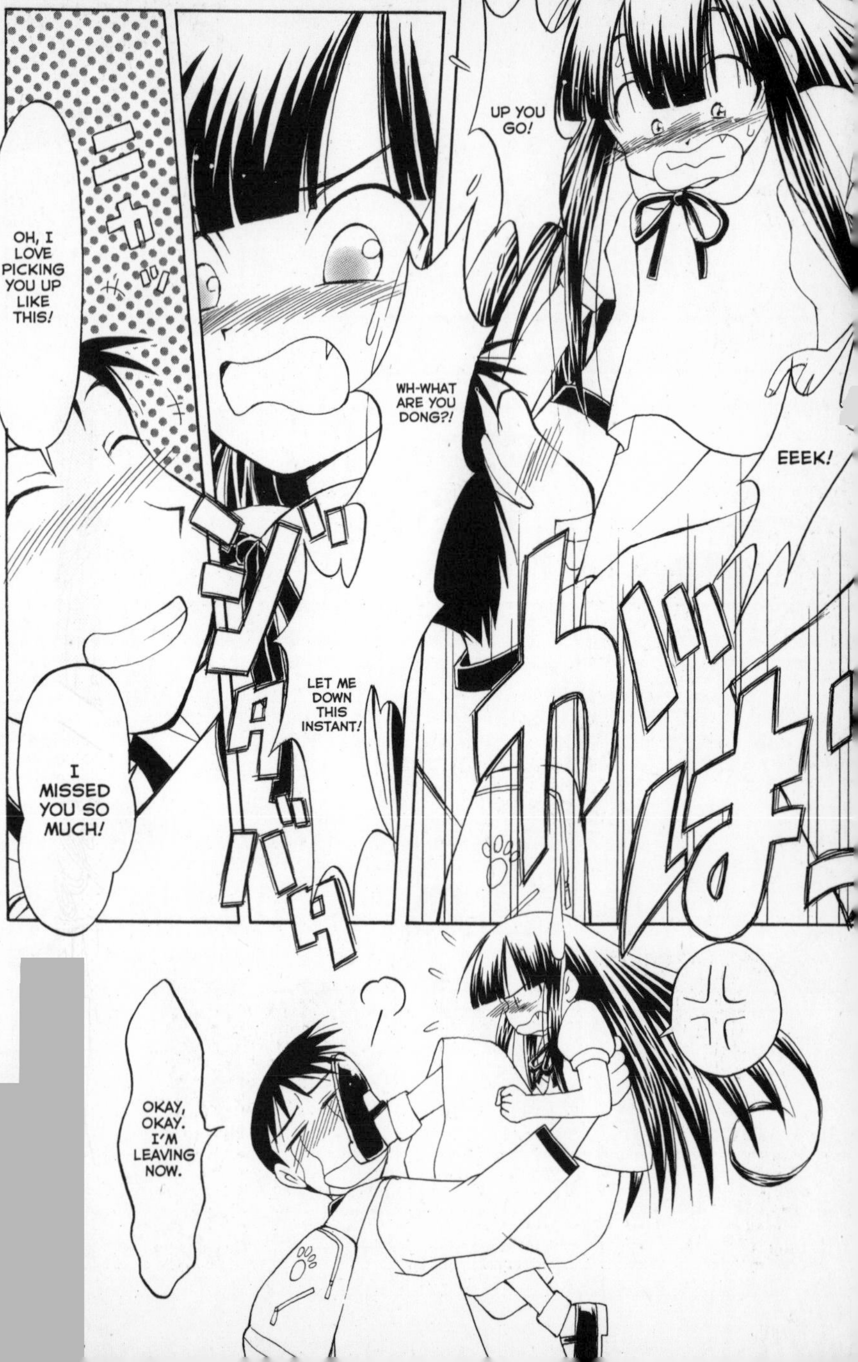
UP YOU GO!
WH-WHAT ARE YOU DONG?!
EEEK!
LET ME DOWN THIS INSTANT!
OH, I LOVE PICKING YOU UP LIKE THIS!
I MISSED YOU SO MUCH!
OKAY, OKAY. I'M LEAVING NOW.

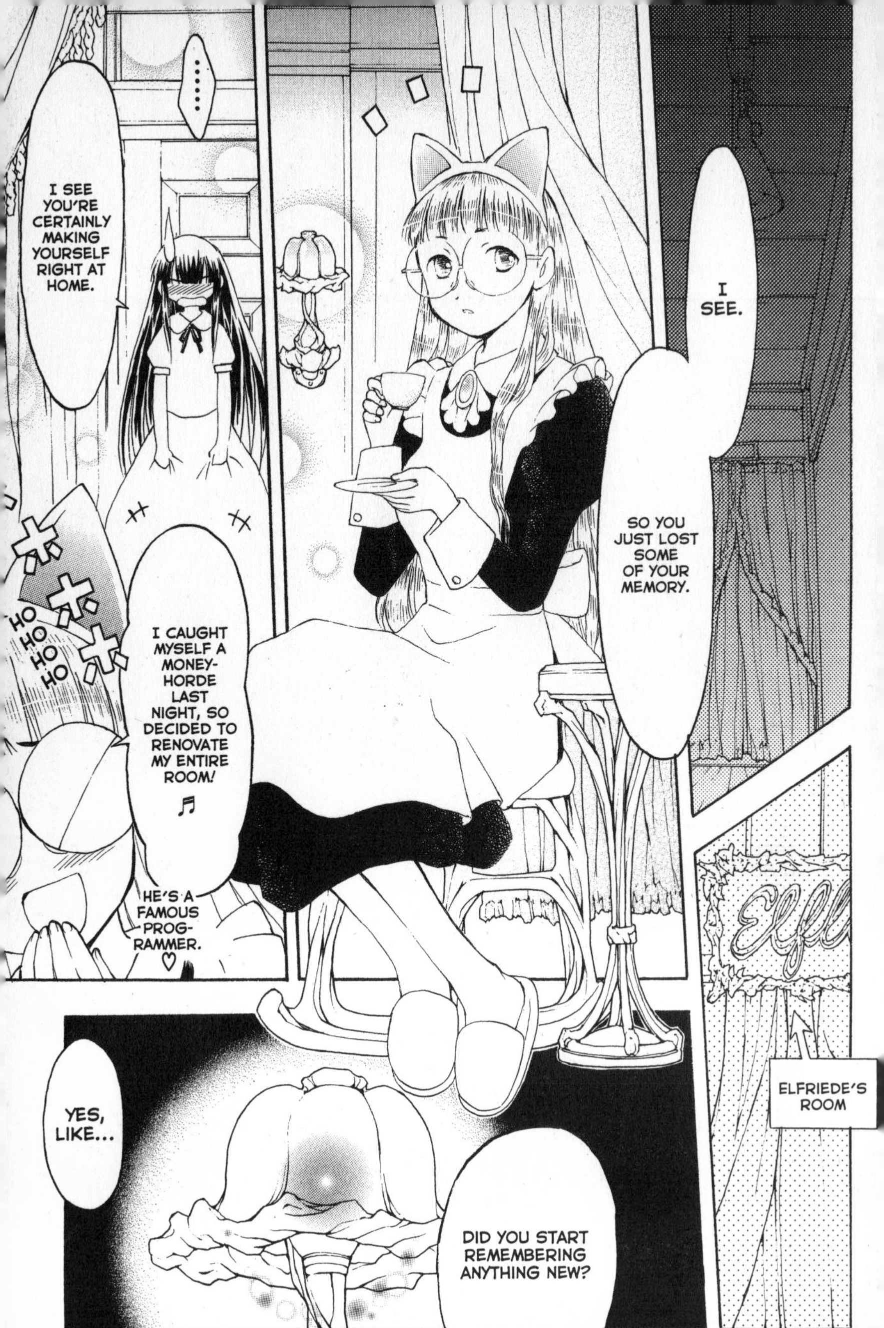
I SEE.
SO YOU JUST LOST SOME OF YOUR MEMORY.
I SEE YOU'RE CERTAINLY MAKING YOURSELF RIGHT AT HOME.
HO HO HO HO
I CAUGHT MYSELF A MONEY-HORDE LAST NIGHT, SO DECIDED TO RENOVATE MY ENTIRE ROOM! ♬
HE'S A FAMOUS PROG-RAMMER. ♡
ELFRIEDE'S ROOM
DID YOU START REMEMBERING ANYTHING NEW?
YES, LIKE...

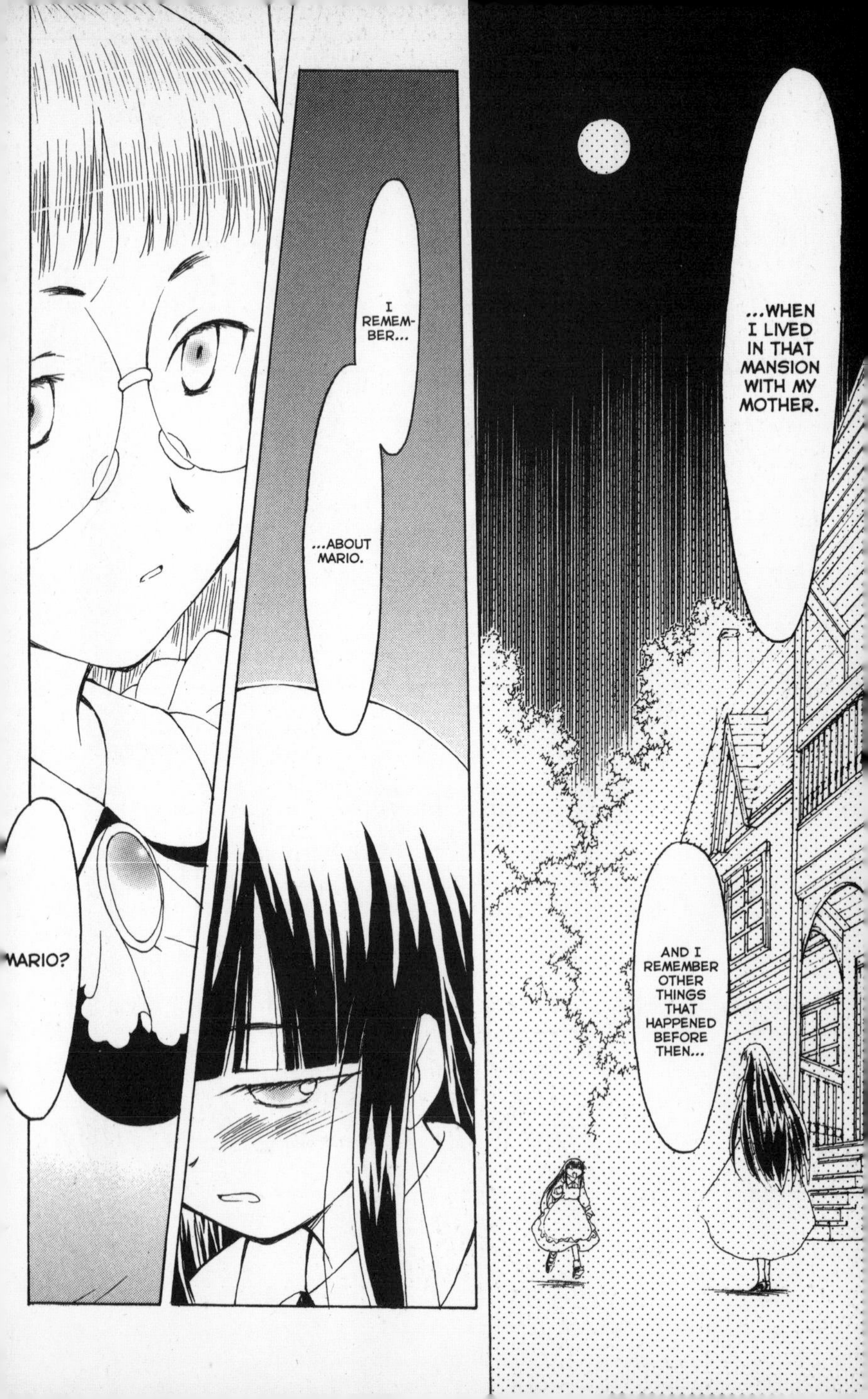
...WHEN I LIVED IN THAT MANSION WITH MY MOTHER.
AND I REMEMBER OTHER THINGS THAT HAPPENED BEFORE THEN...
I REMEMBER...
...ABOUT MARIO.
MARIO?

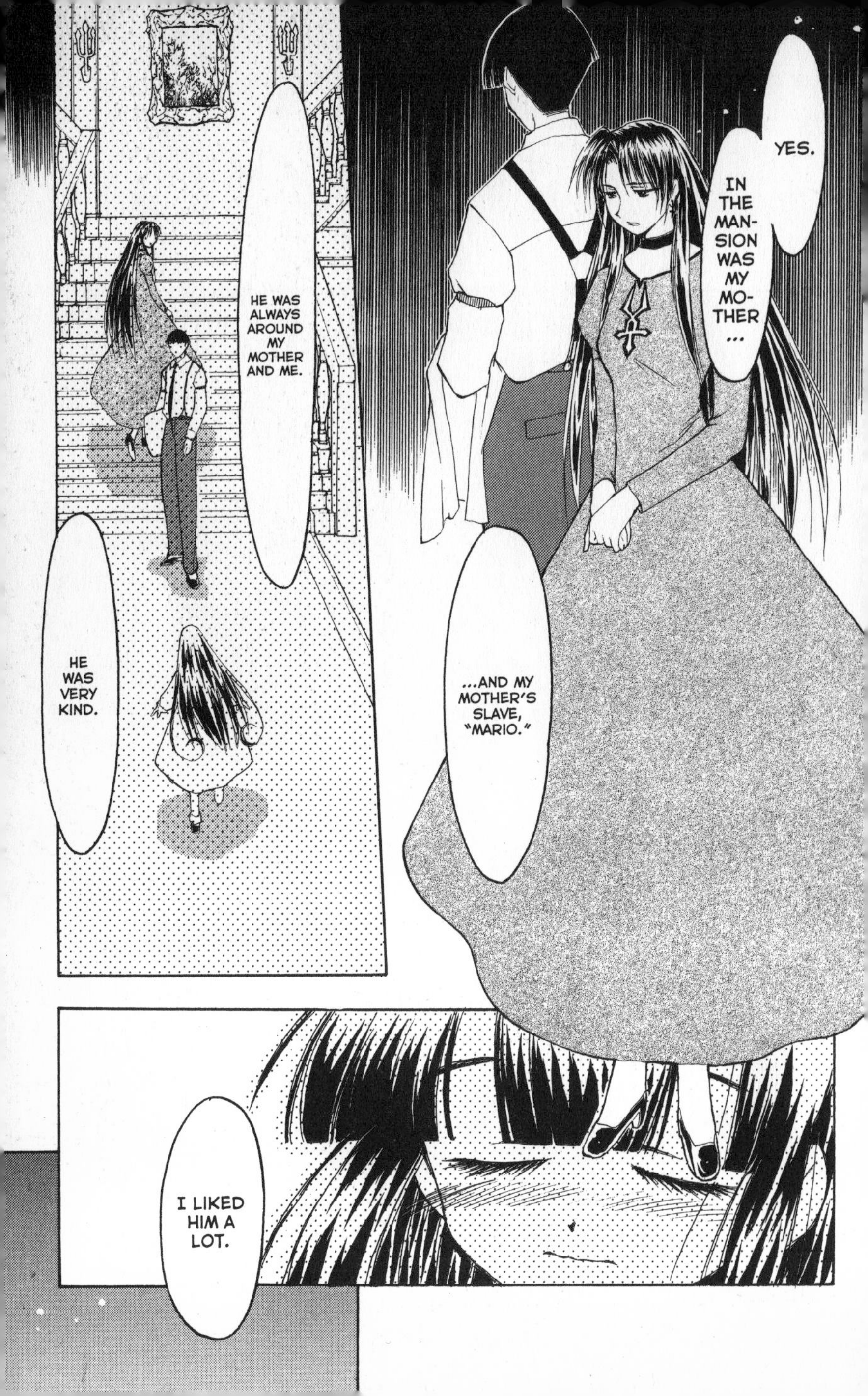
YES.
IN THE MANSION WAS MY MOTHER...
...AND MY MOTHER'S SLAVE, "MARIO."
HE WAS ALWAYS AROUND MY MOTHER AND ME.
HE WAS VERY KIND.
I LIKED HIM A LOT.

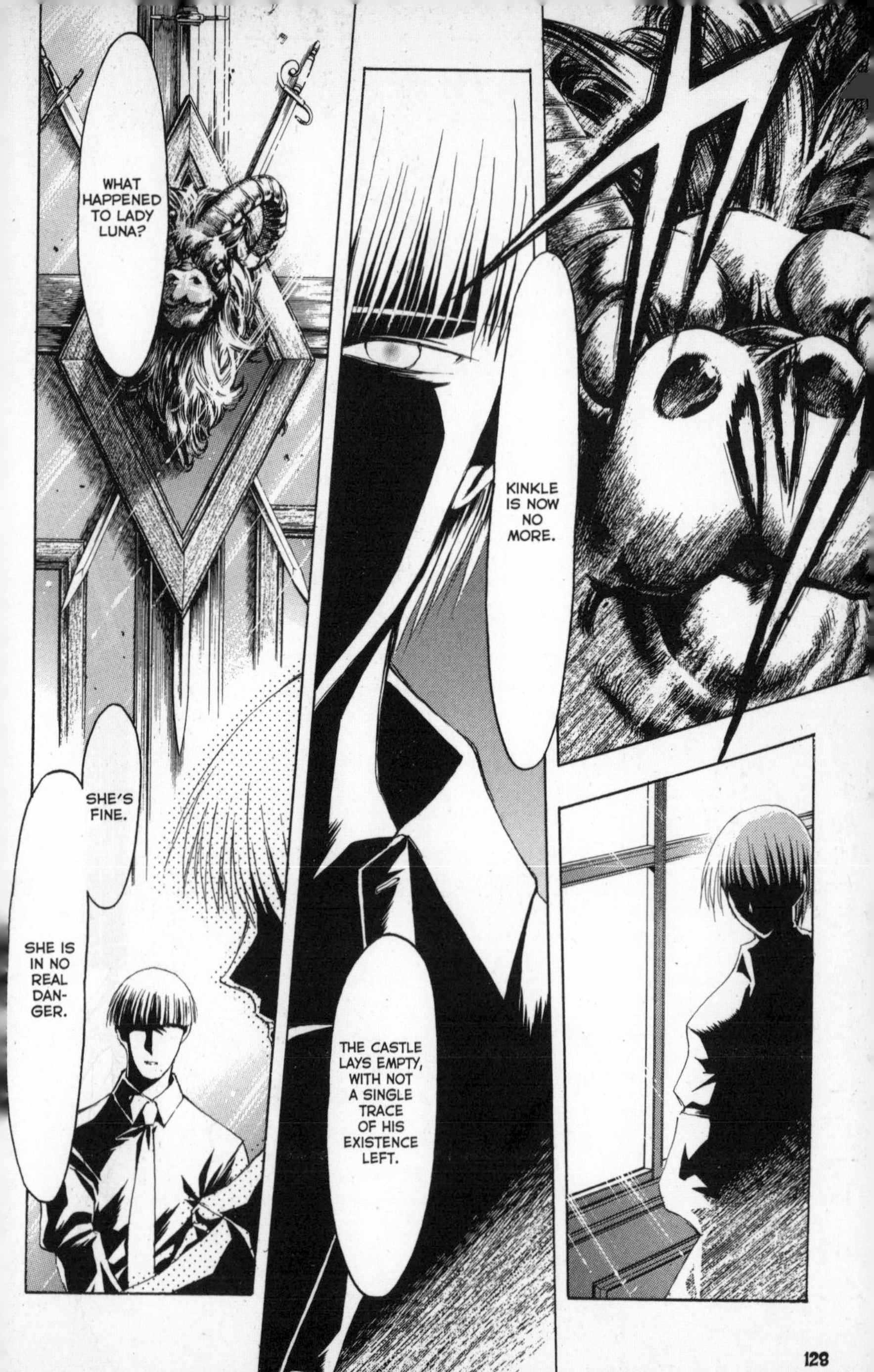
KINKLE IS NOW NO MORE.
THE CASTLE LAYS EMPTY, WITH NOT A SINGLE TRACE OF HIS EXISTENCE LEFT.
WHAT HAPPENED TO LADY LUNA?
SHE'S FINE.
SHE IS IN NO REAL DANGER.

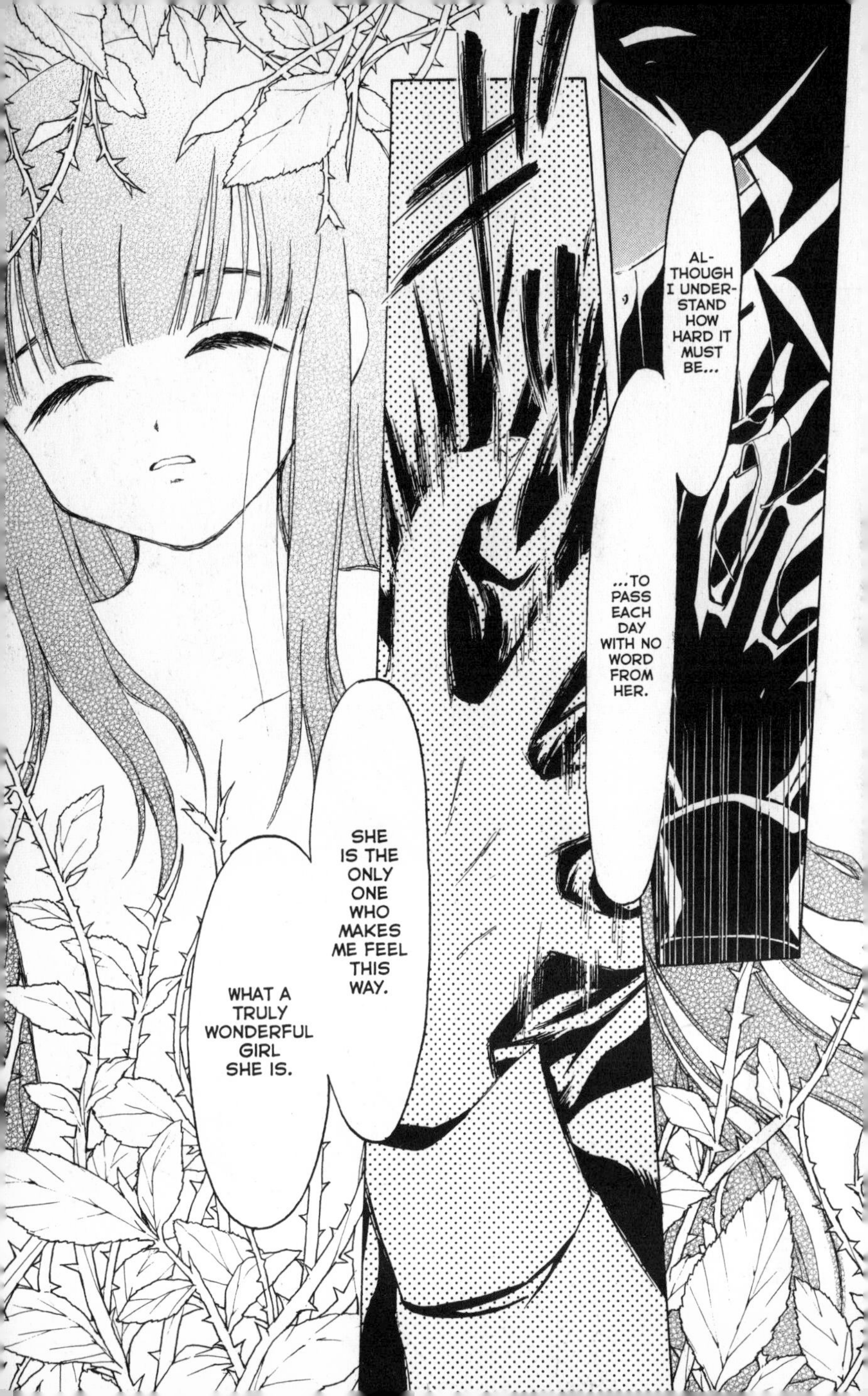
ALTHOUGH I UNDERSTAND HOW HARD IT MUST BE...
...TO PASS EACH DAY WITH NO WORD FROM HER.
SHE IS THE ONLY ONE WHO MAKES ME FEEL THIS WAY.
WHAT A TRULY WONDERFUL GIRL SHE IS.

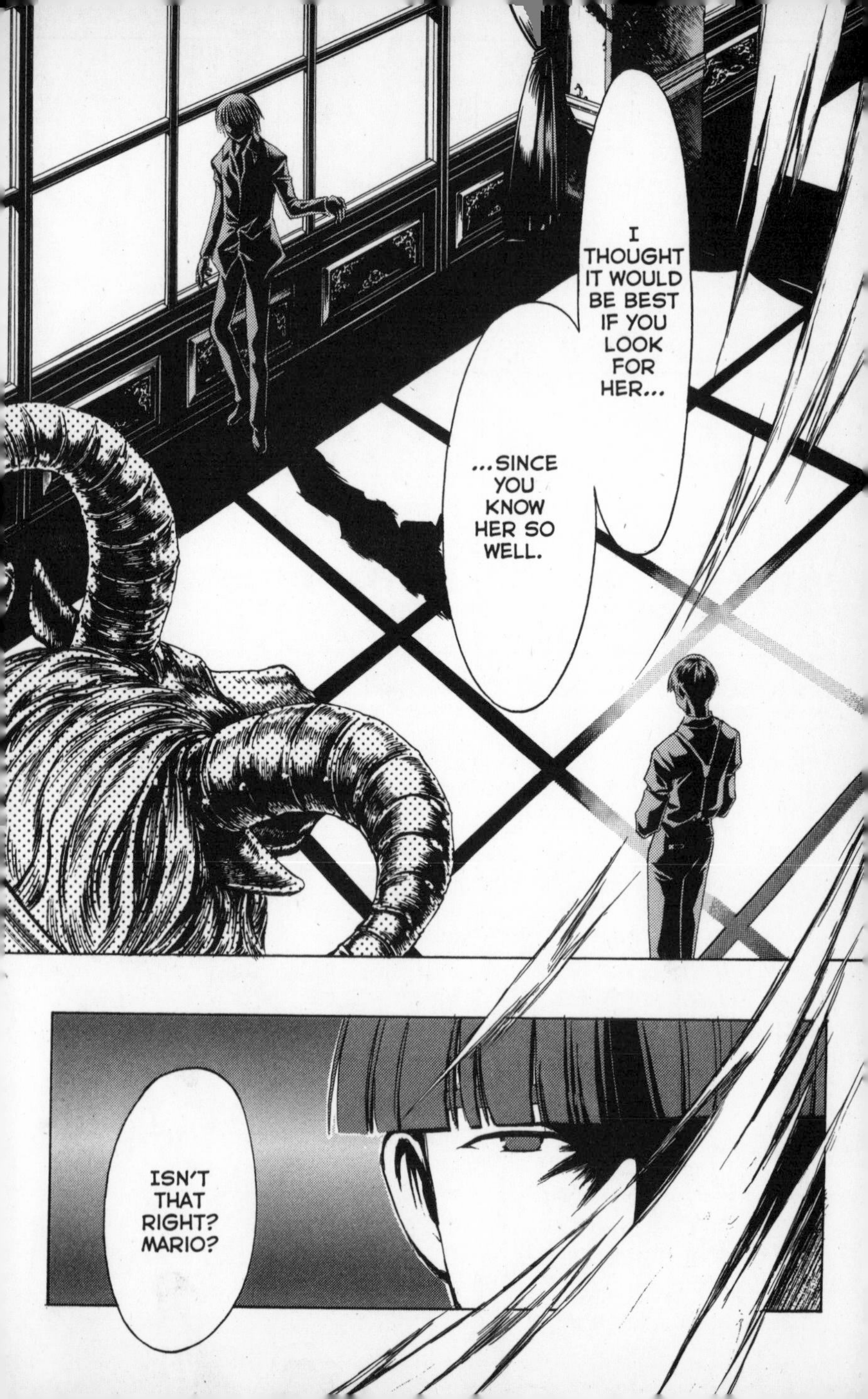
I THOUGHT IT WOULD BE BEST IF YOU LOOK FOR HER...
...SINCE YOU KNOW HER SO WELL.
ISN'T THAT RIGHT? MARIO?

MOON 月詠 PHASE

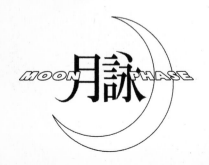

PART 5

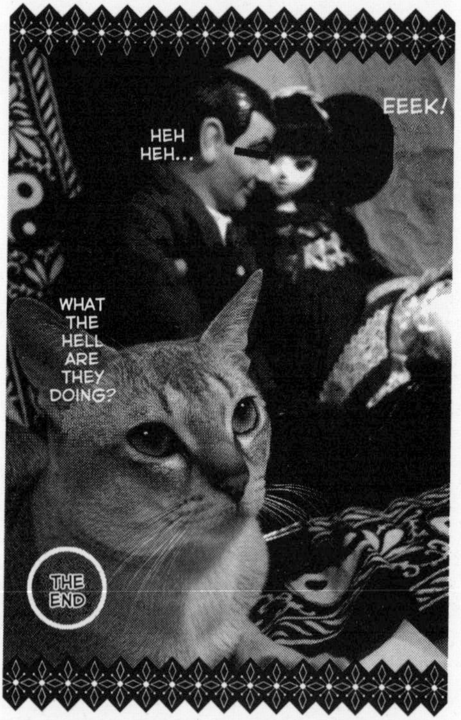
EEEK!
HEH HEH...
WHAT THE HELL ARE THEY DOING?
THE END

(THE HAZUKI DOLL IN THIS PAGE IS CUSTOM- MADE BY BOUKS, CO. LTD. AND IT IS NOT FOR SALE.)

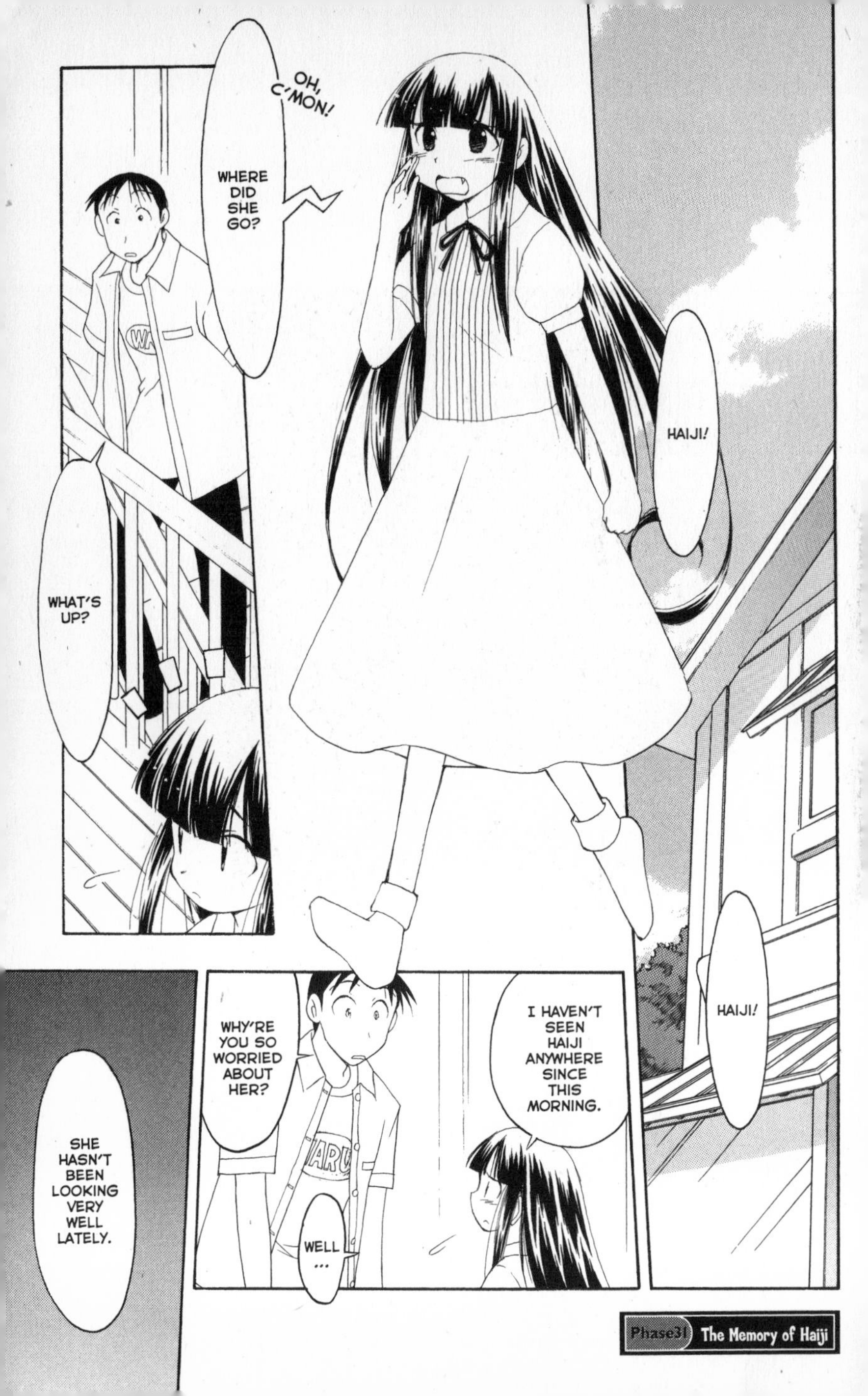
HAIJI!
OH, C'MON!
WHERE DID SHE GO?
WHAT'S UP?
HAIJI!
I HAVEN'T SEEN HAIJI ANYWHERE SINCE THIS MORNING.
WHY'RE YOU SO WORRIED ABOUT HER?
WELL ...
SHE HASN'T BEEN LOOKING VERY WELL LATELY.

Phase31 The Memory of Haiji

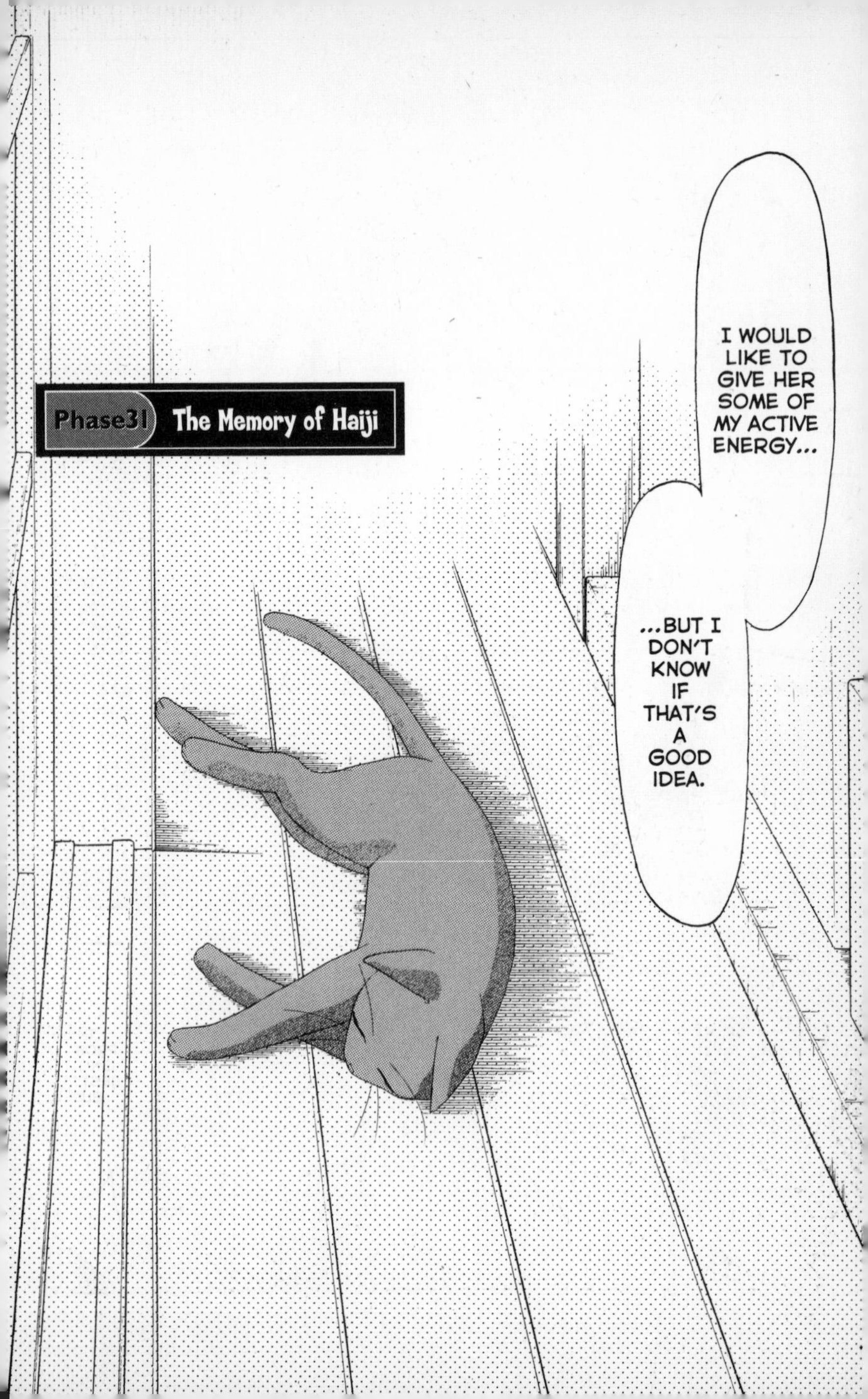
I WOULD LIKE TO GIVE HER SOME OF MY ACTIVE ENERGY...
...BUT I DON'T KNOW IF THAT'S A GOOD IDEA.

Phase31 The Memory of Haiji

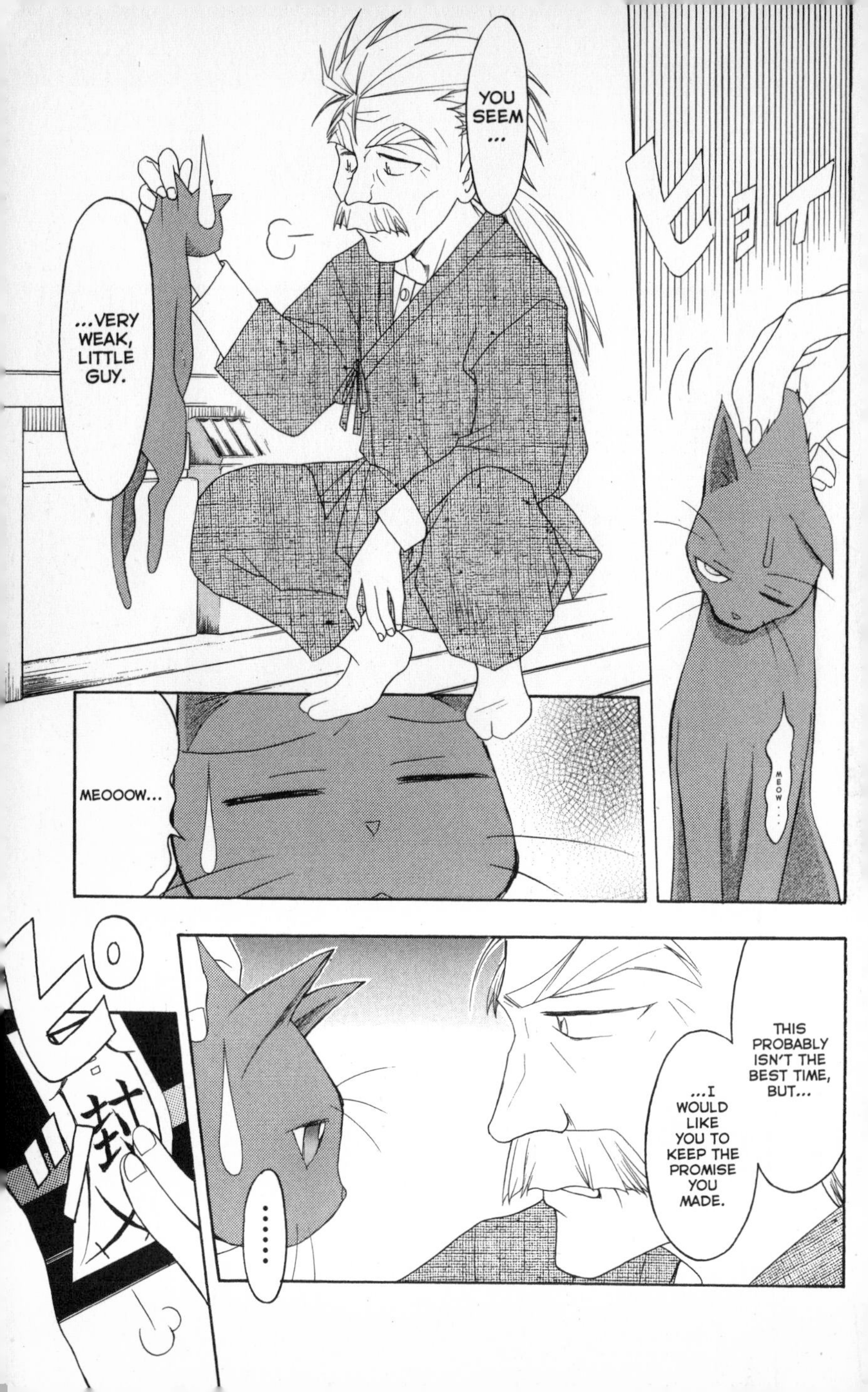

ヒョイ
MEOW...
YOU SEEM...
...VERY WEAK, LITTLE GUY.
MEOOOW...
THIS PROBABLY ISN'T THE BEST TIME, BUT...
...I WOULD LIKE YOU TO KEEP THE PROMISE YOU MADE.
......
ピロ
封

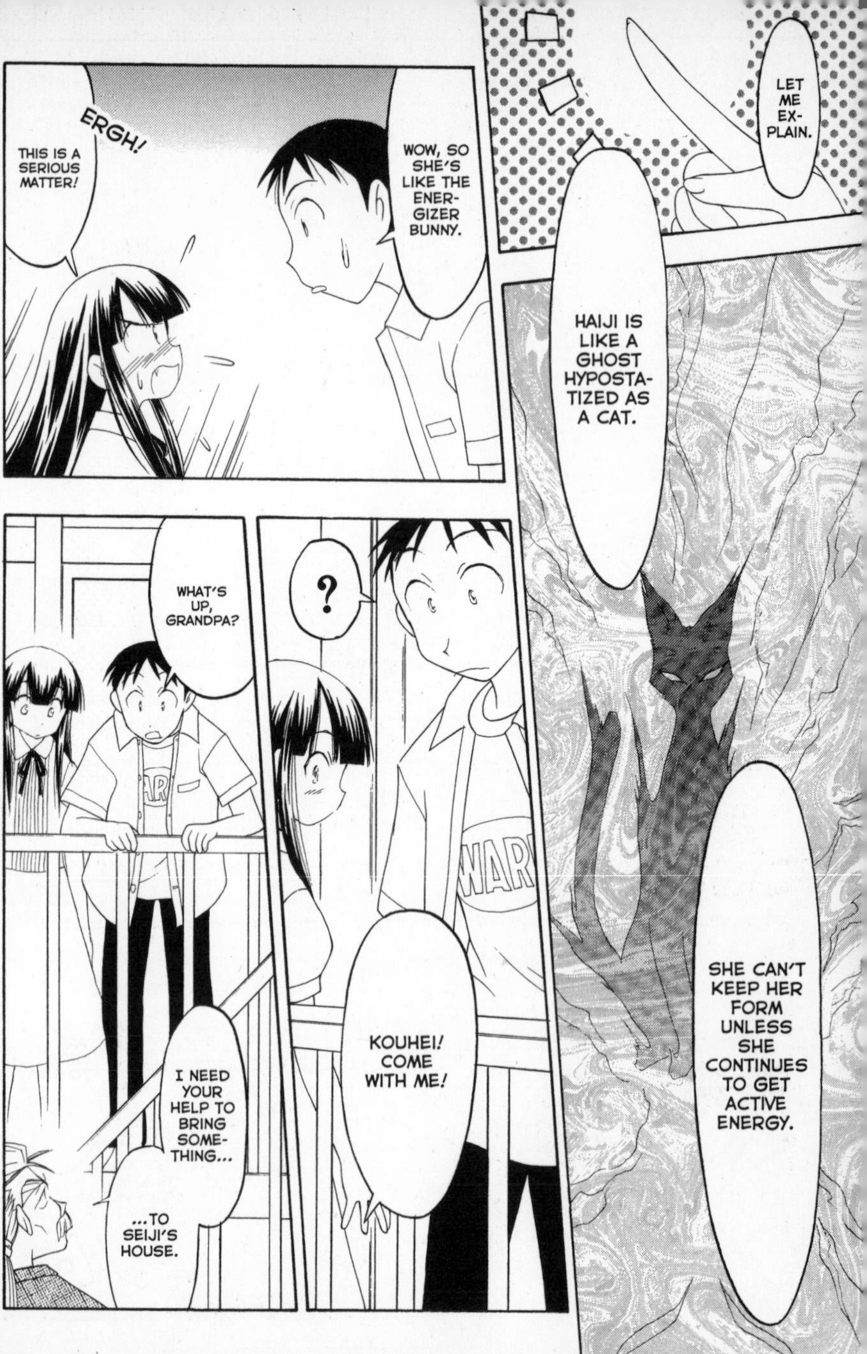
LET ME EXPLAIN.
HAIJI IS LIKE A GHOST HYPOSTATIZED AS A CAT.
SHE CAN'T KEEP HER FORM UNLESS SHE CONTINUES TO GET ACTIVE ENERGY.
WOW, SO SHE'S LIKE THE ENERGIZER BUNNY.
ERGH!
THIS IS A SERIOUS MATTER!
?
KOUHEI! COME WITH ME!
WHAT'S UP, GRANDPA?
I NEED YOUR HELP TO BRING SOMETHING...
...TO SEIJI'S HOUSE.

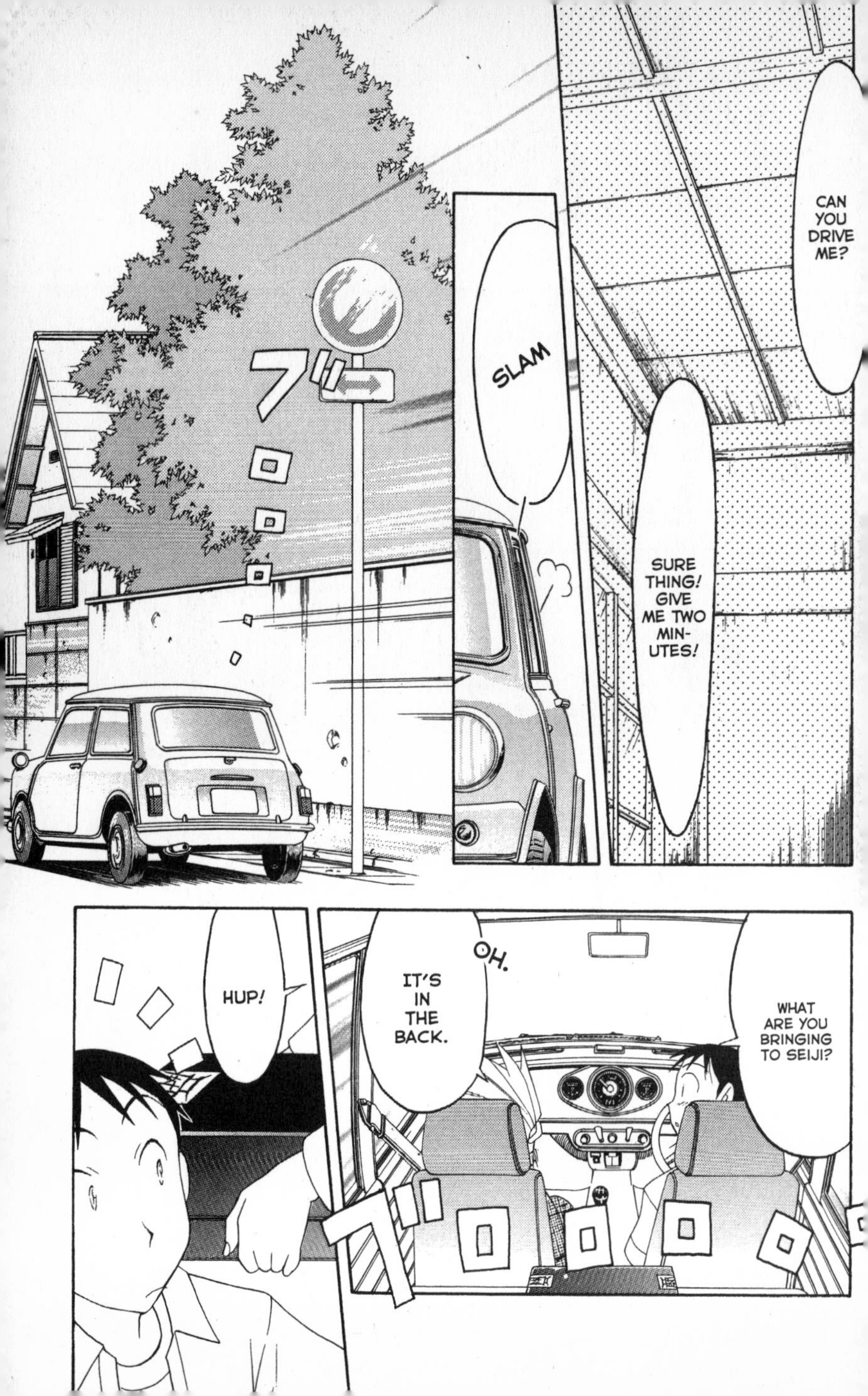
CAN YOU DRIVE ME?
SURE THING! GIVE ME TWO MIN-UTES!
SLAM
WHAT ARE YOU BRINGING TO SEIJI?
OH.
IT'S IN THE BACK.
HUP!

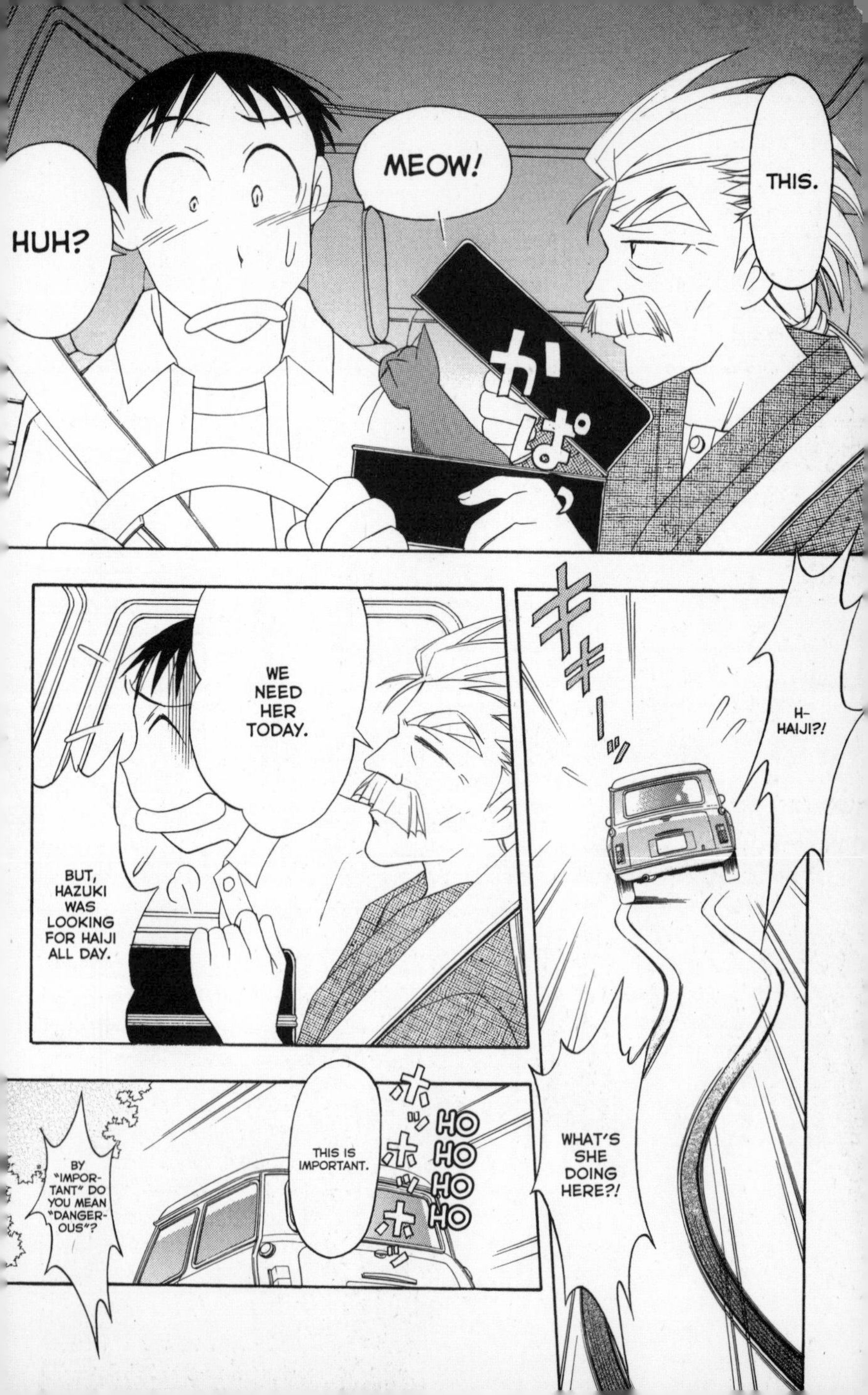
THIS.
MEOW!
HUH?
かぱっ
H-HAIJI?!
WE NEED HER TODAY.
BUT, HAZUKI WAS LOOKING FOR HAIJI ALL DAY.
WHAT'S SHE DOING HERE?!
HO HO HO HO
THIS IS IMPORTANT.
BY "IMPOR-TANT" DO YOU MEAN "DANGER-OUS"?

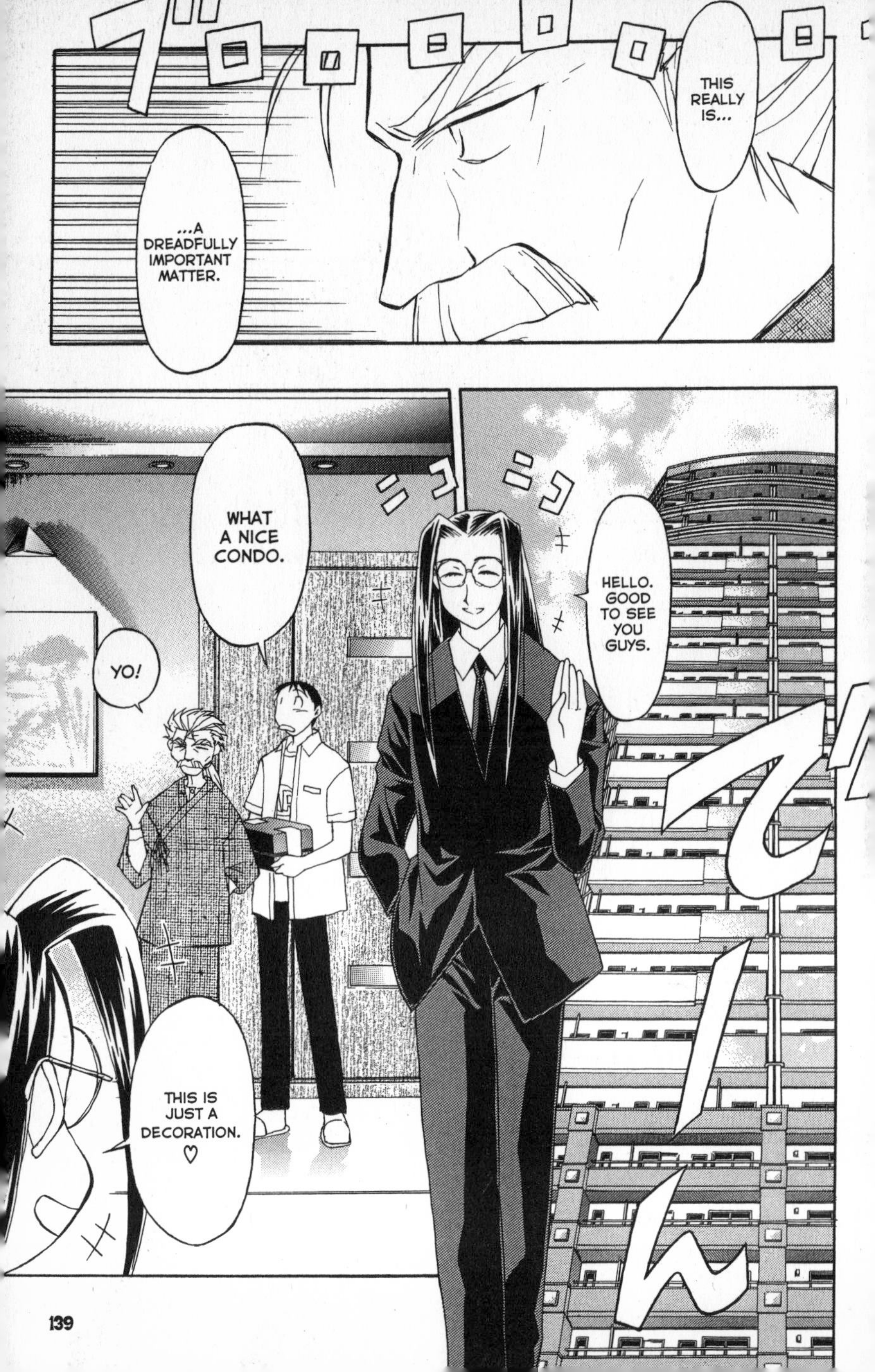
THIS REALLY IS...
...A DREADFULLY IMPORTANT MATTER.
HELLO. GOOD TO SEE YOU GUYS.
WHAT A NICE CONDO.
YO!
THIS IS JUST A DECORATION. ♡

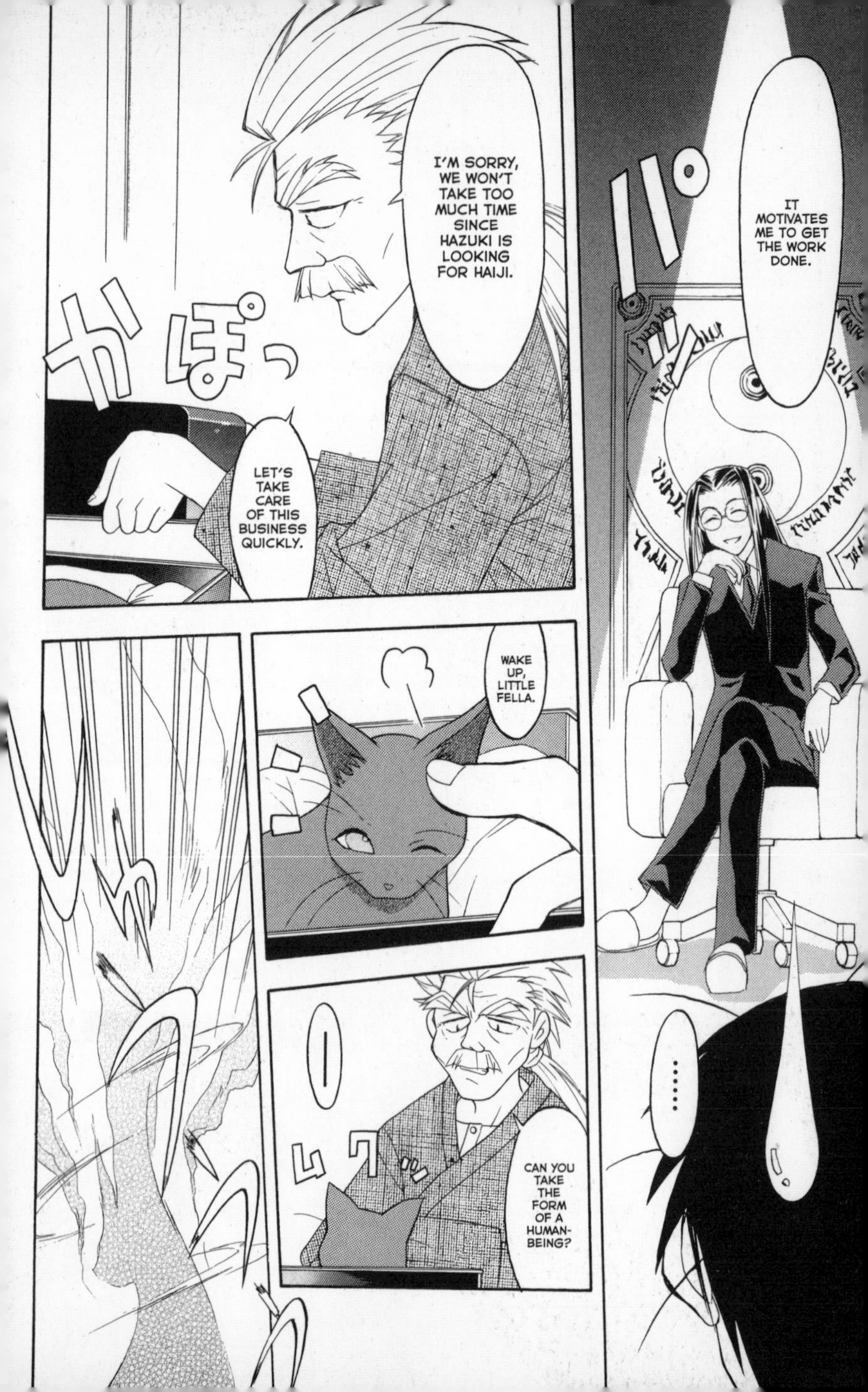
IT MOTIVATES ME TO GET THE WORK DONE.
......
I'M SORRY, WE WON'T TAKE TOO MUCH TIME SINCE HAZUKI IS LOOKING FOR HAIJI.
かぽっ
LET'S TAKE CARE OF THIS BUSINESS QUICKLY.
WAKE UP, LITTLE FELLA.
CAN YOU TAKE THE FORM OF A HUMAN-BEING?

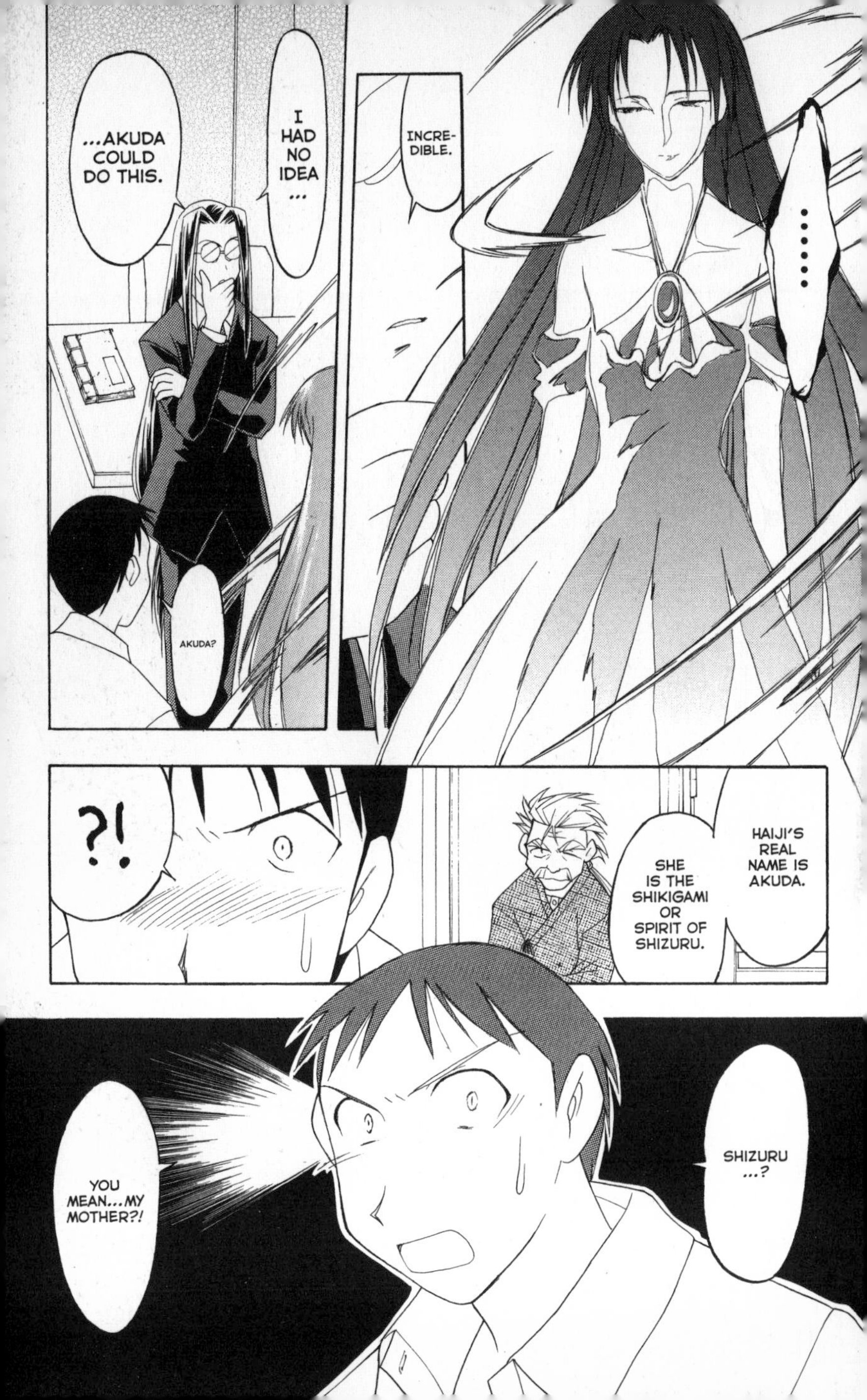
......
INCREDIBLE.
I HAD NO IDEA...
...AKUDA COULD DO THIS.
AKUDA?
HAIJI'S REAL NAME IS AKUDA.
SHE IS THE SHIKIGAMI OR SPIRIT OF SHIZURU.
?!
SHIZURU...?
YOU MEAN...MY MOTHER?!

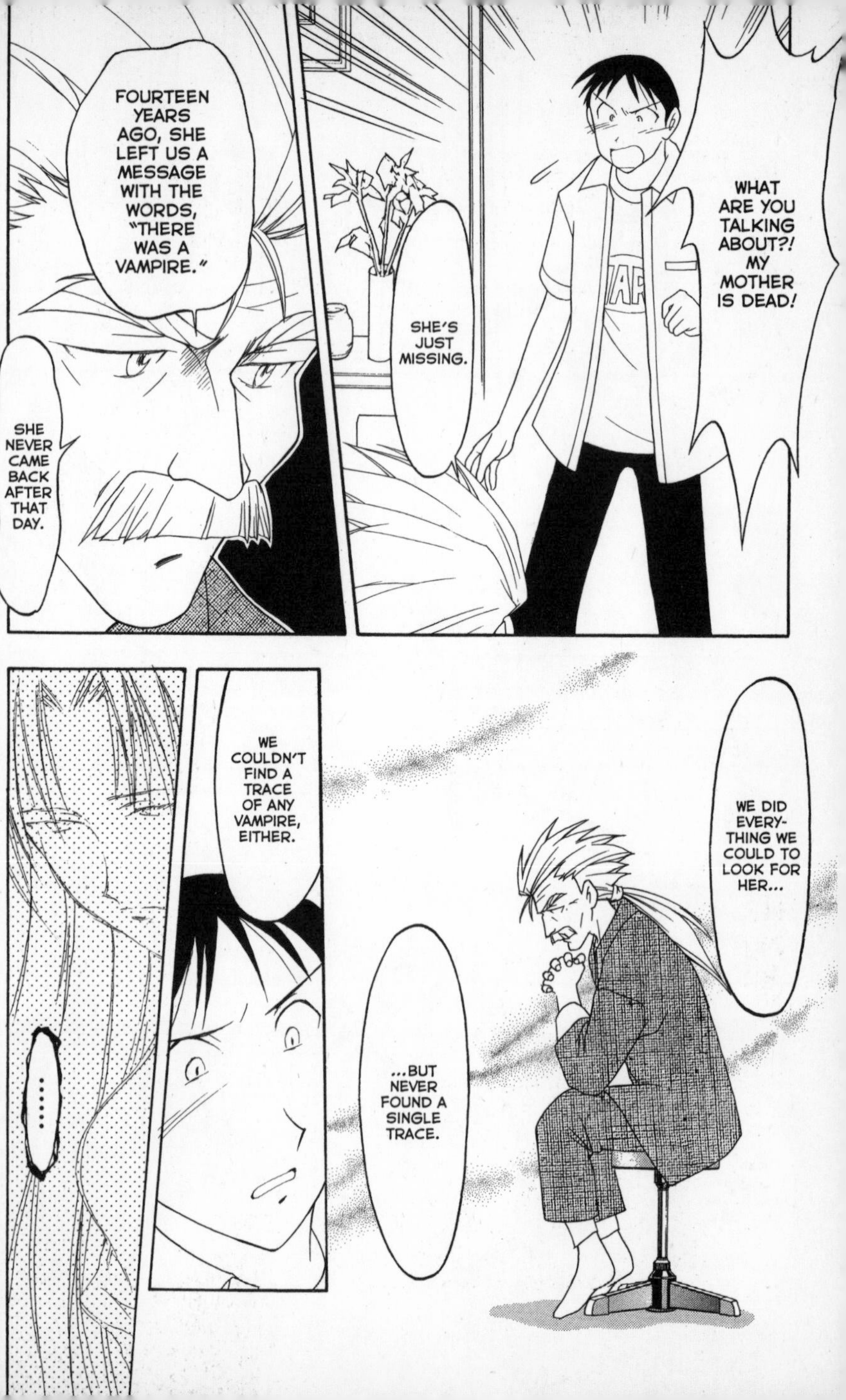
WHAT ARE YOU TALKING ABOUT?! MY MOTHER IS DEAD!
SHE'S JUST MISSING.
FOURTEEN YEARS AGO, SHE LEFT US A MESSAGE WITH THE WORDS, "THERE WAS A VAMPIRE."
SHE NEVER CAME BACK AFTER THAT DAY.
WE DID EVERY-THING WE COULD TO LOOK FOR HER...
...BUT NEVER FOUND A SINGLE TRACE.
WE COULDN'T FIND A TRACE OF ANY VAMPIRE, EITHER.
......

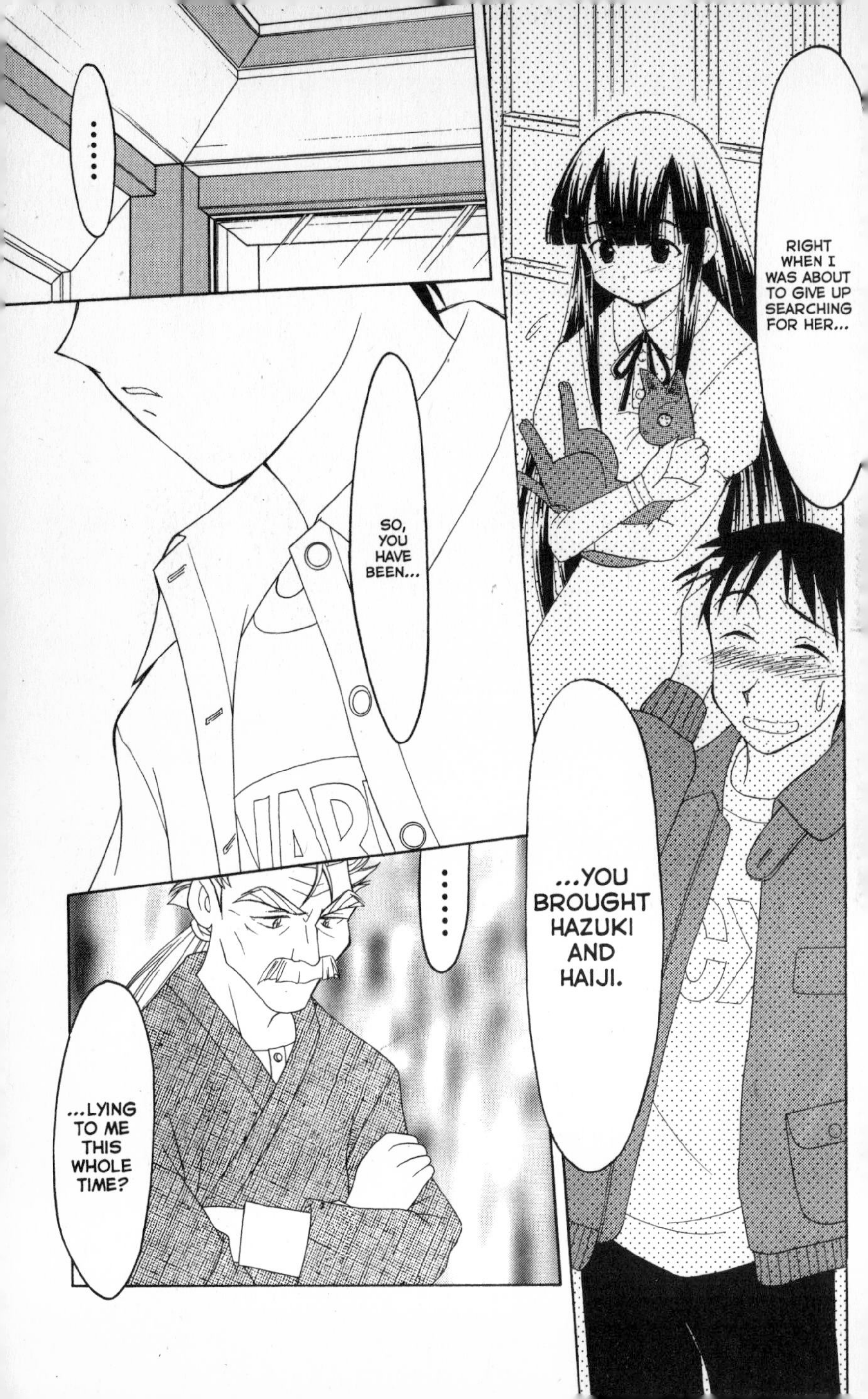
RIGHT WHEN I WAS ABOUT TO GIVE UP SEARCHING FOR HER...
...YOU BROUGHT HAZUKI AND HAIJI.
......
SO, YOU HAVE BEEN...
......
...LYING TO ME THIS WHOLE TIME?

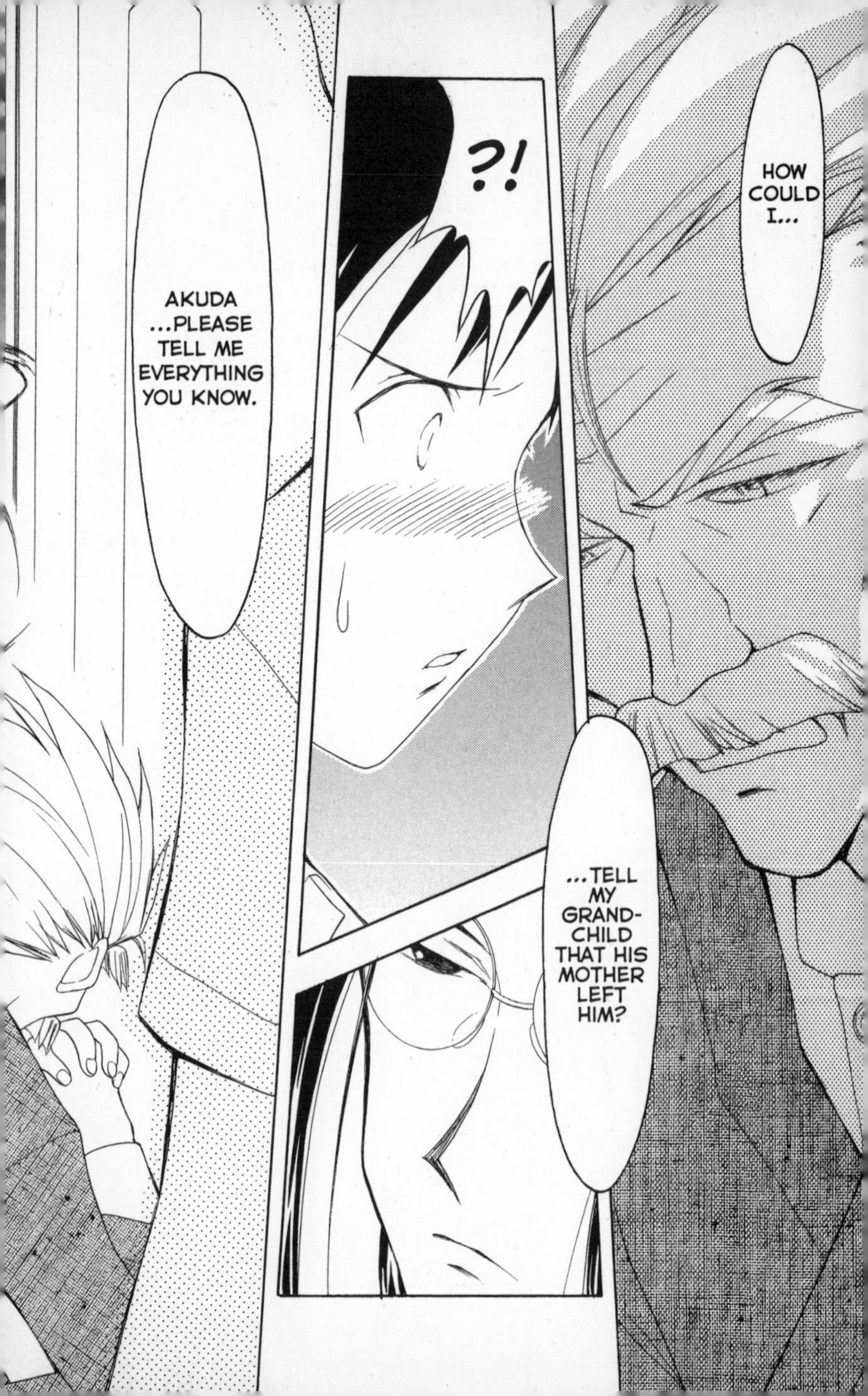
HOW COULD I...
...TELL MY GRAND-CHILD THAT HIS MOTHER LEFT HIM?
?!
AKUDA ...PLEASE TELL ME EVERYTHING YOU KNOW.

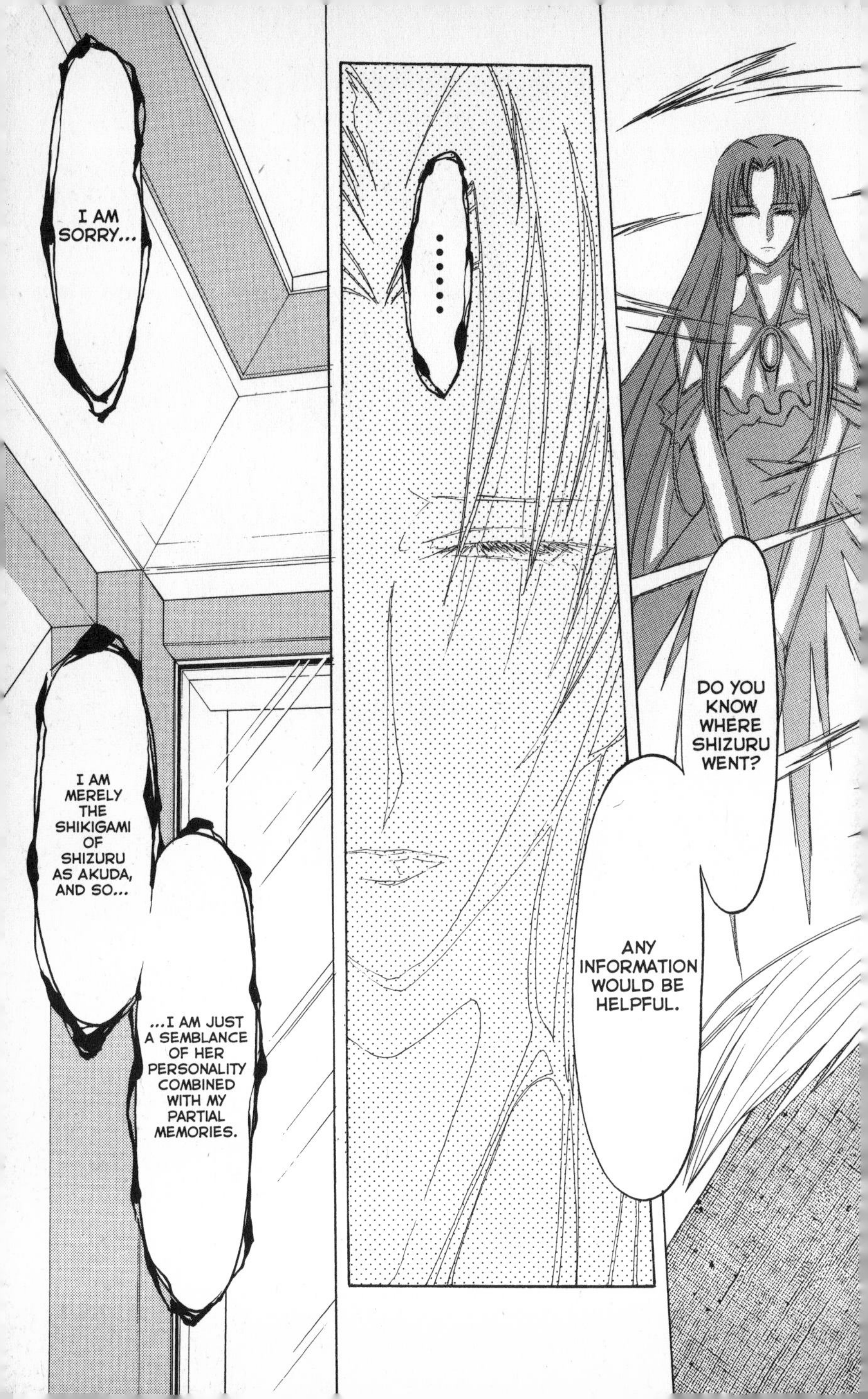
DO YOU KNOW WHERE SHIZURU WENT?
ANY INFORMATION WOULD BE HELPFUL.
......
I AM SORRY...
I AM MERELY THE SHIKIGAMI OF SHIZURU AS AKUDA, AND SO...
...I AM JUST A SEMBLANCE OF HER PERSONALITY COMBINED WITH MY PARTIAL MEMORIES.

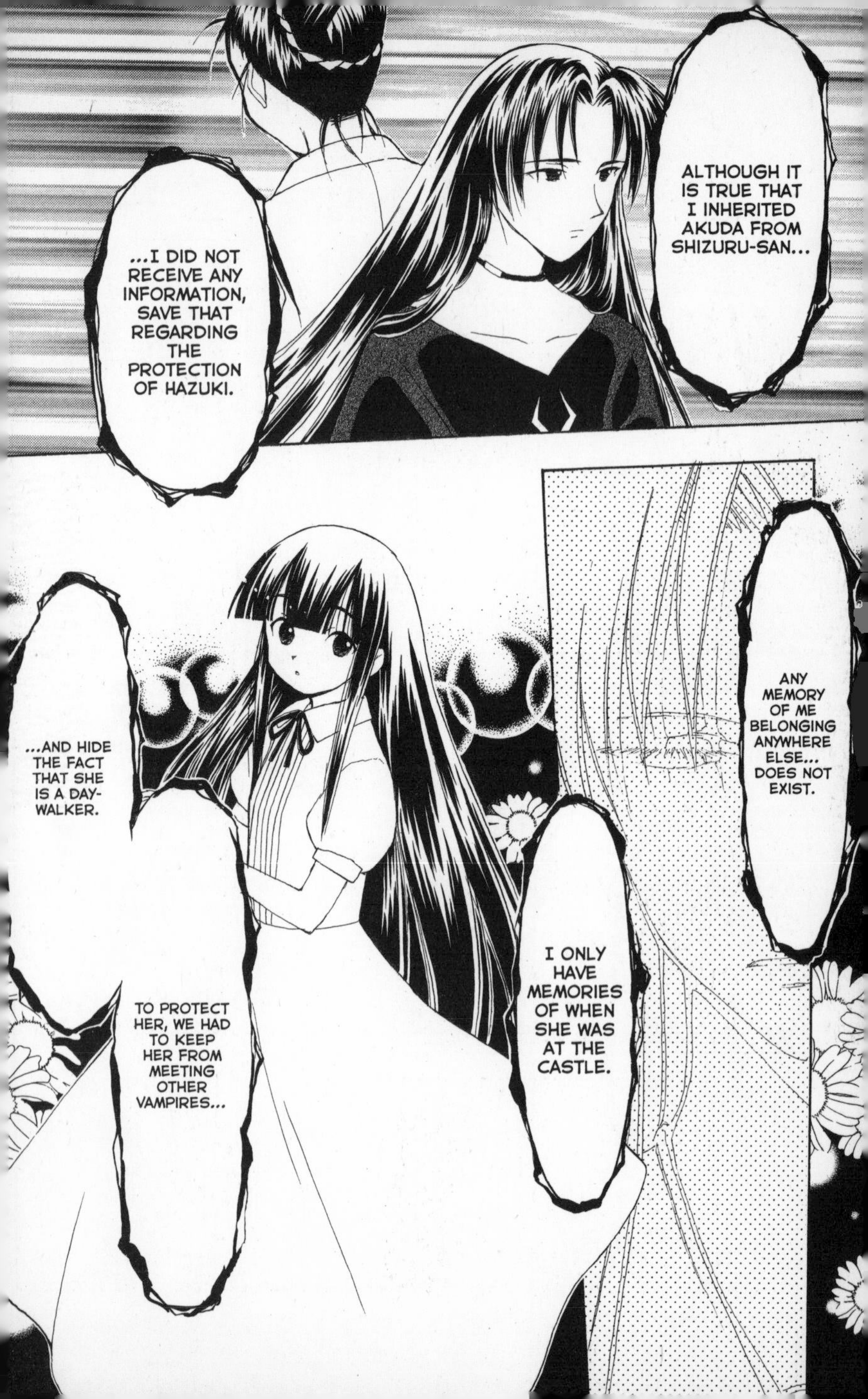
ALTHOUGH IT IS TRUE THAT I INHERITED AKUDA FROM SHIZURU-SAN...
...I DID NOT RECEIVE ANY INFORMATION, SAVE THAT REGARDING THE PROTECTION OF HAZUKI.
ANY MEMORY OF ME BELONGING ANYWHERE ELSE... DOES NOT EXIST.
I ONLY HAVE MEMORIES OF WHEN SHE WAS AT THE CASTLE.
TO PROTECT HER, WE HAD TO KEEP HER FROM MEETING OTHER VAMPIRES...
...AND HIDE THE FACT THAT SHE IS A DAY-WALKER.

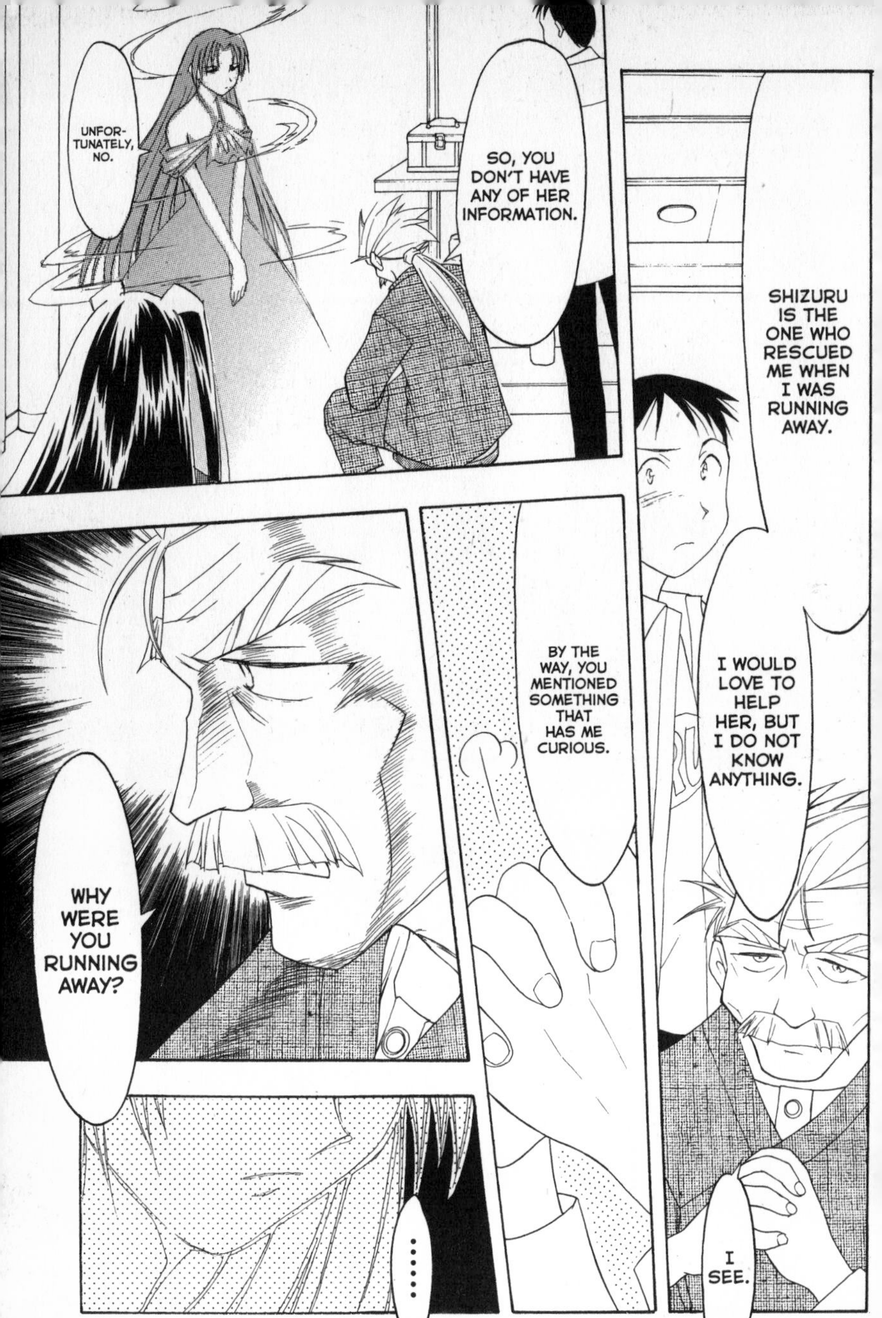
SHIZURU IS THE ONE WHO RESCUED ME WHEN I WAS RUNNING AWAY.
I WOULD LOVE TO HELP HER, BUT I DO NOT KNOW ANYTHING.
I SEE.
SO, YOU DON'T HAVE ANY OF HER INFORMATION.
UNFOR-TUNATELY, NO.
BY THE WAY, YOU MENTIONED SOMETHING THAT HAS ME CURIOUS.
WHY WERE YOU RUNNING AWAY?
......

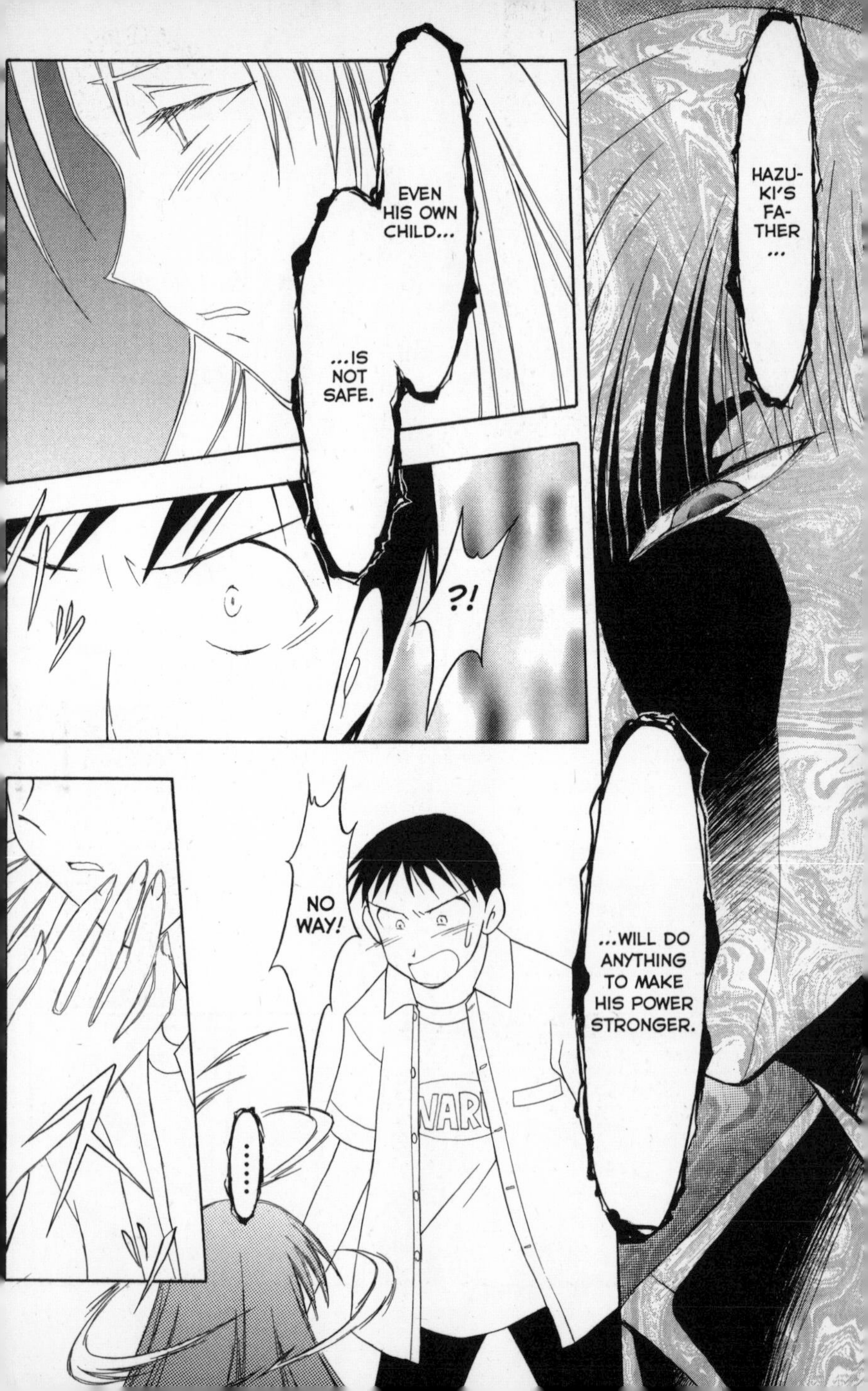
HAZUKI'S FATHER...
...WILL DO ANYTHING TO MAKE HIS POWER STRONGER.
EVEN HIS OWN CHILD...
...IS NOT SAFE.
?!
NO WAY!
......

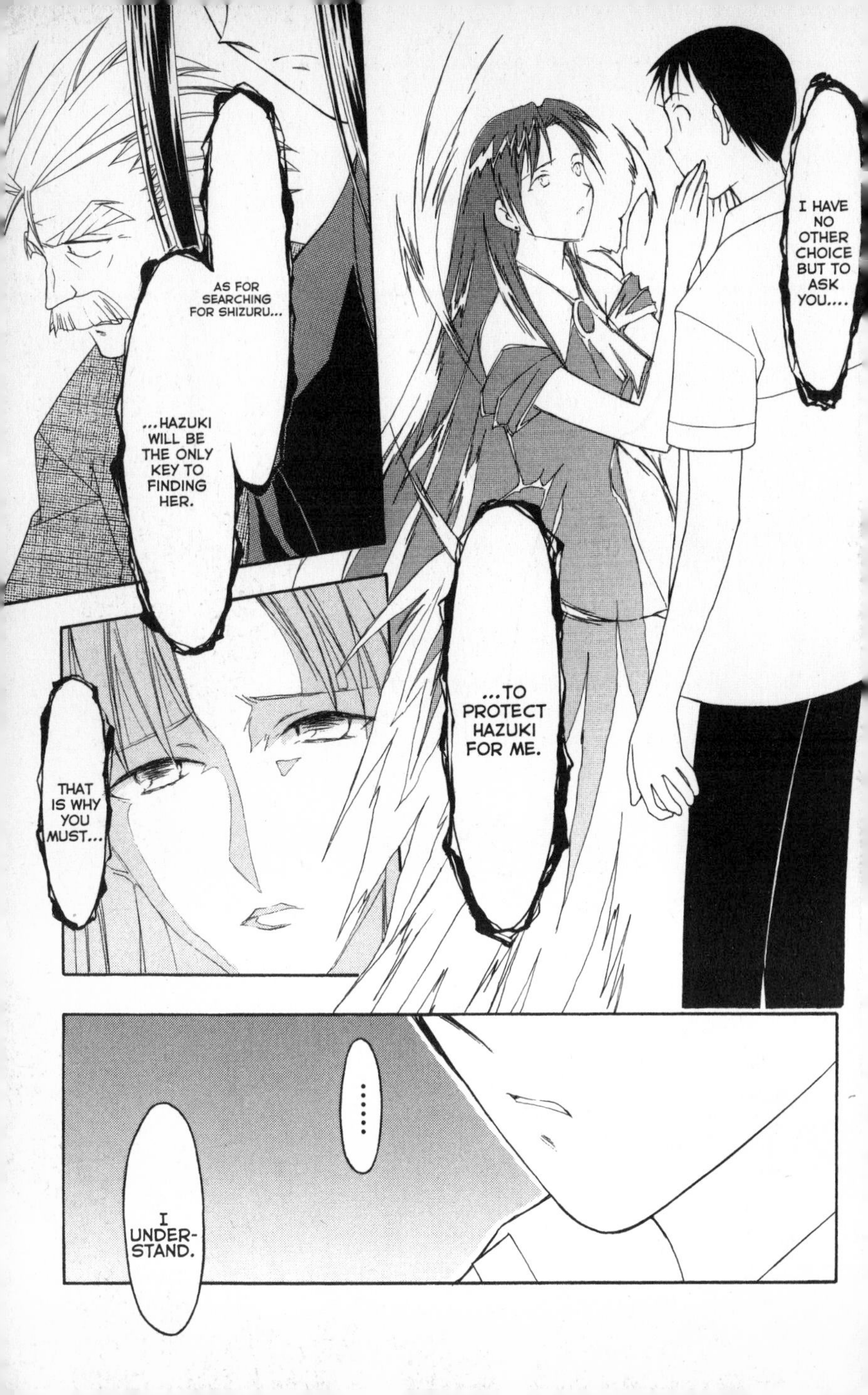
I HAVE NO OTHER CHOICE BUT TO ASK YOU....
...TO PROTECT HAZUKI FOR ME.
AS FOR SEARCHING FOR SHIZURU...
...HAZUKI WILL BE THE ONLY KEY TO FINDING HER.
THAT IS WHY YOU MUST...
......
I UNDER-STAND.

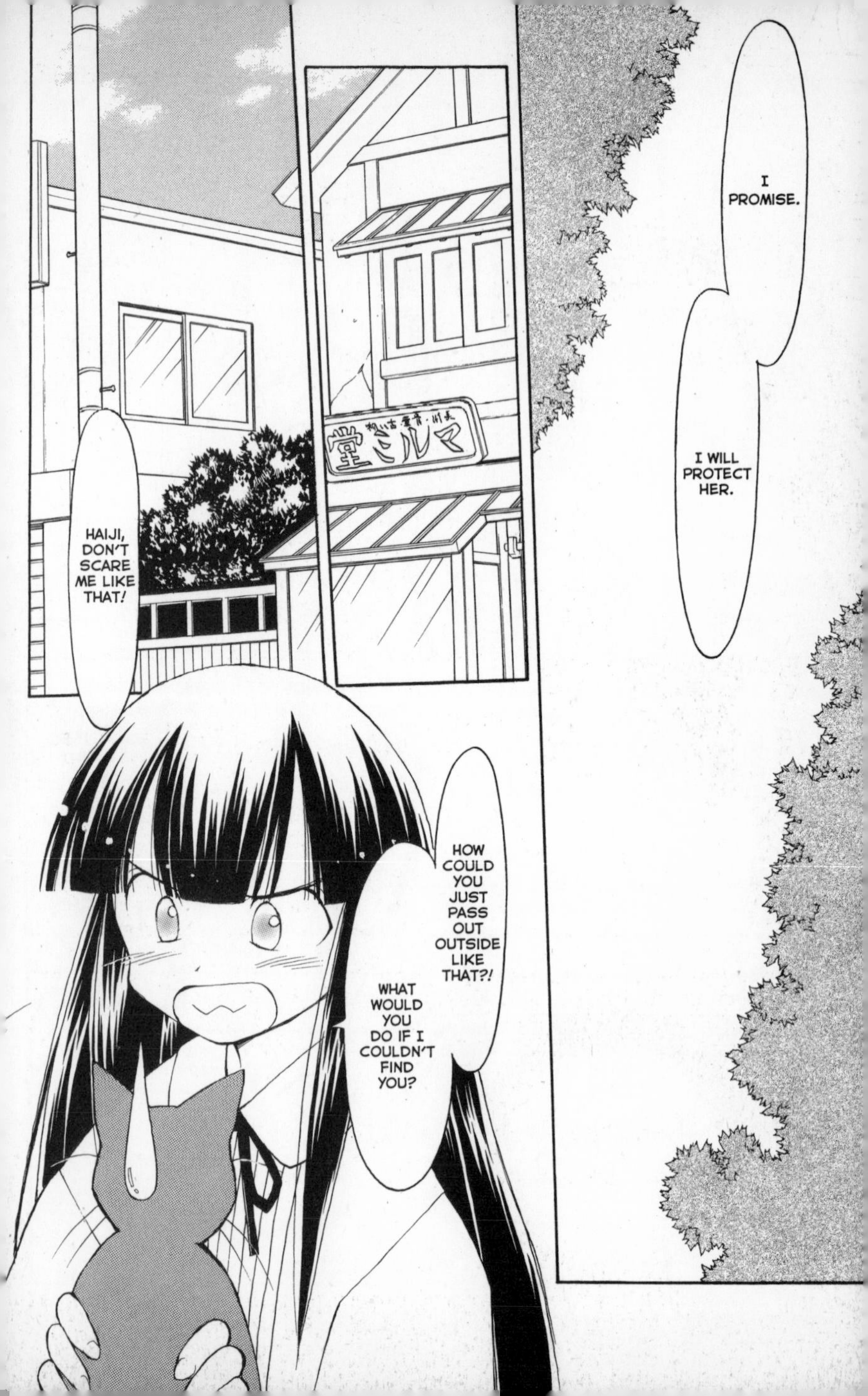
I PROMISE.
I WILL PROTECT HER.
HAIJI, DON'T SCARE ME LIKE THAT!
HOW COULD YOU JUST PASS OUT OUTSIDE LIKE THAT?!
WHAT WOULD YOU DO IF I COULDN'T FIND YOU?

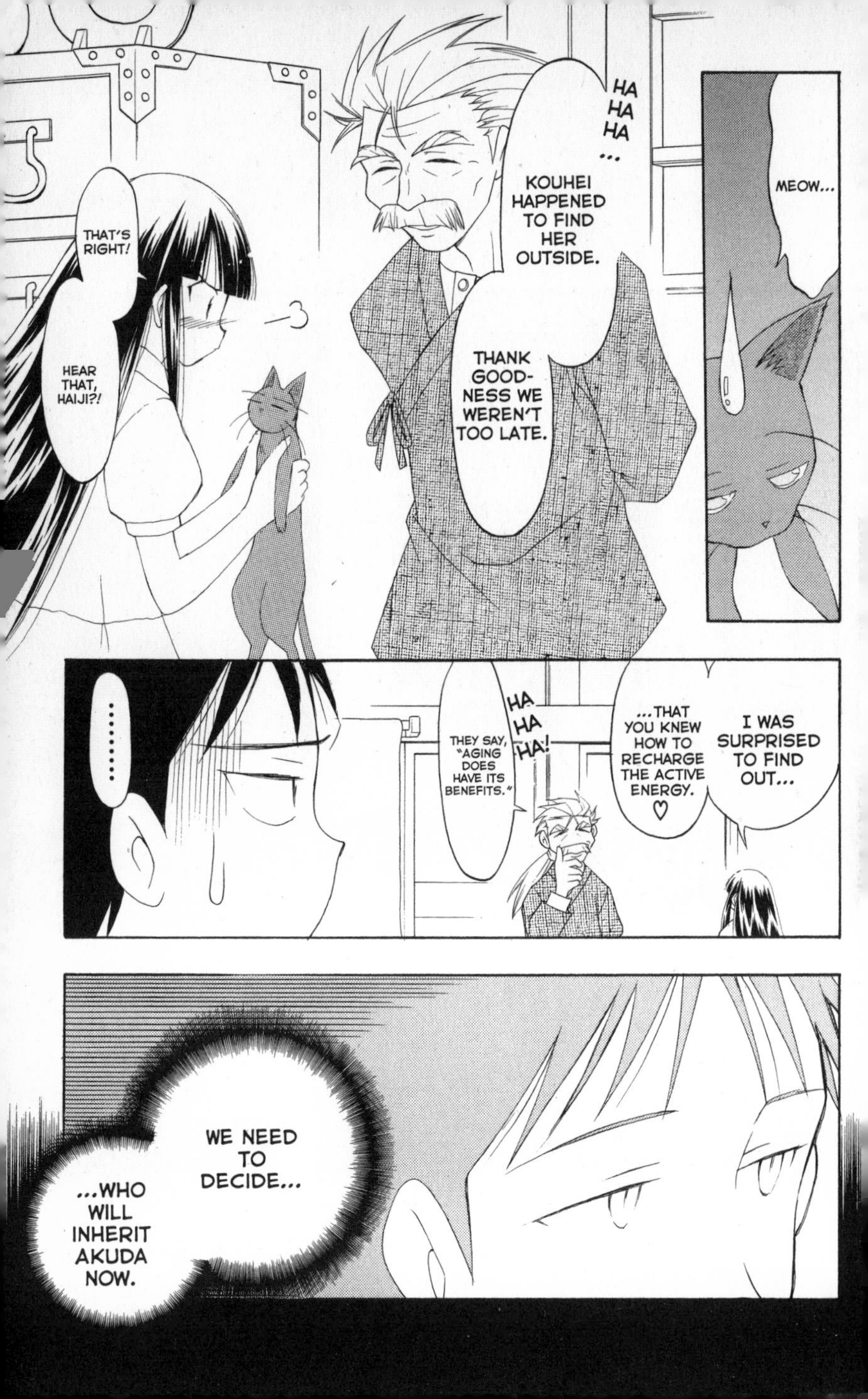
HA HA HA ...
KOUHEI HAPPENED TO FIND HER OUTSIDE.
THANK GOODNESS WE WEREN'T TOO LATE.
THAT'S RIGHT!
HEAR THAT, HAIJI?!
MEOW...
I WAS SURPRISED TO FIND OUT...
...THAT YOU KNEW HOW TO RECHARGE THE ACTIVE ENERGY. ♡
HA HA HA!
THEY SAY, "AGING DOES HAVE ITS BENEFITS."
....
WE NEED TO DECIDE...
...WHO WILL INHERIT AKUDA NOW.

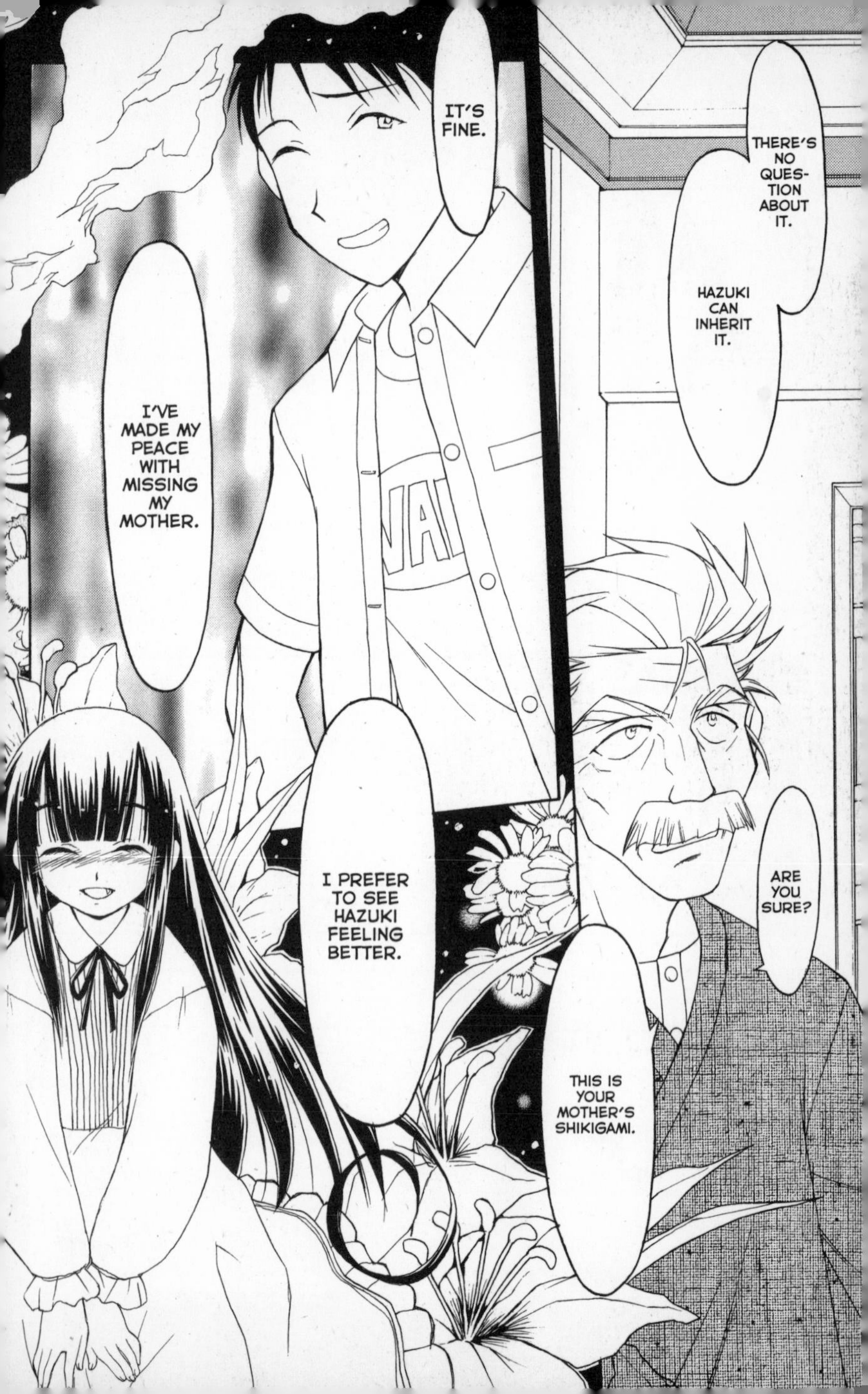
THERE'S NO QUES-TION ABOUT IT.
HAZUKI CAN INHERIT IT.
IT'S FINE.
I'VE MADE MY PEACE WITH MISSING MY MOTHER.
ARE YOU SURE?
THIS IS YOUR MOTHER'S SHIKIGAMI.
I PREFER TO SEE HAZUKI FEELING BETTER.

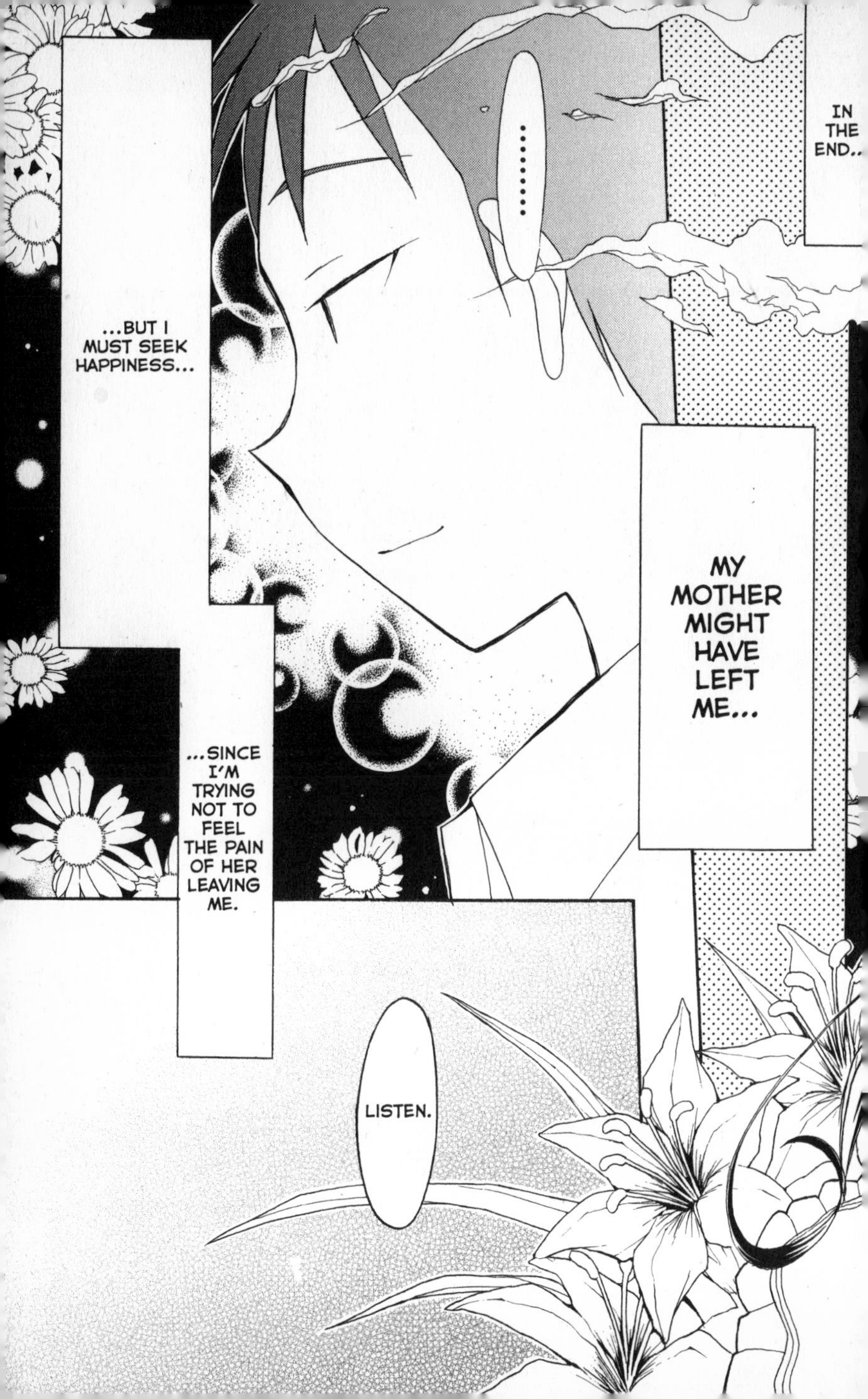
IN THE END...
......
MY MOTHER MIGHT HAVE LEFT ME...
...BUT I MUST SEEK HAPPINESS...
...SINCE I'M TRYING NOT TO FEEL THE PAIN OF HER LEAVING ME.
LISTEN.

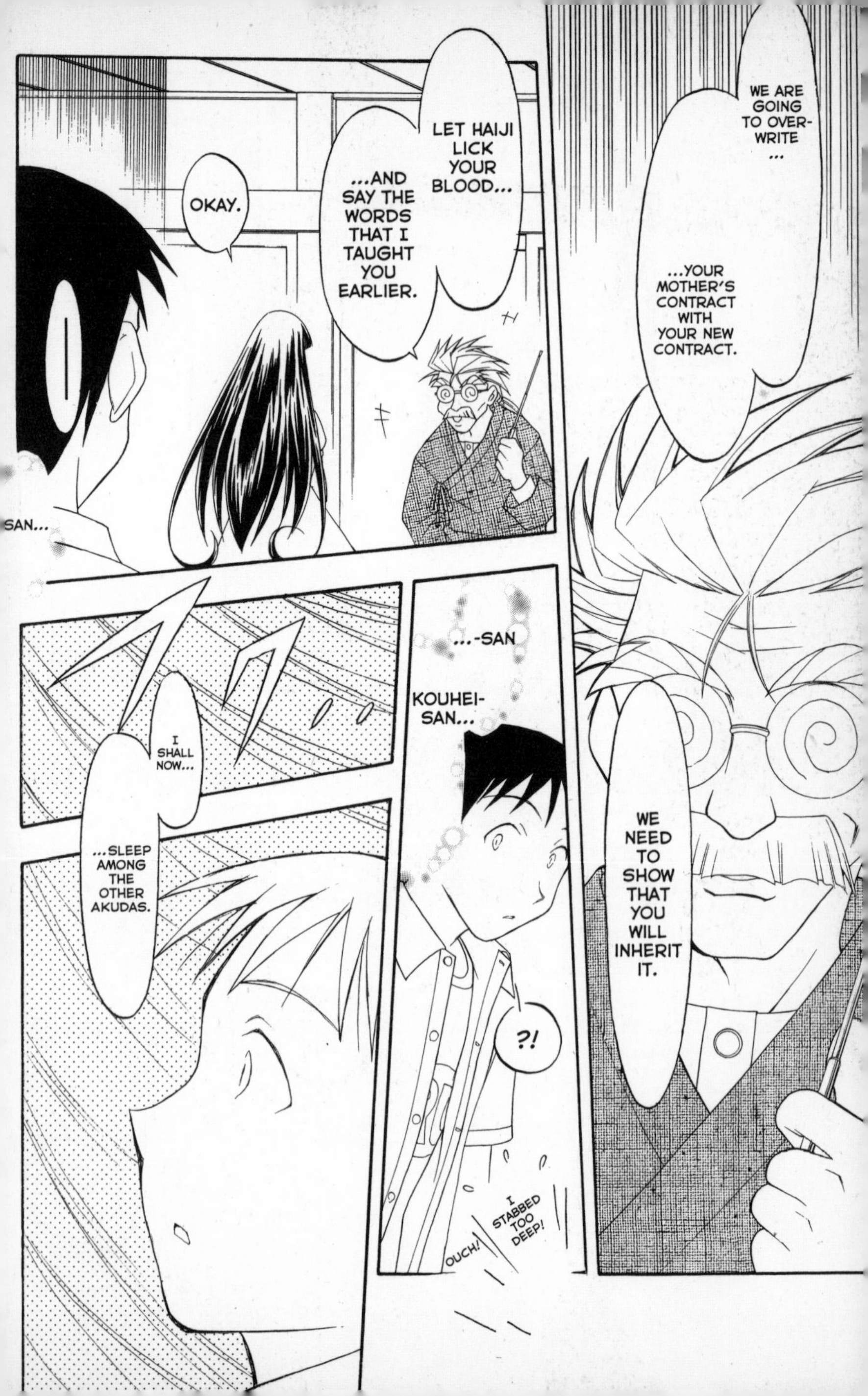

WE ARE GOING TO OVER-WRITE ...
...YOUR MOTHER'S CONTRACT WITH YOUR NEW CONTRACT.
LET HAIJI LICK YOUR BLOOD...
...AND SAY THE WORDS THAT I TAUGHT YOU EARLIER.
OKAY.
SAN...
WE NEED TO SHOW THAT YOU WILL INHERIT IT.
...-SAN
KOUHEI-SAN...
?!
I STABBED TOO DEEP!
OUCH!
I SHALL NOW...
...SLEEP AMONG THE OTHER AKUDAS.

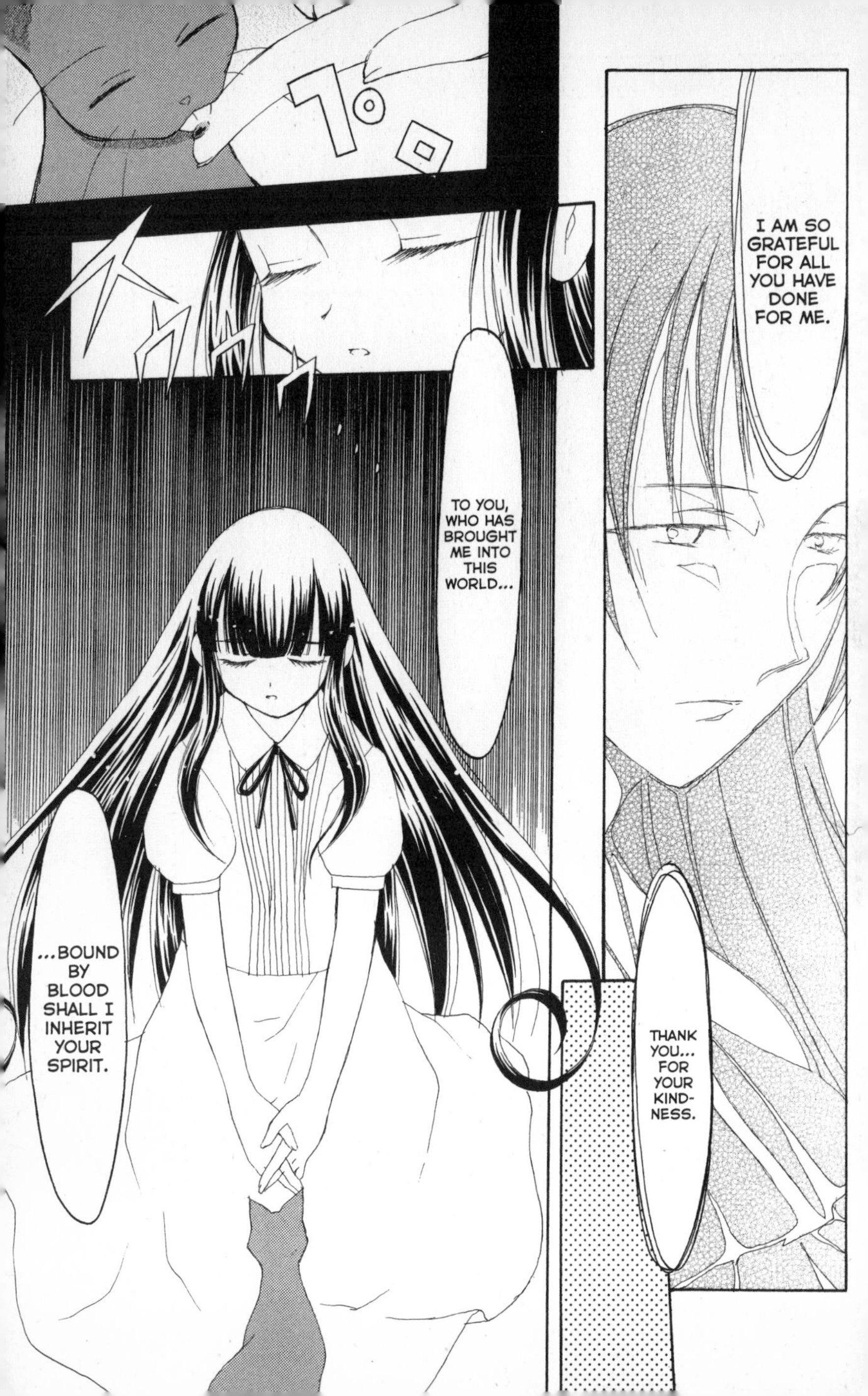
I AM SO GRATEFUL FOR ALL YOU HAVE DONE FOR ME.
TO YOU, WHO HAS BROUGHT ME INTO THIS WORLD...
...BOUND BY BLOOD SHALL I INHERIT YOUR SPIRIT.
THANK YOU... FOR YOUR KIND-NESS.

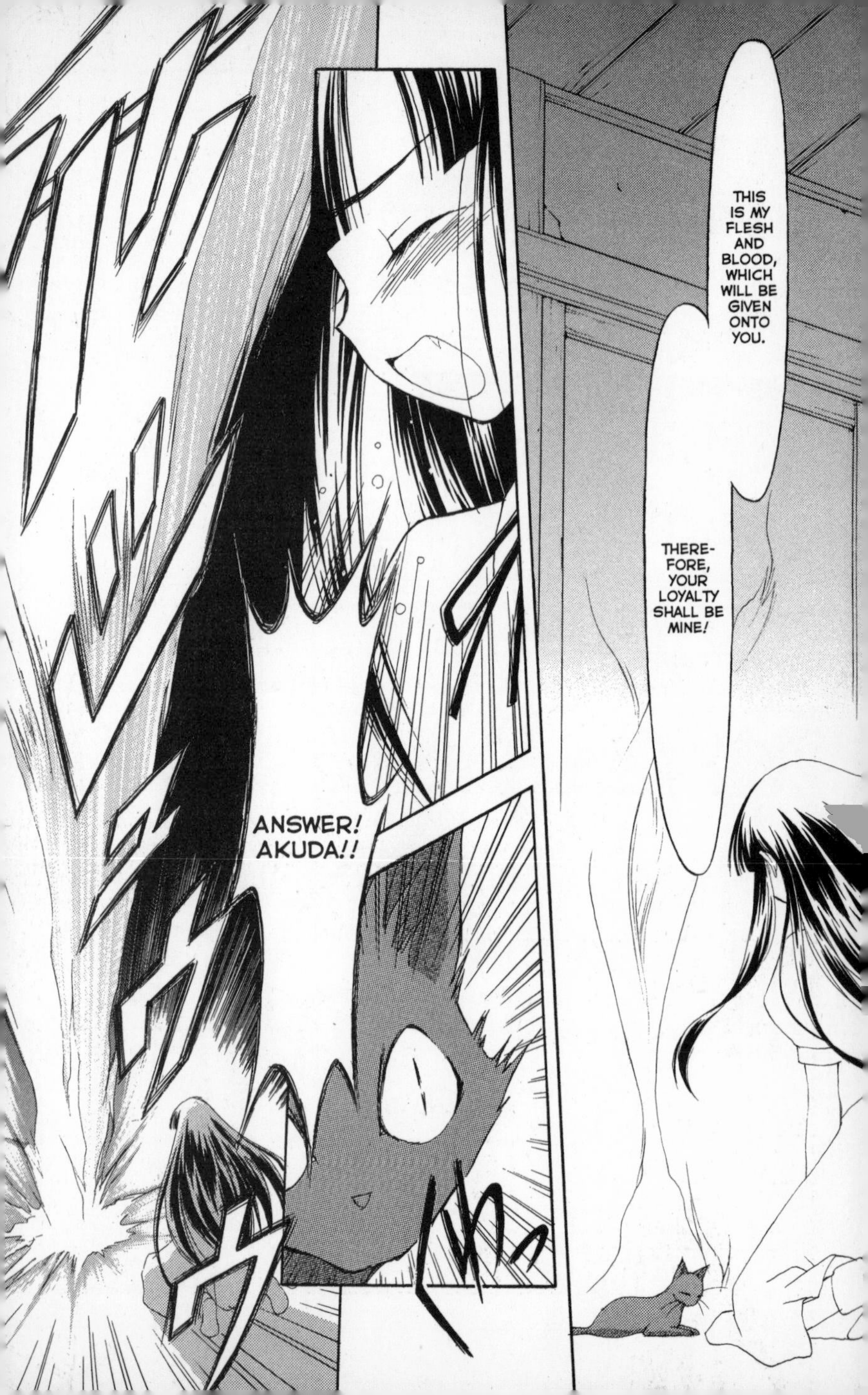
THIS IS MY FLESH AND BLOOD, WHICH WILL BE GIVEN ONTO YOU.
THEREFORE, YOUR LOYALTY SHALL BE MINE!
ANSWER! AKUDA!!

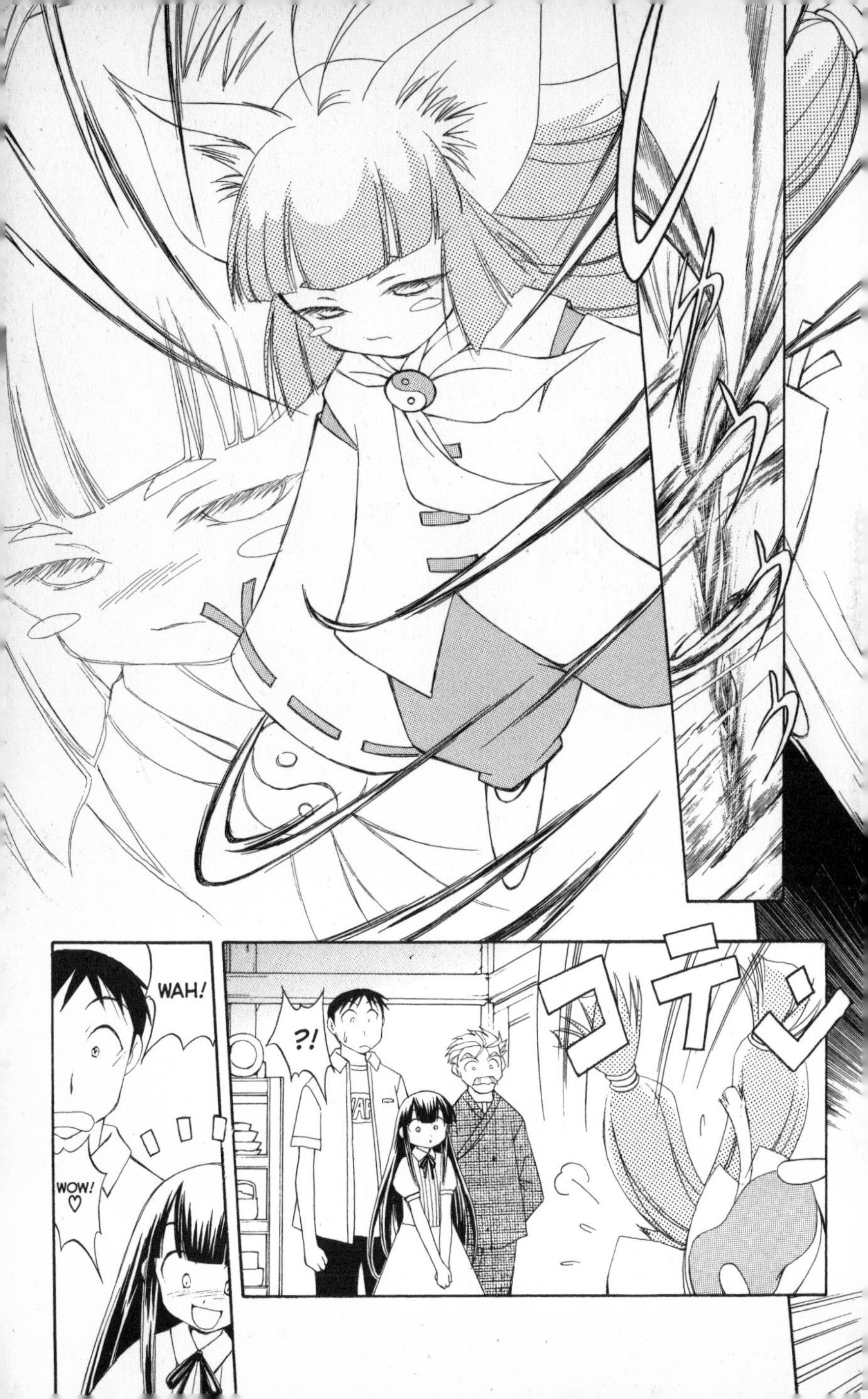
?!
WAH!
WOW! ♡

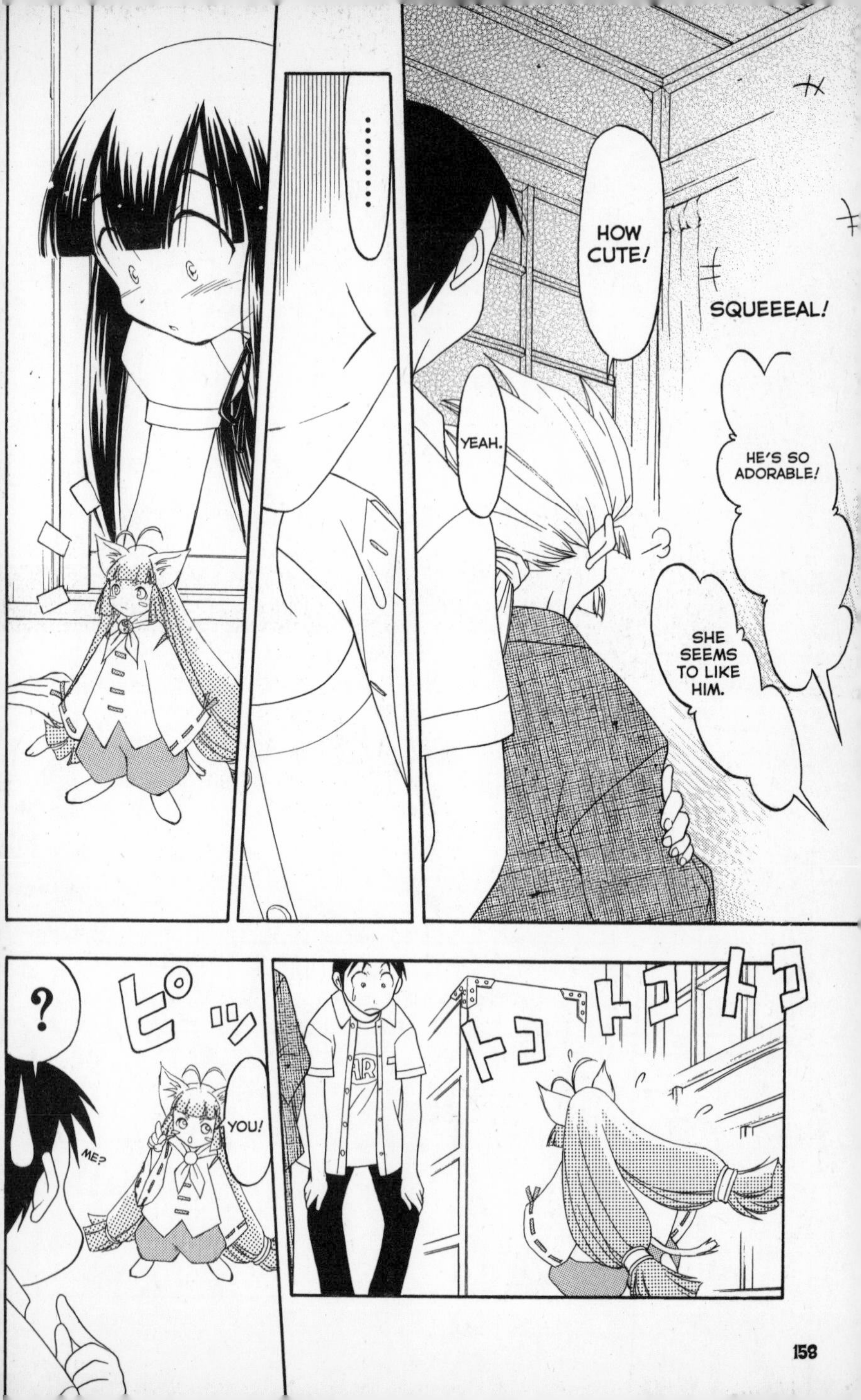
HOW CUTE!
YEAH.
SQUEEEAL!
HE'S SO ADORABLE!
SHE SEEMS TO LIKE HIM.
......
トコトコトコトコ
ピッ
?
YOU!
ME?

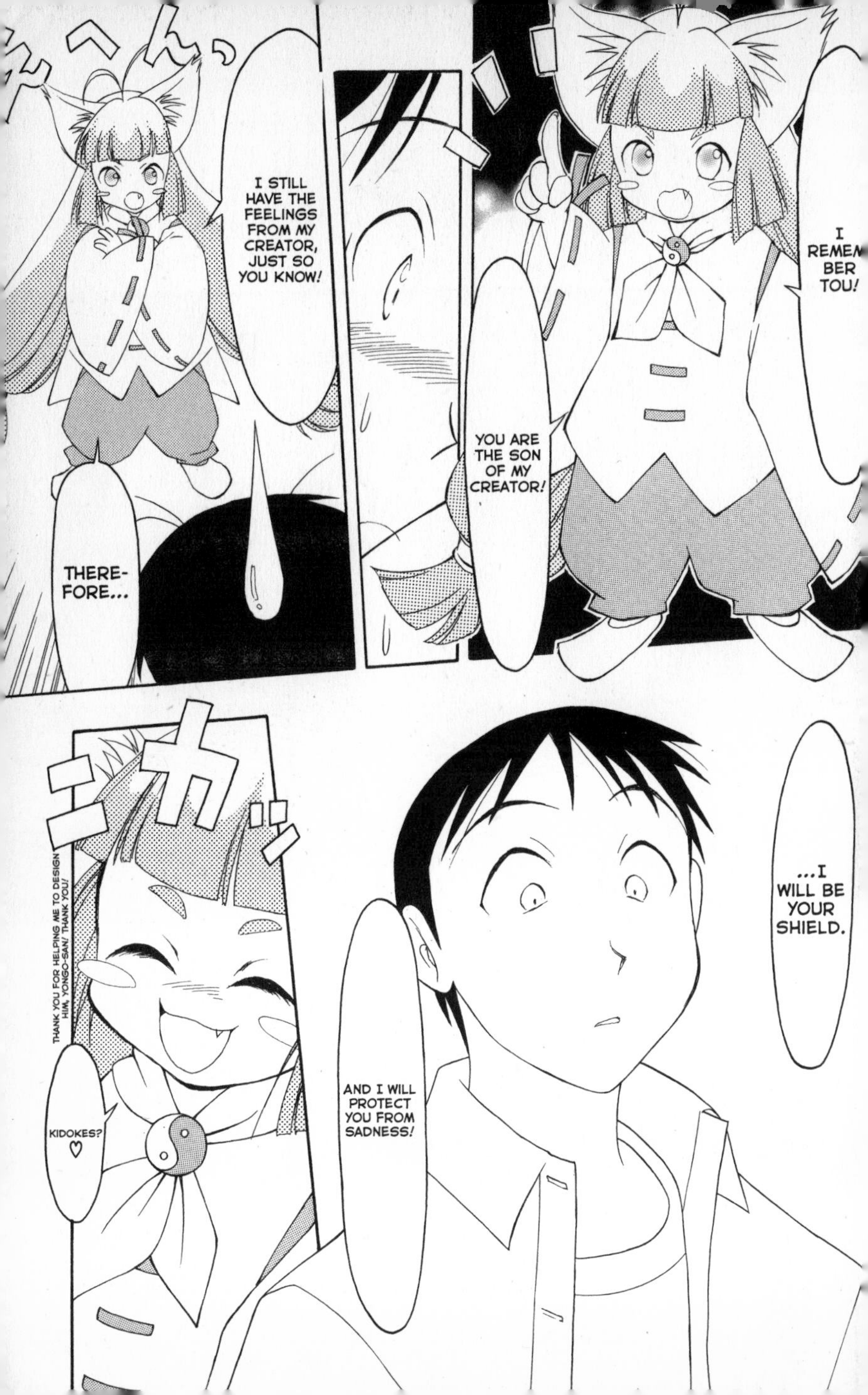
I REMEM BER TOU!
YOU ARE THE SON OF MY CREATOR!
I STILL HAVE THE FEELINGS FROM MY CREATOR, JUST SO YOU KNOW!
THERE-FORE...
...I WILL BE YOUR SHIELD.
AND I WILL PROTECT YOU FROM SADNESS!
KIDOKES? ♡
THANK YOU FOR HELPING ME TO DESIGN HIM, YONGO-SAN! THANK YOU!

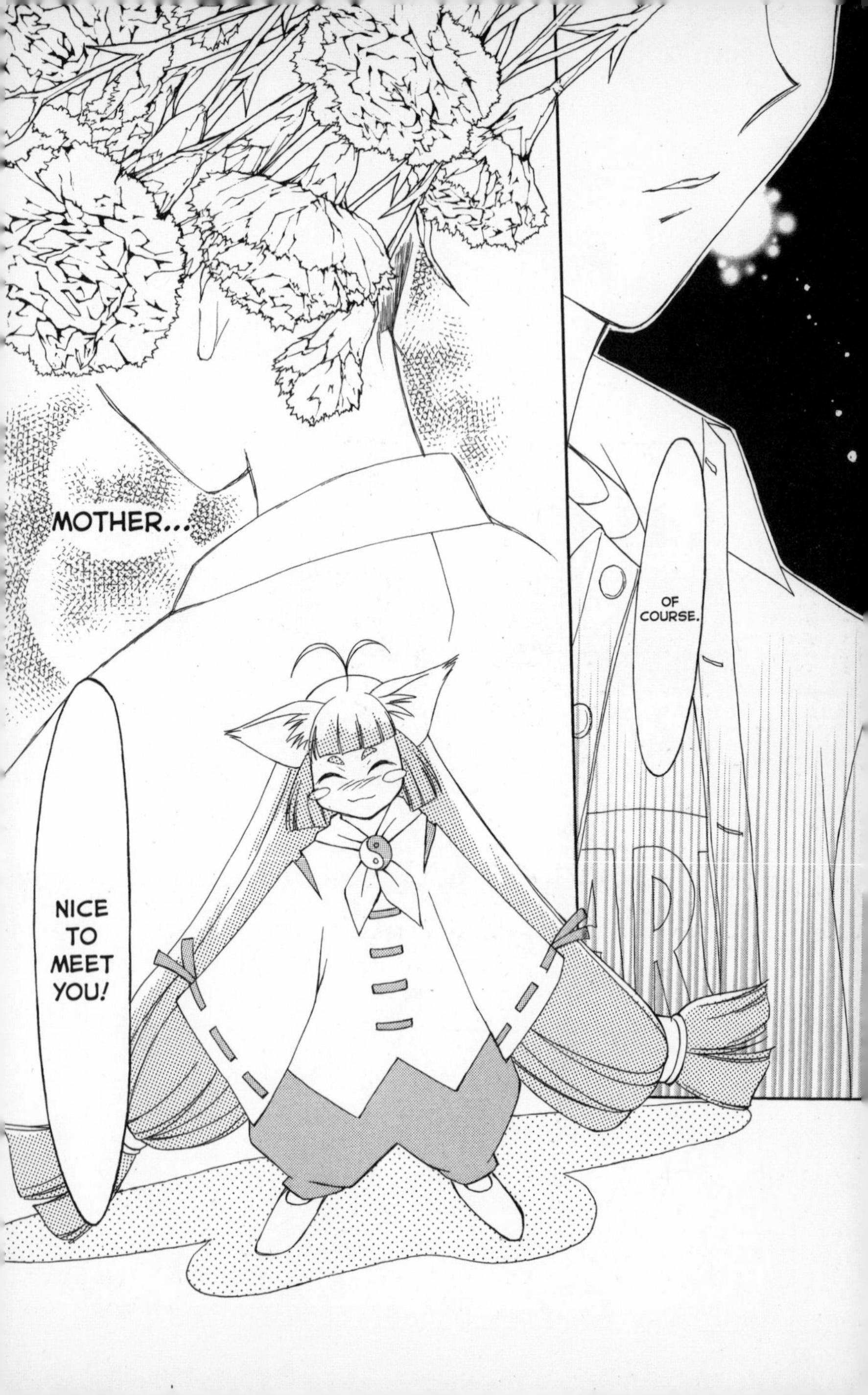
OF COURSE.
MOTHER...
NICE TO MEET YOU!

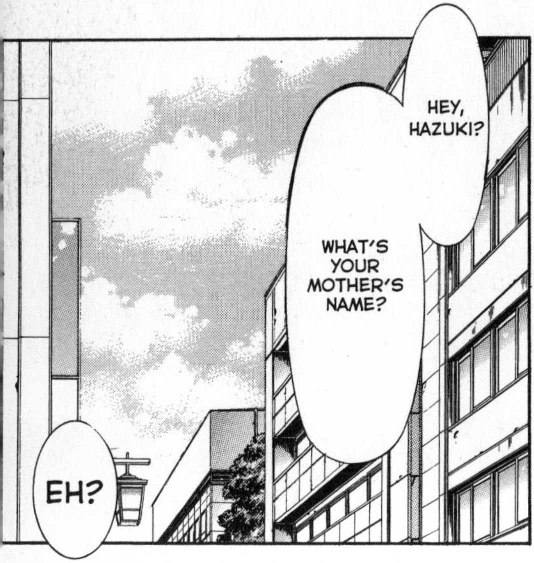
HEY, HAZUKI?
WHAT'S YOUR MOTHER'S NAME?
EH?

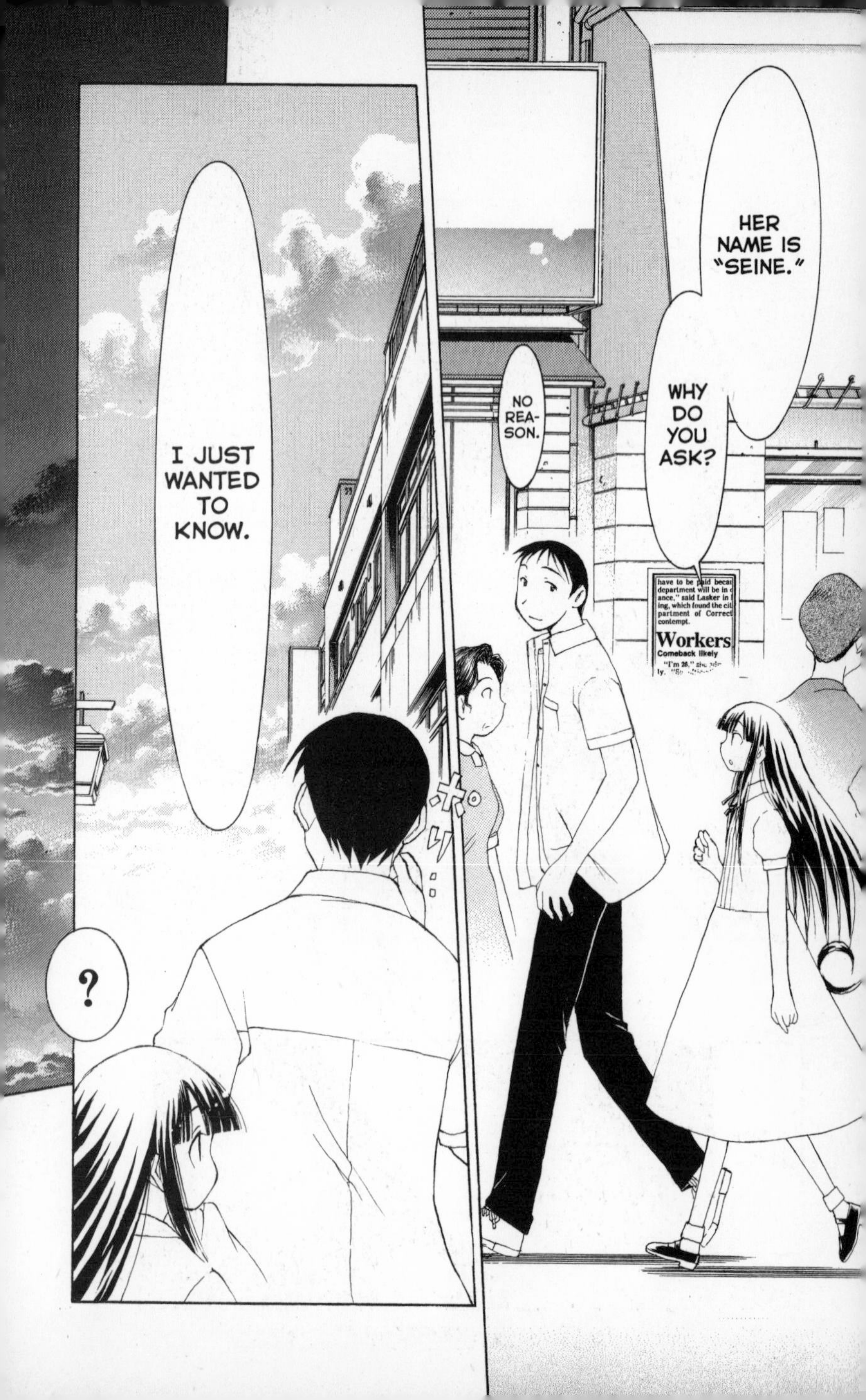
HER NAME IS "SEINE."
WHY DO YOU ASK?
NO REA-SON.
Workers
Comeback likely
I JUST WANTED TO KNOW.
?

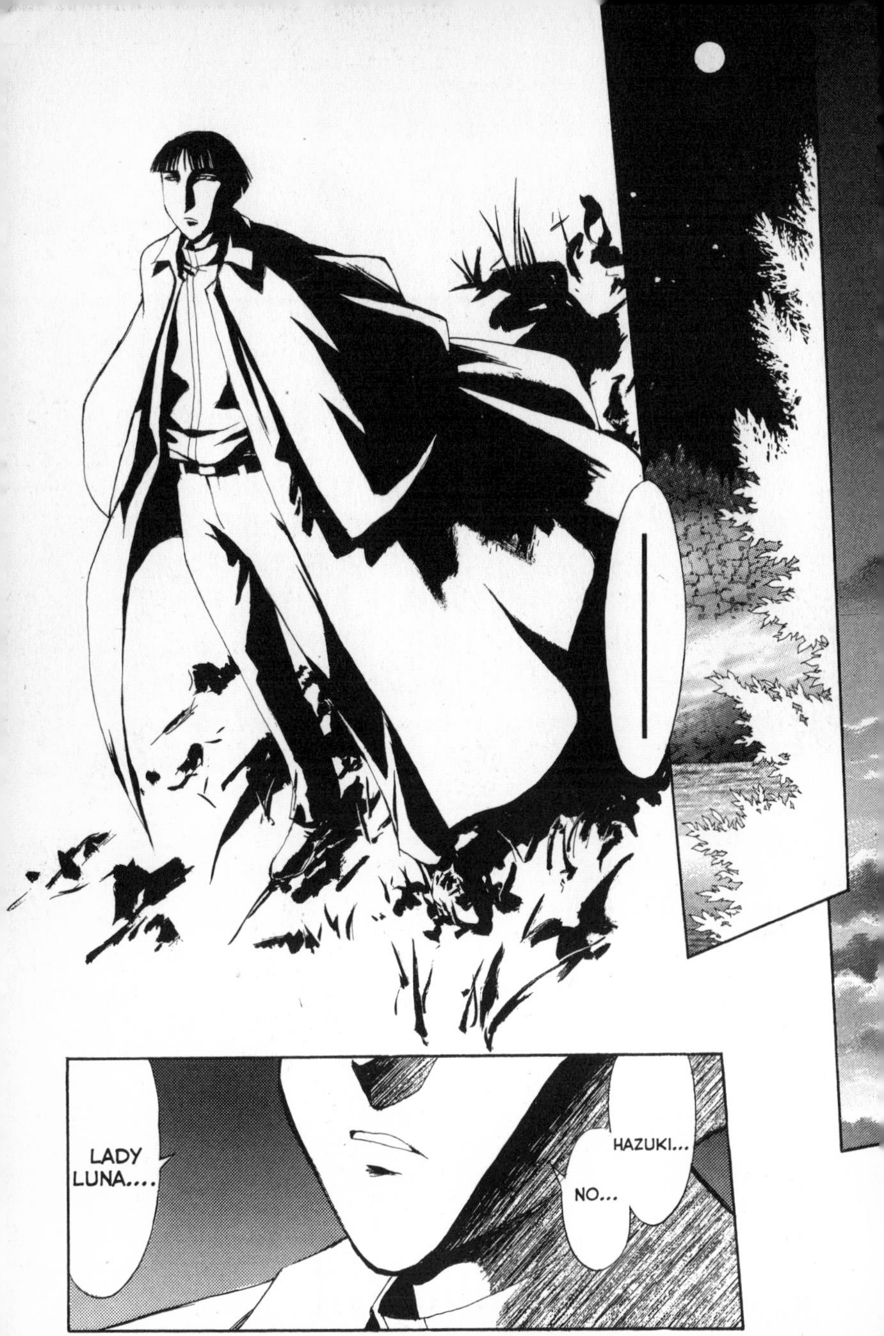
HAZUKI... NO...
LADY LUNA....

NEXT CHARACTER COMMING SOON

IN THE NEXT

TSUKUYOMI

Moon Phase 月詠

THE SHADOW OF COUNT KINKLE'S
REIGN OF TERROR FINALLY LIFTS AS
OUR HEROES STRUGGLE TO FALL
BACK INTO THE REGULAR ROUTINE
OF THINGS. KOUHEI REKINDLES
HIS PHOTOGRAPHER'S SPIRIT AS
HE USES HAZUKI AS HIS LATEST
SUBJECT, MUCH TO THE PLEASURE OF
WORLD RENOWNED PHOTOGRAPHER,
BEAT GRAHAM. ELFRIEDE REVEALS
THE TRAGIC PAST THAT SHAPED
HER TO THE YOUNG WOMAN SHE IS
NOW. AND IN THE DISTANCE, A NEW
THREAT DAWNS ON THE HORIZON...